THE MOONS OF JUPITER II

REDEMPTION

BY APRIL ADAMS

First eBook Edition: February 2015

ISBN: 978-0-98440033-4-8

Cover design by Drop Dead Design.com

ii

*For my Captains,
Bill and Mark
And my Mother Dragons,
Diane and Babs*

iv

TABLE OF CONTENTS

One 1

Two 7

Three 15

Four 27

Five 39

Six 49

Seven 63

8 77

From *The Dream Journal of Hope* 89

Nine 93

One Zero 113

One One 129

One Two 147

One Three 173

One Four 193

One Five 207

From *The Dream Journal of Hope* 231

One Six 233

One Seven 245

One 8 275

One Nine 287

Two Zero 301

Two One 313

Two Two 325

Two Three 343

Two Four 357

Two Five 375

Two Six 385

Two Seven 413

Two 8 427

Epilogue 435

Author's Note 441

ONE

The Ambassador walked into his hotel room, pausing as the door slid closed behind him. After he heard the multitude of locks slide home his thick shoulders slumped under the heavy material of his suit jacket. The Ambassador knew that he was not as high a target as an IGC officer, but he was close.

If he was voted in as a Senator in the next election, he would have to take more precautions, but he would also have better security staff. A staff that would be provided by the IGC rather than his own wallet.

For tonight he was content. He had dined on lobster tails from the frozen waters of Europa accompanied by Golbli garlic truffles and a bottle of golden wine from Atumn Isles of Callisto. His after-dinner Cognac had been complimented with espresso dipped ladyfingers and Chaponese chocolates.

He laid his key card down on the hotel chest of drawers and contemplated his corpulent reflection in the mirror over the dresser, patting his rotund belly in satisfaction. He was getting decidedly fat. The Ambassador did not mind the weight, but was a bit put out at the whispers that followed in his rather large wake.

He ran a hand over his protruding midsection as he looked in the mirror and sighed. He liked the substantial mass that he carried. Something about it made him feel secure, safe inside a suit of fleshy armor, but that security fled when he heard his peers make hushed jibes at his expense.

I'll go to an apothecary as soon as I am home, he thought, disconsolate. *Take care of all this excess. Some of it, anyway.*

He did not mind the tightness of his coat as he peeled it from his body and tossed it on the couch at the end of the bed, though it was a relief to pop the buttons on his vest and drop it on the floor. He wiggled awkwardly out of the rest of his clothes and slipped into pajamas that, though far from loose, were still comfortable.

After using the toilet he chewed a tooth-cleaning tablet and crawled into the hotel bed, scrunching the pillow under his head with a sigh. They had gotten him a satisfactory pillow. He traveled much and it didn't happen often.

Though his portly face was turned towards the window, he did not see the curtain stir. Even if he had, the shift of cloth was so gentle that he would have merely assumed it was due to a draft in the ventilation system.

He considered the events of the evening before he drifted off to sleep. Barin Trey had assured him that he would have IGC backing for his Senate campaign, as well as the funding. The Ambassador knew himself to be neither an ambitious nor an intellectual man, and that Trey was most likely using him. He didn't mind. Senators ate out every night, and they ate well.

The Ambassador closed his eyes, thinking of the restaurants he would frequent as a Senator. Visions of Golblian delicacies danced in his head as he drifted to sleep with a smile on his face.

When his breathing became slow and even, a figure slipped from behind the curtain like a wisp of breeze. The Aridian was female. Her slight, almost stick-like form was topped by a round head and dark eyes so large and round that they took up two-thirds of her face. Her skin was pale gray and straight black hair fell down past her tiny waist. She wore a bit of thin cloth for a dress that tied over her left shoulder.

In her hand was a small black box, not much larger than a key card, with a round knob and a red button.

The Rogue Aridian tiptoed around the bed and did a pirouette, making her tiny dress fan out around her waist like a flower, before she slowly slipped inside the sheets beside the Ambassador - careful not to disturb him. She placed the box under the unused pillow before laying her head down on top of it.

She preferred a knife, and usually carried a sharp, slender blade. It offered a clean, quick kill in most circumstances. The Ambassador, however, was so fat that she thought she could poke him full of holes and never hit anything vital, certainly not before he could raise an alarm. So, the box.

The large man did not stir, save for the rise and fall of his massive chest. His breath was slow, heavy and wet. She breathed in and out slowly, heavy and wet. She slowed her breath until it matched his breath. The Rogue smiled and slipped her foot between the sheets, carefully finding the heel of the Ambassador's foot and touching it gently with her toe.

She had found that the bottom of the heel was always the best part of the body for a touch to go unnoticed. It was covered with thick skin, usually calloused, and yet full of the genetic blueprints she needed.

The Aridian closed her eyes and kept her breath in sync with the body she was touching. That was the hardest part. Her body did all the rest. The change began, the feeling strong and sexual. Her heartbeat quickened and the core of her body began to burn with a pleasurable fire. The Rogue had always wondered what it would be like to Doppelgäng *while* having sex. She hoped to try it someday.

The DNA was drawn from the other body and mimicked, replicating and replicating, just like it should. Then the Rogue Aridian's body began to change, growing everywhere, pushing out in every direction. The tiny dress split and tore into shreds as the body inside it grew relentlessly and the Aridian had a to clamp a hand over her mouth to keep from giggling. Seeing that her hand was now one with chubby fingers that had hair on the knuckles, she had to press tighter, on a face that was also plumping out, to keep from laughing.

She closed eyes that were no longer round and large but more like gray marbles that had been poked into soft dough. She focused on her breath, keeping it in sync with the body she was duplicating. A body that kept growing till she thought it must pop. Her body rounded and began to sink as the mattress gave way beneath the weight.

When the seemingly ever-expanding body finally came to a halt, the Ambassador himself shifted. He was disturbed from his slumber as he felt the unevenness of the mattress, a mattress now sunk in on both sides.

He rolled over, his eyes only partly open. He saw the image of himself and those gray marbles grew wide. The Rogue smiled back at him with his face, waiting.

"Doppelgänger," he whispered.

"Doppelgänger," the Rogue whispered back. It was not enough, the whisper was too soft. She waited.

"Why?" he asked. His word came out reedy and cracking, but it was louder than the whisper, vibrating his vocal cords - and all the Rogue Aridian had been waiting for.

"Why?" she retorted, testing the resonance of the voice, replicating the sound in an instant though the pitch was a bit off. She cleared her throat, a throat now buried in a thick neck. "Why?" she said again, her voice deepening as it took on the tone of the Ambassador, and this time the pitch was a perfect match. She pulled the black box from under her pillow.

His eyes followed her hand as it placed the box over the left side of his chest. When he realized what it was, he made a terrified effort to get away, but his struggle was too late and his bulk too large to move with any sort of speed.

The Rogue pushed the button on the box and there was a soft thump as the G7 pacemaker inside the Ambassador's heart exploded. His body jerked twice and was still.

The Doppelgänger leaned into the face that was melting into laxity now that had it stopped breathing.

"Because I can," she whispered into his dead eyes with her new voice. It was as deep as the body was large.

She clambered out of the bed, tipping over and falling down. She lay on the floor, naked and laughing, trying to get used to her new center of gravity. She pushed herself up and regained her feet, rocking from one side to the other like a weighted balloon until she found her equilibrium.

The Rogue laughed at the body she now had, and then laughed at the strange guffaws that came from her throat. She teetered to the dresser to get some clothes before disposing of the body still in the bed.

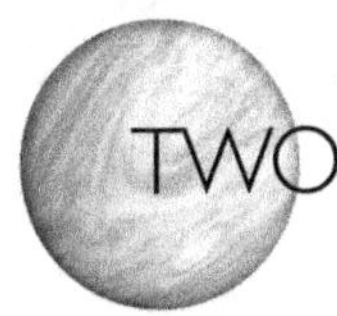

TWO

A pool of light shone down on the three male officers and their Commander aboard the Chimeran Battle Cruiser, *Resurrection.* They were gathered in the officer's mess, which was closed down and dark at this time, for a private meeting that had been hastily called. Officers Jan Petrov, Connor Malone, and Jasyn Issord sat facing a wall inset with a glass flatscreen that was often used by the ship's officers for everything from visual communications to cinematic movies.

Commander Petrov, the ship's Executive Officer, sat straight and tall in the collapsible metal chair, his blue eyes and white-blonde hair shining in the single halogen lamp that lit the meeting. Officer Malone, on the other hand, seemed to absorb the surrounding dark with his ebony skin and only the whites of his eyes shone around his brown irises. Between the two, sat Officer Issord, his smooth olive skin made pale by the halogen bulb and his hazel eyes were dark and thoughtful. He sat straddling a chair turned backwards, his forearms crossed over its low metal back.

JP, the Commander of the ship, walked to the glass panel that was set into the wall and inserted a tiny vid-chip into the small slot at the bottom of the screen. His young face was creamy white, though scattered with freckles, and instead of Chimeran Blue coveralls he wore a heavy, starched cassock robe of a priest, though its blue matched the color of his officer's uniforms. He turned to them, his chin lifted.

"I know I have discussed with you what this job would entail," he said. "But I think you should have a look as well, so you have a better idea of what you are getting into." He ran a slender finger along the edge of the chip and the glass screen flared to life. JP crossed his arms over his chest and watched his officers and their three pairs of eyes as they grew wider and wider.

The image on the screen showed a human male and human female engaged in sexual intercourse. The Commander did not know if the act was particularly violent, or if all intercourse appeared as such. The male was behind the female and was slamming himself into her sex repeatedly. The woman was letting out a guttural shout with each thrust that sounded more like yelps of pain than the forced sounds of pleasure that she was trying to simulate.

Commander Petrov quickly turned his face away. "It looks like he is killing her," he said, his voice deep with emotion.

"It sounds like it, too," Officer Malone agreed. The whites of his eyes seemed to take up the entire upper half of his face while a long-fingered hand came up to cover his mouth and chin.

Officer Issord closed his eyes and tried to swallow but his throat was too dry. "She's going to want *that*?" he asked.

JP shrugged excessively and one of his own slender fingers came up to rest on his upper lip as he thought, his thumb under his chin. "It's barbaric, I know," he admitted. "But it is what will be expected. It is one of the main reasons that they manufacture companion constructs."

"But why?" Malone asked, amazed.

JP shrugged again, though this time not to excess. "It is supposed to be very pleasurable to them."

Issord opened his hazel eyes again to the moving image on the screen. It didn't look like it was enjoyable in the least, for either participant. They both wore expressions of what Jasyn thought of as grim determination.

"And what about us?" he asked. "How would it be for us?"

JP sighed. "That, I cannot tell you." He leaned forward and thumbed the vid-chip. The screen went dark and there was an audible sigh of relief from the officers. "I honestly don't believe it could be as bad as it looks, otherwise they wouldn't do it so frequently."

Issord stared over the back of his chair while Malone and Petrov shot each other a nervous glance. This time, it was their Commander that let out a sigh.

"I chose you especially," he said, eyeing the ones seated before him, "because of all my officers and crew, you three are the most ardent for The Cause, and have the greatest amount of control." He looked at them proudly and nodded. "Greater control than myself, even," he added softly.

The three seated, looking for all the universe like strong and attractive young human males, beamed at their Commander. JP fixed them with a beatific smile from his angelic face and looked at them each in turn with his bright blue eyes.

"But I have to know," he told them, his voice gentle but firm, "if this is something you can do – without question, without hesitation, without so much as a flinch. And I need to know now."

He looked first at his Second in Command. The tall and strikingly handsome Executive Officer lifted his square chin for a moment as if accepting a challenge, then his blue eyes closed slowly and his full lips pressed together. He shook his head.

"I am so sorry," he whispered. "I know how important this is, and because I do, I am afraid I may fail."

JP quickly put a hand on Petrov's shoulder, squeezing it. "You have nothing to be ashamed of, my son," he told him. "And your honesty is as valued as your chastity." Still gripping Petrov's shoulder, the Commander turned his radiant gaze upon the other two officers. Jasyn Issord's hazel eyes looked up from under his dark brows to meet the brilliant blue eyes of his Commander.

"I'll do it," he assured him.

"So will I," echoed Malone, though his voice trembled slightly, making him sound not quite as sure as the Operations Officer.

The Commander beamed at them both, his blue eyes shining from his freckled, boyish face.

"Splendid," he told them, still holding onto the XO's broad shoulder. "We have eyes almost everywhere, and they have been a Godsend. But having eyes *there,* inside the stronghold, will give us great vision indeed."

The young Commander's specialty, other than his training in the pre-Chimeran days, was intelligence. Intelligence that he received through a network of spies. Spies that were greatly trusted and carefully placed. Over the past century, JP had vigilantly constructed a web with strands that went into every division of the InterGalactic Council - including their Financial and Military branches. He even had two agents aboard their precious Dragons.

He had all sorts of instruments, both human and construct, all working for what the Chimeran simply called "the Cause," in all kinds of occupations throughout the galaxies. What he had really been striving towards, for nearly a decade, was to get an agent in place with a high-ranking IGC official or a highly placed employee of the GwenSeven Corporation in the guise of a constructed companion.

The GwenSeven companion droids were notoriously expensive and therefore only bought by people who could afford them, which almost always meant someone in a high position with an equal amount of clout and information.

JP had discussed the possibility with a close group of officers, both male and female, in hopes that an order would be put in for a companion by someone in power. Tonight, his prayers had been answered.

Just an hour ago he had received a communication from an

agent working as a marketing accountant for GwenSeven. An order had been placed for a companion model construct, male. The person who had ordered the construct had been none other than the Lead Chairwoman for the IGC Financial Board and the financier and CFO of the GwenSeven Corporation, Charity de Rossi.

JP nearly fell to his knees and wept with gratitude, but instead threw back his head and laughed and laughed. The Lady Larissa, the stewardess who had delivered the message, looked at him in astonishment, her brown eyes like small saucers in her thin face. Even so, it made her heart race and brim with happiness seeing her Commander so joyous.

The Chimeran had been prepared for such a call, hoping that someday an order would come through from an official of the IGC, the higher the title the better. Never had he imagined, nor could he, that the request would come from not just a high ranking person but one of the two actual directors of the GwenSeven Corporation.

Since the order had been for a male companion, when the call finally came, JP assembled the male officers that had accepted and prepared for this assignment. With the image of the pornographic vid still etched on their minds, he told them who had placed the order. Their eyes, already glassy with shock at the scene they had just witnessed, widened in surprise.

"*The* Charity de Rossi?" Commander Petrov asked, astounded. Security Officer Connor Malone grinned at him.

"Make you want change your mind?" he taunted.

"Definitely not."

The other officers chuckled, though not unkindly. Operations Officer Issord turned his eyes to his Commander, his face drawn.

"How often do you think she'll want to, to...?" he asked, motioning to the now dark glass screen on the wall since his lips seemed unable to form the words. He wasn't nervous, he never was. They had all been told before what would be expected of them, and had taken classes on other things such as manners and customs, dining etiquette and even dancing. Three female officers had taken the same training, in case the request had been for a female. Still, this was the first time he had seen anything having to do with sexual expectations. It looked brutal.

JP shrugged. "Knowing Charity, there is no way to tell. She's horribly depraved and immoral," he told them, making them all flinch. "And for that," he sighed, "I have to admit that someone from Bjorn's hedonistic crew would be a better fit. But, other than that, I trust that any of you would be more able for the mission at hand. You have what it takes to imitate a companion – composure and obedience."

This time Malone motioned to the dark glass. "Is it always like that?" he asked, his mouth dry. "So, so...violent?"

The Commander tapped his bottom lip with a slender finger, thoughtful, before he shook his head. "I don't think so. I asked Larissa to do a search and download for human intercourse," he said, finding himself unable to suppress a smile. "She probably downloaded the first thing she found. I doubt she did a lot of...shopping."

Each seated officer placed a hand over his mouth to hide smiles and soft chortles of laughter, imagining the virtuous Lady Larissa watching the material that they had just viewed.

"On the good side," JP continued, "Charity is extremely busy and probably will not have a lot of time for such activities."

"I hope not," Malone said.

This time the officers could not restrain their nervous laughter and the Commander smiled benevolently at them as if they were children, shaking his head in amusement.

"Well, you should start preparing yourself mentally," he told them, eyeing the two that would be going, "which is why

I showed you the vid. Charity is expecting her order to be ready in ten days, and the trip will take seven of those days in the frigate, which is the fastest vessel we have, other than the fighters. You will need to leave tonight."

"We'll miss the eggs," Officer Malone said, thoughtful. The recent massacre aboard the Beryl Dragon had been successful. A pair of stolen Dragon eggs that had been nicknamed Alexander's Eggs, along with a live Engineer, were on their way to rendezvous with the Chimeran Battle Cruiser, *Resurrection*.

"Yes," JP agreed. "I'm sorry you will miss the excitement of their arrival, but you will have the thrill of this mission, and Mr. Jovak has assured me that he will keep them from hatching until we have Jordans for them. The eggs will be here when you return." He tucked his chin and fixed his blue eyes upon his officers. "And return you will," he assured them. "Whichever one of you is chosen. I am sure of it."

"Yes, sir," Issord and Malone said in unison.

"The only thing you need to take are the micro com-kits, but should they be compromised you need to be ready to improvise."

"Yes, sir."

"You both know the mission, what intel I am after, and the rally point for each system. The only thing I am unsure of," JP confessed, "is how long I will need for you to maintain the ruse. If she proves to be a good source of information, I may have you there for quite a while. Are you prepared for that?"

"Yes, sir."

"She is as capricious as the devil, so you also need to be prepared for her to lose interest or even give you away to someone else."

"Yes, sir," both officers echoed, though Malone raised a hand.

"Yes?" JP asked.

"And if it turns out that she has nothing to offer?" the

Security Officer asked.

The Commander tapped his lips with a finger, his blue eyes thoughtful. "I have considered the possibility," he admitted, "but it is doubtful. I'm sure she has access to the GwenSeven mainframe and, if so, I expect you to find your way in and glean whatever you can. However, should she prove worthless or if you end up where you are unable to access any good or useful information, I want you be prepared to signal for an evac, and have your escape plan predetermined and set. And be ready upon my command, to kill her before you leave."

"Yes, sir."

JP smiled benevolently at his officers. "But first, let us pray."

The officers bowed their heads as the Commander prayed for their safety and success, as well as for the swift and well-deserved deaths of their enemies.

THREE

Galen sat facing a tribunal of judges. Not to defend himself, for once, but to defend the one that he loved, making it more important to the elfin doctor than anything he had ever pled for on his own.

Six judges sat side by side at a long table of polished walnut. They each had a tall crystal goblet, as well as a glass pitcher full of ice water, all sitting on absorbent pads of Golblian cork. Condensation gathered in huge drops before slipping down the sides and running down the stems to soak into the black cork micropads.

It was going to be a long morning for them, and Galen wondered if the hypocrites had filled those pitchers with embargoed Golgothian spirits.

Of all the judges on the P&A Tribunal, each of them a retired aviator or fighter pilot, Galen knew only one, and only by her reputation. Colonel Lizbeth Asti was an ancient thing, with folds of wrinkled skin that hung on her wasted frame like over-washed sheets. She was notorious for having grounded more pilots than Space Madness. Her silver hair was pulled up into a wild knot that sat on her head like a frenzied nest.

"The rules are unmistakable and unambiguous," Colonel Asti croaked out, loud if not tremendously clear. "I see no reason why we should make an exception."

"I have reasons, that I would like to present to you, if I may."

"You're wasting your time, Doctor."

"If not my reasons then possibly a donation would..." Galen

started but Asti brought a skeletal hand down flat on the table so hard that it made it him jump.

"Do not think!" she hissed, bringing her hand up and pointing a bony finger at Galen, "even for a second, about trying to bribe this council."

Galen held up his hands. "Absolutely not," he said, though in fact it had been the course of action he had been hoping for - it certainly would have been the easiest. "I was not speaking of a donation to the council, but one to the school, or any special program that might contribute to helping pilots facing the same problems as the one faced by Ms. de Rossi."

Colonel Asti gave the black-haired elf a suspicious glare before she leaned back and glanced at the other judges. Most gave a slight shake of their head, one of the two male judges simply shrugged.

"The rules are very clear," another of the female judges told him, echoing Asti. She was as gray as the Colonel, but heavyset where Asti was bony, with seemingly more neck than head. Galen wondered how long it had been since she was able to squeeze herself into a cockpit. "Any student or pilot licensed by the council, that uses any kind of Forboden Drugs, will be expelled or have their license revoked. Permanently."

Galen leaned forward in his chair. "Ms. de Rossi then, technically, did not break any rules," he argued. "She was not a student at the time, nor was she a licensed pilot or even in possession of any aircraft."

The judges glanced at one another. Colonel Asti clenched two claw-like hands into fists. "Don't you expect to get her out of this on a loophole!" she spat.

"I wouldn't dream of it," Galen reassured, cursing silently since it was going to be his next ploy. Inwardly he scowled, outwardly he keep his face carefully impassive.

"He is right, though," one of the male judges said softly. "She is neither a licensed pilot nor a student at this point, nor was she at the time of her, ahem, indiscretion."

Lizbeth snorted. "Indiscretion," she sneered.

The judge shrugged. "We have no rules regarding civilians."

The hefty female adjudicator nodded reluctantly in agreement. "We have no jurisdiction over civilians."

Lizbeth glared at each of them in turn from under the folds of skin that were her eyelids. Her fists were clenched so tight that her arms were trembling, making the skin on her bones quiver.

Galen sat back, eyeing them all with his tongue in his cheek as he tried to determine his next course. The judge who had spoken out was one of two male judges. The other four on the bench were women. All accomplished pilots. Fighters. All retired and now adjudicators for the Pilot and Aviator Tribunal for the IGC. Galen knew that even after eons of time, women still had it harder than men. It took more work and determination to rise through the ranks – especially these ranks. Yet, here, they outnumbered them.

The doctor's blue eyes narrowed. There was something else about these women. Though they had more than enough money at their disposal for any age or beauty enhancing treatments, they all looked their natural age, or close to it.

Pride, Galen thought. *They have too much pride.*

"I'm just saying," the elfin doctor continued, "it will be a terrible waste not to let de Rossi continue. She is a genetic anomaly, one that is hardly ever seen, being exactly half human and half elf. She has the speed and reflexes of a human, and the longevity and senses of an elf. Should she make Jordan, and be accepted by a Fledgling, she could be the first female to Captain a Dragon."

At his last remark every woman on the panel shifted, ever so slightly. A straighter back here, a raised chin there, even Lizbeth let her claws unfurl for a moment. Neither male judge seemed to care.

"I'll grant it was a stupid mistake," Galen continued. "But it is one that will not be repeated, even in the case of a loophole."

The judges exchanged glances and Galen sighed heavily.

"Jordan School is the most grueling training there is. She might not make it. Even if she does, a Fledgling might not accept her. All I am asking is that she is given the chance."

One of the female judges cleared her throat. "He does have a point," she conceded.

"What is your interest in this?" Colonel Asti asked suspiciously, her eyes narrowed at the handsome doctor. Galen smiled.

"It is purely scientific."

Lizbeth eyed him a moment longer. "You'll have our answer via Strepcod by the end of the month." She banged a heavy gavel down on the table, dismissing him and sending rivulets of water streaming down the crystal pitchers.

Galen stood and bowed at the panel, keeping his smile hidden. He already knew what the answer would be.

His image, along with the image of the Tribunal Court and its judges, flickered and went out as Jordan Blue turned off the screen with a flick of a burnished steel switch. She had watched the video a dozen times now.

The Jordan of the Blue Fledgling had been all over the human galaxy for the better part of a month, but had spent most of her time circling the planet of Saturn in the first system of the MW1.

She had spent a month with Calyph, working on the first full-sized growing for her Fledgling. It had been amazing: how Cyan was able to grow, what she was able to do to help, and how she could physically feel the growing within herself. It was as if her heart was growing, taking up more space inside her slight frame.

Cyan now had two seats in the cockpit, a proper cabin for Blue, a galley and a latrine. From nose to tail he measured forty-two meters and had a forty-meter wingspan, making him almost twice the size he had been only a few months ago.

With his newly increased size, along with the Jordan being the only living body aboard, he seemed a ghost ship with a skeleton crew– slipping silently from one system to the next, searching.

Jordan Blue, almost a ghost herself and haunted by her thoughts, switched back and forth between manual flight to letting her Fledgling fly at will, talking only to Cyan when she could tell he was distressed by her inner musings.

She looked ghostly enough – a pale white face seemingly suspended in the dark cabin, her body camouflaged by its black Mylar suit that only occasionally reflected back glints of starlight.

The Jordan had her latest set of flight suits made in black Mylar rather than her normal shimmering blue that complemented her Fledgling, out of mourning for those whom she had so recently lost. The first set had been pure black, but so shiny that she felt she looked like some sort of emaciated dominatrix.

The new set had been embedded with silver-edged scales, and bore the number eight stitched into her upper left arm in blue and silver thread, giving at least a slight indication of who she was.

Her platinum blonde hair was piled on her head in a high and smooth pompadour before it was gathered at her neck by a black ribbon and then fell in three perfect coils of white gold over the tops of her shoulder blades.

A double ripple of puckered flesh marred the right side of her otherwise beautiful face. The rest of her skin was creamy white and bright blue eyes peered out over high cheekbones. The scar was the result of a Lethe pipe exploding in her face.

Crushed by her father's refusal to attend her graduation, a graduation with honors that had made aviation history and set a record for the youngest pilot to graduate from IGC Advanced Flight, Lethe was the first and last drug she had ever tried.

True to the nature of the drug, she hardly remembered a thing after her first hit, and had a bit of trouble piecing together much that had happened before. The sweet forgetfulness was short-lived and she woke up some days later in a white room with the scar, an artificial eye, and the most handsome elf she had ever seen.

Galen had been just as enamored with her as she was with him and she stayed with him long after she had recovered from her accident. They had lived together and loved together before her Jordan training, and then after the JTC and her selection by the Blue Fledgling she still returned to the pod they shared every chance she could.

Happier than she had ever thought possible, she soon forgot what and why she had wanted to forget. She had found the love of her life. She had made it through the Jordan training and had been selected by a Fledging on the first Third Generation Dragon to hatch eggs. She was an accomplished pilot and a high-ranking officer in the IGC. She had a new family aboard the Opal Dragon; a brother in Jade, the Jordan of the Green Fledgling, and a sister in Scarlett, the Jordan of the Red Fledgling. Like most sisters, they were often at odds with one another, though Blue never gave it much thought. Captain Brogan was like a father to her.

Then it had all gone to shit.

Galen was dead. Jade was dead. Scarlett had gone mad and had done everything she could to take Blue with her. Brogan, the Commander of the Opal Dragon, was distraught to the point where the ship's overbearing Executive Officer, Commander Blaylock, was making most executive decisions aboard the Dragon.

Blue had gotten away the first chance she could and every chance after. She began patrolling the empty depths of space, looking for answers, but all she found in the darkness was more darkness.

Jordan Scarlett had tried to convince the Blue Jordan that she wasn't real, only a highly made construct that the Chimeran army had managed to get into the ranks of the IGC. Though Blue had no doubts to her own reality, Scarlett had thrown some nasty facts in her scar-ravaged face that had made the Blue Jordan quite uneasy.

The first was a micro-bio that Scarlett had run on Blue's mother that claimed Christa de Rossi only had five daughters. Calyph, the Dragon's Engineer, cleared the bio as soon as they were back aboard the giant living ship that was the Opal Dragon – at least his troll had done so, with the right questions.

Calyph ran a number of biographies on her parents and finally found the answer. A full bio and records check logged in the IGC system, though it had been lengthy, showed that one of Blue's sisters had been missing since the start of the Chimeran Rebellion and, since it had been over one hundred years, was presumed dead.

The Red Jordan's other accusation was that no pilot that had used Lethe would be endorsed, much less licensed by the InterGalactic Council. That accusation Blue found hard to rebut, since the proof of her drug incident was literally clear upon her face.

Again it was Calyph that had come to the rescue. After numerous searches via his troll, the Engineer's historian droid, he had produced the recording of Galen and the Pilot's Tribunal that she had now watched a dozen times.

It didn't make her feel any better.

Galen, only days before his death, had inserted a micro-dot communication chip behind her left ear, and a similar one on the upper edge of his own jawline. Even after his murder, the Jordan and the doctor had been able to communicate – physically as well as audibly. Blue did not know whether it was due to the bond they had shared or the manner of his death, but it was her choice to cut the link and close him off from her eyes and her ears and her body.

His last words to her, however, had been more cryptic than Scarlett's. He had told her to find Faith, and to remember the rings of Saturn.

Finding Faith was no problem. Blue had known that he meant her oldest sister and not some act of religion. But the Jordan had no desire to see a sibling that she felt nothing for and had no memories of – contact with her would be a last resort.

His other message had her stumped. She seemed to remember something about the rings of Saturn, something that had to do with her family, but she couldn't put her finger on what it was.

Jordan Scarlett had now been gone a fortnight, sent off to a farm on a fabricated satellite on the far side of Jupiter. Blue had followed only a couple of days later, glancing at the coordinates that hovered above the dash console as she flew by the moon, wondering if Scarlett had yet eaten everyone alive.

The Blue Jordan passed the moon in a blink on her way to the next planet in MW1 and had circled it one black day after another, flying next to the multi-ringed gas giant as it spun its way with horrendous power through the small solar system. The Jordan hoped that seeing it would jar some buried memory, but for two weeks now she had only been alternately frustrated and bored.

Blue, after cutting off the video, lifted her sapphire-colored eyes to look out the glass eyes of her Fledgling. She held out her hands and immediately they were filled with the soft metal wheel that allowed her to manually take over flight control. Turning and pushing the wheel, she dipped back close to Saturn. Closer than most ships could go, lest they be ripped apart by its crushing gravity and scattered by its whirling winds to become part and prisoner of its infamous rings.

There were Jabret ships in the outer banks, bobbing and weaving like giant water spiders, harvesting select chunks of debris in the seventh ring that were laden with heavy metals.

Blue took Cyan over the sixth ring, then the fifth. She pulled in over the fourth ring and then dipped a wing and dove down through the third, Cyan riding the torrential winds and her deft hand keeping them clear of the racing debris.

Second ring, first ring. She had been through all of them before and had seen nothing out of the ordinary, nothing of note. They looked the same as they had looked the last time around, and the time before that. There was nothing but rubble, varying from huge asteroid-sized chunks to tiny bits, traveling thousands of kilometers per hour, whirling around the gaseous orange ball without cause or care. In some places the rings rose and fell, mountains and valleys of semi-coalesced regolith.

Blue flew between the rings and the planet itself, closer to the gas giant than any human-built ship could ever go, tipping Cyan so that his smooth belly was a boldfaced challenge to the planet's crushing gravity and baleful glare.

She could feel the gravitational pull, a tug upon her craft so insistent that, even cradled safely inside her Dragon Fledgling, she could feel the pull upon her body – relentless and sexual and angry. She let go of the flywheel and it sank back into the silver fleshed dashboard of her living craft.

"Fuck it," she muttered. "Take us out."

She leaned back into her seat, feeling Cyan dip and turn as he maneuvered his silver body and lone passenger through the whirling belts surrounding the glowering gas giant. Titan, Saturn's largest moon, kept a wary eye on them from the darkness.

Her left hand lay limp and motionless in her lap, the wrist enclosed by a smooth band of platinum. The fingers of her right hand trailed along the edge of the band as if absently contemplating triggering her field, or turning back on the link she had previously shared with Galen.

She wondered if he was still with her. Was he really only as far away as the touch of a sensor, or was he fading away into the ether? Was he already gone for good?

The Jordan did not know if his last message had been clipped because he knew that he only had seconds, or if they were purposely cryptic so she would need him to decipher their meaning.

Probably both, she thought caustically.

Looking down, she saw her hand and snatched it back, away from the band. She pushed herself up and out of her molded silver chair.

"Let's head for Jupiter," she told Cyan. "No rush, though. I need time to think."

The Fledgling made a deep purring noise that was a combination of the man-made and installed motor drive gearing up within the area of where his spine should be, and a sound of communication that was purely his own.

The Jordan made her way through his newly enlarged inner cavity towards his belly. There was a small galley there with both refrigeration and cooking equipment but as of yet neither had been used. Blue slid open a stainless steel cupboard door and pulled out a large jar that was plain silver except for numerical bar coding along the side. She jerked open a metal drawer that gave an angry rattle of jostled flatware and selected a large spoon.

Sitting down on one of the small benches along the short table that was bolted to the floor, the Jordan unscrewed the lid of the jar and stuck the spoon inside, extracting a large hunk of peanut butter. She ate it directly off of the spoon, taking her time, considering her options.

It wasn't that she did not want to see Galen, she did – badly. But he hadn't been completely honest with her and she was no longer the over-jubilant trusting soul that she had been only a month ago.

I was so naïve, she thought bitterly, chomping down on the bits of nut inside the paste. *I probably still am. But I'm not ever going to trust anyone so blindly again. Those days are over.*

She wished that Jade, at least, was still around. It had always been easy to talk to the Green Jordan and his advice was always wise and simple. She missed his kind demeanor and boyish smile. His brown hair often hung over his eyes in a way that reminded her of Galen. Blue shook her head, willing away the tears that threatened.

She licked the last of the peanut butter from the spoon and sighed, feeling dejected and empty. She knew that the happy and innocent part of her life was over and the realization made her feel miserable. She tossed the spoon into the galley's dish cleaner where there were only more dirty spoons.

The Jordan glanced aft down the small corridor where her cabin, complete with a bed big enough for two, waited. Other than a few personal items and an extra flight suit, it was empty – and as unused as the equipment in the galley.

Blue headed for the cockpit, thinking absently that it would someday be a bridge. She knew she would be more comfortable in her chair than alone in some strange bed, even one inside her Fledgling. She eased herself into her seat and thought of her dead lover and her lost childhood. She wanted Galen so badly that it made everything inside her hurt, but she wanted answers first.

The Jordan leaned back and the chair moved with her, elongating so that she could stretch out her legs. She turned onto her side and the arms of the chair rose up and folded around her body.

At least she had her Fledgling. The Jordan was sure that he was the one thing that would be hers forever, and for that she was grateful.

"Thank you," she whispered, closing her blue eyes against the night.

Cyan purred in response, taking her where she wanted to go.

FOUR

The frigate gave a lurch just before it landed with a jolt, jarring the only two passengers on board besides the pilot. The Chimeran officers had already changed from their blue uniforms into the plain gray pants and snug black shirts worn by newly made constructs at the main GwenSeven manufacturing plant.

"Sorry" the Chimeran pilot apologized over the com system. "I'm used to docking, not landing."

"Don't worry about it," Security Officer Connor Malone muttered. Operations Officer Jasyn Issord leered at him, his hazel eyes full of merriment.

"If you're scared, say you're scared," he teased. Connor grinned at him.

"I'm scared."

"Are you serious?" Jasyn asked leaning towards the other officer, his dark brows raised high over his hazel eyes. "I was only joking."

Connor laughed nervously. "I'm not worried about what's going to happen to me," he said. "I just want to do a good job. I want to get the Commander what he is after. I don't want to let him down."

Jasyn shrugged as the frigate settled down, hissing and beeping. "Just get whatever intel you can. Personally, I think he wants her dead more than he wants information. Do whatever you have to and get out. How hard can that be?"

"I don't know," Connor said. "You make it sound so easy. I guess I'm not just the same make as you."

Jasyn nodded. He had heard as much before, even from their own Commander. "An intriguing air of detachment," JP had once remarked. The Chimeran knew that he had what was considered an abnormal amount of control over his emotions, especially for a construct. He also knew that it would serve him well should he be selected by the de Rossi woman – and he had the strangest feeling that she certainly would choose him.

"Best of luck gentlemen," the pilot said over the com. "May the One watch over you both."

"And you as well," the officers replied in unison.

The compressed air of the cabin escaped with a hiss as the door was opened. A man's face poked in and looked around. He had close-cropped hair that was reddish-orange, a large nose, and inquisitive eyes with yellow irises. They fixed upon the two officers seated in the frigate.

"This way," he whispered nervously before his head disappeared back through the metal hatch.

Jasyn smirked at the other officer. "This way," he whispered at Connor before he stood up and headed for the door. Connor gave the Operations Officer a good-natured but well placed punch on his right shoulder blade.

The officers stepped from the frigate into the cool night air of Dione – the terraformed moon of Jupiter that was home to the largest GwenSeven construct facility in the universe.

They descended a set of metal stairs to a deserted asphalt tarmac. The concrete was old and broken, with dry, persistent weeds stretching up desperately between the cracks. The area looked like it had been abandoned long ago. The man who had poked his face into their aircraft stood waiting for them at the bottom, his long nose lifted as if testing the air.

"This way," he repeated, and hurried away.

The officers glanced at each other and then followed. The

man led them, scurrying across the darkened tarmac and through the night. They trotted along behind him until a great building began to grow before them in the distance like the rise of a long and jagged black hole.

The three figures kept a swift pace, yet it was half an hour before they met the growing edifice of darkness. All three were dewed with sweat and panting in the thin atmosphere as they stood in the silhouette of the massive shadow. Jasyn filled his lungs with the cool night air as he eyed the building that now took up his whole field of vision from one side to the other.

It was here, he thought, trying to conjure up the memory. *It was in here, somewhere, that the Commander found me. Where he saved me. He said he found me unconscious, bleeding from a blow to the head.*

"Lord Almighty," Connor breathed, looking straight up the side of the unmarked concrete wall before him. "What in the name of the One do they have going on in there?"

The man that had led them there grinned. "You'll see. This way!" He turned to his left and trotted along the side of the building with the officers following close behind. They continued on for what Connor estimated must be a half a klick before their escort brought them to a stop at a steel door inset with a glass pad for a fingerprint read.

The man pulled a gigantic, clanking ring of keys from his pocket. The ring held old-fashioned metal keys, flat plastic key cards, slim glass vials, and a number of severed fingers reeking of formaldehyde.

"Mercy," Connor muttered, turning his face away. Jasyn watched transfixed, though every muscle in his body tensed, as the man selected one of the amputated fingers on his ring and held it against the glass pad.

There was a muffled beep and a clank, and then the steel door swung open.

"This way," the man encouraged, motioning with his hand,

the one devoid of the gruesome key ring.

The Chimeran officers entered a brightly lit hallway and glanced about. The corridor was empty but the man who had led them there gasped, frightened. The officers looked up and down the corridor again but it was empty.

Jasyn's eyes followed the man's gaze to Connor's neck and flinched. Against the smooth black skin of the Chimeran lay a gold chain of linked figure eights. With his jaw clenched, Jasyn reached out and wrapped his fingers around the chain and gave it a sharp pull. It came free with a snap.

Connor's dark eyes went wide and then squeezed shut. "May the One have mercy! I am so sorry!"

Jasyn leaned close to the other Chimeran. "And you're the *Security* Officer!" he hissed, chastising him.

"I am so sorry," Connor said again. "I don't know how I overlooked it. I guess I was so worried about everything else."

Jasyn blew a burst of air out from his bottom lip that went up over his face. He closed his eyes and nodded, understanding. He opened his eyes and pushed the officer's chain into the hand of the man that had brought them from the frigate.

"Drop that down the nearest incinerator," he told him.

The man nodded vigorously as he pocketed the chain. Then he reached over to Jasyn and clipped an identification badge on the left side of his shirt. Jasyn looked down to see a fuzzy picture of himself, his first name printed in bold letters, and a bar code.

The man turned to Connor and clipped one onto the other officer's shirt. Connor gave his own badge a quick glance and took a deep breath to steady himself.

"Thank you," he told the man. The man smiled and nodded and then, as if suddenly remembering what they were about, hurried down the hallway. He motioned for the two officers to follow.

"This way!" he urged.

The man ushered them down a series of passageways, twisting and turning, and then up four flights of concrete stairs and down another corridor. He brought them to another door with a fingerprint keypad on the wall and, to Connor's great relief, the man used his own finger to gain entrance.

The door slid open to reveal a small dining room where five young men were picking up metal trays of used dishes and flatware and pushing them over a tiled countertop and through a square hole in the wall. They all wore the same gray pants and black shirts, and looked at the newcomers with blank curiosity.

"You, and you," the long-nosed escort said, pointing at the two in line at the counter that still had metal trays in their hands. "Come with me." He looked at the Chimeran officers he had brought with him and motioned them away. "You two should get back to your rooms," he commanded with a sudden air of authority.

Jasyn nodded and watched the man lead the two he had chosen back through the door they had just come from without another glance. Then he and Connor turned to face the other three still in the room. Two had blonde hair and one soft brown, though all three were lean and muscular with handsome, sharply angled faces. Of course they had all been manufactured that way.

One of the blondes looked at the two newcomers and grinned like an idiot. The other blonde and the one with brown hair stared hard at the two that had so recently entered. Jasyn and Connor met their steely gaze and gave them a curt nod. The two relaxed noticeably and returned the nod.

A door on the other side of the room opened and a tired looking woman in a rumpled gray suit covered by a white lab coat entered, holding a large acrylic in the crook of her arm. "Okay boys, let's get back to your room," she said, pushing and keeping the door open for them with her free hand.

The five young men filed out, Connor and Jasyn walking directly behind the two that they presumed were from the other Chimeran Battle Cruiser, *Macedonian.* The handsome simpleton and the woman in the lab coat brought up the rear. They didn't go far.

The men in front took the first right hand corridor and slowed as they passed a row of numbered doors with no handles. They reached the last door in the corridor and came to stop. The brown-haired construct pulled his badge from his shirt and held it in front of a small panel next to the door. The door slid open instantly with hardly a whisper. The construct put the badge back on his shirt and went inside, followed by the others.

Jasyn's hazel eyes took in everything at once. A living space with two gray sofas, a glass flatscreen on the wall and a small steel table with a six-button remote, a sleeping area with six bunks, and a door that led to a washroom. It was sparse and utilitarian with tiled white walls and floor.

"Have a good night boys," the woman said from the hallway in a tired but kind voice as she held her own badge next to the panel. The door slid shut and this time there was the unmistakable snick of a bolt sliding home.

One of the blonde constructs hurried to the door and pressed his ear against it, listening. After a few moments he turned away, satisfied. His badge had the name 'Steven' printed in large black letters.

"She's gone," he told the others.

The other blonde construct, Chip, if his badge was correct, sat on one of the sofas and turned on the flatscreen.

The brown-haired construct motioned for Jasyn and Connor to have a seat. "I'm Alan," he told the two officers as they sank down onto a couch. "Out of the way, Chip," he ordered.

Chip flashed him a brilliant smile and obligingly moved to the end of the other sofa without a word. Alan sat down and, when Steven joined him, Chip scooted a little farther away to accommodate him, his eyes going back to the flatscreen as he flipped through the channels with the remote.

"It's good to see you guys," Steven told them.

"You too," Connor agreed. "You guys really have a bead on everything here."

Steven shrugged. "We've been here for a few days. It didn't take long to figure everything out."

"How do you know who we are?" Jasyn asked.

Alan snorted. "Are you kidding?" He looked at Chip. "Chip, turn that damn thing off," he ordered. Chip picked up the remote and turned off the screen. He turned to Alan, a shy smile on his handsome face.

"Is there something else you would like me to do, Alan?" he asked.

Alan shook his head. "No. Go ahead and turn it back on."

"Is there something you would like to watch?"

"No, you pick."

Chip turned the screen back on and turned his blue eyes back to Alan. "Is the volume too loud?"

"No, it's fine," Alan told him, making a shooing gesture at the construct. Chip turned his chiseled face back towards the screen and Alan turned his attention back to the other Chimeran officers.

"I see what you mean," Jasyn said, his voice flat.

"Mercy," Connor whispered. They had been told what to expect, and what would be expected of them, but this was the first time either he or Jasyn had actually seen a live example of what GwenSeven was manufacturing these days - all for consumer demands, of course.

"I know," Steven said, looking at Chip. "It's disgusting."

"It's why we are fighting," Jasyn said, and for the first time he understood the hatred that his Commander harbored for

GwenSeven and the women that had created it. They were playing the One God, and doing a poor job – condemning creatures like Chip to a life of idiot savant servitude.

"Where is Petrov?" Alan demanded.

"Are you sure this room isn't bugged or monitored?" Connor asked, his voice low. Steven nodded.

"We ran a scan, and then staged a fight, just in case," he said, grinning. "We don't have anything to worry about and they certainly aren't worried about us. Why would they? A room full of Chips isn't going to cause any harm."

Chip turned at the sound of his name. "How are you doing, Steven?"

"I'm fine, Chip. Watch your show."

"Would you like to watch it with me? It's about the extinct animals of Earth."

Alan snorted again. "Does it include humans?"

Chip grinned at him, "I don't think so, but it is still very interesting." Alan shook his head and Chip looked questioningly at Steven, who also shook his head. The construct looked at Jasyn and Connor. "Would either of you gentlemen like to watch the program? Though we could watch something else if you wish."

"That's okay," Jasyn said softly.

"No thank you, Chip," Connor said, his own voice barely above a whisper.

Chip turned his attention once again back to the flatscreen.

"Petrov?" Alan urged.

"He couldn't make it," Connor said.

"What does that mean?"

"Commander Petrov was needed aboard the *Resurrection*," Jasyn informed him, closing the subject.

Alan sat back, scowling. "Damn!" he cursed, frustrated.

"He was our blonde-blue," Steven explained. "With him, we would have had the deck fully stacked. Now we'll be taking a chance that The Lung might pick Chip."

Jasyn knew that The Lung was the moniker for Charity de Rossi. And not just on this mission, he had heard her called by that name in the past. Officer Issord looked at the other constructs and for the first time he noticed the differences in the complexions of the Chimeran officers.

His own complexion was a tan olive, his hair black and his eyes hazel. Those hazel eyes glanced first at Connor, with his ebony skin and dark eyes, then to Alan's chestnut hair and green eyes. Steven had a golden skin tone with sandy blonde hair and soft brown eyes. Chip, like Petrov, was very fair with white blonde hair and bright blue eyes.

"I see your point," Jasyn said. He saw Connor's dark eyes traveling over the small group in the same manner. "Did The Lung select any preference when she placed the order?"

Alan shook his head. "No. That's why the Commanders chose a variety."

"Was there *anything* specific about her requisition?" Jasyn asked. It seemed that the other officers were privy to more information than he and Connor had been given.

Alan grinned at him. "I heard that the survey a client is given when they order a new construct consists of nearly a hundred questions. For a companion construct the questionnaire is more detailed and has over three hundred questions. The Lung didn't answer any of them. She simply wrote a note on it asking for a male companion out of the second age bracket."

"That's pretty vague," Jasyn agreed.

"Well," Steven said with a shrug, "at least we have four out of five. Those are pretty good odds."

Connor nodded. "We will just have to pray that the One guides her choice."

Steven and Alan stared at the officer as if he had just told them that he was an ovulating Golgoth.

"Ohhh-kay," Alan said, drawing the word out after a few moments of silence. "Well, she will be here sometime tomorrow night. We should probably get some sleep."

Chip picked up the remote and switched off the flatscreen. "I think that is a wonderful idea, Alan."

Alan rolled his green eyes and pushed himself up off of the couch. Steven followed him into the washroom where Jasyn could hear them joking and laughing. He could hardly believe that they were officers, though he knew that different ships held different levels of discipline. Still, it seemed that they treated Chip in the same manner of the people they were fighting against.

Connor stood and reluctantly headed for the washroom as well. Jasyn followed Chip into the bunkroom where two racks of three metal bunks each were pushed against the right and left walls. Each held a thin mattress and even thinner blankets.

"Where should I sleep, Chip?" Jasyn asked.

"Wherever you would like," he replied, his eyes flicking quickly to the badge on his chest, "Jasyn." He offered Jasyn a shy smile.

"Where do Alan and Steven sleep?" Jasyn asked.

"Over there," Chip said, pointing to the left side of the room. He headed for the bunks on the right. "I sleep up here," he said, motioning with his hand. "On the top."

"Do you mind if I sleep under you?" Jasyn asked.

Chip grinned. "Of course not." He kicked off his shoes and climbed up the side rail to the top bunk.

Jasyn watched him go, his hazel eyes intent. When the construct was settled in his bunk he turned so that the upper-half of his body was hanging off of his bed and looked down at Jasyn.

"Goodnight, Jasyn," he said with a warm, if goofy, smile. Jasyn couldn't help but smile back.

"Goodnight, Chip."

Jasyn sat down on the bottom bunk and pulled off his shoes, then carefully placed them on the floor so as not to be in anyone's way. He climbed up into the middle bunk so Connor would not have to clamber over him, and settled onto the mattress with his hands laced behind his head.

Steven had said they had a four out of five chance of success. As far as Jasyn was concerned, the odds were much slimmer. He knew that each of them had a chance at being selected and carrying out the mission. Their success, however, would be in degrees as varied as their appearances. Officer Issord knew then and there that he was the best shot they had, which made the chances one in five.

JP had always advised his officers on prayer first, action second - though Officer Issord, over the years, had quite often seen the Commander lash out with furious action that was quickly followed by fervent prayer.

Nonetheless, he took the Commander's advice and he closed his eyes to pray, deciding on the action he would take tomorrow. If Chip was the model of what the consumer was after, Jasyn planned on being the model construct by the very next night, when Charity de Rossi was expected to arrive.

FIVE

"When I was your age," Grandpa declared, "the fastest we could make any object fly through space was at 130,000 miles per hour, and the fastest speed that we knew of was the speed of light."

Jeanette listened from her place on Grandpa's rug, her brown eyes wide. "But that is so slow," she whispered.

Grandpa shrugged. "It is now," he told her. "Back then, it was impossibly fast. We called anything faster 'warp speed,' or something like that."

Jeanette rolled over on her back, her small hands clutching her ribcage as she laughed. "Warp speed!" she exclaimed. "Grandpa! You're pulling my leg!"

"I am not!" Grandpa said, bristling.

Jeanette rolled back onto her stomach and her dark brows arched up over her bright brown eyes. "Then how in the world did they get everyone from Earth to Jupiter without dying of old age?" she asked. "It would have taken *forever*."

"They froze 'em," Grandpa told her.

Her wide eyes grew even wider until they were perfectly round. "Do you mean cryo?" she whispered.

"I think that is what they called it," Grandpa admitted.

Jeanette made a face. "They really used to do that? I don't believe it. It is so...so barbaric!"

Grandpa threw back his head and cawed laughter at ceiling through his old and broken teeth. "Girl, you have no idea what barbaric is! I can't believe you even know the word!"

"Of course I do," she declared. "I know lots of words, and I know Cryo was outlawed before I was born!"

"It was?"

"Yes!"

"Why?"

Jeanette's tiny shoulders pulled up in a shrug. "I think it was because too many people died from it."

Grandpa rubbed his chin thoughtfully, feeling the white stubble that had to be at least two days worth of growth. He was pretty sure they still froze people, but his memory was pretty hazy these days and even his grasp on the present was a tenuous one. He thought he had just shaved that morning.

"You'll have to ask your Aunt Johanna," he told the girl on the rug.

"I will. I like Auntie Jo."

"Is that so?"

"Yes. She always tells me the truth – everyone else still treats me like a baby. And Sean says she's a real ass-kicker."

"Don't you start using that language," Grandpa scolded, his bushy white eyebrows knotting over his bleary blue eyes.

"I'm only saying what Sean said!" Jeanette told him before hiding a giggle behind a slim fingered hand, now only slightly chubby. Her once round face was beginning to thin but was still soft with youthful innocence.

Grandpa wondered, as he always did, how old she was. *Still a child*, he thought. *I know that much. But for how much longer?*

She would be a beautiful girl someday, and fortunate. Many girls who favored their father's looks were not so lucky. Jeanette was a beautiful girl that would undoubtedly be a beautiful woman. One with a creamy smooth complexion, dark curls and flashing dark eyes - a spitting image of her Aunt.

A spitting image of... Grandpa thought hard but could not remember. The face was a blur and the name....

The old man felt a lump rise in his throat and a bulge of terror tighten in his belly. There was something horrifying about that. He knew he was forgetting something that should never be forgotten. The realization filled him with sorrow and fear.

Jeanette wiggled around on Grandpa's itchy rug, trying to get comfortable. Same old rug, brand new pod. John and Rebecca had finished unpacking his things for him just a few hours ago and were now working on unpacking their own things in the pod across the hall. Grandpa could hear Sean complaining even through the expensive new walls.

New klick, new pod. Grandpa wondered how many times he had moved in his lifetime and decided it would be ridiculous to try and count. Usually he had a pod in a building close to John and Rebecca and sometimes it was even in the same building, if it could be arranged, but even then it was often on a different floor. Never right 'cross the hall.

Rebecca had told him it was so he could help keep an eye on the children. They could come to his pod after school or whatever dance/ball/music practice they had. Grandpa knew better. His mind might be getting mushy but it wasn't entirely gone, not yet anyway. The children were most likely to be keeping an eye on *him*.

Both the children were old enough and the school close enough for them to ride the link to Grandpa's new pod by themselves. He supposed that it gave them someplace to go where they would not be alone until their parents got home.

At least I'm not entirely useless, he thought. *Not yet.*

His days were already muddled because of different schools and schedules, early release, late start, dance class, gaming circles and spheres. Who knew what else? Not him. They just showed up and it was easy to be there because he was always there.

He wasn't about to learn their routines. It was hard enough to manage even without considering their parents' schedules - and why they worked Grandpa never knew. Johanna made more than they ever thought she would, more than they could dream of making even though they were both well-paid professionals.

They had worked, of course, while Johanna was in flight school, taking care of their family along with the costs of her tuition. They had not expected the way or speed with which she would climb to the top, and Grandpa supposed they did not see the need to leave their jobs once there was more money than they could spend.

"Okay then, Miss Smartypants," Grandpa said, watching Jeanette perk up on the rug. "Can you tell me why your parents still work?"

Jeanette swung her legs around with a childlike grace and then tucked them under her butt so that she was sitting up. To Grandpa she looked as bright and fragile as a firefly, just before he tried to recall what a firefly was.

"They believe in what they do," she told Grandpa as if it were the most obvious thing in the world.

"Is that so?" he asked softly, wondering if the child in front of him was really still a child or if his bleary eyes and his mushy brain were playing tricks on him.

"Of course. They think that everyone can and should make a difference, no matter how small."

"How small a difference, or how small a person?"

Jeanette giggled, showing her age. "I never thought about that before, Grandpa! Both, I suppose."

Grandpa gave her a gap-toothed smile. "And what are you doing to make a difference, little Jean?" Jeanette laughed and the sound was like music to his ears. Most people grimaced when Grandpa smiled. He knew his teeth had seen better days the better part of a century ago.

"I'm keeping you company Grandpa! But tomorrow, I'll make you cupcakes!"

"I like cupcakes," Grandpa informed her.

"Who doesn't?" Jeanette laughed. "If we don't have the stuff to make them you can walk me to the market. It's right on the other side of the park."

"Maybe I could take you to the park?" Grandpa asked.

Jeanette made a face. "It's a baby park," she told him. Then her face brightened. "But you will like it Grandpa."

"Why, do you think I'm a baby? If so, maybe you can push me on the swings."

Jeanette fell back over on the floor, laughing. "Nooo, Grandpa! I just think you will like it out there." She sat up, her face exquisitely serious but her eyes still twinkling. "There is grass and trees and a big, blue sky!"

"Blue sky?" Grandpa let out a low whistle as Jeanette nodded, her dark eyes shining. "I haven't seen the sky for a long time," he admitted.

"Sean and I had never seen real sky, until today. When Mom and Dad were moving you up here, we laid on the grass and stared at it for an hour."

"I'll bet," he said. Grandpa nodded and rubbed his unshaven chin. "I think I'm actually looking forward to that myself."

"Really?" Jeanette asked. She knew that Grandpa never left his pod unless it was to move into another one. She thought that there might be something that he was afraid of outside, though she would never say it or ask outright. Then she remembered something Sean had told her.

"It's the safest neighborhood there is," she informed him. "And Sean said that there are no street people." Jeanette wasn't sure what he had meant by that, but she hoped it might be something that reassured Grandpa. She watched him closely for his reaction.

Grandpa grunted, but didn't say anything about the street

people. The pod was quiet and even the pod across the hall seemed to be bereft of the sounds of moving crates, the squeak of the helper droid, and Sean's constant grumbling.

"Do you start your new school tomorrow?" he asked.

"No, Grandpa. No school tomorrow. Tomorrow I'm going to make you cupcakes! But for now, I'm going to head home." She stood up and rubbed her butt. "It's quiet over there, which means it's probably safe to go back."

"Do you think you are a big enough girl to get your Grandpa a glass of water from the fridge?"

"Of course!" She bounded away with the energy of a puppy and was back in moments with a tall glass of his special water.

"Thank you little Jean," Grandpa said, carefully taking the glass from her with both hands.

"You're welcome, Grandpa," she said. She planted a kiss on his cheek and then drew back quickly, rubbing her lips with the back of her hand. "Ow, Grandpa!" she scolded. "You feel like a cactus!"

"Do you know what cactus is?" he asked.

Jeanette frowned at him. "Well, no," she admitted. "But I've seen pictures."

Grandpa threw back his head and crowed laughter. After a moment Jeanette joined him, laughing even as she trounced out of his pod, her dark curls bouncing and the door closing behind her.

♋

The Aridian ran her

No, his *hands. My hands are his hands now*

over her

his

new body. Her newly enlarged body.

By gods I am huge! she thought with elation as she touched the different pieces and parts. *What a body I have!*

The Rogue Doppelgänger had never taken such an enormous body before. She thought at first that she would be disgusted, but then found that she was fascinated, even stimulated.

She felt unable to stop running her hands over the expanse of flesh that encircled her. It was heavy, it was protective, it was provocatively sexual. Grinning, she rotated her hips and shook her wide bottom. She ran thick-fingered hands all over her new form until they were in her pants. The Aridian, laughing and gyrating, fell heavily on the hotel bed, thrashing like a watery leviathan in its death throes. She lay there for a while, her flesh quivering and panting heavily.

Not a lot of stamina with this much body, she thought, feeling her enlarged heart work twice as hard at what should be a simple job. *It needs less activity and more rest.*

After almost half an hour of catching her breath, she finally gave a guttural laugh and heaved the upper portion of her body forward, trying to propel it from the bed. It took three tries to get up, which wasn't helped by her booming gales of laughter.

When she finally struggled to her feet, the Aridian - wearing the heavy cloak of the Ambassador's body - found the man's acrylic and browsed through his contacts and appointments.

His meetings, she was not surprised to discover, were useless. His associations, however, were as promising as she had hoped. The gray marbles that now served as her eyes searched through the different categories of the Ambassador's connections, many of which were political and powerful.

She had only been running through the contacts – names and positions and distinctions - for ten minutes, not even through the first list yet, when there was a deep rumble from her protruding belly.

"Shush," she told it, giving the bulge a few reassuring pats. "I'll feed you in a little bit. There's work to be done first."

The belly gave a petulant grumble and was silent, but only for another minute. The Aridian touched the gingerish moustache on her upper lip and kept reading, sometimes absently pulling at a bushy gingerish eyebrow. She was just finishing the first list of contacts, which included foreign relations that were non-human/non-elfin, when her stomach growled at her, more insistently this time.

The Aridian sighed.

"How inconvenient," she muttered with the Ambassador's deep voice, but thought that a small snack might not be out of the question. She could certainly take the acrylic with her. With only a small bit of difficulty she was able to get up and struggle into a coat. She poked chubby feet into a pair of shoes and tucked the acrylic under a heavy arm.

"Yes," she said as she left the room to find a restaurant in the hotel tower, "a little snack is just what I need. I can work and eat at the same time."

The idea of eating while working filled her with a strange sort of pleasure.

"Yes, yes," she agreed with herself as she boarded the hotel tower's main lifts. Much to her delight, she found a whole floor of restaurants and, with a hankering for something salty, selected one specializing in fished meats and touched the button.

The lift stopped along the way to pick up a pair of stylishly dressed men with two beautiful construct women before it opened upon the restaurant. The Ambassador held out a beefy arm, letting the others out before him.

"Thank you," both women intoned as their gentlemen led them into the reception area of the establishment. The Ambassador bowed graciously and the Aridian was glad that her head was down because the gray eyes went wide as he almost lost his balance and toppled over. The Rogue shifted her weight back quickly, throwing out an arm to steady the cumbersome body.

The gray eyes glanced around furtively but no one had noticed. She tapped a heavy fist on her barrel of a chest and cleared her throat in which she hoped was a most dignified manner. She exited the lift and was met in the lobby by a beautiful Indasian hostess.

"Ambassador Channing," the hostess greeted warmly. "How lovely it is to see you tonight. Right this way please."

She turned and began to negotiate her way through the tables at a leisurely pace that would be comfortable for the near obese figure of the Ambassador.

The Aridian noticed that another Indasian hostess, identical to the first, stepped up to welcome the restaurant's next patrons. She followed the first hostess wearing the cumbersome body, trying not to bump hips or belly on the backs of people's chairs. It wasn't easy.

"Here we are," the girl announced, holding a hand out to a booth table with a large bench seat.

"Thank you," the Ambassador panted, wiggling the ample bottom into the booth and sitting down with great relief. The Aridian found herself as suddenly tired as she was famished.

"Good evening, sir," the construct waiter said, replacing the hostess who disappeared back to the lobby and handing the Rogue a brightly lit holo menu. "Can I start you out with something?"

"Certainly," the Ambassador rumbled. The Aridian was about to ask for sardines, just a little snack of course, when the Ambassador's belly gave her an irritable twinge. It knew it was too hungry for just a snack. The Rogue drummed her fingers on the belly and perused the holo pictures that floated above the menu.

"Which is larger?" the Ambassador asked the waiter, looking

up at the handsome construct. "The gamlin trout or the sanai bass?"

"Most definitely the bass," the waiter said.

The Ambassador nodded. "I thought so. Then I will take the bass," he said, handing the waiter the flat panel of the holo menu. "With lots of butter."

The waiter accepted the menu with a bow and tapped on it, placing the order.

"And jelly noodles," the Ambassador added.

The waiter bowed and tapped again on the menu.

"And fried chitkrins on the side. And collards."

The waiter bowed again and the Rogue put a finger to the mustached lip before it could order more food.

"Anything to drink, sir?"

"A glass of ivor wine." The Ambassador's fingers wiggled. "Better make that a bottle," he said.

"Very good," the waiter said as he scrolled and typed on the menu. He bowed one more time before hurrying away to get the order that had already been started.

The Aridian sighed and placed the Ambassador's acrylic on the table and went back to work, carefully cataloging the man's associations and marking them for future use.

The food arrived quickly and she noticed that it was quite enjoyable to eat while one worked and, though the acrylic got a bit greasy, by the time she was done with her first dessert she had a list of people to contact.

The initial calls would have to be done delicately. It would not do to be thrown into prison.

The Rogue was not privy to the details of IGC law, but she was sure that if her own people would condemn her to death for doppelgänging, the InterGalactic Council might be more than a bit perturbed at her for murdering and then masquerading as the Ambassador of Tro-lit. Not to mention high-jacking a Dragon Fledgling and selling it on the black market.

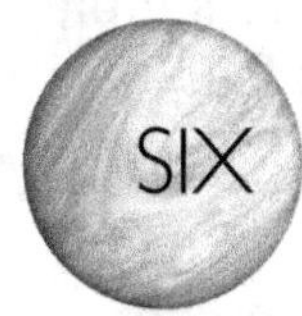

Jasyn followed Chip everywhere the next day, trying to mimic every movement and mannerism. Chip seemed delighted, though Jasyn had no way of knowing if the construct was truly pleased or if he was just programmed to respond that way. He did notice, however, that the construct would display disappointment at times - giving him a broader range of emotions, though it was usually replaced by his standard simpleton grin within seconds.

After lunch, when they had a bit of downtime back in their quarters, he took a seat next to Chip on the couch before the construct could turn on the flatscreen.

"Hey, Chip."

The construct turned his blue eyes to the Chimeran officer sitting next to him. "Hey, Jasyn," he replied, smiling. "Are you having a good time?"

"Yes, thank you. I'm learning a lot."

"Me, too."

"Really?"

"Yes, all the time." He grinned at Jasyn's startled expression. "Why does that surprise you?"

"I don't know," Jasyn said, not wanting to hurt Chip's innocent feelings. "I guess I figured you already knew everything you needed to know."

Chip surprised Jasyn again by laughing. The sound was warm and beguiling.

"Of course I don't know everything! No one can know

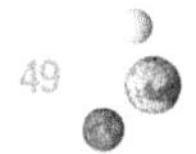

everything, and that is what life is all about. Constant learning is your own personal evolution."

Officer Issord felt as if he had been struck. Chip was simple, but not a dummy. Jasyn didn't know if that made him feel better for the construct, or worse.

"Are you worried at all that your," Jasyn began but then had to pause and swallow before he continued, "that your owner will expect you to already know something that you don't?"

Chip smiled warmly. "No. I think, when the time comes, I will know what to do or they will tell me." He reached out and put a comforting hand on Jasyn's knee, his face full of concern. "Just remember that there is no shame admitting that you don't know. No one knows *everything*. We are all always learning."

Jasyn smiled. "Thank you, Chip."

"You're welcome, Jasyn. Would you like to watch a program?"

"No thanks, I think I'll go lay down for a while."

"Okay."

Jasyn headed for the sleeping area as the glass panel in the wall flared to life. Alan and Steven were sitting on the floor with their backs to the wall, talking softly. Connor was laying on his bunk with his eyes closed, his lips moving in silent prayer. Jasyn said a quick prayer for him.

Jasyn feared the day would last forever but the five constructs were gathered up just after the evening meal and ushered away by a group of women, four humans and one elf. The human women all had short, dark hair and dark eyes. The elf had blonde hair pulled into a tight bun on the back of her head and high arched brows over almond-shaped blue eyes. They all wore matching white lab coats.

Though the women were quiet, there was a taut hum of excitement that swirled about them like an electrical current. They knew full well who was on their way to select a construct that evening. They accompanied the young men down what seemed like an endless amount of corridors, making right and left turns until Jasyn was sure they must be in another part of the compound.

What little scenery they had, of white paneled walls and gray linoleum flooring, changed at one of the turns to polished wood floors and walls covered with holographic light. They came to a stop at an ornately carved wooden door and the elfin woman removed her badge and held it against a panel that was inset into the wall. There was the sound of a lock sliding back and the woman pushed open the door.

The room beyond was plush and painted in warm colors. The lighting was soft and ambient. Thick carpet covered the floor and art that was abstract but eye-pleasing was hung on the walls. There were five small couches, each just large enough to hold two people comfortably.

The women directed each construct to a separate couch and went to work on them – combing hair, buffing fingernails, straightening clothes. They each had a damp cloth that they used to dab at the constructs wherever they thought was appropriate or needed, in the same manner a mother would use with a child. It was also the same manner in which any retailer would polish up his goods for sale. Jasyn didn't know which was worse since both thoughts disgusted him equally.

The Operations Officer thought the whole experience humiliating and for the second time found himself empathizing with JP and his hatred for the de Rossis. He bore it all patiently, wondering how Alan and Steven were taking it. He figured they were either enjoying it thoroughly or were completely incensed. He knew Connor was probably terrified. Chip seemed to be having a great time.

Just as the women were putting on what Jasyn hoped were the finishing touches, the elfin woman straightened, putting a hand to her ear.

"Not here?" she asked, alarmed. "But why?" The woman closed her almond-shaped eyes, listening. "Yes, sir," she said.

She dropped her hand and turned to the other women that were waiting anxiously, their faces drawn.

The woman who had been attending to Jasyn was the first to speak. "What is it, Kate?" she asked. "Is something wrong?"

"Ms. de Rossi will be arriving shortly," Kate informed them, "but she doesn't want to meet them here. We need to take them to the Conjunct."

"What?"

"But why?"

"I don't understand!"

Each woman was openly distraught and confused. Kate held up a hand, shaking her head. "I have no idea," she told them. "I just know that we need to get them over there as quickly as possible."

Each woman regained her composure and as a group they ushered the constructs to their feet and from the room. Keeping a swift pace, they exchanged the wood floors and holographic lighting for tiled corridors lit with fluorescents that ran along the bottoms as well as the tops of the walls.

They reached an intersection in the corridor and Kate, who Jasyn discerned was either the leader or had some sort of seniority, brought them to a halt. She seemed undecided as to which hall to take.

"Through Dev?" the woman next to Jasyn asked.

The one next to Chip also looked at the fair elf woman. "It would be the fastest way," she told her. The elfin woman pressed her thin lips together and nodded. She took the corridor to the right, everyone else following quickly.

The group left the hall and descended a wide staircase that led to a great room where people were working at desks, talking on comsets, and typing into small computers made of glass. They were the first people Jasyn had seen that were not wearing lab coats. On one side of the room was a small gathering of elves deep in discussion around a holo table who was projecting a full-size color image of a female elf.

Most conversation in the room paused as the group passed through, watched by eyes round with surprise, before the talk picked up again in hurried whispers. Jasyn felt heat rising in the hollows of his cheeks and hoped it wouldn't give him away. He looked at Chip who gave him a nervous smile.

At least it's not just me, he thought with relief, seeing that even Chip was not comfortable being the sudden center of attention in such a large group of strangers. Jasyn was relieved when they had finally traversed the room and left through a wide passageway on the other side, leaving the surprised faces and hushed whispers behind.

The five constructs and their chaperones passed through a broad walkway with a high, arched roof made of glass. Jasyn looked through it at the sky outside that was turning a pale pinkish-orange. He guessed that they must be leaving one wing of the compound and entering yet another.

From the glass hallway they entered the next building. They passed through a number of corridors floored with polished stone and then into another series of passages floored with white tile. Finally, they reached a large industrial looking pair of double doors with no handles or knobs.

Kate pulled off her badge and held it against a small panel to the right of the doors and they swung open on silent hinges. The room beyond was so vast and so dark that Jasyn could not see any walls, only a concrete floor with a pathway of light that came from a series of halogen bulbs hanging from an unseen ceiling.

The women led them across the cold floor with its blobs of light until even the door they had come through had disappeared from sight. They reached a brighter spot where the light pooled onto the concrete floor in a wide circle and Kate brought the group to a halt.

They herded the young men into a line so that they were standing shoulder to shoulder and then stepped back to examine them. Kate shook her blonde head, her arched brows coming down over her angled blue eyes, and the other women shuffled each construct a bit until they were half a meter apart. The elf nodded and the women went to work making last minute adjustments on the constructs, brushing at their hair with their fingertips and smoothing out any wrinkles in their clothes.

Jasyn could see why the women had been surprised at having to bring the constructs to such a place. Rather than the intimate room where a client could obviously chat comfortably for a while with a prospective purchase, they were in a space that looked more like an interrogation area, possibly less cozy.

The women had lined them up with Alan on the far left, then Steven, Connor, Jasyn, and finally Chip. Jasyn was about to steal a glance at Officer Malone when he heard a clamor of noise coming from somewhere in front of him.

Far ahead in the darkness, there was a hollow clunk as a hanging halogen bulb came to life, then another, and another, lighting a path for someone to follow. As the sequence of thunking sounds and lights reached the constructs, Jasyn was able to discern the approach of voices.

Most of the voices were soft, though one stood out in contrast to the others, almost as if it were ignoring them, or simply talking above them without regard to what they were saying. The noise grew into a din and then formed itself into a band of people, hastening to keep up with the clear voice that cut through the dark like the prow of a ship. The group came to an abrupt halt when they saw the line of young men, and each chattering tongue fell silent.

The chaperone women promptly finished their grooming and stood aside as the woman known as The Lung, called such for the money she breathed into the IGC, stepped into their pool of light.

Her golden hair was curled and piled and pinned artfully onto the top of her head and jewels sparkled on her ears, throat, and hands. She wore a long, flowing dress of silver cloth lined with gold.

Kate stepped forward to greet her but Charity held up a hand, silencing the woman before she could utter a word.

"Well, well, well!" Charity exclaimed. "What do we have here?" She sauntered up to Alan and eyed him appraisingly with a salacious smile. "Very nice," she remarked, her green eyes meeting his. Alan gave her a bit of a smile but she was already moving to stand in front of Steven.

"Nice," she remarked again with a nonchalance one might use in discussing the weather. She had barely paused to look him up and down before she moved on again and stopped in front of Connor.

Jasyn felt his heart thudding much too hard in his chest and he breathed in slowly through his nose, mentally calming himself, slowing his heart rate. It was all happening so fast now. At least Alan and Steven had already been passed by, which meant his odds were getting better.

Now, Charity had stopped in front of Connor, a lecherous smile making its way across her porcelain features.

"Oh, my," Charity breathed. "How *very* nice!"

Again Jasyn felt his heart rate begin to rise and again he slowed it down, one of his unique abilities he had that had gotten him to where he was, both in the Chimeran ranks as well as where he was standing at the moment.

No, the Operations Officer thought bitterly, praying silently. *Not Connor. Even Chip would be a better choice.* He knew that the other officer from the *Resurrection* was not up to the task.

Charity leaned back slightly with her left shoulder. "Are we currently making any models with goatees?" she asked.

"Facial hair of any sort is not standard," Kate informed her. "It is by preference and strictly by order only."

Charity nodded thoughtfully. "I see. But it might do to throw one into the mix now and then, just to give one an idea."

"Yes, ma'am," Kate replied.

"I'll mention it to my sister," Charity said, almost absently as she began to move down the line. She eyed Jasyn as she strolled by. "Nice. Very nice."

Jasyn's heart sank as she moved passed him. She was already in front of Chip when she turned her head back towards the Chimeran officer, her light brows drawn together. Charity cocked her head, examining his features. Jasyn gave her what he thought was his best imitation of one of Chip's smiles.

Charity's face lit up and she stepped back in front of the olive-skinned Chimeran, moving closer to him this time. "Well, well, well," she said softly. "What do we have here?" Her eyes, green and mischievous, traveled over his face and down his body. She looked down at his badge and trilled laughter. "I'll take him!" she announced, then turned on her heel and walked away, returning down the path of lights while the majority of her entourage hurried to keep up.

Jasyn watched her disappear, her voice going with her, as Kate came up to him and removed his badge. She held out a hand towards the two people from Charity's party that had remained behind, indicating that he was to go to them. He walked towards them, glancing back at the other constructs.

Connor's expression was one of joyous relief. The other two officers looked stoic, their expressions unreadable. Chip gave Jasyn an encouraging grin as the constructs were rounded up by the human women and herded away.

Jasyn turned his face to look at his new escorts. Both were women that had brown eyes and masses of brown hair that hung down their backs, woven into intricate designs. Their faces were elfin, with high-arched, dark brows, but their ears were round. They smiled at him encouragingly as well, though they were obviously anxious to get going. One held out a hand in the direction Charity had gone, inviting him to follow that same path. Jasyn went forward and did not look back.

The two escorts fell into step with him, one on each side, as they hurried over the circles of light on the concrete floor. One said something to him in the elfin tongue and he shook his head. He had understood what she had said, but knew he was better off playing as dumb as he could get away with. It would give less away.

"We must hurry," she repeated, this time in Anglicus. "We have a long journey ahead of us."

Jasyn smiled and nodded. *The Last Castle,* he thought, his heart thumping. *After all these years, we are finally going to know where it is.*

They led him through the building and finally out a door that was large enough for a jet to pass through. Night was falling and dusk was quickly becoming a memory on the horizon. He caught a glimpse of Charity's main party ahead of him, heading for what looked like another building.

It was long and tall, with white walls and an enormous G7 emblazoned on the side in gleaming gold paint. The dry wind whipped at them as they crossed the concrete area to the next building and it wasn't until they began to enter it, by walking up a broad ramp, that Jasyn realized that it wasn't a building at all. It was a ship.

Officer Issord couldn't help but gawk as his escorts hustled him aboard. The ship was nearly as large as a Battle Cruiser, but instead of narrow hallways of riveted steel and harsh fluorescent lighting, there were acres of plush carpet and a gentle light came from the sconces that adorned the polished wood walls. Antique tables held bowls of fresh flowers and soft music played from unseen speakers.

There were numerous people moving about, though they looked more like a household staff than any sort of flight crew. Charity was nowhere to be seen.

"Come on," one of his attendants chirped. "We need to get settled so we can take off. Ms. de Rossi is in a dreadful hurry."

They led him down carpeted hallways amid the dance of the hurried staff and into a room that looked like a small library. It was a comfortable room with overstuffed sofas and reading chairs, a holo fireplace with a merry green fire, and shelves lined with amber-colored acrylic volumes.

He was directed to a seat as his consorts plopped down onto a sofa. One touched her ear and let someone in the bridge know that they were all set. She looked at Jasyn when she was done.

"I'm sorry," she apologized, "I'm Diana."

"And I am Persie," the other said with a smile.

"Pleased to meet you," Jasyn said.

"Sorry about the rush," Diana said. "Charity may seem very nonchalant, but she has a very tight schedule to keep."

"Where is Ms. de Rossi?" Jasyn asked. Saying her name out loud to strangers felt odd enough. He certainly wasn't ready to start calling her by her first name unless she insisted on it. He hoped she wouldn't.

"Probably in the drawing room," Persie said.

"Or her bedroom," Diana said.

"Or the bar," they both said together and then giggled like children, their hands coming up to cover their mouths. Jasyn couldn't help but like them. At first he had thought they were twins, or possibly constructs since they looked so alike. On closer inspection he realized that Diana had slightly darker hair, and her almond-shaped eyes were almost black, rather than brown, like Persie's.

The ship gave a shudder as all of the legs of the aircraft pulled in and all the ports sealed. There was a gentle lurch as the craft lifted into the air and then a sickening feeling as it shot up into space and artificial gravity replaced true gravity, though the feeling only lasted for a moment.

"Can I get you something?" Diana asked once the ship was smoothly scorching through space. "Something to eat or drink?"

"No, thank you," Jasyn replied.

"Well then," Persie said, "let me take you to a guest bedroom where you can lie down and rest. I know it is evening where we just left so your body clock will probably be used to winding down sometime soon, and we won't be to our destination for another twenty hours."

Both women rose from their seats and headed for the door. Jasyn followed them, mentally calculating how far they could go in twenty hours at a top speed for a Luxury Cruiser and then trying to imagine what moon would be in that range. It was next to impossible to tell without knowing which direction they had gone, but at least he knew that The Distant Shore was within twenty hours of Dione. He felt that he was already off to a good start.

Keeping his expression stoic, Jasyn followed Persie and Diana back out into the hall where butler droids were busy carting food and drinks to another part of the ship. The three of them moved through the current of robotic as well as human staff members until they reached a circular room with a wide ivory staircase with gilded risers that curved up along one wall. A chandelier bedecked with hundreds of crystal teardrops hung from the ceiling in the center of the room, throwing soft light in every direction.

Diana had her foot on the bottom stair when she stopped abruptly, putting a hand to her ear. Her dark eyes flicked over to Jasyn who, along with Persie, had stopped at the bottom of the staircase.

"Yes," she said. "Of course." She turned to Persie. "She wants to see him."

"She does?"

"Yes, in the bar. Come on, Jasyn," Diana said, indicating the direction with a twitch of her head.

Jasyn turned and followed Persie, who was already heading

away, her dark woven hair swinging across her back.

Why does she sound surprised that Charity wants to see me? he wondered as he glanced at Diana. *They both seem surprised.* A strange, unpleasant feeling began to form in the pit of his stomach.

"This craft is so large," he said to Persie, trying to get a clue as to what was going on by making what he hoped was simple conversation, "and so many servants. Is there going to be a party?"

Persie made a gentle snorting noise and clapped a hand over a giggle. "Goodness no," she said, even as three butlers in matching tuxedoes stepped politely aside for them to pass, though the hallway was quite wide. "There is hardly anyone on board right now, which is a bit odd. Charity usually has a few hundred people on board the ship, but right now it is only staff."

"This was a private trip, just to get you," Diana added, as if the news should impress him. "There are quite a few people scheduled to board at our next stop, after we drop you off, of course."

Jasyn felt his back stiffen and his heart sink. He was about to ask if he was to be dropped off somewhere with Ms. de Rossi when they reached the end of the hall where two double doors of ivory gilded with gold and silver stood open to the room beyond.

With a tight throat, he followed Persie into a vast, circular room of white and glass and chrome. It could house a party of one, possibly two, hundred people comfortably but at the moment it was mostly empty.

In the very center of the room was a round ottoman that was three meters across, and covered with a patchwork cloth of varying shades of white and ivory. It was surrounded by an enormous, white sofa that curved into a circle around the ottoman. Small sections of the circle were missing to allow one to pass through the couch to the seating area. All around the gargantuan sofa were numerous high tables of polished chrome flanked with tall, narrow seats of white leather.

Along the circumference of the great room was a short wall of glass brick topped with a polished chrome counter. White plastique barstools stood along the massive, curved chrome bar. On the far side were tiers of glass shelves holding hundreds of bottles of liquor, wine, and champagne. Jasyn's eyes traveled up the wall of bottles and he saw that the room had a second level that looked down onto the lower floor from a glass balcony above. He searched out the way up and saw that there was a glass staircase just to his right, beyond one of the many security guards that flanked the door.

The room was softly lit from beneath the opaque glass floor and from above the opaque glass ceiling and rebounded off all of the polished chrome, bathing the giant room in cool, silver light.

Charity was reclined on the round sofa while attendants and personal assistants fluttered around her like nervous butterflies. Besides the security guards that stood at the entrance to the room, two patrolled the balcony above. Another pair stood watch a few meters away from where Charity was lounging and giving constant instructions to the young woman refilling the crystal glass in her outstretched, jeweled hand.

She caught sight of Jasyn and waved for him to join her. Persie led the way around the tables and chairs and through a section in the couch and Diana brought up the rear of their little party.

Charity was babbling to a worried looking attendant when they reached her and she patted a spot close to her, indicating a place for Jasyn to sit. The only other people sitting were two young women in business suits wearing viable comsets and square eyeglasses with small black frames. They each held what looked like a square pane of smooth glass and kept their attention fixed on Ms. de Rossi. The attendant left as soon as

Charity was done and the brilliant, bejeweled woman turned her attention to the young man who had joined her on the couch.

"Jasyn, darling, can I offer you something to drink?"

"Water, please," Jasyn said, just to be polite.

Charity trilled laughter and raised a hand and another attendant went hurrying off. "So pure," she remarked. "You are the perfect match." She took a sip of her drink, her green eyes sparkling at him from over the rim of her crystal glass.

Jasyn smiled at her. "For you?"

Charity's brows shot up and she leaned into her drink to keep from spitting it back out, trilling laughter once more, though this time more hearty and genuine. "Heaven's no!" she exclaimed when she had composed herself. "As delightful as you look, I could never do that to you."

Two butlers arrived - one with a silver tray table, which he set up next to Jasyn, and another with a silver tray that held a pitcher of water and heavy crystal glass, along with a bowl made of cut glass brimming with blood-red raspberries. He filled the water glass for Jasyn before he and the other butler hastened away.

"I intend to give you as a gift," Charity informed him. Jasyn, his mouth suddenly dry, took the glass from the tray and took a long drink before putting it back. "Don't worry," she said, smiling her mischievous smile. "You're going to love the person you will be going to – you were practically made for each other."

Jasyn tried to keep his face set with Chip-like optimism as he felt his heart plunge. Diana had been correct, he was going to be dropped somewhere, with someone else. He could only hope that he would be going to someone important and that the mission would not be a total loss, but his hope was small and fleeting.

As if reading his thoughts, Charity's smile turned into a smirk. "Change your mind about that drink?" she asked.

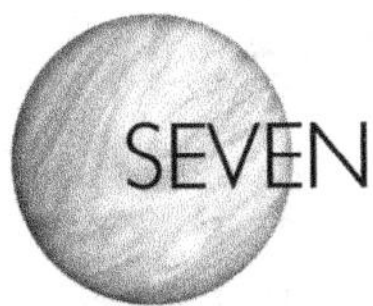

SEVEN

Calyph watched Jordan Blue enter Fledgling Bay and make her way towards the gate in the detfleck, the neck-high wall of sparkling flecks of color that would pulverize anyone trying to pass through it. The elfin Engineer, already on the other side of the detfleck, sat on a molded metal chair facing a pair of Fledgling Dragons, his face turned to watch the Jordan. His troll squatted close by in autumnal silence.

Both Fledglings were a matte silver in color but the larger one had a blue sheen that ran over his metal skin while his smaller brother gave off a crimson glow. The smaller of the two was nineteen meters long with a twelve meter wingspan while the Blue Fledgling was over twice the size of his brother, including a larger belly and raised dorsal line, due to the growing that Calyph had initiated a month earlier.

The troll, a droid Calyph had acquired decades ago, was ancient and clunky but – true to his kind – stored the histories of the galaxies in his metal bulk. He was also incredibly useful to the Engineer in his metallurgy.

Calyph's blue eyes watched the Jordan slip through the expanse of the bay like a sliver of night – her lithe form encased by a sparkling black flight suit and black boots that came up to her knees.

The Engineer watched a group of crewmen greet her respectfully as she walked by them towards the security gate. Her response, usually a mischievous smile accompanied by a playful remark, was now just a slight jerk of her head in acknowledgment. Calyph thought she looked like some archaic plaything; a marionette or a mechanical wind-up toy that was slowly breaking down. The group watched her go, shaking their heads sadly, obviously remembering the Jordan that she had been not so long ago.

Calyph remembered a different woman as well, one that usually had him aroused within seconds. Her sexuality had always been in the way she would lean towards him, or touch him teasingly with the tip of a finger, or in her whispered innuendos. She was so different from Jordan Scarlett, whose sensuality seemed to emanate from her eyes, along with every curve in her body.

The Engineer closed his slanted blue eyes and felt a shiver run up his spine as he thought of Scarlett's body, and the memory of those curves under his hand. Her skin was so smooth and so warm. So different from the cold metal he was used to working. His blue eyes popped open.

So different than Tara, he thought suddenly. *Tara was always more like Jordan Blue, all skin and bones.*

He wondered if that was why he had found Blue so attractive at first. So seductive. Now he found her terrifying. He smirked, realizing that she had that in common with Tara as well. He watched warily as she handed her sidearm over to the guard. Medical security gave her the once over to gain access to the far side of the detfleck; checking her mouth, her DNA, her prints.

She gave the armed guard a half-hearted whistle and he returned her sidearm to her. She dropped it into the holster slung below her right hip and strode past him and the doctor towards where the elfin Engineer waited. When she reached Calyph and the Fledglings she stopped, her sapphire eyes flicking back and forth from the troll to the Engineer.

"What are you doing here?" she asked, curt.

Calyph suppressed a sigh. "Good morning, Jordan," he said politely. "How are you?"

The Jordan's head jerked as she quickly looked away and looked back at the Engineer, as if slighted by his amiable greeting. "I haven't changed since yesterday," she informed him. "Or the day before. What are you doing here?" she repeated.

Calyph squirmed internally. *She doesn't know,* he thought, discouraged. *The Captain should have told her.* But he knew that the Captain of the Opal Dragon had been out of sorts lately - just as much as the Jordan. Still, he didn't want to be the one to tell her. The Engineer took a deep breath.

"We need to proceed with Fledge's growing," he told the Jordan.

"So?" she demanded, then frowned at him as she considered his choice of words. "When you say 'we,' do you mean you and your troll?"

Calyph sighed. "Yes, but I mean you as well."

Blue's frown deepened. "What in the hell do you need me for?"

"I need a Jordan to grow a Fledgling."

"Why?"

Calyph's blue eyes grew wide. "Because I need to get inside him. Don't you remember? From when we grew Cyan?" It had only been a few weeks ago that that they had worked together on his growing – granted a lot had happened in those few weeks – but Calyph would be amazed if she didn't recall what they had done.

"I remember," Blue said, looking at her newly grown Fledgling. She glanced at his brother, who was noticeably smaller, before fixing her eyes on the Engineer. "He won't let you inside?"

"No."

"What makes you think he'll let me inside?"

"Won't he?"

"Why should he?"

Calyph's face fell, perplexed. "You are a Jordan of the Opal Dragon."

Blue snorted. "So? He detests me, just as much as or just because Scarlett detested me. He carries the same feelings as his mistress."

"But you're a Jordan," Calyph said, as if it should explain everything. "You should be able to get inside."

"So what? From what I can guess, you've been inside the Red Jordan. Why shouldn't you be able to get inside her Fledgling?"

Calyph blushed from the bottom of his neck to the tips of his pointed ears. "I haven't tried. I *wouldn't* try," he told her, though his heartbeat quickened and his mind raced with the possibility. "Fledglings bond to their Jordans. They are loyal to that bond. They disdain contact with anyone outside of their family unless that contact is encouraged by their Jordan. It's hardly possible to communicate with a Dragon of any age unless it is through their Jordan, or their Captain."

Jordan Blue almost told Calyph that if he was right, then he could go see if the Captain would oblige. She knew, however, that her taunt would be insubordinate to her Commander. Besides, the Captain was not well.

Instead, the Jordan crossed her thin arms over her chest. "Is that so?" she asked.

Calyph looked at the pale body encased in shimmering black and shrugged. "As far as I know."

Blue turned her gaze towards Fledge, the Fledgling Dragon that squatted on the silver tarmac next to her own Fledgling, Cyan. "Do you want to grow?" she demanded, raising her voice. "Feel like letting me inside you?"

The Jordan paused for a second before she cocked her head at the Engineer, her expression both expectant and triumphant. Calyph looked back, waiting.

"He says no," she told him. "On both counts."

"Does he actually talk to you?"

"No, the communication is more of a feeling, and his feelings are clear. He doesn't want anything to do with me."

The high-arched brows of the Engineer drew together. "Then you need to talk him into it," he told her.

Blue looked as if she were on the verge of laughing. "Talk him into it?" she asked. "He's as stubborn as his bitch of a Jordan!"

"This is important!"

Jordan Blue huffed. "Why should I care?"

Calyph closed his eyes and blew out a sigh through pursed lips, his shoulders sagging. His lips pressed together and when he finally drew another breath though his nose he fixed his own elfin blue eyes on the half-elf pilot.

"I know you are angry," Calyph told the Jordan, averting his eyes quickly as her body stiffened. "As to the rest of your feelings, I can't imagine what you must be going through." The Engineer drew another deep breath and looked back at Blue, meeting her cold glare. "But you have to know that we have to go on. To hold on to what we feel will be our destruction. To move on with what we could only possibly hope for will be our redemption."

Jordan Blue, her arms still crossed across her chest, felt the muscles in her jaw loosen so much that she thought it might drop open. She listened to Calyph's words again as they echoed inside her head. After a moment of reflection, she straightened and nodded, her own lips pressed tightly together.

"You're right," she admitted.

The Jordan turned and approached the Red Fledgling. She reached up and put her hand upon his silver belly, just aft of his nose.

"You need to let me in," she told him, her voice low and

obliging and caustic all at once. Calyph's eyes went back and forth between the Jordan and the Fledgling in the pause that ensued. The Jordan frowned suddenly and turned her hand, cracking her knuckles on the Fledgling's metal skin, producing a dull clunking sound. "Fine!" she spat. "And when Scarlett comes back, *you* can tell her why you're so puny. She will be *so* proud to be the Jordan of the smaller, weaker Fledgling!"

Calyph's blue eyes widened, waiting. He could sense that the troll was watching as well, cataloguing the event in silence.

The Blue Jordan's smug smile was all the answer he really needed as she turned her scarred face towards him.

"He doesn't like it," she said. "But he'll do it. Let me know when you're ready."

Calyph smiled. "I have all the materials, just let me get set up."

Blue nodded. "Fine."

ɞɛʒʓ

Just like the first time, when Calyph had performed his first growing on Cyan, Blue sat on the silver floor of Fledgling Bay. This time, however, she wore a flight suit of sparkling black instead of sparkling blue, the one-piece suit seeming to absorb as much light as it reflected. Her platinum hair was still pulled back in the high pompadour that she favored, and separated at the back of her neck into a few large curls.

Her hands were empty this time, but there were a number of long, cylindrical rods of metal neatly lined up on the floor next to her. Calyph, again, had spent the morning carefully separating and laying them out in the order they would be used.

Blue watched as the troll shot a gray beam of light out from one of its limbs and raised a long rod of lithium up with its field. Calyph, holding up a hand but without touching the rod, took the bar from the troll's field. The metal hovered three meters off the ground as Calyph guided it over the Red Fledgling in a field of his own making. He placed it on top of Fledge's left wing. The bar jutted out from the shoulder of the Fledgling, longer than the wing by nearly two meters.

The troll produced a leveling field of red light that blinked off when Calyph had the bar perfectly lined up. Then the troll and the Jordan simply watched. Calyph, his eyes fixed on the metal rod, slowly brought his right hand up to shoulder level.

Blue watched as the lithium softened, the bottom flattening slightly, before it began to unroll down the wing like a piece of dough on a baker's board. It melded with the wing itself, stretching and lengthening and hardening as it did. It was the same as when Cyan had his growing.

Again, Calyph worked tirelessly, though it seemed to go much quicker this time. He took a late lunch break, sitting with Blue in the Mess Hall with a smattering of crewmembers that had just been relieved from the first shift of the day. The Jordan got a plate of food for herself that she didn't eat, but just picked at listlessly as she waited for the Engineer.

"The way you move those bars of lithium," she said thoughtfully, "you move them without touching them, and without a field generator."

Calyph shrugged. "It's something all Engineers can do."

"Can you do that with anything?"

The elf shook his head and finished the bite of protein wrap he was chewing. "No, just with metals."

"And you can change their form," she said, idly drawing designs in her food with her fork. "Make them melt or harden."

Calyph nodded. "That's just temperature control. But, yes." The Jordan nodded, still playing with her food. "Can I ask you something?" he asked.

Blue looked up and Calyph noticed with a start that for the first time her eyes were not a perfect match. They were close –

so close that only elfin eyesight would pick it up, and even then only at close range, like he was now. The artificial one, the one in the scarred half of her face, was the same sapphire blue as before. The other was a shade, just a touch, lighter.

"Sure," she answered, bringing his attention back to what he had been thinking before he noticed her eyes. He cleared his throat.

"You said before that your communication with the Fledglings is based on a feeling you get from them."

"That's right."

"Is it just in response to questions?"

Blue shook her platinum curls. "No. I can tell how they feel in general, especially when they are distressed. And I can feel Cyan more than Fledge. Our bond is stronger."

Calyph sucked at the straw in his drink and put the cup down on the table. "Can you tell how he feels about me?"

Blue smirked at him, the right side of her face puckering around her scars. "Fledge? He trusts you," she said. "Because Scarlett trusted you."

Calyph looked away as if embarrassed. He finished chewing what was in his mouth and then dropped the remains of his wrap down on the plate. "Well, let's get back," he said, rising from his seat.

"You're not going to finish?" Blue asked, indicating his half-eaten wrap. He shook his head.

"I'm not that hungry."

"I know the feeling."

Blue scooped up his remaining plate of food and stacked it on her own plate and dropped the lot of it down the trash chute on their way out of the Mess.

"Do you remember what comes next?" Calyph asked as they went through the security gate in the detfleck fence.

Blue had to wait to answer since the doc was looking into

her mouth with a flashbeam. When he was done she whistled at the guard and he let her through. The guard handed over her sidearm and she dropped it into the holster on her hip. She turned to Calyph, who was now undergoing the same scrutiny.

"Yeah, I take your troll inside of Fledge."

"That's right," Calyph said, holding his wrist out for the carbon DNA scan. "I don't have a ladder this time - I found a hover jack – but you can ride it up with me if you want." The doc checked the chip that was embedded in the flesh between his thumb and index finger before handing the Engineer his credentials card.

Blue shook her head. "That's okay. I'll watch from the ground this time."

Calyph let out a low whistle and the guard let him pass. "Just thought I would offer."

The two walked past Fledge, his body lumpy with the metals that Calyph had already fused to his metallic skin. The troll was just finishing the clean-up from the morning's business.

The droid had gathered up all of the leftover metal and then separated the scraps into piles of identical compounds. The troll, using a short-range laser and a field manipulator, then melted each group and reformed it into smooth rods and bars for easier handling.

The Jordan and the Engineer waited as it moved the bars and rods, which would later be transported to storage or Calyph's personal cabin, to the side of the work area. Its head swiveled in their direction, its optic bar trained on Jordan Blue.

"Are you ready?" it asked, its voice metallic and gravelly.

"As ready as I'm gonna be," the Jordan sighed.

She walked up to the metal-robed Fledgling and waited. When nothing happened, she reached up and rapped on his side with her knuckles. Calyph, judging by the heavy clunking sound it made, thought it must hurt like hell on her hand but the Jordan didn't seem to notice. He watched, expectant, but nothing happened.

"Well?" Blue demanded, her voice rising. "Are you going to let me in?" Calyph's almond-shaped eyes went back and forth between the Fledgling and the Jordan. Still nothing. Blue gave Fledge a single, angry rap with the back of her fist. "Do you have any idea how ridiculous you look?" When still nothing happened the Jordan scowled. "Fine!" she spat. "Stay that way!"

To Calyph's amazement she turned to stalk away but, as she did so, the metal on Fledge's side rippled. A set of uneven ridges protruded from the Fledgling's side as he tried to make a ladder for the Jordan to climb. Blue turned and regarded the Fledgling for moment with her arms crossed in front of her chest and a smirk on the ragged side of her face as his hood slid open, moving roughly over and around the new metal. Then she grabbed the first rung and began hauling herself up.

Calyph motioned to the troll and it fired the thrusters located underneath its metal bulk, lifting itself up into the air next to the ascending Jordan. Blue climbed inside and dropped a knee down into the pilot's seat, the only seat at present, and eyed the dash console with a bewildered frown.

At first she thought Fledge had gotten warped somehow from what Calyph had done, then she realized that all of the controls were backwards. The controls in Cyan were all on the other side because Blue was right-handed. Seeing them reversed for the left-handed Jordan Scarlett made them look skewed and unfamiliar.

The troll settled its bulk down into the small space behind the Jordan but she was already rising to her feet, knowing that she wasn't needed except for a few words.

"Okay," she told the Fledgling, "I'm out of here, but you need to let the troll stay inside." She could feel Fledge's pang of discomfort at the thought, a sort of mental grumbling, and it brought a crystal clear image to Blue's mind – she had seen

Scarlett plenty of times have to submit to something she didn't want to do and his feeling was as sharp as Scarlett's glare. "Bitch all you want," Blue said. "The troll stays. It won't take long and you'll feel better afterwards. At least you'll look a whole lot better."

She felt a wave of amusement from Cyan, followed by a wave of resentment from Fledge that made her grin. *Just like Scarlett,* she thought. *She doesn't like amusement at her expense either.*

The Jordan swung a leg out of the cockpit and, as her foot found the top ridge of metal, the head of the droid rotated towards her.

"Any words regarding Calyph's testicles?" it asked.

"What?" Blue asked, frozen and staring. She thought that maybe the damned thing was malfunctioning. A second later she laughed, recalling what she had told Cyan when he was grown and she had left the droid inside of him. "No," she told the troll with a lop-sided grin, "His balls are safe. For now, at least."

The troll's head turned away as she descended the misshapen rungs and then dropped to the floor. The hood over the cockpit slid closed and the irregular ridges of metal melted back into the side of the Fledgling.

"All set?" Calyph asked.

"I think your troll might be developing a sense of humor," she told him.

Calyph shook his head. "Trolls don't have humor."

The Jordan shrugged to show her indifference. "Anyway, he's all set." She walked away and leaned against Cyan's leg, watching as Calyph placed the blocks of diamond glass over Fledge's eyes and then climbed onto the hover jack before it rose into the air. Calyph maneuvered the lift forward until he could place his hand on Fledge's nose.

The air seemed to go still and then, in the seconds that

followed, Fledge began to swell as the metal that covered his body melted and melded, smoothing out as the Dragon Fledgling grew and grew.

Blue could feel a rise of heat, mostly on her face, as if she were facing a furnace or a bonfire. Then Cyan wrapped a protective field around her and her body began to cool. His act of protection brought out a feeling of sadness in her, followed by a sentiment of confusion from him.

"It's not you," the Jordan said, reassuring him. She sighed and shook her head, confused and angry. "I just don't know what's going on with anything right now. I feel so lost and I can't seem to figure anything out." The field that enveloped her body filled with waves of consolation. "Don't worry," she said, pushing back with her shoulder as if she could nudge him, "I'll figure it out. Eventually."

The field dissipated and the Jordan's blue eyes flicked up to take in the other Fledgling, now smooth and shiny and as large as her own. Fledge seemed to swell as much with pride as with his growing and Blue could feel an emotional field coming from him as well. It was reluctant appreciation.

Blue laughed. "Just like Scarlett!" she scolded softly, thinking of the time she had rescued the other Jordan from the clutches of the Chimera. Fledge was able to share the feeling of the memory and his appreciation became a tad less begrudging. Blue shook her head, grinning, and looked at the Engineer. "Well?" she asked.

Calyph smiled and his shoulders sagged with exhaustion. "Get my troll out of there, and take him out for a flight."

"The troll?" Blue asked.

Calyph gave her an exasperated look. "Take Fledge out on a flight. Like you did right after we grew Cyan. The temperature out there," he said, jerking his head towards the bay door, "is pretty close to absolute zero. It will help permanently solidify all of the alloys."

Blue eyed the newly grown Fledgling who, even as he was opening the cockpit to release the troll, was listening to their conversation and regarding her with a sensation of increasing suspicion.

Going inside was one thing, flying him was quite another.

Jordan Blue sighed. "Don't worry!" she admonished the Fledgling with a scowl. "I'll take Cyan and you can follow. Good enough?"

She could tell from the wave of begrudging acceptance that it would indeed, be good enough.

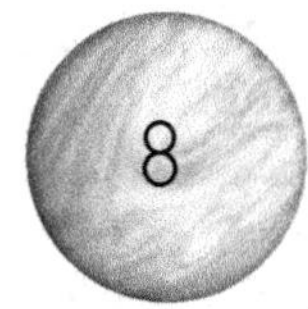

8

Charity's craft was too monstrous to dock with the villa, so a tender had been readied to take the smallest part of Charity's entourage down to the villa's secondary berth. When the smaller transport craft had finally docked and the seals had been released, Jasyn followed Charity, along with her lead security man and two assistants, out of the small commuter craft and into a large, round room pocked with corridors.

The group was greeted by another security team and ushered into a circular glass elevator that was wrapped with a clear, spiral staircase. The ride down was short and before Jasyn could take in his surroundings, Charity was flowing out of the lift and onto a raised foyer of gleaming black marble. The foyer steps descended into an expansive room of black and white that rolled out before a wall of starry night.

A young woman, a PA by the look of her square glasses, with brown hair and wearing a brown skirt and suit jacket, stood waiting by a small onyx cocktail bar.

There was only one other person in the room, a woman in white with long gold and brown hair, staring out into the inky black space beyond the glass wall. Jasyn fixed a dopey smile on his face to hide the fact that his heart was pounding as he looked around, taking it all in before his eyes darted back to the figure at the window.

"Sister!" Charity gushed as she flowed down the marble steps. The woman at the window turned and at the sight of her Jasyn could feel something hitch inside his chest that was not entirely pleasant. He turned his face away, hoping that his wild thinking was camouflaged by his dopey smile.

Sister?

Jasyn's mind raced. Charity de Rossi had five sisters, but was only close with one as far as anyone knew. Jasyn looked back and met the woman's eyes as her gaze fixed upon him and she studied him momentarily from across the room before they glided across the rest of Charity's entourage. Again he felt that uncomfortable hitching in his chest and he looked away, knowing that she could be none other than Faith de Rossi - the Chief Executive Officer of the GwenSeven Corporation.

Was this where he was going? Could Charity possibly be giving him to her sister? Jasyn felt sick with the possibility. It had taken determination to summon the nerve of having to serve Charity de Rossi, but he had been given a bit of time to get used to the idea. But Faith?

He had learned from his Commander that these women were monsters. JP despised them both, but where he had always spoken of Charity as being lascivious and depraved, he had spoken of Faith as being calculating and cold. The thought of having to touch her, and most likely much more than that, was loathsome. But the opportunity that the Chimera would have would be divine. A sign from the One himself, JP would have said.

Jasyn was vaguely aware of security coming and going and then Charity was calling out to him, summoning him, to join her and the heathen woman that had the audacity to play the One before the eyes of the Almighty himself.

Jasyn realized that his jaw was clenched and made an effort to relax it as he walked down the foyer steps. Full of righteous indignation but cloaked with the smile he had learned from Chip, the Chimeran officer stood before the two women as they talked about him as if he were a piece of furniture that Charity had picked up on sale at the local shopping mall. He could feel the other woman's eyes traveling all over him; appraising, assessing, judging. Between her restless stare and Charity's drawling voice he felt at that moment he could gladly strangle them both.

Control, he thought. *Control. Remember why you are here.*

As if he could forget.

He looked back and forth between the two women without really seeing them as they chatted. He was afraid that he might not be able to control his expression should he let his eyes focus on either of them.

Then Faith touched him, running her hand down his arm and he felt a tingle that followed her fingers like a trail of electricity. He caught her hand in his own to stop her from touching him, and then brought it to his mouth before he let it go. The same tingle ran across his lips.

Of course, he thought. *What else would you feel when touching the person that had created you? Shaped you and made you and gave you life?* JP had told him once that she was like a heathen deity, evil and cruel, who offered only slavery rather than salvation. It made him want to shudder.

Jasyn only had to endure the torment a moment longer before Faith's PA was beckoning to him and leading him away. She looked as severe as any woman crewmember aboard the *Resurrection,* but was indisputably human.

She waved Charity's female servants towards another room and led him back into the lift and up to the next floor where he was ushered into a room full of glass monitors and subjected to a security scan.

Jasyn remained calm, knowing there was nothing they could find. He was as pure as possible, without a single prosthetic and not so much as a micro-transmitter. He had learned to flinch his upper cheek to simulate a wink and could whistle through his teeth. If he did both quickly they were hardly noticeable unless under the greatest scrutiny. He was asked to do neither since they already knew he was not human.

After the body scan and a carbon check, the PA led him back

downstairs, this time taking the staircase that encircled the lift. He followed her across the foyer, the sounds of the sisters talking floating on the air as she led him through a door and into a bedroom.

The room was curved, like the room they had come from, and had the same glass wall. The largest bed he had ever seen dominated the room, the headboard only visible by the way it blacked out the stars on the far side of the glass. It was flanked by night tables and reading chairs. Past the reading chair on the right side of the room was a monstrosity of mirrors that made his stomach clench.

What vanity, he thought, utterly disgusted. Closer to him, also on the right side of the room, was a wide opening to a darkened area that he supposed was a bathroom or a closet.

"Make yourself comfortable," the PA said without bothering to introduce herself. "But do not disturb Ms. de Rossi while she is with her sister." She paused and eyed him for a moment. "Are you hungry?"

Jasyn shook his head. He didn't think he could eat even if he had been starving.

"Alright. If you change your mind, put your finger over the green glow on that nightstand and it will give you coms with the kitchen." The PA paused again and gave him a doubtful gaze. "Do you know what that means?" she asked. Jasyn nodded slowly. "Good. Order anything you like and they will bring it here." The woman looked around as if unsure what else she could offer. "Go ahead and take a shower if you want," she said, gesturing towards the dimly lit hall. "These talks with Charity usually last for hours, so you have quite a bit of time. Get some rest, I guess. If you need anything else, the brown holo on the nightstand will page me."

She tapped her right ear and Jasyn noticed for the first time that she had a golden device wrapped securely around it, ending in a small wire that came up over the lobe and ended at the entrance to her ear canal.

The woman's brown eyes narrowed behind the square black frames of her eyeglasses. "I trust that you know what not to touch?" she asked, her shoulders tight under her brown suit jacket.

I sure do, he thought. *It's what I'll be going through the first chance I get.* But Jasyn simply nodded quickly and she seemed to relax somewhat.

"Well, alright then. Clean up and get some rest. Ms. de Rossi will be in later." She gazed at the construct for a moment more and then left, closing the door behind her.

Jasyn let his eyes travel over the room once she was gone, slowly this time, his heart pounding like it never had before. *Control,* he thought absently. *Control.* His body relaxed and he looked around. He almost grinned as he was filled with elation from the outcome of his situation and then stopped himself, realizing that it was quite possible he was being monitored by cameras.

He walked around the room, letting his fingers trail over the backs of the chairs, his eyes falling nervously on the giant bed covered in copper and gold, velvet and satin, and piled high with pillows in a multitude of sizes. His heart rate picked up again as he eyed the bed and he consciously slowed it down.

He stopped before the vanity and looked at himself reflected in dozens of mirrors before looking away in disgust. *She must love to see herself from every angle,* he thought. Though, now that he had time to reflect, decided that she hadn't looked that bad. Certainly not as evil and menacing as he had imagined.

More like a benign cancer, he thought, *rather than an ogre from a fairy tale. Still, that doesn't change who she is.*

He walked passed the nightstand that the PA had pointed out and noticed that it had a drawer. Using the tip of his finger, he slid the drawer open and looked inside. The only thing in there was an old fashioned book. Yellowed pages were bound into a hard cover that read *Dream Journal*, embossed in a flowy script.

He closed the drawer and crossed the room to the dimly lit hallway and touched the light panel on the wall. He found an oversized bathroom with a large, round soaking tub and a separate walk-in shower encased in marble. Beyond the door to a small room with a toilet, was another room that Jasyn imagined what a woman's clothing store must look like.

The room was almost as large as the bedroom, but the walls were lined with dresses and suits that hung close together in neat rows. There were slanting shelves that went from the floor to the ceiling and held shoes in every style and color. In the center of the room was a chest of drawers and a padded bench covered in gold velvet that was large enough for two people to sleep on comfortably.

Curious, he opened the top drawer. Seeing delicate undergarments, he shut it quickly, feeling the color rise in his cheeks. Having nothing left to explore or do, Jasyn left the closet and, after a moment of indecision, stripped off his clothes and got in the shower.

It was a semi-circular room of pale marble with enough nozzles and knobs to make it look like a control room of sorts. When he got it working, the hot water felt good and he realized that he hadn't had a shower since the G7 distribution center. It already felt like a lifetime ago.

After he had showered, he puzzled with the body dryer trying to figure out how it worked only to find once he was dry that his hair stood around his head in a ridiculous puff of black. He went to the sink to wet his hair and smoothed it down.

Having nothing left to do, he pulled on his only pair of underwear and slipped into the gigantic bed. He smoothed the sheets down around him and tried not to think about what he was going to have to do. He laced his hands behind his head and tried to focus on how lucky he was that the mission had taken such a fortuitous turn, and all that he would be able to accomplish for the Cause.

He tried to recall all that he knew about the de Rossi sisters, which wasn't much more than the same history that everyone else knew. JP spoke of them infrequently, calling them monsters when he did. They didn't seem too monstrous, as far as Jasyn could tell. Charity seemed to be nothing more than a vapid socialite and Faith… well, with Faith he would just have to wait and see.

Thinking of such things, he drifted off to sleep. He awoke with a jolt as he heard a faint grinding noise. He pushed himself up off a drift of golden pillows and saw that a curved metal shield was rising beyond the wall of glass. It stopped half a meter from the ceiling, closing off the view but still letting in an innocuous amount of starlight, tinged pink-gold by the gas giant that loomed in the east, its swirling colors like melting caramel.

A second later the door to the room swung open and Faith strode in, the door swinging closed behind her. She went by the bed without a glance and Jasyn could hear her movements coming from the adjoining room. He sat up, suddenly nervous.

Control, he thought, closing his eyes and breathing deep. *Control.* After what seemed like an endless number of minutes Faith de Rossi came back in the room.

"Jesus!" she exclaimed, her hand fluttering up to her throat, clearly startled to see him in her bed.

Jasyn smiled, feeling more at ease, knowing that she was caught off her guard, and for the first time since he had arrived at her villa, really took the time to take a look at her. His hazel eyes traveled over her body and over the angles and curves of her face - and he felt his breath catch in his throat.

He had no idea why, other than the fact that she was hardly dressed - wearing only a thin camisole of copper-colored silk. Her face was more ordinary than striking, certainly not as statuesque as Charity, but there was something about her that made him feel strange in a way that he could not describe.

Something that I haven't felt in a long time, Jasyn thought, even though he could not identify what that feeling actually was. His eyes ran down the line of her neck, her skin bathed in a rosy glow from the light outside, making it as smooth as molten gold.

"You scared the shit out of me!" she accused him, laughing softly once the scare had passed.

"I'm sorry," he apologized.

Faith cupped her right elbow with her left hand. She ran the smooth nail of her right thumb over her lips, thinking.

That's not right, Jasyn thought, the idea rising in his mind like a bubble, though he had no clue why the action seemed so off to him. He tried to remember everything he had ever learned about Faith de Rossi, all of the vids and holos he had seen about her.

She asked him something about Charity and he answered as best he could but his brain was jumbled with images and words and all were incongruent. But while his mind worked furiously, his eyes traveled over her body once more and he found himself pushing back the covers, inviting her into the bed.

Oddly enough, she seemed as nervous as he felt. She slipped into the sheets as if she were afraid to touch him, though her body was right next to his. She watched him carefully, her golden brown eyes wide.

Thinking of the sex vid that JP had shown him made his stomach lurch. Realizing that he had no idea how to get to that point, made him want to laugh.

They looked at each other in silence as the seconds ticked away.

"I'm not really sure how to start," he told her. Faith seemed to relax and her smile was warm.

"Why don't you start by kissing me," she told him, "and we'll see where it goes from there."

Jasyn drew a deep breath and leaned down to kiss her, stealing himself against the jolt, remembering the feeling of electricity from her previous touch. But instead of a shock, there was only the soft give of her lips against his and the feeling it produced flooded him with warmth.

He drew back quickly, surprised.

The warmth seemed to flow through his head, as if a vessel in his brain had popped, or melted, flooding his skull with hot liquid.

Faith regarded him, perplexed, and then smiled. After a moment of hesitation Jasyn leaned down to kiss her again and, once again, he was flooded with warmth - though this time it traveled throughout his entire body. It was accompanied by another feeling that took him longer to identify. Desire.

He reached out a hand to slip around her back and found his whole body responded and took over, pulling her form tight against his own.

Suddenly, he found himself fighting to control the emotions that he could feel warring within him. There was a loathing, an icy forcefulness made from nearly a hundred years of cold anger. And there was a heat, a need that burned away at the ice, but it was slow. Part of him wanted to pull away in terror, another part wanted to strike out in anger. Then there was another part, a part that was so foreign and yet so powerful, that wanted to touch her so much that he would become part of her.

He reached up with his other hand to touch her face, full of craving and curiosity. He ran his fingertips from her cheek to her neck, his thumb trailing along the pulse in her throat, and he thought about how easy it would be to kill her. To close off the flow the blood to her brain, to crush her fragile windpipe, to stop her breath, stop what she had been doing to so many for so long.

Then she rose up against him, opening her mouth to his, pushing her slender neck into his hand as if inviting him to break it. Instead, his hand found the strap to her camisole and he pulled sharply, snapping it. He could feel her hands at the back of his head, her fingers entwined in his hair, trying to pull him closer, tighter.

It surprised him that she was not frightened, and even more so in the way that she clung to him as if he were there to save her rather than to kill her. But what startled Jasyn the most was the way that his own body answered.

He abruptly became aware of small sounds coming from the back of her throat and he almost stopped, thinking he was hurting her and part of him hoping that it was true. Then he realized that the sounds, though small and timid, were not sounds of fear or pain. They were sounds of *wanting*.

The fire that now raged inside did not burn away the ice within – but, for the time being, the ice was overcome. Jasyn pushed Faith down into the satin pillows and let himself succumb to the moment. For the first time in his memory, he let himself lose control. The fire raged through his entire body, relentless and consuming. He was filled with her scent, her touch, her taste - and his ears were aware only of the small sounds that she made. The sounds of wanting.

ᘓᘔ

Later, their bodies damp with sweat, Jasyn lay tangled with her in the copper sheets, feeling like he had been hit by a meteor. He looked at the woman known as Faith de Rossi, the monster he had been after for a time that spanned over nine decades.

He brushed away a strand of hair from her face and, looking into her brown and gold eyes, he saw that they had tears in them. Before he could say anything she kissed the corner of his mouth and turned over, pressing her back into his chest and pulling his arm over her body like a blanket.

After a while he could feel her breathing become slow and deep and he knew that she had fallen asleep. He lay still for as long as he could, trying to assimilate what had just happened.

Had Chip been right? Did he simply know what to do when the time came? Or was it something more? Had he just betrayed his people? Of course, even JP had known what would be expected of him, that was the whole reason for showing the officers the clip that had frightened them all so much. But was he supposed to feel the way he did? Was he supposed to enjoy it?

Jasyn didn't think so. He was pretty sure it was supposed to be awful. Part of the job and something to be taken with a grain of salt. He carefully withdrew his arm from where it encircled Faith's body, but not away from it entirely. He let a hand rest on her hip and then carefully moved it to her elbow. Then, pausing to listen to her slow breathing, he let his fingers travel up and down the length of her arm. He pressed his lips to the back of her shoulder where it met her neck and closed his eyes, inhaling deeply. He let his hand close gently over her arm as it ran over her skin.

It's so smooth, he thought, wonderingly. *Too smooth*, he thought, and a frown creased his brows. He ran his hand again over the skin of her upper arm and the same thought echoed. *It's too smooth.*

Before he could figure out why, Faith stirred and murmured something. He thought it might be a name, but certainly not his. He froze, not knowing how she would feel about being awoken. But she turned and this time her murmur *was* his name, and it made him smile. She ran her hand up his own arm then his shoulder and then, reaching his face, pulled it down to her own.

Jasyn felt his body respond in the same way it had the first time, possibly faster knowing what it had in store. He tried to rein in his increasing passion, in case the kiss was all that she was after. But as soon as he heard the sounds of wanting coming from her throat, he knew he would be unable to stop.

Late in the night or early in the morning, after he had

fallen asleep for while, he awoke and found himself stroking her skin once again. And though this time he tried to be more gentle and not wake her, awaken she did. Pressing into him, her mouth open and wanting as if it was starving for him, she brought him fully awake as well.

FROM

The Dream Journal of Hope

I open my eyes and I see black. I feel the staccato of the pebbled pavement under my cheek and my nostrils are filled with its rich wet smell. It is rank with the tarry scent of industry and the heavy weight of nostalgia.

My eyelashes brush against the wet ground and come to a tickling rest on the tops of my cheeks. My eyelids flutter and I push myself up, my skin splattered with freckles or blood, I am not sure which in the ashy light.

The breeze whispers that the fall is coming, the fall is coming.

I am lying on a patch of asphalt, a broken road that ends only inches in front of me, giving way to knobs of grass that are filled with sand then it is just the wet sand that drops in miniature mountains towards an angry shore.

The ocean roars in my ears like a poetry reading, off-key and desperate, moving closer and crashing harder till I am quaking with trepidation. I try to ignore the reading of the waves as they gnash their teeth and focus instead on the raw true poetry of the sea – the unseen calm, the crashing storm, rolling blue, heavy with innumerable corpses. The stink of rotting fish.

I am wet but not cold, dreamnumb as I gather my wet dress around my white limbs and wait.

When the skies break apart it is chaos, but there is a feeling of tranquility that billows in to fill the void as the universe begins to mend itself.

The storm has left everything still and quiet and I sit under a tree with great, dripping leaves and see the sun reflected in a million puddles.

The pools of water are flat and glassy and smooth as mirrors. My eye catches movement in one of the mirror-puddles and I turn my head, hoping it is you, but it is not. It is a girl and I realize that I have seen her before, but only in my dreams.

She moves through my subconscious more and more, following me with the stealth of a cat. Sometimes crossing beaches, sometimes traversing forests, sometimes climbing rocks. Her clothes are as black as death and her hair as red as blood. If others in my dreams ever spy her she is desperately ignored, as though the watcher fears for his life.

I get up from beneath the tree and walk away, my bare feet sinking into the wet sand. I am looking for you, as I always do, looking for the key. I see movement far up the beach and my breath catches in my throat as I realize how close you are.

I try to walk faster but I am sinking, sinking in the wet sand. I go deeper with each step – to my ankles then my shins then my knees. I begin to flounder and suddenly I am pulling myself out of the sand with my hands, crawling, crawling away from the lapping waves and up into the mounds of sand-choked grass hills that guard the beach.

I try to remember how close the pavement is, knowing that it is firm and safe and I can run on it but I don't know where the road went or why I was ever on it in the first place.

I stand on the sporadic mounds of weedy grass and my eyes scan the horizon, looking for you. There is a forest ahead and a flicker of movement and I try to run but my legs are heavy like bags of sand and try as I might they move slowly so slowly and a cry of frustration escapes my lips and I fall forward, catching myself on my hands scraping my palms and jarring the bones in my arms because it is blacktop I am on the asphalt again and I push myself up and now I finally can run.

I run down the road still wet from the rain, feeling each pebble that bites my feet as I tear through the air and burst into the forest where the asphalt is taken over by pine needles and the wind is exchanged for branches that whip at my face but it is okay because I am almost there I have almost caught you and as you run I chase and I realize now that it is not you, it is the girl and though my lungs are burning I run faster and think that somehow she is more important and that I must catch her.

She runs like a deer, darting through the rain-soaked woodland and I pursue like a lion, my mane like a halo of flames and I am almost upon her when I am thrown violently to the ground. My bones quiver viciously all the way to the roots of my teeth and I realize that I have collided with something.

I stand up and, reaching out with my fingertips, feel a wall of glass in front of me. The girl stops on the other side and turns and looks at me before running off again and I know I cannot reach her. I cannot follow her and I cannot find you and the frustration fills me till I am ready to explode with it and I bang on the glass with the palms of my hands, hoping that it shatters, even if it cuts me to pieces.

Hitting the glass again and again I scream like a child in the throes of a temper tantrum. Desperate, I move to swing my arms again and suddenly see that the glass is now a mirror. I am staring at my own reflection. My hair is wild nest of copper-colored corkscrews, which is nothing out of the ordinary and my green eyes are wild and my feet are bare, neither of which hold much surprise. But my belly is huge, round and swollen.

I wake up, my nightgown and hair wet and stuck to my face and body and I am sure that is from my race through the rain-sodden woods but it is just sweat. In a panic my hands search out my belly and feel it over and over but it is flat and smooth and I am alone.

NINE

Bjorn absently fastened the buttons on the front of his Chimeran blue coverall, the mechanics of dressing in his officer's uniform long ago made into a rote act of his daily routine. The coin-sized gold medallions crossed his broad chest in a diagonal from his right hip to his left shoulder. The epaulettes on his shoulders were simple, merely straps of cloth held in place by another set of gold medallion-like buttons, yet they showed that he was not only an officer, but the Commander of the ship.

After a quick examination of himself in the mirror above his bureau, the Commander left his cabin and headed for the bridge, slightly unsettled by the quiet atmosphere aboard. He had lost thirty crewmembers in the attack of the Opal Dragon, and that was after fifteen had already been killed in the escape of the Red Jordan.

Bjorn had always been discouraged by the loss of life and liked it even less when those in question were Chimeran, his kind being harder to come by these days. What he hated the most was losing someone under his command. Bjorn had learned to accept death as a part of life, having been a leader in a war for his people that had lasted for nearly a hundred years, but he always felt personally accountable for his own crew - their well being was his concern and their safety was his responsibility.

The silence of the fallen crewmembers followed him through the corridors of the Chimeran Battle Cruiser *Macedonian.* There were no whispering ghosts, no sighing breeze that called out blame, just a vacuum of souls. The feeling was eerie and made him feel physically ill.

Throwing off the nagging ache at their loss and determined to drive on, the Commander entered the brightly lit bridge, nodded to everyone as they greeted him respectfully, and took his seat on the raised platform behind the astrogator and coms man.

The only bright star in his sky at present, and the one loss he did not mourn, was that of Rohn Stojacovik, his Second in Command. Though Stoj had been with him since the start of the revolution, the bastard had gone from increasingly insubordinate to damn near mutinous. Bjorn had been ready to send him packing or wring his neck. The Red Jordan had done him a favor. Still, the Executive Officer would have to be replaced.

Bjorn's first choice would be the Red Jordan herself, but the thought of it almost made the Commander laugh out loud. He had a better chance at getting Scarlett physically under him than serving under him. Both thoughts were as appealing as they were arousing. Bjorn gave his head a quick shake to clear it.

Settling into his chair, Bjorn opened his mouth to ask Aaron at the coms for a report but Aaron was already turning his chair to face the Commander.

"Sir?" Aaron asked, his blue eyes wider than normal and somewhat anxious.

Bjorn regarded him with raised brows, curious at what might have his coms man disturbed. Then he saw the nervous twitch at the corner of Aaron's mouth and knew what was coming. He sighed.

"Yes?"

"Sir, I have the Commander of the Battle Cruiser *Resurrection* online requesting conference with you."

Requesting? I'm sure demanding would be closer to the truth,

Bjorn thought, as he nodded at Aaron. "Put him through."

"Would you like his holo or on your screen?"

"On the screen, please."

I don't think I could handle a full holo of JP right now, he thought. By the look of relief on Aaron's face, neither could he. Most of Bjorn's crew did not take too well to the other Chimeran Commander. Half of them were terrified of him, the other half found him devout to the point of hilarity, and absolutely everyone thought he was crazy. Bjorn agreed with all of them, on all counts.

He swiveled his chair to the right so that he was facing a plate of hyper-glass nearly a meter wide and half a meter high. The glass became opaque, turning pearly white before it was filled with a crystal clear image of what looked like a teenage boy with smooth auburn hair wearing a priest's collar and robe.

Blue eyes burned with feverish intensity in a boyishly handsome face that was lightly spattered with freckles.

Bjorn, however, knew that it was simply the high collar of JP's coverall that made him look priestly, and the boy he was looking at was over a hundred years old. Not quite as old as Bjorn, but close. JP's normally porcelain skin was ruddy with rage and his perfect features were tight with fury.

"They betrayed us!" he sputtered as soon as he saw Bjorn on the video link. "The humans betrayed us!" The boy's expression alone was enough to lift Bjorn's spirits immediately.

"Hello, JP," he said warmly. *Why is it that everyone forgets the niceties? If I am the only civilized being left in the universe, then this universe is in worse trouble than I feared.* "And how is everything on your end?" he asked, though he had a good idea after having a look at the young-faced Commander.

"My end?" JP demanded, furious. "My end is missing a pair of Dragon eggs!"

Bjorn almost laughed aloud at JP's phrasing, and was barely

able to stifle the smirk that rose threateningly to the surface of his own features. "That's odd," he said. "The information I had been given was that the extraction had been successful."

He watched the other Commander shake with rage and Bjorn quickly made a fist so tight that his short nails bit painfully into his palm. He knew it would be a dangerous thing to laugh, not for himself, but for anyone who might be standing close to the other Commander. It was most likely Jasyn or Petrov, and Bjorn did not want to be responsible for either of their deaths.

"The extraction *was* successful," JP informed him, seething. "It was the delivery that went awry. The humans betrayed us!"

Bjorn sighed. He tapped a long finger on the arm of his chair, thoughtful. His mission to draw out the Opal Dragon had been a success, partly. The Dragon had been drawn, but not to much avail. The Chimerans were not able to control the situation in the slightest, nor were they able to hold onto the Fledgling they had captured. The only achievement had been proving that a Dragon really could be drawn, and providing a colossal distraction while the mission aboard the Beryl Dragon was carried out.

It had been very satisfying to learn that the attack in Beryl Dragon had been a success, to say the least. The Chimeran military had finally been able to plan and execute a major offensive based on a prediction of how the enemy would react. The success in the prediction itself being the greatest triumph. Yet now that victory had been taken from them as well.

"That the humans deceived us is obvious," Bjorn agreed with a flip of his hand, "if the eggs did not reach you." His full lips pressed together and he gave his head a shake. "But you must also consider that Elanor might have been involved as well."

JP's eyes grew wide and round – like a child's blue teacups on porcelain saucers. "No," he whispered. "She wouldn't."

"Was her body in the transport?" Bjorn asked.

"No."

Bjorn scowled, his lips now no more than a tight line. Of all the First Seven, JP suffered the most from a lack of imagination. The green-eyed Commander suspected that JP, being the last of the Seven, had been rushed in production. "Then you must consider the fact that she was most likely involved."

JP looked away from the screen, his face pained as he considered Bjorn's words. "The One save her soul if she was," he whispered.

Bjorn smirked without realizing it. *The One save her ass if Petrov finds her for you,* he thought.

JP looked sharply back at the screen, his eyes narrow with suspicion as if hearing Bjorn's thought from eight dozen light years away. The lips of the green-eyed Commander twitched.

"I don't have the eggs," he assured the devout Commander. "Or Elanor, if that is what you are thinking."

"It most certainly is not!" JP snapped. "But I would like to hear where you think they might be!"

Bjorn leaned forward in his chair. "Isn't it obvious?"

JP scowled at him. "No! How could I?"

Bjorn was finding it harder not to laugh. *I knew they rushed your damned model,* he thought. *You have less imagination than Petrov, and he's Second Run.* He sat back and blew out a long breath through pursed lips.

"It's the other faction," he said. "It has to be."

JP's blue eyes lit up and looked heavenward, scanning the ceiling of wherever he was in his own ship, most likely his own cabin. Bjorn didn't think the other Commander often wanted others privy to his conversations.

"Of course!" he agreed after a considerable time. "The other faction!" He and Bjorn had already discussed the fact that there was another entity in the universe, another group other than the Chimera and the IGC that was gathering power, getting ready to make a play for control. So far the suspected faction had remained anonymous. "Do you think it could be the girls?"

Bjorn knew that JP meant the de Rossi sisters when he referred to "the girls." He also knew that they were as much girls as he and JP were boys. "Faith and Charity?" he asked. Bjorn shrugged. "They could be."

"But why?"

Bjorn smirked. "I don't know. But they certainly have the means, and they are completely unpredictable."

Unlike us. We're as predictable as the weather on Venus.

"What do you think they are up to?" JP asked, truly puzzled. "What would they do with Dragon eggs?"

Bjorn shrugged. "I haven't the slightest idea. Sell them to us? Back to the IGC?"

JP cocked his head, thinking. "Why would they sell them? They are the last two people in the universe that need money."

Bjorn shrugged. "I don't know. Maybe they don't want money. Maybe they want to trade them for something else."

JP nodded slowly. "Maybe," he agreed, his voice soft and thoughtful. Then he fixed his blue eyes on Bjorn. "We might be able to find out soon enough," he said, giving the green-eyed Commander a sly smile.

Bjorn took the bait like a starved mackerel. "Why? What have you done?"

"Nothing yet. But Jasyn was chosen by Charity."

Bjorn let the words settle over him and his smile was broad but bittersweet. The Commander felt a strange mixture of exhilaration and disappointment.

"Something wrong?" JP asked, measuring the unease in the countenance of the other Commander.

"I was hoping to take Jasyn as my Second," he admitted. He had always liked Officer Issord. He was incredibly bright, quiet, and uniquely obedient. Also, there was something very comfortable about the Operations Officer. Something that felt familiar, like a distant relative that was rarely seen but whose company was always enjoyed. Bjorn sighed. "But if he got in, I'm glad. He'll do a good job."

JP cocked his head, smiling. "And?"

"And what?" Bjorn asked, a furrow forming between his blonde eyebrows.

JP shrugged, a smug smile set into his porcelain features.

Bjorn stared back at him, relaxing as he understood what the other Commander might be implying. "Do you think I am jealous?" he asked. He shook his head and laughed before the other Commander could answer. "Jealous of being Charity's sexual companion?" He shrugged. "I hadn't really considered it until now. Maybe I am. Just a little. You know how I felt about her."

Or maybe you don't. Your eyes were always fixed heavenward.

"Anyway," Bjorn continued. "Someone in your crew is bending Charity, hopefully to some end, and I am short an Executive Officer. If Jasyn is unavailable, I am at odds with whom to choose for my Second in Command. Maybe I should contact Nora."

JP leaned forward. "Nora Dijon?" he asked. "From Noa's crew?"

"She was one of the most passionate forerunners of the Cause."

"I know, but she hasn't been spaceborne for a long time, and I'm not sure Noa will want to give her up."

"David?" Bjorn asked. "Unless you think I should draw an officer from another Chimeran ship? I don't know enough of the satellite officers well enough, though I could bring a few on board the *Mace* for a probationary period."

JP leaned back, placing his palms together as if in prayer and touching the tips of his fingers to his lips. "No," he said, his blue eyes serious and far away. "I think David might make for a fine Executive Officer. Promote him on a provisional basis and see how he does. I would be interested to see how he fares under your command." The Chimeran's steely-blue gaze became focused once again as he trained his stare upon Bjorn. "And do we continue in the same direction? I will acquire the eggs and you will acquire Jordans?"

Bjorn straightened, sure once again. "Absolutely."

JP cocked his auburn head and a smile played at the corners of his full lips. "And are you pursuing those that would most likely make good Jordans, or those that are already Jordans?"

Bjorn frowned at him. "I am pursuing those that could most help The Cause."

JP laughed softly but did not say any more. He could gauge Bjorn's volatile temper as well as the green-eyed Commander could judge his own. "I can only hope that you are being led by your head," he said, carefully – though not carefully enough. "The one that makes the logical decisions," he added with a smirk.

"Maybe I am led by hope," Bjorn retorted calmly with a smirk of his own.

JP did not miss the slight and streaks of red snaked up over his pale jaw like flames. "Just get the Jordans we need!" he hissed.

Bjorn gave him a placating smile in response. "Of course. And you make sure they have the Fledglings they need."

"I will," JP promised through clenched teeth, the angry flush settling in his porcelain cheeks like a brush fire in a snowbank.

"And keep me updated on Officer Issord," Bjorn told JP as the Commander, furious, cut the transmission. "And Elanor," Bjorn whispered to the empty glass screen.

The Commander of the Battle Cruiser *Macedonian* leaned

back in his chair. The bleeps from the consoles, the click of Olivia's nails on the navigation dash, and the soft voices of his crew all joined and wrapped him in a comforting blanket of serenity.

Bjorn placed a finger against his lips and measured the responsibility entrusted to him regarding the current mission of the Chimeran people to end the reign of tyranny and oppression of the governing force of the civilized galaxies; the gods-be-damned InterGalactic Council. He considered for what must have been the hundredth time how he was going to get a pilot so well trained that he or she could fly the new Fledgling Dragons once they were hatched.

Only one person came to mind. The same person that he had thought about so much over the past weeks that she had become an obsession. The Red Jordan of the Opal Dragon. Named Scarlett.

෴

Jasyn watched Faith walk away, his feelings so split that he remained rooted to the spot where he stood in the dining room with their half-finished meal still hot upon the table. Part of him was relieved. He knew that he had to start gathering intel as soon as possible and, even more, he needed a bit of time to assimilate what had happened over the past twenty-four hours, and how he felt about it.

Yet another part, a very powerful part, wanted her to stay. He wanted to touch her, to smell her, to press his lips against hers and feel their bodies move together like they had the night before.

Faith was joined first by Penny as she walked through the living room, then by her head of security – the steely-eyed Geary. Faith turned her head towards the man saying words that Jasyn could not hear and the man nodded respectfully, though he looked none too pleased and threw a scorching glance back at Jasyn as he held a finger to his ear and spoke into his comset.

As Faith and her PA, along with the security escort, entered the lift at the center of the foyer and started to rise, someone came bounding down the stairs that encircled the elevator. It was a young man with brown hair and brown eyes in a black suit with a white shirt and a comset fitted tight into his right ear.

His eyes found Jasyn and he smiled as he approached the construct, holding out his right hand amiably.

"Hi," he said by way of introduction. "I'm Tom."

"I'm Jasyn," the construct replied, shaking the security man's hand.

"Geary said I'm to show you around while they're gone."

"Really?" Jasyn asked, his dark brows arching up over his hazel eyes. "Well, that was certainly nice of him."

Tom laughed. "No offense, but I'm sure it wasn't his idea. I have the feeling that if he had his way, even Charity wouldn't be able to visit without being shackled."

Jasyn liked Tom immediately. "What are you supposed to show me?" he asked.

Tom shrugged. "Geary wasn't specific, one of the reasons that I think that it wasn't his idea," he confided to Jasyn. "He didn't sound too excited about it. He just told me to show you around and keep an eye on you."

"Well," Jasyn said, thinking. "I saw most of the villa today, the two bottom floors anyway."

"Then you've seen most of it. Some pool, huh?"

Jasyn nodded. "I've never seen anything like it," he said, which was true.

Tom chuckled. "No kidding. Well, it's still pretty early. Do you want to take a look around upstairs?" he asked. "There isn't much, but at least you would have had a full expedition of the place before turning in tonight."

Jasyn smiled. "I would like that."

"Come on, then." Tom turned and led the way up the stairs that circled the lift to the third floor, giving Jasyn an informal tour. He pointed down the hall that led towards the staff's quarters, which took up half of the upper story of the villa. "That's where we live, for the most part."

"I came through here yesterday," Jasyn remarked as they passed through a small section slightly off the center of the third floor. It was the dock through where the construct had passed the day before when he had arrived with Charity. Tom nodded in agreement as he led Jasyn to the other side of the docking area.

"And this," he said as he held his palm over a pad next to a steel door, "is security." The door slid open to show a darkened room full of slim, glass monitors. A man with dark skin and dark eyes turned as they entered, acknowledged Tom with a nod, and then turned his attention back to the monitors.

"Hey!" Jasyn exclaimed, his enthusiasm child-like as his eyes swept the bank of monitors, "there's the pool!" He catalogued each viewpoint as best he could while Tom grinned at him.

"That's right," the security man said. "Every inch of the villa is under constant surveillance. Inside and out."

Though the construct was ecstatic, Jasyn frowned as if he were confused. "I don't see where I slept last night," he told Tom, his eyes traveling over the bank of monitors. "At least, I don't think I do."

Tom laughed and clapped Jasyn on the back. "Right again! The one place in the villa that is kept isolated is Ms. de Rossi's personal quarters. For privacy's sake." He gave Jasyn a knowing grin that the construct carefully returned, though much more tentative and nervous, which made Tom laugh again.

"You must work all the time," Jasyn said. "With someone watching the villa and someone guarding Ms. de Rossi."

Tom shook his head. "No, not so much. The villa is more secure than you could imagine. The top and bottom are covered with an alloy owned by GwenSeven, one so rare that it is not even sold, and it can close up like a clam. Most of our work is monitoring anything that gets close to the villa, along with who and what comes inside, which is easy. The hard part is guarding Ms. de Rossi herself when she is on the move – which is a lot. We have a team of twelve, though most are usually on personal guard. We take shifts with everything else."

"Oh," Jasyn said, hoping he sounded confused and unsure.

Security team of twelve, the construct considered carefully. *Impregnable base. Ingress and egress closely monitored.* He meticulously cataloged everything he could see along with everything Tom gave him, committing it all to memory. *Constant personal detail on Faith, who is out and exposed most of the time. Jeez, Tom,* he thought. *Is there anything else you want to tell me? Want to give me the keys to the safe or, better yet, why don't you tell me where she keeps the GwenSeven Mainframe?*

Tom leaned against a chair and crossed his arms over his chest.

"Well, what else would you like to see, my friend?"

The Mainframe.

Jasyn smiled nervously. "I don't know. What else is out here? Are we all alone? Out here in space?"

"No," Tom told him. "This villa is part of a community, there are other villas that connect to The Commons."

"The Commons?"

"Yeah. It's a large area, enclosed of course, of parks and shops and eateries in the middle of all the villas."

"Oh. Do you go there a lot?"

Tom chuckled. "No. We only go there as an escort, and Ms. de Rossi doesn't spend much of her time in leisure."

"What does that mean?" Jasyn asked, though he already knew. Still, it made Tom smile, which was what he was after.

"It means that she doesn't do much more than work," Tom informed him. "But we'll have some time to kill before she gets back. I can show it to you if you want."

Jasyn's face lit up. "Really?"

"Sure. We can go tomorrow."

"I'd like that," he said, smiling.

"Great!" Tom straightened and held out a hand towards the door, ushering Jasyn from the room full of monitors. "It will be a nice change of pace to get out for a while." He followed Jasyn to the stairs that encircled the lift. Jasyn smiled at him.

"Thank you," he said. "I can find my way from here."

Tom grinned. "Great. I'll come and get you after breakfast tomorrow."

Jasyn nodded in appreciation and headed down the stairs. He paused in the living room long enough to pick up his new acrylic before he headed for Faith's bedroom. Looking under the lever that served as a doorknob he saw a magnetic lock, which he slid closed with his thumb.

Feeling more secure than he had for nearly a week, he shucked off his clothes and slid into the giant bed. He toyed with the acrylic in a way he had not dared before, when he thought he might be seen. Manipulating its universal sensor and private transmitter, Jasyn was able to connect the acrylic to an outside line. Determining the safest route, and since the device was not strong enough to send a direct message to the *Resurrection*, he bounced a message to JP off a Chimeran relay point on the moon of Io.

Fire in the kitchen, the message read. *Nothing to worry about – however, the chef will be serving brain, rather than lung.*

Jasyn deleted the message once it had been sent, cleared its history, and powered down the acrylic before setting it aside on the night table. He placed his hands behind his head and stared at the ceiling, taking the time to sort out the conflicting feelings he had endured over the last twenty-four hours.

Unfortunately, all he could think of was the body that should be laying next to his, under his, entwined with his. Try as he might, he could not make sense of his feelings. The last thing on his mind as he dozed off was Faith, cradling her elbow in her hand, running the nail of her right thumb over the smooth curve of her lips.

◌੪ॐ੭◌

The next morning after breakfast, Jasyn explored The Commons with Tom and another security guard as an escort. Tom did most of the talking while the other guard kept watch, following a pace or two behind as they strolled through manicured gardens and quiet streets lined with shops.

The Chimeran found that it was not difficult to play the part of a freshly made construct. He simply acted as if he didn't know anything and was amazed by everything. Tom treated him like a child, with respect but still like a child. Jasyn did not mind. It made it easy to ask questions without raising suspicions and Tom was a goldmine of information.

"How many people live in the villas?" Jasyn asked.

"It varies," Tom told him. "But there are one hundred and twenty-eight villas. Mostly couples, though there are some families as well as a few people that live alone. But even those who live alone, like Ms. de Rossi, always have live-in staff. So roughly five hundred people, give or take a few."

"Wow," Jasyn said, his hazel eyes traveling over the glass storefronts that encased items that were as ridiculous as they were costly. He spied a mother and daughter in matching red coats point at miniature figures in a storefront window. "It must be expensive to live here."

Tom nodded. "It is. A lot of famous people live here."

"Like holo-stars?"

Tom laughed. "Actually, there are a few, but many are corporate executives or IGC Officials."

"What does that mean?" Jasyn asked, feeling a thrill run up his spine. He knew full well what Tom meant and found a deep pleasure for the first time in controlling his heart rate.

Tom grinned and shook his head. "Government people," he explained trying to use the simplest terms he could. "People who make big decisions for other people."

I couldn't have said it better myself, Jasyn thought. His hazel eyes took in the tree-lined avenue, the smartly dressed women shopping together, couples sipping hot beverages out of delicate china cups at an outdoor café, a man sitting on a bench smoking a vapor cigarette and reading the news on an acrylic.

Good lord, he thought. *Talk about the mother lode. One friction bomb could take out this whole satellite.*

His eyes lingered over the people on the street as he realized that they were most likely not the ones he was after. These were the ones left behind while the important people went to work. Left behind like him.

Something destructive would best be done on a day when those important people were at home. A holiday – that would do it. A holiday that people spend at home, even the important ones.

"It seems so quiet," Jasyn remarked. "Is it always like this?"

Tom shook his head. "It's like this a lot, especially during the day. More people are out at night, especially on the level above where there are more restaurants and nightclubs."

Jasyn looked up but all he could see was a simulated blue sky with a scatter of dainty clouds.

"Over the winter holidays," Tom continued, "it is really busy,

both down here and on the upper level."

Paydirt.

"What is winter?" Jasyn asked - just to please Tom, who was more than happy to share as he directed the construct down the main street.

"It's a time on rotational planets that tilt on an axis, making it colder than normal for a certain time period." He thought of telling Jasyn that there was even artificial snowfall in the Commons during the winter holidays, but he figured that if the construct didn't know what winter was, he certainly would have no concept of snow.

They explored a few more streets and even went into a few shops, including a jeweler's boutique that specialized in precious metals.

Jasyn asked the jeweler to show him a collection of necklaces inside a glass case that were displayed on a long box covered in black velvet. He had only seen Faith dressed twice and had already noticed that she liked to wear heavy-looking chains of gold. One caught his eye that was alternating links of gold and silver, the links alternately oval and round and varied in size.

"Ladies," Jasyn asked Tom, pronouncing the word slowly, "like to receive jewelry as gifts?"

Tom laughed. "They sure do! But if you are thinking about Ms. de Rossi, she is not like most ladies. Besides, you might want to talk to Penny about something like that. That's more her area."

Jasyn nodded and thanked the jeweler and told him he would be back. There were hushed whispers from the only other two people in the shop as he and Tom left. Tom pointed out a few more things on their return trip and they were back at Faith's villa before lunchtime.

Jasyn had a quick meal in the kitchen watching Cook and her assistant, Bowe, stock the pantries and the refrigerated compartments. When he was done he took his plate and glass to the oversized dishcleaner but Cook whisked them from his hands and waved him away before he could even open it. He thanked them both and went downstairs to the pool.

He descended the spiral staircase, walking carefully down into the darkness. He held onto the stair rail, ready for the moment of vertigo that he knew was going to swallow him, even if it was only momentary.

It rose up to meet him as he reached the bottom, the toe of his foot feeling around, uncertain if there was another step. One foot found the solid surface and then the other was down as the vertigo swept through him, making his body want to sway. His hand tightened around the rail until the sensation passed and his eyes traveled the room, taking it all in.

The bottom stair ended on a circular platform of black marble. Beyond it, the rounded bottom of the villa disappeared into a pool, encased entirely in a hyper-diamond shell that was more clear than any glass. The black marble floor continued behind the lift where molded glass chairs were available for reclining and stacks of thick, black towels waited for the brave swimmers. The curved walls were of the same ultra-clear hyper-diamond, the ceiling a darkened mirror. The darkness of the space under and around him was broken by the distant sparkle of a billion stars.

The stars were reflected in the ceiling and again on the polished floor, doubling their number and then doubling it again.

Everything is a mirror here, Jasyn thought.

His eyes traveled over the pool and across the ceiling and he suddenly thought of the craze of mirrors upstairs that made up Faith's vanity.

So many mirrors. It's important to know the real from reflection.

The Chimeran cocked his head, puzzled by his last thought,

feeling that it was important. He mulled it over, trying to decipher where the impression had come from, before giving up and pulling off his shoes and clothes, tossing them onto the black marble floor. He stripped down to his undershorts and put a tentative foot in the water. It was as warm as a tub.

He felt along the bottom, making his way out until it was deep enough to swim. He swam out to what he thought was the center of the pool, then saw that he still had a ways to go. It was much larger than he had first thought.

Everything here is deceptive.

It felt good to be able to stretch his muscles and get his blood flowing. He loved to swim but, being almost always spacebourne, was rarely afforded the opportunity. He was about to swim back towards the platform and climb out when something caught his eye. At first he thought it might be the movement of the water. Then, as he slowly treaded in place and waited for the ripples to smooth out, he thought it might be an imperfection in the glass.

There was a large dark blur at the bottom of the pool, blotting out the stars. He took a deep breath and dove under, pulling for the bottom. It was deeper than it looked, which was no surprise, and he pulled harder. He kicked until his legs burned and, reaching out, his hand touched something large and rough and curved. He had only that moment.

He flipped his body and pushed off of the bottom of the pool with his feet, shooting back up to the top, his lungs burning. He broke the surface with a splash, took a gulp of air and shook a spray of warm droplets from his hair. He pedaled his feet, treading water as he looked down at the star-studded darkness beneath him. He considered going back down and changed his mind.

Jasyn swam back to the raised foyer and climbed out. He dried off with one of the heavy black towels and wrapped another around his shoulders before sitting on one of the molded glass chairs. It was warm and comfortable. He settled back into it, his hazel eyes quick and restless.

He watched the ripples on the pool die down until the water was glassy once more, the universe caught still and encapsulated. Returned to the womb by Faith de Rossi. He felt heat emanating from the chair, warming him. When he was dry, and his mind had gone over as many options as he was able to conceive, he dressed and went upstairs to retrieve his acrylic.

ONE ZERO

John walked through the security monitor as he entered the stout yet sparkling building of concrete and hyper-glass that was the IGC Pilot Training Center for the Upper Klick of Three Mile on Io. The spec-onyx doorframe took an eye scan of his left retina, clocking him in for work as efficiently as it scanned him for weapons.

Mike, his new partner, was already in their private office looking over the list of sign-ups for the next training quarter. Mike was the only flight instructor at the school that was younger than John, and the only other trainer qualified to teach pilots all the way up to an IGC fighter clearance.

He was over-skilled, overly cocky, and John had liked him instantly. When John had asked Mike why he wasn't a pilot himself, the young man had rolled up his sleeve, exposing an arm covered, like the rest of him, in smooth skin so dark it was nearly black as pitch.

Seeing nothing out of the ordinary, John had regarded the man with raised brows and a shrug. "So?" he asked.

Mike flashed him a grin, showing a row of bright white teeth. "Underneath that beautiful near-ebony skin, my friend, is more metal than the IGC will allow for fighter status."

John nodded, understanding. He knew that the government's policy on pilots and prosthetics was stringent.

"Lost the whole arm in a skiing accident when I was in college," Mike continued. "I thought it was going to kill me – the loss of my future career, not the loss of my arm. I knew even then that I wanted to be a pilot."

"You can still be a pilot," John had told him but Mike had laughed.

"Doing what? Flying cargo cogs full of plastic shit and computer rip-chips from Titan to Europa?" Mike's laugh was hearty but bittersweet. "No thanks. I'm a fighter pilot in my heart. If I can't fly with the big boys, I'm going to teach them. It's the least I can do."

John's brown eyes crinkled at the corners as he gave him a knowing smile. "I know the feeling," he admitted.

This time Mike's laugh had been genuine and without a trace of bitterness. "And you? Too much family competition?"

John had echoed Mike's hearty laugh at that. He knew his family name always preceded him. He shook his head. "No," he had said. "I'm a family man." Mike had simply nodded and clapped him on the back, understanding.

Today, as John entered, Mike looked up at him from the glass screen of his compute board, flashing his white teeth in his usual grin.

"More sign-ups?" John, asked, already familiar with that particular smile.

"More, indeed," Mike told him. John recognized the sly gleam in the man's dark eyes as well.

"Waiting list?" he asked, though he already knew the answer.

John had recently moved to the upper klick with his family that included an ancient grandfather and a teenage son named Sean. After Sean's first day at his new school, John's work – the only IGC authorized fighter pilot school in the Upper Klick - had been inundated with applications by what John assumed must be every boy in Sean's grade and at least half in the grades above and below his towheaded son.

There had even been a number of applications from girls,

which always brought a smile to John's face. Female pilots, especially the tenacious ones, always made him think of his sister - though he had never met one that was even close to being as tenacious or as bad-tempered as Johanna.

Unfortunately for Sean's classmates, the minimum age for flight school was sixteen standard human years. That meant that over ninety-nine percent of the kids went onto a waiting list.

"The waiting list indeed," Mike told his partner. "If I had known the response we would get having you here, I would have encouraged the company long ago to hire someone famous."

John smiled and put the sim-leather case that held his personal acrylic on his desk. "You mean like a holo star? Gina Stardell perhaps? Or a socialite? Maybe you could get Charity de Rossi. I'm sure she is one hell of a pilot."

Mike hooted laughter. "I doubt that, but I think plenty of men would still be willing to pay the tuition just for a glimpse down the neck of her flight suit."

John's smile widened as he dropped his weight into his chair. "Do you think there is a man in the seven systems that hasn't had a look at Charity de Rossi's cleavage?"

"I haven't!" Mike argued with a good-natured frown. "Not up close and personal, anyway," he added.

Before they could continue their discussion regarding the neckline of the galaxy's most notable socialite, a baritone chime sounded over the open com in their office.

"Mr. Mattatock?" a woman's voice inquired.

John looked up towards the source of the voice - a micro speaker hidden behind a lamp sconce.

"Yes, Lina?"

"Your wife is on the outside line, would you like me to put her through to your personal, or take a message?"

"Put her through on my personal, please." John fished his personal comset out of his shirt pocket, wondering why Rebecca didn't call him directly, until he saw the two colors running along the edge of the normally clear device, showing that he had two messages waiting.

Damn, he thought as he hooked the set over his ear, turning it on. Rebecca was already there.

"John?"

"I'm here. Is everything okay?"

"Yes, it's just that I'm on my way to the school to pick up Jeanette."

"Is everything okay?" John asked again, interrupting, worried. He rose up from his chair, leaning over his desk with his weight on his splayed fingers.

"Yes, she's fine…it's just," Rebecca stopped and he could hear her laughing softly, which put him more at ease. "It's father-daughter day for her grade, a take-your-daughter-to-work kind of thing." John smiled and sat back down in his chair, relieved, while Rebecca continued. "The notice went out a few weeks ago, before she started, which is why we didn't know. If it is too much trouble, I can take a half-day, or maybe she will be okay with Grandpa until Sean gets home…"

"No," John said quickly. "It won't be any trouble." He could hear Rebecca's sigh of relief over the comset. He knew how she felt. Grandpa had seemed a little off lately. Well, more off than usual. "Do you want me to get her?"

"No, that's okay, I'm almost there. I'll take the Q and drop her off on my way to work."

"That would be great, I'll meet you outside."

"John?"

"Yes?"

"Thanks."

"Of course," he said frowning. "Love you."

"Love you too."

He cut the link, pulled the comset off his ear, and tossed it onto his desk. He didn't know how some people could walk around with theirs on all day.

"Charity de Rossi coming in?" Mike joked.

John laughed. "Better. My daughter."

ᚼᚱᚢ

Jeanette was her typical bundle of energy and smiles and dark bouncing curls. As usual, it made John's heart swell to twice its normal size when he saw her.

"Daddy!" she squealed as she ran to him. He lifted her high, kissing her cheeks and giving her a big squeeze before setting her on her feet again. He kissed Rebecca as she handed him Jeanette's canvas school bag along with the dance bag made of black ripstop with holos of pink shoes dancing along the sides and decorated with streamers of pink ribbon.

He put his arm through the strap of each as Jeanette slipped her tiny hand into his. He was glad that neither was a diaper bag. He had found the years of diapers and bottles long, tedious, and smelly. They certainly weren't his favorite.

"Thanks again," Rebecca told him.

"It's really no problem," he assured her.

"I know, it's just..."

"Grandpa?" he asked. Rebecca nodded as if she felt guilty, her eyes not meeting his. John touched her gently on the chin. "You don't feel good about leaving the kids with him these days do you?"

"Not for too long. Especially..." she trailed off looking meaningfully at Jeanette before finally meeting his eyes of brown with her own eyes that were large and blue. "I'm worried about him, John."

John nodded. "I know."

"If something happened," she said shaking her head, "while the children were there..." she trailed off again, frowning. "Sean would be okay but," she looked back at Jeanette who scowled at her mother.

"Are you guys worried that Grandpa might keel over and I won't know what to do?"

John scooped her back up and tickled her, making her squeal. "That is exactly what we are worried about," he told her.

"I know how to call the e-line," she assured her parents. "And Sean says that in the Upper Klick they are at your door within seconds!"

"Well," her mother told her, kissing her cheek, "hopefully we won't have the need for the e-line."

Jeanette giggled. "I'm sure we won't. There's nothing wrong with Grandpa."

Her parents exchanged glances that said they were not so sure but John kissed her dark curls before putting her back on her feet. "I hope you are right, Sweetheart," he told her.

"Of course I am. Now, are you going to teach me how to fly a jet today?"

John laughed. "If that is what you want to do," he told her - but the look he got from Rebecca told him that he better not. He gave his wife a kiss. "Afraid she's going to run off and join The Legion?" he asked.

Rebecca gave him a smack on the arm and a kiss on his bearded cheek. "I don't think that's such a far-fetched idea, considering your family."

John shook his head, chuckling. He took up Jeanette's hand again and led her into the building as Rebecca turned and headed back to catch a ride on the Q, but she was smiling too.

"Jeanette," John said as he dropped her bags onto the chair

behind his desk, "this is my partner, Lieutenant Mitchell."

Jeanette held out her hand. "Pleased to meet you, Lieutenant Mitchell," she said politely, offering a tiny curtsey along with her hand.

"The pleasure is mine little lady," Mike told her, shaking her small hand. "Do you like to dance?" he asked, seeing the bag with the shoes dancing along the sides. She nodded enthusiastically. "Yes, but today my daddy is going to teach me to be a star-fighter."

"Is that so?" Mike asked, looking up at John, whose eyes were gleaming. "Well, there is a lot to learn if you want to be a star-fighter, so you better get started."

"Do we have anything that needs my attention first?" John asked.

"Nah! We don't even have anything that needs *my* attention first. I'd like to watch the next star-fighter here have her first lesson."

Jeanette bounced up and down, clapping her hands.

"Come on," John told her, leading the way from the office he shared with Mike to a corridor that led away from the administrative section of the building. "Let's go for ride, shall we?"

Jeanette looked ready to explode with excitement. "We're going in a real jet?" she asked. John laughed.

"Not yet," he told her as Mike followed them down the corridor. "We are going to go into what is called a simulator. It's a pretend jet, but it will look very real. It even moves and shakes – so it feels very real – so if you get scared you need to tell me right away and I will turn it off."

"I won't be afraid, Daddy," Jeanette declared, shaking her dark curls emphatically.

They came to a pair of double steel doors and he pulled his badge from his shirt pocket and flashed it at the pad on the wall. The doors swung open and Jeanette followed her father through, her head swiveling to take everything in and her dark eyes wide as she looked around.

They were in a very big room crowded with wires and machines. In the very middle of the room was what looked to Jeanette like the front half of a space shuttle. Lieutenant Mitchell moved around behind the shuttle, turning on more lights. Her daddy twisted a handle on the shuttle door and pulled it hard, swinging the door up and open.

"Climb in little fighter," he instructed. Jeanette bounded inside and onto the seat like an eager puppy while her father went around and climbed in on the other side. "Put your arms through the harness," he told her, showing her by sticking his arms through his own harness. "Good. Then fit the buckles together over your tummy, and over…" John laughed, seeing that the chest strap was going to go across her nose.

John unbuckled his own harness so that he could lean over and adjust Jeanette's strap as low as it would go, and tightening it where he could. He could hear Mike's laugh over the com system and knew that his partner was watching them on the monitor. He got back into his own harness and palmed the button that closed the doors.

"Wow," Jeanette breathed, her brown eyes traveling over all of the controls. To her it seemed like an endless and inscrutable amount of switches and levers and dials. "How do you remember everything?" she whispered. Her father laughed.

"One at a time," he told her. "For today, the only thing you need to know is the yoke, sometimes called the joystick."

"The joystick?" she asked.

"Yes. You can't miss it, it's the only stick in here."

"This one?" she asked, putting a hand on the bar of metal that jutted up from the floor in front of her knees.

"That's the one!" her father said. "Go ahead," he

encouraged, smiling. "Take hold of it." Jeanette leaned forward as far as her safety straps would allow and grasped the metal bar in her small, slightly chubby fingers, nearly bursting with excitement. "Now," he told her, "when you push it forward, it will make your fighter go down. When you pull it back it will make your fighter go up. Left is left and right is right. You do know your left from your right, don't you?"

"Daddy!" she scolded, letting him know that she was well aware of which was right and which was left.

"Okay," he said. "Do you feel the trigger under your finger?"

"Yes!"

"Good. That will fire a laser pulse, but your missiles are right here," he said leaning over and tapping a red button on the top of the stick.

"Left, right, laser pulse, missiles, got it."

John laughed. "Well then, little miss," he said, "why don't you take us in for our first battle?" John reached up near the ceiling of the simulator and flipped a switch that threw them into darkness while the area in front of them took on the appearance of the nose of a fighter jet streaking through space.

Jeanette squealed and dove into the black of space like an otter diving into water. John was worried that she might be scared once the first attack came but she dug in with a determined expression and fought amazingly well, especially for a child of not quite ten. John had to restart the program twice. The first time her ship was blown to bits within seconds and the second time it was within minutes. Though she fought doggedly for the better part of thirty minutes on her third try, the virtual fighter craft had simply sustained too much damage to remain viably active.

For John, he could not remember the last time he had laughed so hard or so much. The sides of his body and his cheeks both ached. He released the latches on his safety harness and leaned over to let his daughter out of her restraints.

"It's over already?" she exclaimed, disappointed.

"It is for me - you're a crazy flyer! I'll be spacesick if I stay in here!"

"Can I keep going?" Jeanette asked, placing her hand protectively over the buckle on her safety harness. "Please?"

John looked at her with a lopsided smile under his beard. "Sure, if you want. But I will be right outside, watching you on the monitor, and I will be able to hear you in here. When you are ready to stop just let go of the joystick and tell me you are done."

"I will, Daddy!"

John climbed out, shut his door and joined Mike on the instructor's dais next to the bank of monitors that showed the inside of the jet, the simulation of oncoming fighters, and readouts of damage and predictable outcome. He thumbed the coms switch.

"Ready?" he asked.

"Ready!" Jeanette called back.

John started the program again and leaned against the bank of monitors with his arms crossed over his chest, watching. On her next ship, she made it through the starfight with her ship not only intact, but practically unscathed. Jeanette's squeals of delight could be heard coming from the simulator, even with the coms off and the doors shut.

John thumbed the coms switch. "Good job, honey. How about going with me to the cafeteria and grabbing a snack?"

Jeanette's voice came back through the speaker vents, tiny and pleading. "Can I keep playing? Pleeeeease?"

Mike looked at John, grinning from ear to ear and mouthed the word, *playing.*

John rolled his eyes and leaned towards the coms dash. "Of course, Sweetheart. Are you ready to move on to the next program?"

"Yes, yes, yes!"

Smiling, John started up the next simulated attack and ran his index finger over the light that read *Restart upon Failure* and turned to his partner.

"I think I have an idea," he said with a grin.

"Are you going to offer her my job?" Mike asked.

"Hilarious," John said dismissively. "You know that list we have?"

"The wait list?"

John nodded. "How do you think the company would feel about starting a new program? We could call it the Junior Pilot Program. Flying only simulators until they are old enough for the jets, and if they are too young for a simulator it could be all classroom instruction."

Mike looked at his partner, his dark eyes gleaming. "How do I think the company would feel about making a lot of money right away?" He pressed his lips together and shook his head slowly from side to side, feigning uncertainty and fighting a smile. "I don't know, John. Is that something companies like to do?"

John opened his mouth to continue but Mike pointed at the monitors. Jeanette had beaten the second simulation on her third try. "I'll be damned," John whispered. He started the next sequence without his daughter having to ask. The sound of her cheers from inside the simulation shuttle let him know that she was thrilled.

Again he ran his finger over the control to restart the program when failed, though this time he also set the program to move to the next level if completed. Jeanette had all day to play and he was sure that he was onto something.

"You were saying?" Mike encouraged, his dark face all innocence.

John leaned towards him as if sharing a secret. "This could be huge," he said, his voice quiet. "Not only would the company get an amazing influx of revenue, but imagine the head start these pilots would have. They aren't allowed to enlist before they are sixteen, because of flight regulations, but practically their entire first year is spent in a classroom so they can get their permit…"

"And another six months are spent in the simulators…" Mike continued for him, nodding.

"If these kids could get their permits and paperwork done by the time they are sixteen and could actually start flying by then," John continued, "they would have a leg up on every other pilot in the galaxy."

"And what parent wouldn't be willing to pay through the nose for their boy…"

"Or girl!"

"Or girl," Mike acquiesced with a deferential nod, "to be ahead of every other cadet in the civilized systems?"

The two instructors leaned closer, sharing their thoughts and getting increasingly keyed up with each new idea. The conversation rose and fell as they plotted the success of the program, what it would mean to the company and to the community, not to mention the instructors that had come up with and started the whole plan.

"We could even…" John said excitedly when Mike held up a hand, cutting him off and then pointing to one of the monitors, the whites of his eyes showing all the way around his dark irises.

John whirled, suddenly fearful that something had happened to Jeanette. He could hear her shouting from inside the simulator, but they were sounds of elation and victory. His eyes scanned the monitors, unbelieving.

"Jesus," he whispered, leaning back.

"Did you teach her that?" Mike asked.

John shook his head, unable to speak or draw his gaze from the screen as he watched his nine-year old daughter simulate a barrel roll, firing a missile at each pivot point. It kept her ship untouched while delivering a direct hit to each oncoming ship that she caught in her sights.

At the same instant, the eyes of both instructors sought out the training level. The glowing red number was seven. Their heads turned until their eyes met.

"It's usually six months before a cadet can make it through that program," Mike said with a trace of disbelief in his voice. He narrowed his dark eyes at John in good-humored suspicion but his partner was looking at the monitor that showed Jeanette inside the simulator. "Are you sure you never taught..." he started but John was shaking his head, already walking towards the simulator.

"No," he said, not sure if Mike could hear the quaver in his voice and not caring. "Not ever." The fact that Jeanette was literally *killing* at the simulated fight that took cadet pilots half a year or more to beat was disturbing enough, even worse was the expression on her face.

John circled the mock fighter craft and slapped his palm against the hydraulic lever. The training jet sank down with a hiss and John lifted the hatch on the pilot's side. He saw that his hands were shaking.

The snarl that he had seen on his daughter's face was not full of hatred or aggression and probably would have looked adorable to Mike or nearly anyone else. But John had seen it before - on his sister, Johanna. It was a snarl of determination and gratification that usually came when she was in any kind of fight. Jeanette was the perfect mirror of Johanna when she had been the same age. That expression customarily meant that someone had just got punched in the mouth, or kicked in the balls.

He pulled the door open and for a second he was terrified that it *would* be Johanna inside, snarling at him.

"School is out little starfighter!" he called, his voice cracking. He looked into the simulator and saw only his daughter there. Her cheeks were pink and her brown eyes were not defiant or angry, just brimming with disappointment that the fun had to end.

"Already?" Jeanette asked.

"Already?" John echoed. "You fought through lunch!"

"I did?"

"Yes, you did."

"Did I do a good job?"

John laughed as he pulled her out, planting a kiss on her cheek. "You did fabulous," he told her. "In all my years of training, you are the only starfighter I have ever met that giggles when they are hit by enemy fire."

Jeanette's laughter pealed like a chime of bells as he put her on her feet. "I *am* hungry," she admitted.

"I'm sure you are," her father agreed. "Star-fighting can really work up an appetite. I'll clock out early today and we'll get something to eat before I take you to dance class." His heart finally stopped hydraulic-hammering in his chest. He waved at Mike and his partner nodded in agreement, his dark eyes gleaming.

"Was I really good, Daddy?" Jeanette asked as they left the big room with the pretend jet wired to the floor.

"Yes," John told her, sighing a little, his scare and surprise now fading into pride. "You were very, *very* good."

Jeanette clapped her hands. "Can I tell Sean how good?"

"Yes," her father said, tousling her dark curls. "But not your mother."

Jeanette's dark brows drew together, making a seam in her otherwise perfectly smooth brow. "But why not?"

John squatted down so that they were eye to eye. "Because Mommy is not all that keen on star-fighting," he told her.

"Okay," Jeanette said, smiling with the knowledge that they were sharing a secret. "What about Grandpa?"

"Yes," he said. "You can absolutely tell Grandpa."

Jeanette clapped her hands and squealed with delight.

ONE ONE

Jasyn sat in the living room of Faith's villa. He kept perfectly still – on the outside. On the inside, his emotions were in turmoil. His acrylic lay on his lap, over legs that wanted to bounce erratically with nervous energy, but he forced himself to be still.

Something was wrong with him. Had he considered himself a machine, he would think that he was malfunctioning. The irony was not lost on him. His lips twisted into a smirk as he brought his right hand to his mouth and his teeth bit down on the nail of his thumb and nibbled at it.

Everything had started out fine, better than fine. He could imagine JP closing his brilliant blue eyes and uttering prayers of thanks to the One every time he received intel from Officer Issord.

But now things were spiraling out of control, and the Operations Officer of the Chimeran Battle Cruiser *Resurrection* knew that he was to blame.

He couldn't pinpoint the exact moment it started. It would be like trying to pinpoint the start of a storm that grew with each second to become a swirling hurricane. Was it the first breath of a breeze, just enough to whisper through one's hair and run teasingly across the scalp? Or was it even less - as gentle as the beat of a butterfly's wing, something that would roll into the future and result in a cataclysmic act of the One?

If that was the case, Jasyn knew that it must have started the very first night, when he first laid his eyes on Faith. If not at that moment, then the second he pressed his lips against hers. Something strange had happened inside himself that night, something that he still could not identify.

When Faith was away on business, which felt like all the time, his discipline as a Chimeran Officer could be observed with his every move – masked by the simple smile he had adopted from Chip. Every thought and every movement was based on his predetermined course of action and executed with precision. Upon his first tour of the villa he was able to establish that there was not a single weak spot where it could be penetrated with ease, other than from inside. After his first trip from the villa with Faith he was able to break down the components of her security team and mentally diagram the quickest way to disable it. It was as simple and rote as field-stripping a laser rifle.

Faith de Rossi was aloof with everyone, though she tried not to be with him, giving him attention when she could. But even when she was home she was working. He had not been at the villa for much more than a few weeks before he watched in amazement one night as Faith transformed the vanity in her bedroom from the maze of mirrors into a maze of monitors and touchpads.

Jasyn had been sitting in the wing chair with his acrylic when Faith had gotten a call and, with a sigh, she dropped down onto her vanity bench and ran her slender fingers up along the outer right edge of the largest mirror. She did not seem concerned in the slightest that he was practically right next to her.

The mirrors, he had thought, looking down at his acrylic, feigning disinterest. *I knew it. This whole place is a gods-forsaken hall of mirrors.*

On her next business trip it only took him a few minutes to figure out the simple trigger mechanisms. He transformed it himself and stared in awe as he realized that it was not just a computer with multiple screens. He was looking at the

GwenSeven Mainframe, and much more.

Normally – or, at least, during most of the day - the vanity was a mess of reflective glass in all different shapes and sizes. When transformed, the panes of glass turned, flipped, or faded to reveal everything from compute monitors and galactic coms screens, to real-time video feeds.

After he had gotten comfortable enough not to worry about a security team crashing through the door, and though he was always on alert, Jasyn spent an entire night one time watching the live feeds. He cataloged each place in a secure window on his acrylic each time he figured out from where the video was being transmitted.

Most of the people and places that were being monitored made perfect sense – embassies and councils and the like. Others seemed random or trivial – children playing games in a park, a green blip on a radar monitor, a girl with pinkish-blonde hair in front of a computer monitor in an otherwise darkened room.

He dourly saw that four of the video feeds were coming from Chimeran bases or ships, though he was somewhat relieved that none of them were coming from the Battle Cruiser *Resurrection*. Other people and places he could not identify, but was sure that Faith had her reasons. One transmission he watched for an hour, knowing that it was coming from a ship but not recognizing anything or anyone the least bit familiar. Then out of the blue he recognized the similarity of the crew uniforms and realized that the transmission was coming from on board a Dragon.

Jasyn spent another entire night reading over a month of Faith's coms history. All of it was fascinating to him in its own way - especially the way she commanded everyone to whom she spoke. He pored over transmissions of construct approvals, monetary deals, biometric acquisitions, land and space acquisitions, where and when she wanted people or projects moved, whom she wanted terminated. It was later, after going through a folder marked *Replies and Results,* that Jasyn realized when she ordered a termination it had nothing to do with employment.

All of the knowledge that he acquired was passed back to JP aboard the *Resurrection*, at every chance he was afforded. Faith was regularly gone for days on end, giving him plenty of time as well as opportunity.

When she was gone, the Chimeran Officer's job was easy. Almost too easy. Not just from all of the time he was given to carry out his mission as a spy and a relay, but because he was able to do it without distraction. But when she was there, he *and his mission* would begin to fall apart. He found himself less and less interested in gleaning information – and more and more interested in the seemingly trivial things she would share with him about herself and the few people in her life.

Without Faith around, he was in complete control of his thoughts and emotions. But when she *was* there, and especially when she was close to him, everything blew apart like paper pages in a cyclone.

Over a century of training, of preparation, of acquired hatred – dissolved in her presence. When she was within his sight he wanted nothing more than to be near her. To wrap her in his arms, to feel her body under his hands, to press his lips against her skin and close his eyes. He was consumed by her. The physical pull was difficult but tolerable. What was worse was that when she was next to him he felt deprived of his mental faculties. He seemed to lose all control of his senses when she was around - and the most absurd things would come tumbling out of his mouth before he could stop them.

On the first actual day they spent together, he accompanied Faith to The Commons – the commercial hub of the wealthy satellite community that Tom had shown him on her first trip away. Jasyn had returned to the jeweler's and bought her the necklace he had seen. Unbelievingly, even as he was mentally dissecting her security detail, he was fastening jewelry around her neck and blurting out that he would not let anything happen to her. He promised that he would keep her safe.

He told himself later that it was only part of the ruse, nothing could be further from the truth and that he was just playing the game. But he knew that he really did feel - deep down inside – that it was true. He had bought the necklace because he had wanted to please her, and a part of him feared that he would really protect her in an instinctive manner if she were threatened.

Every time she was with him it was the same.

Then she would leave for business, and he would spend hours filled with a longing emptiness, and then anger. He would be furious that she left him, that she treated him like an inconsequential pet to be left behind. Then he would come back to himself and remember that *that* in itself was the entire reason for his presence at the villa – to stop this woman from creating people to be used as playthings.

Jasyn thought time and again that it would be best to simply finish collecting what information he could, and then kill her and be done with it. He was certain that it could be done, especially if he struck in the night. Eliminating Geary first would be crucial, and the most difficult. The man was tireless, always on watch and always on alert. Once he was gone, however, picking off the rest would be a breeze. He could have a rendezvous capsule pick him up and be back on the *Resurrection* in just over forty hours.

If they sent an extraction team he could not only be gone with the GwenSeven goods – he would only need the hard drive from the Mainframe – but he could also leave a bomb in return, one large enough to destroy the entire satellite.

But those thoughts and feelings only occurred when she was gone.

Then Faith would return, her body wound as tight as a spring and her face just as tense, led by Geary and followed by assistants – Penny always in the forefront either speaking rapidly into a comset or tapping notes onto her acrylic in her hurried but precise manner.

As soon as she entered the room Jasyn would find himself rooted to the carpet, or the chair, momentarily paralyzed like a frightened animal until her eyes met his own. There would be a single second that bore into them both, a chasm that would open wide and then snap shut. He would see her whole body relax, a tiny smile at the corner of her lips, and feel the same softening in himself. Seeing the warmth in her eyes at the sight of him would make his entire soul dissolve.

The storm grew within, thundering and clashing until it shook him to his core.

Oddly enough, he felt that it was his acrylic that saved him when the worst storms threatened. The damn thing was a bottomless well of information. He could research any database he found. The ones constructed by humans were ridiculously simple to hack into. AI systems were a little more tricky, but he knew most of the tricks they used – having a fabricated brain of his own helped - and he was simply able to figure out the rest.

His first night alone he was tempted to use the acrylic to try and find a way into the security system of the satellite community in an effort to find out the names of those that lived in all of the villas. On a whim he checked to see if the community had a central concierge and, lo and behold, it certainly did. Jasyn used a back-door program to get a list of tenants, which he promptly sent to JP. Within his first week of living at the villa, his mission was already one of the most successful ones the Chimera had ever run.

The acrylic was also good for all kinds of entertainment; movies, music and games and more things that he had yet to explore. He didn't necessarily care for the movies, even though the picture was incredibly dimensional for a flat screen, but Faith would occasionally load one for him and he would watch it to please her. Most of the movies were old, pre-rebellion era. He supposed that they had some meaning since she would look at him quizzically afterwards, gauging his reaction. He would always tell her that he liked them, though there were few that he enjoyed. It was the same with the music – he only listened to what she chose and he liked some but was ambivalent about most. It was the gaming that he really was keen on.

He loaded numerous games and beat them all quickly. Then he found that he could engage in games that other people were playing and play against them in real time. The first one he tried (amused by its name - Chimera Battle) was a simulated jet fighter game. Despite having actually fought in the Chimeran Rebellion for almost a hundred years, he never served as a pilot. He was instantly decimated, and instantly hooked. The more he played the more he grew in skill and, as he mastered Chimera Battle, he began trying others. Golgoth Invasion was another fighter simulation, but he also enjoyed IGC Commission and Lost Earth, which were strategy games.

There was another game called Storm Chaser that reminded Jasyn of an Astrogator that had worked aboard the *Resurrection*, many decades ago. His name was Jarec, and he had the palest skin that Jasyn had ever seen on any species, even Chimeran. His skin had the milky white color of the Commander's, but without the freckles or ruddy flush. Jasyn had remarked upon it one time but Jarec had laughed and waved him off.

"It was common with my run," he had remarked offhandedly, meaning the batch of constructs that had been manufactured at the same time. "I was lucky to be brown-brown," he had told Jasyn, referring to the color of his hair and eyes. "The brown-blues had some sort of light sensitivity and had to be recycled."

Jasyn did not know if that meant the constructs were sent back to be given new eyes, or new skin, or if they were entirely recycled. He didn't ask.

Jarec had been fascinated with storms. Planet storms that ranged from simple electrical thunder storms to tornadoes and hurricanes that would tear a swath of destruction across the landscape. He was enthralled by space storms that encompassed everything from meteor showers to red light shock waves. The man had watched more doc-vids and live feeds than anyone the Operations Officer had ever met.

"You know," he told Jasyn one night when they had sat next to each other during the dinner meal, "I think black holes are a type of space storm, but no one has ever classified them as such."

"Really?" Jasyn asked.

"Yes," he said. "Come see me tonight during my shift. I have some amazing images that I captured from the GW."

Jasyn had the same shift that night in the bridge and took a break from his own work to visit the Astrogator. Jarec, excited, pulled up a picture of a black hole on the glass of the holo screen in front of him.

"You see this right here?" he asked, pointing to the sphere of pure black sunk into the background of stars. He ran his finger along the edge of the sphere where the light of the stars disappeared.

Jasyn tilted his head, examining the picture and focusing on where Jarec was pointing. "The event horizon," he remarked. "It's the point of no return, where the gravity is so strong that even light cannot escape."

Jarec nodded excitedly. "Yes, yes!" he agreed. "It is a gravitational singularity where the curvature of space-time becomes infinite."

Jasyn grinned at the Astrogator. "That's more than I can wrap my head around," the Operations Officer admitted. Jarec became even more excited by his response.

"I know, right? Now look at this." He changed the image on the screen to one of a swirling mass of white cloud over the blue ocean of a planet or moon, Jasyn was not sure which. "This," Jarec informed him, "is a tropical cyclone. It is a wild storm that forms over water and then edges over the land only to rip up anything in its path. See this part here?" he asked, tapping on the dark eddy in the otherwise white blanket of clouds.

Jasyn nodded. "It looks like the event horizon of a black hole," he agreed. "But I can't imagine how they could be the same thing."

"It's called the eye," Jarec told him. "The eye of the storm." He sat back in his chair and looked up at the Operations Officer. "The thing is," he confided, "that while this incredibly powerful storm destroys everything around it, the center is supposed to be very calm – almost a safe haven."

Officer Issord had grinned and shook his head. "Where are you going with this?" he asked.

Jarec had placed a finger over his lips, thinking before he answered. "I'm not really sure," he admitted.

The Operations Officer had laughed in surprise, and the Astrogator had laughed heartily with him.

"I just can't help making the comparison," Jarec said. "Something about them is so intriguing, and I think that the phenomenon must be related somehow. They are the same, but opposite. With the black hole, the space around it is safe. It's when you cross the event horizon, into the eye, that everything is torn apart. With the cyclone..."

"The eye is where you are safe," Jasyn finished.

Jarec nodded approvingly at the success of his lesson and leaned back, lacing his hands behind his head. He let out a whoosh of air through his pursed, pale lips. "If I figure it out, I might be famous someday," he said, his voice tinged with hope. "I could be known as the Chimeran that discovered the Relativity of the Eye."

Jasyn had clapped him on the back, chuckling. "I think

that you have too much time on your hands," he informed the Astrogator and Jarec had given him an apologetic smile and a slight shrug.

"I have to do something while I am on duty," he said. "Unless I have somewhere to take us, it gets a little dull."

"Understood," Jasyn agreed. "And I hope that, in time, the revelation befalls you, as well as your fame."

Jarec had grinned at him, though he never found the time to make his great discovery. He had time for many other discussions with the Operations Officer regarding storms and his research, but only for another few months. One night he was simply too close to JP when the Commander had been given a piece of bad news.

The Astrogator's head, with brown hair and brown eyes, had rolled across the floor of the bridge spraying blood – his mouth slightly open in surprise. He hadn't even been the one to give the Commander the news. The other officers were not too surprised. They had seen it happen before.

Jasyn had thought about the Astrogator from time to time, but even more now that he was the one with so much time on his own hands. The Chimeran officer was growing increasingly comfortable with Faith but increasingly uncomfortable with the way she would leave him behind. Even more so with his own feelings that being left behind would trigger. She left him often, and she was usually gone for days on end. He hated it more each time. Jasyn began to take notice of the conflict raging within himself and likened it to the tropical storm Jarec had shown him years ago.

He knew that the first breath of wind had begun to blow on the first night he had seen her, had kissed her, had lain with her. At that point it was barely a breeze and about as harmless. At the time he did not foresee the day that the wind would pick up, change direction, and grow into a deadly gale. A force that would lead to certain disaster.

ଔଞଜ

The Chimeran Battle Cruiser *Macedonian* decelerated as it neared Europa, braking so hard that the outside of the ship glowed red with heat as it entered the atmosphere. Bjorn gripped the armrests of his chair, his knuckles turning white.

He knew that it wasn't necessary to hold on so tightly, the chair was bolted to the floor of the bridge and he had a safety web across the lower half of his body, but he supposed it was instinctive to brace oneself as one's center of gravity was shifted so violently. He was quite sure that he should not be able to feel anything at all, much less a gravitational shift, and feared that the *Mace* was falling into a state of disrepair.

The Commander flinched inwardly, knowing that there was nothing to be done at present for his beloved ship. He had lost all but two of his mechanics during the attack of the Opal Dragon, and the ones that were still alive were busy enough just keeping the damn thing from breaking down altogether.

A dozen mechs, ten Chimeran and two humans that supported the Cause, were waiting for him on Europa. One more, from the *Resurrection*, was also scheduled to rendezvous with the *Mace* while they were there. Maybe together they could get the old girl ship-shape again. He hoped so.

Bjorn released the webbing from across his lap as soon as the Flight Chief had the ship stable, cruising towards Europa at what looked like a forty-five degree angle in the opposite direction.

Though many supported the Cause, both secretly and openly, it would still not do to drive a Chimeran Battle Cruiser right up to the largest inhabited moon in the Jupiter System. So the *Mace* veered away, heading for one of Jupiter's smaller, unnamed and unmanned moons.

"Master Helioch!" Bjorn called.

"Yes sir!" Helioch answered.

"Have the transport shuttle prepared, and have a steward lay out some civilian clothes in my billet." He turned and flashed a smile of perfect white teeth at Helioch. "I'm going shopping," Bjorn informed his Quartermaster.

Helioch nodded as he fitted a comset over his right ear. "Yes, sir!" he agreed, looking the Commander up and down. "You haven't been planet side for quite some time," he cautioned with a smirk. "Aren't you worried that what you have might be out of style on Europa?"

Bjorn favored him with a confident smile. "It doesn't matter, Master Helioch. I make anything look good."

"Yes, sir!" Helioch agreed with a grin, already dispatching orders into his headset.

Six hours later, Bjorn was walking along a promenade of shops in a prestigious part of Svenborga, a vacation community for the very rich on the moon of Europa - artfully made to look like an alpine village.

The town was quaint and quiet, a delicate reproduction of a snowy mountain town on pre-apocalyptic Earth. The A-frame buildings were crossed with beams that gave the appearance of tree wood over plaster. The streets were fabricated plastique made to look like stone cobbles.

He had a small escort of bodyguards; one by his side, two that trailed behind, and two that walked on the other side of the street. The one at his side was his personal bodyguard, Julian. The construct was broad-shouldered and lean, with dark blonde hair and dark blue eyes that never stopped moving.

Bjorn's gaze traveled over the signs until he found the shop he was looking for and literally had to duck inside, lest his head clip the top of the simulated wood doorframe. Real metal bells hung from the door and jingled as he entered, followed by Julian. The others took up posts outside along the street. They drew a few curious looks from the people window-shopping, but no real interest. It was an exclusive town and bodyguards were not uncommon.

Julian took the place in with a sweep of his dark blue eyes. The room was small and lined with faux wood shelves. On the shelves were small plastique figures of people and droids. There was a woman in a light sky-blue jacket and matching skirt tapping numbers onto a pane of glass behind a wooden counter. An ornately carved wooden door led to a back room.

The woman straightened when she heard the bells and looked up to greet them but Julian had already turned to the window, his eyes darting up and down the sidewalks and storefronts. She was tall, with pale skin, pale hair and pale blue eyes over high, prominent cheekbones. Bjorn remembered her kind from Earth, though this woman had been greatly enhanced. She wore no shirt under her tight suit coat.

"Hello," she announced, her pale eyes wandering over Bjorn with obvious appreciation. "And how may I help you?" The Chimeran Commander flashed her a smile that made her ample chest heave.

"Hello… Astrid," he said as he spied the name in blue light that floated over her left breast. "I'm looking for a troll."

"Well!" she exclaimed, slightly breathless. "You have come to the right place. Are you looking for skin?"

"I beg your pardon?"

"Are you looking for a construct model, or a traditional droid?"

Bjorn placed his forearm arm along the simulated wood counter and leaned forward, laying his hand over her fingers, evoking a coy smile.

"You will have to forgive me," he said. The woman gave him a look that said she would forgive him anything. "I'm not a local," he confided, "and I am quite out of date, as you can see by my clothes."

"I hadn't noticed," Astrid assured him, turning her hand over beneath his and stroking his palm lightly. "But if you are uncomfortable, you can take them off. I can have a new outfit delivered...in an hour?"

Bjorn actually paused a moment to consider. The way she was stroking his hand left no room for doubt. But it only lasted a moment. The green-eyed Commander gave his head a small shake to clear it, then picked up the lady's hand and kissed the backs of her fingers, making her inhale sharply.

"Thank you so much for your gracious offer and, had I the time, I would stay here long enough for you to order me an entire wardrobe. But I am here on a cruise and the Captain is a rather grouchy old bastard who would have my nether parts if I were to be late getting back to the ship. I'm afraid I only have time for a quick bit of shopping."

Astrid sighed but accepted his apology with a smile. "Very well," she said, donning a businesslike air. "We offer two types of trolls, the traditional metal droid - and all of ours are the highest quality stainless steel with a titanium alloy - or the newer construct variety."

"Construct variety?"

The woman nodded. "Yes, GwenSeven now has a whole line of trolls."

"Of course they do," Bjorn murmured.

"Standard models come in human, but an elfin model can be special-ordered, and both male and female are available."

"Female," Bjorn said without hesitation and the woman's smile widened.

"Human or elf?"

"Human."

Astrid beamed as if being personally complemented. "Would you like to see what we have in stock, or look at a holo log and order one to be delivered?" She batted dark lashes at him. "Do you live here on Europa perhaps?"

Bjorn gave her a conciliatory smile. "I don't even live in this system, which I am now finding quite unfortunate. I'll have to see what you have in stock." The woman nodded as if she had expected his answer and turned, illuminating a holo board along the plank counter.

Seven holos of women in white jumpsuits stood on the counter in front of the Commander, each holo half a meter tall. The figures were all human, as he had requested, with a variety of hair colors, body styles and facial features. Each figure turned to the left in unison, back to face front, and then to the right.

Bjorn leaned back to examine each one, though as his eyes raced over the figures it took him only a second to decide.

"That one," he said pointing.

"A brunette," Astrid remarked, sounding disappointed. A tiny line formed between her light brows as she tapped on a glass plate to her left. The holos of the women disappeared and Bjorn gave the woman a rapacious smile.

"I don't want to be attracted to my droid now, do I?"

Astrid nodded appreciatively at his foresight as he handed her a fake credentials card attached to a real account. "You do accept IGC credits still?"

Astrid took his card, running her fingers along his hand, her pale blue eyes never leaving his bright green ones. "I'll take anything you want to give me," she murmured, slowly coaxing the card from his grasp before glancing at the name. "Mr. Roder," she added with a coy smile. "Any clothes?" she asked.

Bjorn laughed. "I'm afraid I really don't have the time."

Astrid's laugh joined his own. "Not for you," she said. "I meant for your droid."

"Ah!" Bjorn exclaimed, grinning. "I guess you have me a bit distracted. Yes. If you have an outfit that is all red, I'll take it."

"Certainly," Astrid acquiesced with a smile, running his card across the glass behind the counter before handing it back to the Commander.

In less than a minute, the door to the back opened and a shapely woman with dark hair that hung down her back in sculpted waves entered. She wore a white jumpsuit with the GwenSeven logo embroidered in blue thread over the heart, or where her heart would be if she had been human.

She was more petite than the Red Jordan, and certainly not as full figured, but she was close enough for Bjorn and she brought a wide smile to his full lips. Another woman followed the troll, holding onto a black box tied with a white ribbon. Tall and pale and blonde like Astrid, she held out the box proudly.

"Here is the..." she started, and then faltered as her eyes landed on the striking figure of the Chimeran Commander. Astrid scowled at her furiously and snatched the box from her hands, practically shoving the woman back through the door.

"Yes, I know," she said. "Thank you Ingrid. That will be all!"

The woman was still trying to peek out from behind the door even as she was being propelled backwards and having the door shut on her. Gathering a deep breath to compose herself, Astrid tossed her blonde hair with an air of authority and handed the box to Bjorn, along with a metal card with a rolling holo.

"The instructions for use and care are all here on the card," she instructed. "As well as my personal comlink number," she added, lowering her voice. "Should you require anything else, please do not hesitate to contact me directly."

Bjorn flashed her smile of perfect white teeth. "Thank you, Astrid. I will certainly do so, the first chance I get."

Astrid beamed, her chest swelling as Bjorn turned to his new troll. She had strange golden eyes that reflected the different colors in the room.

"What do I call her?" Bjorn asked.

"Whatever you like," Astrid said from behind him.

The Chimeran was at a loss. He certainly could not name her Scarlett, though that was the only thing that came to mind. "Julian?" he called over his shoulder. His bodyguard, quiet and motionless other than the constant darting of his dark blue eyes, looked at his Commander.

"Sir?"

"My imagination fails me at the moment. Can you think of an appropriate name for our new consort?"

Julian took in the droid with a single sweep of his discerning blue eyes. "Lucy," he said without pause or emotion, his piercing gaze turning back to the window and scanning the street once again.

Bjorn smiled. "Well Lucy, shall we?"

"Go?" Lucy asked.

"Yes, go."

"If that is what you require," the droid said dispassionately.

Bjorn could hear Astrid laugh softy. "If you are looking for an opinion, I am afraid you are going to have to stick with a real woman."

"In the meantime?"

"Just tell her what to do."

Bjorn chuckled. "Very well. Come on, Lucy, we are going." Lucy took a single step and stood next to him, waiting. Bjorn turned and held up the metal card with Astrid's number on it. "Thank you for your service today, Astrid," he said, tucking the card into a pocket on the inside of his coat.

"You are most welcome. Please let me know if there is any way I can service you in the future, Mr. Roder."

Bjorn gave her a nod before he pushed open the door and walked through it. Lucy followed as if tied by a string, as did Julian, the guard's stoic features not showing the surprise he felt.

He knew that the Commander had a much better imagination than his second-run guard. And, in the fifty years he had been Bjorn's personal bodyguard, he had never seen the Commander turn down an offer for sex. Not once. Not until today.

# ONE TWO

Jordan Blue patrolled Saturn with both Fledglings until she knew every ring, inside and out. Though something about the rings tugged at her insides, a mute insistence that they were important to her somehow, the sight of them did nothing to jar her memory. She toyed with the idea of opening the com-link with Galen, often just to see if he would still be there, but discarded the idea every time. She felt terribly lonely without him but she wanted answers first, and she was determined to get them on her own.

Though Blue hated the idea, she finally decided to go to the one person she thought might have some answers – her eldest sister. The Jordan took both Fledglings on a patrol that took them to the far side of Jupiter, close to the moon of Callisto.

The trip was uneventful until she neared her destination. As she closed the distance a strange feeling overtook her. Though she had the coordinates for the satellite community where Faith lived, as soon as Cyan had rounded the gas giant with Fledge following close behind, she no longer felt that she needed them. It was as if she were being drawn to her destination. Cyan seemed to feel it too, she could tell.

"What do you suppose that is all about?" Blue asked aloud to the empty air. Cyan did not respond, though she could sense a feeling of amusement coming from him. From Fledge there was nothing as far as she could tell. The Red Fledgling had grown friendlier towards her, even a bit attached, though he was still hard for her to read.

She had the satellite community in her sights – to her it looked like a cluster of semi-flattened metal grapes, suspended by a vine of titanium hanging from a great ellipsoid of hyper-diamond – when there was a flare of light on the console, indicating that an outside source was trying to establish a line of communication with her ship.

The Jordan leaned forward and touched the light.

"You have coms," she announced. "This is Jordan Blue of the IGC Dragon 787."

"Good afternoon, Jordan," a respectful voice replied. "Are you stopping at Iron Rose, or just passing by?"

"I had planned on stopping. I was hoping to pay a visit to my sister," Blue said. "She is a resident."

"Name?"

"Faith de Rossi."

"Are you expected?"

Blue pressed her lips together. Though the voice on the other end could not see her, she did not want him to hear the smile in her voice. "I don't believe so, and I don't have her comset code. Could you please put me through to her, or give me her personal line?"

"I am afraid that I cannot put you through directly," the voice answered, "but I can have reception put you through to her security."

"That will be fine."

The Jordan sat back in her seat and waited. A few seconds later there was a flash on the console.

"This is Tom Reynolds of de Rossi security," a voice announced from the dash. "How may I help you?"

"This is Jordan Blue. I would like clearance to dock with the villa."

There was a pause before the voice spoke again. "Did you say *Jordan* Blue?"

Blue rolled her eyes. "Yes."

A series of clicks ensued and Blue could imagine cameras being trained on the Fledglings, though they were keeping a respectable distance from the satellite. The voice came back on over the com-line, doubtful and suspicious.

"Do you have business with Ms. de Rossi?"

The Jordan blew out a great breath, annoyed. "No, I'm her sister. I would like to speak with her."

"You're her *sister*?"

Blue's hands clenched in front of her black-clad form. What kind of idiots did Faith have working for her?

"Yes," she said, exasperated. "I am Noel de Rossi. Is my sister there?" A short silence followed and she guessed he must be checking records before he spoke again.

"I'm sorry, Ms. de Rossi is not here. But she is expected to arrive within the hour and you *are* listed for pre-clearance. Would you like to come in and wait?"

Blue sighed. "Sure, why not?"

"The villa is…"

"That's okay," Blue told him. "I know where I am going."

"Excellent. Please use the upper dock."

"Roger that."

The Jordan took the Fledglings in towards the satellite, heading for the bottom grape on the bunch.

"Hang back here, Fledge," she commanded once they were only two klicks from the villa. Fledge obligingly wheeled and braked until he was hovering at a near standstill, a crimson glow in the darkness. She took Cyan in closer until she was nearly up against the enormous flattened sphere of the villa. The bottom two thirds appeared to be made of clear hyper-diamond wedged into a titanium casing that looked as if it could close over the entire villa like a steel sock.

She guided Cyan up until they were over the metal-encased top, her eyes searching out the ports. Calyph had told her that it would become harder to exit via the cockpit hood after Cyan's first growing and then completely impossible after his next growing, and that they should practice docking.

"There," she said, first spying the markings of a large port and then another smaller one nearly fifty meters higher. "I need you to get me in there. Do you think you can?"

Cyan made a grumbling sound that translated to the fact that not only was he indeed able to dock, but a little insulted that she had asked.

Blue grinned and stood up out of her chair. She smoothed down the sparkling black material of her flight suit and headed towards the galley. Cyan glided up to the villa until it nudged his silver skin, and then pressed himself against it. A part of his side bulged out and melted over the three-meter high oval on the metal casing that denoted the dock-port.

"After I am in, go back and hang with Fledge," she instructed.

The silver skin began to dissolve away in the center, making a hole that grew until the entire oval door was exposed. Cyan waited that way, his side kissing the villa like a suckerfish attached to a shark. The Jordan almost leaned forward to knock on the side when she felt the bitter cold emanating from the steel, chilling her face. She laughed softly at her shortsightedness, knowing that the metal was so far beyond freezing that it would have taken the skin off her knuckles. She was going to ask Cyan to ping the villa when the door irised open.

A young man with brown hair and brown eyes in a black suit with a white shirt stood waiting for her. A comset was wrapped tightly around his right ear. Another man in the same garb stood behind him, though he was more broad-shouldered, his hair was darker, and he was not quite as tall.

"Hello Jordan Blue," the young man greeted. "I am Tom Reynolds, current command of Ms. de Rossi's security team."

He held a hand out to her and her first wild thought was that he was expecting a tip. Then she realized that the hand was to assist her to walk out of Cyan and into the villa's docking area. She had to bite her bottom lip to keep from laughing but she slipped her small hand into Tom's and stepped as gracefully as she could into the sterile room that was obviously nothing more than an airlock.

"Why, thank you," she said, airily. She didn't know how her sister lived, but the experience so far was filling her with an equal mixture of amusement and disgust.

The second man walked passed them as the door irised closed and he passed his finger along the top and then the bottom of the door, sealing the airlocks.

"Alright," Blue said, dispensing with the pleasantries as her eyes moved across the empty room. "Where do you want me to wait?"

"I will be happy to escort you downstairs, ma'am. But first," Tom paused and the Jordan looked at him, arching a brow. He swallowed and continued. "Your sidearm, please."

Blue smirked, her smile pushing at the rippled scars in the skin of her right cheek as she pulled her pistol from the holster and handed it to him, butt first.

"Thank you," Tom said, handing it to the other man as he passed by. He held a hand out towards the open door of the waiting lift, inviting her inside. "Please," he said smiling. "After you."

The Jordan entered the lift with Tom and the door slid closed. It started down, going at an angle. They exited the lift onto a floor that looked too industrial to Blue to be her sister's living quarters.

"This is the security and staff level," Tom explained, as if hearing her thoughts. He held out his hand again, inviting her toward another lift. Blue shook her head in response and moved towards the staircase.

Something about the place was making her feel strange. It seemed to move around her in rhythmic waves – something that alarmed her at first, but it was a comfortable feeling. Almost a familiar feeling. Besides, she knew that if there were any sort of danger, Cyan would warn her. She paused, feeling the pulse about her body, then went down the steps, Tom following close behind.

She stopped on the next level, her eyes traveling over the expanse of black marble and white rugs and furniture. This, she thought, is where Faith lives. She looked down the curve of the staircase as it continued down around the elevator to where is disappeared into darkness.

"Would you like to sit down?" Tom offered, but Blue shook her platinum coils. She cocked her head, as if listening for something. He was about to inquire if she would like something to drink when she turned sharply.

"What's downstairs?" she asked.

"The pool."

After a pause, as if listening again, the Jordan continued her descent down the stairs that spiraled around the lift, Tom escorting her politely. She reached the bottom and looked around, her blue eyes wide.

"I know, right?" Tom said, watching her expression. "It's like being left out in space, isn't it?"

Blue nodded as her eyes traveled over the pool and around the starry expanse that surrounded her. She took a tentative step along the foyer platform, avoiding where it sank down into the water. Behind the lift and encircling staircase was an area of more polished black marble with chairs that were nearly invisible in the dark. She walked to the glass wall and looked out into the black.

"I'll wait here," she said.

"Can I get you anything?"

"No," she said, crossing her arms over her chest. "Thank you," she added after a moment.

Tom paused at the stairs and looked at her, smiling. "You favor your sister's looks, you know," he told the Jordan.

Blue turned her face back towards him, her brows raised. "Faith?" she asked, but Tom shook his head.

"Charity."

Blue's brows went up even higher. "You're kidding."

Tom gave her a small smile as he shook his head. "You look better."

Blue grunted and turned her attention back to the dark beyond the glass, shaking her own head.

"Just holler if you need anything," Tom said.

The Jordan nodded but did not turn back around. Once Tom had gone back up the stairs she walked around the staircase and gazed at the pool. That strange feeling she was getting seemed to emanate from the water. She crouched down and was about to reach down and touch it but she could hear a quiet turmoil coming from the floor above her. Frowning, Jordan Blue rose back up and walked back to the wall of glass and waited.

Hearing the hushed noise of the commotion upstairs, she was unexpectedly filled with doubt about whether she had made the right decision by coming to see Faith. The doubt grew quickly, making her anxious. Then, as if in response, something soothed her, calming her nerves. She suspected it must be Cyan, keeping watch on her.

Moments later she could sense as well as hear someone coming down the stairs. She knew without turning whom it would be. There was a moment of silence and the Jordan felt her skin prickle.

"Hello, Noel."

"Hello," Blue responded, still intrigued by Cyan's way of calming her and – even more so - mystified by the feeling coming from the pool. It was distracting her from the reason she had come, but she could not ignore it. "This place is strange," she remarked. "There is something familiar about it, though I've never been here or anyplace like it. There is a smell here, a warmth that is oddly comforting."

Faith cleared her throat and the Jordan could sense her sister's discomfort.

"I'd heard you'd taken to wearing black."

Blue wanted to gag at her sister's attempt at small talk but instead answered without looking at her. "I'm in mourning."

"I heard. I'm sorry for your loss."

The Jordan huffed but still did not turn. Losing Jade had been horrible. Losing Galen even worse.

"Whose loss do you mourn the most?" Faith asked.

Noel took a deep breath and let it out slowly. "My own." There was another uncomfortable silence before the woman spoke again.

"I'm glad you're here."

"Are you?"

"Of course. Why wouldn't I be?"

The Jordan turned and smiled crookedly. "My dear *sister*," she sneered. "Don't act like we have ever been close. We've hardly ever seen each other."

Faith, who looked only vaguely familiar to the Jordan, lifted her chin. "You may not have seen much of me, but I've seen plenty of you. I've been with you a lot more than you know."

Jordan Blue's eyes narrowed in suspicion, making her scar pull taut and shiny. "What do you mean by that?"

Faith shrugged. "I came to see you quite a bit when you were younger. Almost every week when you were really young, only slightly less when you were still too little to remember.

Elem and secondary. Saw you at parochial and flight. I went to all of your graduations. I even visited the Lido moon and checked in on you a few times during your Jordan training."

"You did?" That was a surprise. Noel had never suspected that anyone in her family gave a second thought as to what she was doing.

"I did."

"Why didn't you ever speak to me?"

Faith walked over to a lounger and sat on the edge of the black leather padding that cushioned the molded glass chair, crossing her legs. The Jordan's wide blue eyes, one natural and one a perfect copy made of hyper-optic glass, followed her. "I didn't know what to say, or how you would feel about me. Like you said, it's not like we were ever close. But I was watching over you."

Blue felt anger lance through her body and when she spoke her voice was low and accusing. "You hired Galen to watch me."

"Is that what this visit is about?"

Blue tensed, her flight suit shifting and tightening about her form, the thin black fabric rippling and casting back the reflection of the stars. Something about this woman made her withdraw mentally, as if she harbored feelings of

abandonment

anger, but she had no idea why, other that the fact that the woman had been using Galen to spy on her. She was loathe to share anything with this supposed sister of hers, but why play games? Faith was right, Blue wanted to know. It was the only thing she had come for.

"Yes."

Faith's shoulders moved in a small shrug. "Galen was already working for the company. I saw him at your graduation from Advanced DS Flight and told him to keep an eye on you. It was a good thing, since you had your...accident that night." Her tawny eyes drifted towards the vast expanse of the pool, the water as black as the night around it. "I didn't tell him to fall in love with you. That was his doing entirely."

Noel turned away and looked out through the wall of glass.

"Is he...with you now?" Faith asked.

The Jordan shrugged, the movement throwing glints of light off her darkened form. "I wouldn't know."

"You haven't seen him since you...turned him off?"

Blue felt her body jerk as if stung. "No." Her lip curled up away from her teeth. "Why? Did you want to speak with him?"

"No. I was just curious." Faith toyed with the rings on the index finger of her left hand, twisting them nervously. "Would you like something to drink?" Faith asked abruptly, deciding that she certainly needed something. Noel shook her head, making her blonde coils tremble between her shoulder blades. "What about something to eat? You look dreadfully thin."

Noel looked at Faith from over her shoulder, smiling with half of her mouth. "I could use a bite." She couldn't remember the last time she had eaten. She usually didn't care, but her mind felt like it was getting fuzzy and she felt she needed to have her wits about her, especially talking to this woman.

Faith ran a finger along the edge of the gold cuff on her wrist before bringing it up to her lips. "Penny, please have Mari make some sunbutter sandwiches. And send down some champagne for me."

The Jordan smiled at her sister again from over her shoulder. Maybe they had something in common after all. "I like champagne too," she told her.

Faith returned her smile. "I know."

Noel grunted and turned back towards the outer darkness.

There was a clatter of footsteps and a different security man came down the stairs carrying a bottle of champagne and two glasses. He was much more intense than Tom, and coiled like a razorspring. He watched Noel warily as he uncorked the bottle. When it popped Noel shot him a quick glance.

"One of his guys took my sidearm," she remarked.

"How do you know it was one of his guys? Maybe this man is my butler."

Noel snorted. "Please." She turned her face away again. "What's with them, anyway? Do they think I want to kill you?"

"They assume that everyone is trying to kill me. It's one of the reasons that I am still alive."

The Jordan's military training had taught her the same thing – stay alert stay alive. Only she didn't have to pay people to do it for her. Then again, she was not occupied with running the largest corporation in the universe. She tried to muster some respect for her sister, but it wasn't easy.

"Would you like a glass?" Faith asked.

"No, thank you."

The security man put the empty glass down on the table next to the lounger. "Mari should have the sandwiches done shortly," he informed Faith. "Is there anything else you need?"

"Thank you, Geary. That should be fine."

The security man gave his employer a slight nod and took the stairs quickly, leaving silence in his wake. The silence did not last long. In less than a minute he was again descending the staircase, slower and more carefully this time. His powerful yet deft hands carried a tray of sandwiches, sliced fruit, and glasses of water and milk, which he set down on a side table.

"Please," Faith said, calling out to the wraith facing the darkness. "Sit down and have something to eat."

Noel turned from the glass wall, hesitated for a moment, then walked to the empty lounger and sat down on its edge, facing the woman she felt that she bore no resemblance to but supposedly shared some sort of background with, namely parental. She picked up a sandwich and took a bite.

"I'm sorry I didn't have peanut butter," Faith apologized.

The Jordan smiled around a mouth full of food. "How do you know I like peanut butter?"

Faith hid her smile in a sip of champagne before putting it down on the tray. "I have eyes everywhere."

The Jordan took the glass of milk from the tray and washed down a mouthful of sandwich. "Via Galen?" she accused, not attempting to keep the bitterness from her voice. The half-elf pilot assumed that it had to be the recently deceased, bright-eyed elfin doctor, since her penchant for peanut butter had evolved quite recently. The thought that her lover had been some sort of spy made a sick clamminess creep over her back. But Faith shook her head.

"He refused to divulge any personal information about you, which I was not pleased with, but he did keep steadily reporting his progress on the Thermopylae, so I kept him employed."

Noel munched on her sandwich, thoughtful. If that was true, it was going to make her feel a hell of a lot better. Maybe enough to restore the link and bring him back. If she could. "Did you want to speak with him?"

"At some point if you could...arrange a meeting, I would. Not right now. Tonight I would like to talk to just you. I really am glad you are here, I wasn't just making polite conversation. I've been meaning to talk to you about something, something very important. This is just sooner than I expected."

Noel watched her sister twist the rings on her fingers nervously and waited for her to get on with it. She tore off a bite of the sandwich and chewed it up, waiting.

"So, what the fuck is it?" she finally asked.

Faith laughed and picked up her champagne glass. She took a long drink and looked at the girl sitting across from her. They were almost knee to knee and she could see Faith glance at her eyes, from one to the other. Most people who knew that one eye was a prosthetic did that, surprised at how well they matched.

"I want you to leave the IGC."

Noel choked, throwing a hand over her mouth as she coughed out half-chewed chunks of sunbutter and bread. Faith rose quickly to pound her on the back, or more if it was needed. The Jordan was laughing more than choking and waved her sister away until she sat back down.

Faith crossed her legs and waited for the Jordan's laughter to subside. Noel realized her sister wasn't joking and stopped laughing straight away.

"You're serious?"

Faith nodded.

"Are you insane?"

Faith smirked. "More than a few people have asked me that before, but I doubt it."

"Leave the IGC and do what?" Noel asked her, grinning. "Retire?" She laughed aloud and stuffed the rest of the sandwich in her mouth, shaking her head. Faith waited until she had swallowed, she didn't want her choking again.

"No, but I think it's time you joined the company. Joined your family."

"You're crazy," Blue told her. "I'd never leave my Fledgling."

"I wouldn't want you to. I would want you to bring him. In fact, I'd like you to bring all the Fledglings."

The Jordan frowned and she felt her heartbeat begin to pick up, a quick thudding in her narrow chest. "What do you mean, *all*?"

"The red one, as well as your own. I'm working on attaining the green one."

The Jordan's mouth sagged, her jaw hanging open. "You can't be serious," she whispered.

"I am."

Jordan Blue sat back so fast she nearly toppled over, keeping upright only by fastening a hand around her knee. "Cyan," she whispered. "Fledge. *And* Verdana?" She took a deep breath and looked back at her sister, her blue eyes bright with curiosity. "And you think I could fly all of them?"

"You are already assuming control of the Red Fledgling, aren't you? In the absence of the Red Jordan, of course."

Noel blinked rapidly, surprised by what her sister knew and then her lip curled up in an expression of dry amusement. "I'm trying, but he is as stubborn as his mistress. I have gotten him to fly with me, occasionally, but only for training and growing while Scarlett recovers."

Faith waved a hand as she sipped her drink, signaling that the facts were inconsequential. "He will be yours soon enough. The green one as well, as soon as it can be brought around."

Noel was damned curious to know where her sister might acquire a Dragon Fledgling that had all but disappeared from the known universe but something else troubled her much more.

"What exactly would you want with a squad of Fledglings?" she asked, her eyes narrow and her voice low.

"The short story? To overthrow the IGC."

Noel stared at her sister in stunned silence before voicing a cackle of nervous laughter. "You *are* insane."

Faith shrugged and sipped from her flute of champagne. "Anyone might say so. But you do not know what I know, nor have you lived through what I have survived." She fixed her eyes on her sister. "Do you know what a Singularity is?"

Noel shrugged, the previous look of shock draining from her face as she considered the question. "It's a mathematical term, having to do with a system breakdown. In the military we call it a goat-fuck."

Faith pressed her lips tightly together. "I'll take your word for it. It is also a term used to denote a time when there will be an equal fusion of the artificial and the organic."

Frowning, Noel plucked up another sandwich and dug into it with small, white teeth. She was starting to feel that she was in over her head. She felt that her life, so simple until just a short time ago, was becoming more complicated by the day. Though she had always jumped at every challenge with enthusiasm, for the first time she wondered if she was up to the task.

Faith took a deep breath, carefully rolling the flute of champagne between the palms of her hands.

"A Singularity was reached on Earth in their recorded year of 2030, when artificial intelligence finally matched human intelligence. Once that happened, it passed human standards within seconds and then within minutes all hell broke loose. The result was almost the destruction of the human race – not by the machines themselves but by war fought between the humans who thought the machines should be destroyed and the humans who thought that we should merge with them."

Noel listened, her blue eyes wide and interested. She had only the vaguest recollection of human history. She swallowed. "So who won?"

Faith shrugged. "Winning is only a matter of perception." She took a sip from her glass and continued. "Another Singularity was reached in the Year of the Third Dragon, as the elves call it. 3888, by human standard years."

The Jordan's nod was almost enthusiastic. This part of history she knew. "The Rebellion."

"Yes, when artificial emotion matched human emotion."

Noel took a bite of sandwich before pointing it at her sister in an accusatory manner. "When the life-forms *you* created realized what they were being used for, and decided to wipe out real humanity."

Faith shook her head. "They already knew what they were, they just realized what they could be. What they wanted to be.

I think every advanced life form, us included, reaches that at some point in their existence."

Noel sat back, commiserating with the constructs though she didn't want to – she had been fighting them for a number of years and the conflicting feelings roiled inside her like a poison. "They were being used." She shot an accusatory glance at Faith but the older woman only nodded, her face solemn.

"In the game of life there are only players and pawns. Whichever one you are is entirely up to you. Despite any background or circumstance, everyone must decide for themselves which one they want to be."

"Use or be used?" Jordan Blue asked, disgusted.

"Yes."

The Jordan frowned. "What if there are people that don't decide? Or choose not to play?"

Faith sighed. "Then they are pawns by default. They constantly mourn their fortune and play the victim, but it is still by their own choice that they are the victim."

Noel's sandwich had been worn down to the crust and she turned it around in her hands before tossing it back onto the plate. She brushed her hands on the thighs of her black flight suit, dusting off crumbs.

"What does any of this have to do with me or the IGC?"

Faith straightened, breathing deep as she squared her shoulders. "A Singularity is coming again. Intelligence, emotion, technology, desire – it is all reaching a breaking point – critical mass, if that is the term you prefer - and nothing is going to stop it. The Council will fight it and, for the first time in my life, I will fight the Council."

The Jordan's eyes grew wider as she listened. "When you say fight, do you mean voicing your opposition or actually fighting?" she asked.

"Why do you think I want a squad of Fledglings?"

Noel's mouth dropped open and then closed. Images of herself leading a fleet of Dragons flickered through her mind, along with images of herself being executed. She looked away, breathless. "You are suggesting treason. I could be sentenced to a firing squad if I ever even related this to anyone."

"One of the reasons I know that this conversation will remain private."

Blue glared at Faith. "Still," she argued, frowning. "You think having a handful of Dragon Fledglings will give you control of the universe?"

"I don't want control of the universe, I just want to see that control change hands. The IGC should have been deposed half a century ago. GwenSeven already has more control of this universe than most people know. Hell, more than most people suspect. We do not have a military, however, though our allies are working on that."

"Allies?" Noel asked, startled.

Faith nodded. "I'm not just some raving lunatic. There are entire populations that have had enough of the Council and their tyranny."

Noel stared blindly at the woman across from her. She knew that not every species held a seat on the council, but she had never considered why. Tyranny? What did the IGC do besides fight the Chimera?

"Having an elite force of fighters would make up the backbone of the new militia and put us on equal ground," Faith told her. "It would give us a level playing field, as the expression goes. The Dragons have been the greatest military threat in centuries, but I don't believe they would attack their own children."

"Nor do I think any Fledgling would attack its own mother!"

Faith nodded. "That bond is what I am counting on. If I can create a stand-off of military power, or have a show of force that would prevent an offensive against us, the fighting should be minimal, the loss of life slight."

Yeah, Noel thought. *Slight. And what if those slighted are people I know? People I care about?*

"How do you know of the bond?" Noel asked.

"I have eyes everywhere," Faith repeated, but this time her voice was quieter, more somber.

The Jordan's mouth was suddenly very dry. She took a long swig of milk from the glass, draining it, but held onto it, rolling it between her hands. "You want me to *fight* for you? What makes you think I even would?"

"Because you… I mean we, we are family."

"The Hell we are!"

Faith's brow furrowed deeply in sudden anger. "Who do you think paid for all of your schooling, including flight schools? Father never would, I can tell you that!"

Blue recoiled as if she had been slapped. Twice. The jab about their father stung, but the implication of her schooling filled her with horror.

"Are you the reason I made it through?" she demanded, filled with anger. "You and your money?"

Faith closed her eyes and sighed, regaining her composure. "No. I covered all of the costs but I never paid to have you accepted at any school or promoted to any rank. You got to where you are now on your own merits and earned all of your own accolades." Blue relaxed markedly and Faith reached out and placed a hand on the Jordan's knee and, though the girl flinched at her touch, she did not pull away. "I care deeply for you," Faith told her earnestly, "more than you can imagine. And the ties that we have, that all of us sisters have, it is *our* bond. It runs deeper than some loyalty to a council that cannot be trusted."

"You don't understand," Noel argued. "The IGC is the only family that I have ever really known."

It was true. She felt closer to Jordan Scarlett, a woman that had despised and berated her for the last five years (though even then she had just chalked it up to sibling rivalry), than to the woman sitting across from her.

"You are *not* family to them," Faith said, her voice cold. "You are not even a person to them."

"I am a respected officer," Noel argued, feeling the tension rise and coil around their bodies.

"Respected," Faith scoffed. "They don't respect you, only what you can do for them. You don't even have a name! You are a number and a color! You are a pawn in their game – they think nothing of you!"

"That's not true!"

"Don't fool yourself! I told you that in this universe you are either a player or a pawn, and right now you are the latter. The IGC is moving you like a piece on a holo board. You're going to have to decide for yourself if you want to keep playing their game."

"I'm a *Jordan* for Christ's sake!"

"Which is nothing compared to what you would be," Faith said, her voice cooling, becoming patient. "Nothing compared to what you *could* be. GwenSeven controls Galactic Commerce. Charity holds Universal Finance in her grasp. You would hold a position equal to ours in the new military. Not as a Jordan, or even a Captain, but as an Admiral. You and your Dragons."

Again the images of leading a fleet of Dragons – Cyan full grown and trailed by Fledge and even Verdana – warred with images of prison and torture.

"You're talking treason!" Noel hissed.

"I'm talking about the future," Faith said, perfectly calm. "A future that you cannot stop but one that you can participate in. As a player, rather than a pawn."

It was too much for Noel to take in and process all at once. She stood up quickly, almost panicky, shaking her head. "I can't listen to this," she said, refusing to make eye contact with her sister. She placed her empty milk glass on the table. "Thank you for...for...for giving me so much to digest," she said. She gave her an awkward smile as she turned and hurried for the stairs, eager to be gone.

Faith rose to her feet but her sister was already fleeing, almost at the stairs. She called after her quickly, almost desperately. "Did you ever wonder who ordered the hit that cost Galen his life?"

Noel froze with her hand on the rail, her body tense. When she finally answered her voice was heavy with emotion. "You were the only one I had considered."

"I would do no such thing!" Faith admonished. She looked at the slender form of the Jordan and sighed. "But the IGC would not think twice about terminating those that they see as a threat, even a future threat, such as the people that are close to their key officers." Noel shook her blonde curls and started up the first few steps, deciding that she had heard enough. "They have done it before," Faith called to her retreating form, "just ask your fellow Jordan."

The Blue Jordan stiffened as if she had been given an electric shock. She paused as the words sank in and then bolted up the stairs without looking back.

Noel took the stairs two at a time, trying to put as much distance between herself and her sister that she could. Put a distance between the words and the suggestions and the accusations that she had made. The staircase spiraled up around the lift that rose from the glass pool at the bottom of the villa.

The Jordan reached the middle level, the main living floor, and stopped - her blue eyes darting around the room. She didn't know how large her sister's household or security staff might be, but it seemed like they all had to be there right now, looking like villagers from a fairy tale, terrified but determined to stand against some invading beast.

The only one who didn't look terrified was Faith's main security man, who stood by the lift looking terribly smug. He held out her weapon, the laser pistol she had given Tom, butt first. Blue decided his look wasn't as smug as it was challenging, almost daring her to take a shot at him. The Jordan snatched the weapon from his hand and jammed it into the holster that hung on her hip, the black of the gun disappearing against the black of her flight suit.

Without a word she walked past him and continued up the stairs to the top level of the villa. Tom, along with the other man she had seen upon her arrival, waited by the door to the second lift. Though he had been polite to the point of cheerfulness when she had first arrived, he looked as though he had been chastised into submission since, though he was no less polite.

Tom extended his arm, holding it out towards the open lift. "If you please?" he offered. "The main dock is still in use by Ms. de Rossi's craft. I will be glad to accompany you to the second dock."

"That won't be necessary," the Jordan told him as she strode by and entered the lift. Regardless, the man stepped inside before it began to rise. The Jordan blew out a great breath as the lift rose at an angle. "I'm sorry if I got you into trouble," she apologized quickly without looking at him.

Tom smiled. "Don't worry about me," he assured her. The lift angled up and outwards, coming to stop at the small room with the airlock.

"Cyan?" Blue asked aloud.

Tom cocked his head at her. "Your Fledgling?" he asked. "Will you need..." he began but Blue shook her head, cutting him off.

"He's already here," she said brusquely, walking toward the airlock and past the surprised security man. Reaching up, she passed a finger along the top row of rivets, releasing the lock.

She leaned down to release the bottom but Tom, recovered from his shock, was already running a hand along the bottom for her. She stood aside as he straightened, giving her a sheepish smile.

"Sorry," he apologized. "I would have taken care of all this for you but I didn't realize that your craft would get here so quickly."

"Hmm," was all the Jordan could offer in return. Tom reached for the control pad next to the lock without taking his eyes off of the Blue Jordan.

"Is there anything else you need?" he asked. "For your trip?"

Blue frowned at him. "No. I'm sure I'll be fine."

Tom nodded, his smiling face only slightly downcast. "Of course," he agreed, placing his index finger into the read slot that would release the door. The lock spiraled open and Blue expected him to look inside, to grab a peek at the inside of a Fledgling Dragon, but his eyes remained fixed on her.

"Thanks," she told him, nonplussed as she walked by him and stepped into Cyan's break cabin, just aft of the galley. Tom's eyes followed her inside.

"Anytime," he said, giving her the sheepish grin once again. Blue frowned as the airlock spiraled closed on his side and Cyan's side melted closed on her side. She shook her head and strode through the galley to a cockpit that at present would not fit more than two pilots, maybe an Astrogator as well - if he were a small one.

She dropped down into her seat and Cyan, feeling her intent even before she could speak the words, was already disengaging from the villa and dropping away into the black. She would have told him to get her the hell out of there, but he already knew, and shot off into space, his brother trailing in a flash of crimson light.

Blue put her head in her hands, squeezing it tightly as if

trying to keep it from exploding. She had gone looking to her eldest sister for answers, but all she had gotten were more questions and, worse, more doubt. Even fear. The Jordan cursed aloud, thinking that she could not possibly feel fear at this point. Not when she was finally taking control of her life.

I am, she assured herself. *I am the one in control now. I am the one making the decisions. I am not a goddamned pawn!* The fingers of her left hand caressed the platinum band that encased her right wrist before she pulled them sharply away.

The Jordan sat and thought and stewed until she thought she might go mad.

Leave the IGC? Her sister was certainly crazy. Lead a military against the IGC? Blue laughed out loud. The idea! Her smile fell as she thought of what her sister had said about Galen and what was his obvious assassination. He hadn't been robbed or taken by a crime of opportunity. He had been gunned down in cold blood in the pod they had shared for more than two years.

Would the IGC really target an innocent civilian if they thought that person might interfere with the life of a b-class officer? Had they? Tears sprang, hot and unwelcome, to her eyes. Both eyes.

She could not think of leaving the IGC. She certainly could not think of rebelling. *Of mutiny.* Still, if they had killed Galen... He was the only person outside of her family that she had ever loved. The only one to have ever loved her. Unconditionally.

Or so she had thought. A hoarse sob escaped her lips, hot air heaving out into her lap like vomit. She choked and shook, trying to control herself. After a few minutes she took a slow calming breath, drawing herself up.

Her right hand hovered about her mouth for a moment, either undecided or gathering strength. Suddenly, it shot out to the platinum band that encased her wrist as if trying to accomplish its task before the other hand knew what it was up to or before her brain could stop her.

Furtive but quick, her index finger triggered the link.

Instantly, in the empty seat next to the Jordan, appeared an image in flickering blue light.

The image was that of a male elf, of young but otherwise indiscriminate age, with dark hair just long enough to hang in front of bright blue eyes. His smile was broad and warm and full of love.

"Hello, Sweetheart."

Jordan Blue, despite how angry she was and how angry she had been for a long time, smiled - even as a sob broke from her lips.

"Dammit, Galen!" she cursed.

"Did you miss me?"

Blue smiled, unable to help herself, though she pressed her lips as tightly together as she could, trying to hide it. The apparition of bluish ghostly light grinned.

"You did, didn't you?"

Blue sighed and smiled at him through her tears. "Of course I did!" She leaned towards him scowling and pointing a thin finger at his chest. "But you are still in the shithouse!"

Galen's blue and ghostly image drew back, shocked. "Why?"

"You lied to me!"

"I did not."

Blue's fist clenched. "You did!"

Galen sighed. "I might have omitted things or *obscured* things that I thought might hurt you. But I never lied to you."

"But why?" Blue demanded. "Why didn't you tell me? I thought we shared everything."

The ghostly elf winced, obviously pained by her statement. "I am hundreds of years older than you, Noel," he explained. "At least I was. What did you think I should do? Have many long nights in front of a fireplace with a bottle of elfish red while

I regurgitated my life to you? You would have been asleep in seconds! Besides, I never thought you were that interested in my past."

The Jordan sighed. "No shit. Boyhood, wet dreams, degrees and doctorates, blah blah fucking blah." She leaned towards the flickering blue figure again, angry. "But you must have known that I might be interested in the fact that you worked for my sister. Or maybe the fact that you were dead!"

Galen's image smiled sheepishly. "Sorry."

"That's it? Just, sorry?"

Galen shrugged, humble and apologetic. "It never seemed like the right time."

Blue leaned back in her seat and wiped the tears from her face with the back of her hand. "I hate what has happened to me," she told him, shaking her head and not looking at his eyes. "But what I hate more, *what shames me*, was what an idiot I was, trusting everybody." Her voice cracked and broke as she fought off the sobs. "I feel like such a fool!"

Galen looked as if he had been struck. He leaned over and placed a ghostly hand over Noel's knee. She flinched, but held still.

"You were never an idiot," he told her. "Or a fool." She turned her face from him, wiping away the tears that seemed to come faster now that the dam had broken. Galen squeezed her leg, she could see it and she could *feel* it. "You were just like we all are when we start out – full of hope."

"And does everyone go though what I did?"

Galen offered her a small smile. "Maybe not to that extreme, or with such shocking speed, though for some it is even worse." Blue shuddered at the thought and Galen caressed the thigh of her flight suit, trying to offer some comfort. "I hoped I could protect you from that. I always wanted to protect you from that – the harsh realities of life. I hoped you would never lose your purity and innocence. Your faith."

Blue choked off another sob. "Yeah, well that all kind of went to shit when you died, did it not?"

"Trust me," Galen said, "I didn't go willingly. I actually went after that big bastard with a thermite gun."

The Jordan cocked her head, piqued. "The old one in the front table?"

"Yes."

Blue tipped her head back into her seat, laughing and redirecting her tears from their course down her cheeks and instead towards her ears. "You're lucky it didn't blow up in your face. You should have run!"

"That was my first thought, but I knew he would have chased me down. My only option to get away was to get *far* away. I made a break for the Thermopylae. When I knew that he was after you too, I tried to kill him."

Noel finally turned her head to look him in the eye. "Well, you did. Eventually, but just soon enough. Thanks for that."

Galen smiled. "Anytime."

"Well then I guess there is just one more thing for us to consider."

"Which is?"

"What the hell is going on, and what the hell we are going to do about it."

Galen grinned. "That's actually two things."

Blue rolled her eyes. "Always have to be genius, don't you?"

ONE THREE

Jeanette dropped her bags on the floor of Grandpa's pod by the door. "Grandpa!" she called loudly. "I'm home! Or here, anyway!"

Jeanette giggled as Grandpa shuffled out of the kitchen. *No, she realized immediately. He is not shuffling. He is walking straight and tall. He is just walking carefully because he is holding a cup of coffee.* She watched him come into the living room with her dark eyes round with surprise and delight.

"Hey there, Little Jean!" he called back, smiling. "How was school today?"

"Magnificent!"

"Magnificent?"

"Yes! I love my new school! I miss my old friends but I have made new ones and they are super-cool!"

"That's *wonderful*, honey," Grandpa beamed.

"And my new dance school isn't in some half-abandoned strip mall," she said. "It's at The Pyramid!"

"The Pyramid?" Grandpa asked, sitting down in his favorite chair.

"Yes!" Jeanette exclaimed, clapping her small hands. "It's a mall, made of dark and sparkling glass and in the shape of a pyramid!"

"Is that so?"

"Yes! And *everyone* goes there! Adults, teenagers, and even kids my age! Can you imagine me taking martial arts?" she demanded and then rocked back on her heels, laughing at the thought before she continued without his answer. "There are restaurants and shopping and arcades. Some of my friends even like to play games in the arcades. Can you believe that? Girls that game, in fighting games!"

"Is that a strange thing for girls to do?" Grandpa asked.

Jeanette threw back her head and trilled laughter. "Of course it is!" She dropped down onto Grandpa's rug and lay on her side, propping up her heart-shaped face with a tiny hand. "I've even seen the type of spa that Auntie Jo likes to go to," she told Grandpa with a smile that was a little bit sly.

"Really?" Grandpa asked.

"Yes, really!" Jeanette answered before hiding a giggle in her hand. "And you know what?" she asked, sitting up as if she had just remembered something important.

"What?"

"I looked up what you were telling me about space travel," she confessed.

"You did?"

"Yes, and you were right! There was a velocity called 'warp-speed' a long time ago!"

"There was? I mean, of course there was! Do you think I'm crazy?"

Jeanette rolled on her back, laughing. "No! But I did think you were joking with me. It turns out that it was the first human attempt at creating wormholes."

"Is that so?"

"Yes. They were not able to create an actual tunnel through space, as they had originally intended, but they were able to create a bubble in space-time that was large enough to put a spacecraft inside, and push that bubble along, creating a worm-hole as they went." Jeanette giggled again. "They called it warp-speed at first, though I think that was sort of a joke based on a movie or something they had around at that time. It was officially called Sphere Drive. It was the first successful way that the moons of Jupiter were settled by those from Earth."

Grandpa nodded thoughtfully, rubbing the smooth skin on his shaved chin as his eyes drifted upwards. He did not recall the research or the news of the Sphere Drive, but he could recall the movies about warp speed with perfect clarity. It was all coming back to him. Slowly but surely, it was all coming back.

"So what does this mean? You want to be a travel agent?"

Jeanette laughed and made a face. "No, Grandpa!" she admonished. "I want to go myself!"

Grandpa smiled at her. "Well, you are young now, but when you are older maybe your parents will let you go to school abroad. Maybe study on Europa!"

Jeanette rolled on her back, holding her narrow ribcage as she laughed. "Europa! Mom would never let me go! Besides, I don't want to just visit some nearby moon. I want to see it all!" She took a deep breath, her eyes bright and hopeful. "Maybe I will be a starfighter someday," she gushed. "Like Auntie Jo!"

Grandpa wanted to throw back his head and caw at the ceiling, but he knew that it would hurt her feelings. Instead, he pressed his lips together and looked at the little girl in front of him – her rosy cheeks and dark curls – and wondered if Johanna had ever been so sweet. Now he did throw back his head and cackle, unable to stop himself, but Jeanette – sweet Jeanette - only smiled.

"What, Grandpa?" she asked. "What's so funny?"

"I was just thinking of your Auntie Jo," he confessed. "I was wondering if she was ever as sweet as you."

"And?"

Grandpa cawed laughter once again. "Not even close! She was born with teeth, and I don't mean that figuratively, the girl was born with *teeth*! The doctor said she bit him!"

This time Jeanette joined him as he laughed, both of them holding their sides. When their chortles died down into giggles, Grandpa looked at the girl with great fondness.

"Now," he said. "I have the feeling you are after something."

Jeanette smiled sweetly, her cheeks still bright and pink. "Weeellll," she started, tilting her head and twirling a dark curl around a finger that was now only slightly plump, "I did want to ask you something, I mean I *do* want to ask you something. I wanted to know if you would tell me about the Zealots."

The young girl froze and looked at the grizzled man in front of her, expectant and hopeful.

Grandpa's wrinkled lips puckered and he let out a low whistle. "Religion is a powerful subject. A lot of people are very touchy about it."

"I know," Jeanette confided in reserved tone. "Which is why you are the only person I can ask about it."

Grandpa nodded, trying not beam at her but knowing that he could not stop. "Well then, little Jean, what would you like to know?"

Jeanette let out a rush of breath, her dark eyes wide. "I don't even know. I don't really know anything about the Zealots." She swung her legs around under her body so that she was sitting up on the rug and favored Grandpa with a smile. "But I am sure that *you* do. I'm sure you know a lot – if not everything!"

"Don't flatter me, little miss," he warned, though he was grinning from ear to ear. "But I will tell you what I know."

Jeanette's grin mirrored his own, though hers had more teeth. "So?" she prompted. "What happened?"

"So," Grandpa said, his voice deep and determined, the way it always was when he started a story. "A long time ago, there were many religions and people believed a great many things – about God, other gods, themselves and the universe."

Jeanette wiggled into a cross-legged position on the rug. She could tell that this was going to be good.

"After the humans and the elves had made their first encounter, about a decade before the First Year of the First Dragon, the different races were still getting to know each other. They had different languages, different foods, different religions."

"A culture gap," Jeanette said.

"Very good!" Grandpa exclaimed, surprised. Jeanette beamed at him and he narrowed his blue eyes at her in suspicion. "I think you might know a lot more than you let on, little miss."

Jeanette smiled. "I had heard of it but never really knew what it meant until now. Keep going, Grandpa."

Grandpa cleared his throat. "Well, us humans were very eager to bridge that gap, and some of us thought that religion might be the best way. The elves already had a few religions of their own that were very similar to ours. Same...story lines if you would. So a group of people got together..."

"The Zealots?" Jeanette asked.

Grandpa shook his head. "Not yet. I can't remember what they called themselves when they first started out – my father called them 'New Age Crazies.'" Jeanette giggled as Grandpa continued. "But these people that got together took all of the stories and made them into *one* story. One religion."

"Ohhhh."

"Now, this got a lot of people very excited. A good deal of the elves were behind it, which makes me think that their stories were the ones that stayed more intact, but many humans were in it as well. Many, many human religions joined this new religion, this blend of religions. But there were a few that would have none of it."

"The Catholics," Jeanette said, pronouncing the word slowly and carefully.

"That's right, but they were not the only ones. The people of Israel and Islam, if I am not mistaken, refused the new religion, but were too busy fighting amongst themselves to give much of a fight to these up-and-comers , who called their sect The One, or True Religion."

"What happened to the Catholics?" Jeanette asked.

Grandpa's blue eyes narrowed as he examined his granddaughter. "Why are you so interested in this?"

Jeanette's young face became serious and she paused, deciding if it was something she should share. "It's one of my new friends," she confessed after a few moments. "I think she might be one, a Catholic I mean."

Grandpa's face became stern. "And why do you want to know?" he asked. "Will it change how you feel about her?"

Jeanette shook her head emphatically, her dark curls moving in a frenzy. "No, no, no – it's nothing like that! I just...I just don't want to be stupid," she said softly. Jeanette sighed and it was the sigh of a person much older than nine or ten years. "I don't want to say the wrong thing," she confessed.

Grandpa's expression softened. The girl's heart was tender after all. And she was old enough to hear about the past. How much of the past, he was not sure. But he knew that she was old enough to deserve answers. Some of them.

"Well, like most religions, the One Religion had a lot of good people with good intentions. Also, like most religions, it had people who thought that their religion was the only right one and felt that anyone who said otherwise should be stopped from saying anything all." He took a sip of his coffee, watching his granddaughter to see if she got his meaning. He could tell by her expression that she did.

"Those were the Zealots, weren't they?"

Grandpa nodded. "Yes. The ones that were the most fanatical, the most zealous, about the new religion. They began burning churches of the other religions. They hunted down and tortured and killed those that wouldn't convert."

"Convert?"

"Change from their old religion to the One Religion."

"Oh. And the Catholics?"

"The Catholics tried to put a stop to what the New Age Crazies were doing. It was called the Crusade of Truth, by both sides."

"And?" Jeanette asked. "What happened?"

"The Catholics were slow to decide and slow to action, and started their crusade too late – after the One Religion had amassed an incredible number of Zealot Disciples."

"And?"

"The Catholics were slaughtered, honey."

The color drained from Jeanette's face, though she did not look surprised. She nodded gravely at her Grandpa. "And?" she whispered.

"The Zealots forbade the Catholics and all others to openly practice their religions, under the penalty of death, and created a militant branch within their own sect that would enforce that law."

Jeanette was wordless for a while, thoughtful. "There were other religions?" she asked. "Others that refused to join?"

Grandpa nodded. "A few of the religions on Earth, what were called the Eastern Religions, joined together with two similar elfin religions to create the Zenarchists."

"Did they fight the Zealots?"

"No. They simply told the Zealots that they would not join, and that they were to be left alone."

"Didn't the Zealots fight them?"

"Not outright," Grandpa said. "The Zealots burned their temples, those that they could find, but not much else."

"Why?" Jeanette asked. "Why were they not hunted and

killed like the Catholics were?"

Grandpa took a sip of coffee and tried to remember. A lot had been coming back to him, but not everything. *Not yet,* he thought. *Not yet.*

"I'm not sure, Little Jean," he confessed. "But I think it had something to do with physics."

"Physics? Like what Sean studies in school?"

That surprised Grandpa. "Sean studies physics? I thought he studied biology!"

Jeanette made a sour face and rolled her eyes, her head of dark curls tilting back as far as her small neck would allow. "He's a nerd," she said with a good deal of adolescent contempt. "He studies everything!"

Grandpa threw back his own head and cackled at the ceiling.

CS80

Jordan Blue looked through the hyper-diamond eyes of her Fledgling and into the star-studded blackness of space. Her knee bounced with nervous energy and her fingers drummed rapidly on the armrest of her pilot's chair, pattering like a steady rain.

Galen's ghostly image sat in the chair next to hers, tinged blue and somewhat transparent. His eyes were more blue than ever, and they watched her, his high-arched brows furrowed in concern.

"What's bothering you?" he asked.

"My sister."

"Which one?"

Blue scowled at him. "Faith."

"Why?"

"I want to know how she knows so much."

Galen smiled "She's been around a long time. A long, *long* time."

"But I haven't," Blue remarked, her sapphire eyes turning away from him to gaze back out into the darkness. When she spoke again, her voice was barely above a whisper. "How does she know so much about me?" After a moment of thought she turned to Galen and her faintly almond-shaped eyes narrowed in suspicion. "Are you sure that you never told her anything about me?"

Galen sighed. "The last time I discussed you with your sister was shortly after your accident, maybe two days after you had woken up. I'm not sure of the date but it certainly wasn't recently."

Blue turned her eyes once again to the darkness. Her fingers stopped their drumming and she brought her right hand to her mouth and chewed at her thumbnail in consternation.

"Before that, what did you say about me?"

Galen's form made a rippling movement, like a holo in a power surge, as he shrugged. "I had told her about your accident, but that you were okay. I let her know what I intended to do concerning your procedure. A few days later, I let her know what I wasn't going to do regarding both your face and being her sort of pseudo-spy."

With her thumbnail still caught between her teeth, Blue raised one finger and stroked the scar tissue that rippled across her right cheek. It was what Galen was referring to –what he hadn't done was give her a skin graft to remove the scar. He had told her at the time that he couldn't - but the truth was that he wouldn't. He thought her face was perfect the way it was.

"Two days after you had woken up, I knew I was in love with you," Galen said, his voice low. "I let Faith know that I would still watch over you, but that I wouldn't relate any personal information about you outside of general health or well being."

Blue grunted. "How did she take it?"

Galen smirked. "Are you kidding? She was furious, though she recovered rather quickly. She still wanted me to continue my work on the Thermopylae. I was relieved, since I still wanted the project. I felt I was getting close."

"And if she had made you choose?" Blue asked without looking at him.

"I would have walked away from it without a second thought," he said firmly. "But not from you."

Blue snorted. "You knew already that you loved me?"

Galen looked at her, a small crease forming between his dark, arched brows. "Without a doubt. How long was it before you knew you loved me?"

The Jordan's hard expression faltered. "Less than five minutes after I woke up," she said softly.

Galen reached over and laid a hand over her thigh. Blue stared out into the dark as the silence enveloped them. When she spoke again her voice was still quiet, so low that Galen thought she might be talking to herself.

"Faith has a spy aboard the Dragon," she murmured. It was almost impossible for her to believe, but she did. She had to. Her mind raced and twisted, trying to narrow down the possibilities. The worst of it was that it had to be someone that the Jordan knew, which made it even more difficult to swallow, but also had to be true. "She knows too much about me," Blue whispered.

Faith had a wealth of information at her fingertips, that much was obvious, but what disturbed the Jordan the most, what gnawed at the edges of her psyche, was that Faith had known about Blue's newfound penchant for peanut butter. That was personal information that had surfaced recently. Very recently. Only someone aboard the Dragon would know, someone she knew well.

"Are you *sure* you haven't been in contact with her?" Blue asked, facing Galen once again. He gave her a look of exasperation and disgust.

"You mean since I've been dead?"

Blue frowned, recalling the first time she had eaten the pasty mush. It had actually been in the middle of a starfight, her mind fading away as her body burned up its fat stores and slipping her into a state of drug-induced forgetful lethargy.

She remembered Galen's hand, Galen's ghostly hand, upending the pilot's kit bag and rummaging through the contents for something that could help her. She had forgotten that he had been dead, even then, and now the realization made her stomach lurch.

The Jordan looked away and started drumming her fingers again.

She had found the paste nasty at first, and then developed a taste for it since it was an easy snack and she could eat it with damn near everything, or nothing at all. She searched through her mind in the same manner that Galen had searched that upended kit bag back then.

Who else knows I like peanut butter besides Galen? The cook aboard the Dragon? Duh. But why in the seven systems would anyone want a cook as a spy? To discover that everyone lines up for sirloin on Sunday but mysteriously disappears to the Atrium on the nights they serve strg-toast?

Blue bit her lip, thinking. *Who else?* She never sat or talked with hardly anyone these days and nights, even the other officers, but Faith had known. The Jordan thought back to her meeting with her sister, replaying the scene in her mind. When Blue had asked Faith how she knew that she liked peanut butter the bitch had told her that she had eyes everywhere.

But first she had smiled.

Faith had tried to hide that smile in her glass of champagne but the Jordan had seen it. She said it again later in their conversation, the Jordan was sure of it.

"She thinks she is pretty damn clever about something," Blue muttered.

Calyph, she thought suddenly. *Calyph knows I like peanut butter.*

The Jordan laughed out loud, the sound light and echoey in the ghostly loneliness of the cockpit. The thought of Calyph being a spy for anyone was hilarious. She bit her lip in frustration and shook her head, making her platinum coils tremor.

"She obviously thinks that I don't know or couldn't figure it out on my own, otherwise she wouldn't have said anything. That it would be the last person I would suspect. Shit, maybe it is the damned cook! Fuck!"

Blue slammed her fist down on her knee, making Galen jump in his seat. She blew out a deep breath between her teeth, trying to keep her rising anger at bay.

I have eyes everywhere.

Was Faith suggesting that she had more than one spy? Well, of course she had more than one spy. Blue was sure that her sister had spies spread out all over every civilized galaxy and then some. But was she impugning that she had more than one spy aboard the Dragon? Blue suddenly was filled with the terrifying thought that maybe everyone on her mother ship was reporting to her sister. She rolled her shoulders back, forcing herself to relax and ward off the paranoia that was creeping up on her.

She could see Galen from the corner of her eye, cocking his head, watching her. She closed her eyes so she could concentrate.

I have eyes everywhere.

And that damned smile.

I have eyes...

Blue felt her mouth go dry and her own eyes popped open. They widened, losing their almond shape until they were perfectly round and she leaned forward with her mouth open as if she were going to retch. She felt like she might.

Nothing came out of course, since the sunbutter sandwiches and talks of treason had been fed to her eighteen hours ago. The sandwiches were long digested but the hints of insurrection and promises of redemption lingered. They roiled in her cramped belly like sea-water. Yet it was not the thought of the mutiny being asked of her that had her insides heaving, but the mutiny done upon her. She turned her face to the bluish and ghostly image of her love.

"When?" she gasped, her body still hunched over, unable to straighten.

"When what?"

"My procedure."

Galen cocked his head, not understanding.

"When did you put in my prosthetic?"

Galen looked away as he considered her question, then looked back at her. "Two days after your accident. I had taken a high-res pic as well as the measurements of your undamaged eye and did a wave-line submit for a match. I wanted to perform the surgery before I woke you up from sedation, to spare you any additional trauma."

"You had already spoken to Faith?"

"Yes." His form flickered as he frowned, wondering where she was going.

Blue closed her eyes. She could feel tears coalescing under the lids, blobs of hot saline. "Where?" she asked.

"Excuse me?"

"Where did you get my new eye?"

Galen's ghost paled. "From the company," he whispered. He

did not have to tell her which company, she already knew.

Blue pressed her lips together so tight that they all but disappeared and she shook her head slowly from side to side. The elfin doctor trembled, the words tumbling out fast as he tried to explain.

"It was a medical submit that went directly to the G7-5 factory," Galen said quickly. "I knew it was the only place where I would get a perfect match and the best quality. But I sent the request straight to MedCen. I didn't get the eye from Faith." He paused and swallowed. "Not directly."

"You didn't have to," the Jordan hissed. "She knew what you were doing. She knew what *she* was doing."

Blue gripped the armrests of her chair and screamed in fury, gathering all her strength before pushing herself up and out. She strode from the small cockpit towards the galley, alternately screaming and shouting profanities as she went. Galen leapt from his seat and quickly followed her past the kitchen area where he watched her yank the first aid kit off of the wall, scattering instruments and bandages and tubes all over the counter.

"What are you doing?" he asked, unnerved and trying to keep his voice at a normal timbre.

"Getting ready to play!" Blue spat, her eyes searching the counter.

"What?"

"I'm done being a pawn," she said, her voice shaking with rage. She made another noise that was a furious amalgamation of shout and scream as she pounded her fist against the counter before she turned her glare upon the ghostly visage of her lover.

"She made it out to sound like I was a pawn of the IGC," she barked, her voice livid and her scar standing out like an angry exclamation on her face. "But it's her! I'm *her* pawn. Or both of theirs! I don't know and I don't care - I'm done! I'm out!"

She picked up a roll of gauze with one hand and used the other hand to jerk open a utensil drawer. "Too big, too big," she muttered, her eyes scanning the metal contents. "Aha!" she exclaimed, victorious.

She snatched up a small, round coffee spoon and slammed the drawer closed with her hip before sidling past Galen's ghostly form.

"What are you doing, Jordan?" he demanded, following her down the cramped hall to the one meter square room that was her lavatory. His voice was high and pitchy as he fought against the terror she might be planning. "You don't know for sure if she tampered with it. Get back to the Dragon. Have Westerson check you out or, better yet, go see Chang. For God's sake don't do anything crazy!"

"It's a little late for that," she said, her own voice firm but soft, facing her reflection in the small mirror. She dropped the roll of gauze next to the sink, freeing up her left hand.

Galen shook his head, his bluish-black hair whipping across his face, and opened his mouth to argue. Then he realized what she meant to do.

Before he could even flinch, the Jordan moved with the speed for which she was becoming famous. In a single fluid motion she used her left hand to raise her right eyelid and with her right hand she slid the rounded edge of the spoon over the ball of her right eye.

"No!" Galen shouted in a near scream of panic, but she was already driving the spoon deeper, her face tight with resolve.

The pain was slight at first, not much more than an extreme discomfort, until the spoon began to sever the filaments that held the prosthetic in place and blood began to encircle the hyper-glass optic before it gathered and ran down her cheek.

Blue gathered her courage and pressed harder, vaguely hearing Galen shouting behind her, terrified and panic-stricken. When the bowl of the spoon had all but disappeared into her eye socket, Blue pushed the handle up, using it as a lever against the arch of bone over her right eye. There was a feeling of resistance, a taut and dogged suction, as if her socket was not so ready to release its tenant.

The Jordan ground her teeth and pushed harder and it began to give. She screamed as more filaments snapped, one with a horrible metallic twang that she felt go through the back of her head and all the way down her spine. Finally, with a terrible squelching noise, the orb came out.

It did not pop out as she had hoped, fairly clean and free. Instead it toppled down her face, clumps of tissue clinging to the back. It came to a stop on her lower cheek where it was caught up and hung by one last strand - the thickest of the optic fibers though even it was hard to see – just a miniscule strand of silver, sparkling where it wasn't coated with thick drops of red.

"Get...it...OUT!" she screamed at Galen.

Blood welled up in the socket and then poured down over her cheek. She grabbed at the roll of gauze as she fell backwards, her knees buckling. She staggered, trying to keep her feet as her body began to go into shock, but her legs seemed far away and utterly useless.

Galen, standing behind her, caught the Jordan as she fell. He hooked his hands under her arms as he hefted her up like a drowning swimmer, back-peddling and dragging her from the bathroom and back towards the galley while she profanely ranted about players and games.

Stepping into the small kitchen area, Galen wrapped one arm around her middle to keep her upright while he used the other to pluck two items off the surface of the countertop before sweeping the rest away, sending the remainders of the discarded first aid kit to clatter discordantly all over the galley floor.

The ghost of the elfin doctor hoisted the Jordan up onto the counter with ease. "Christ," he muttered. "You hardly weigh any more than I do." He eased her down gently so that she was lying like a patient on a table. Blue said something incoherent and held up her hand, the end of the gauze roll streaming out from between her fingers.

"Really?" Galen demanded, angry. "Gauze? You were just going to stuff yourself full of gauze?" He cursed in elfin and Noel laughed drunkenly, only half understanding what he said.

He dropped the two items he had retrieved from the medical kit, a laser curette and a small pair of scissors, down on the counter next to her head. Taking hold of her chin, he turned her face so he could have a better look. Grimacing at the mess but as determined as the Jordan, he took hold of the silver filament and pulled gently, sliding it out through the tiny hole in the back of her eye socket.

Blue screamed.

Galen didn't know whether it was in pain or simply at the horrible sensation of pulling that went deep into her skull.

"Don't worry," he told her, putting the gauze into her socket, "you did most of the work. It's almost done."

Her body, already in shock, started to go limp as she lost consciousness. Galen reached for the surgical scissors and watched in horror as his hand, already ghostly, passed through the scissors and into the counter. He stared at Blue in terror, blood seeping insistently into the gauze as her consciousness ebbed away.

"Shit," he whispered. "Noel!" he shouted. The Jordan's eyelids fluttered and a bit of his substance reformed, but not enough. "Dammit!" His eyes darted around the medical mess on the floor before they found what he was after.

Just as she began to fade away again, so did he. His ghostly image leaned down until he was nose to nose with the body on the counter.

"NOEL!" he shouted into her face with all the force he could muster. "JORDAN! WAKE UP!"

Blue's eyes flew open and Galen made a dive for the floor, his fingers closing over a small white packet and, to his great relief, picking it up. Blue moaned and weakly waved her hand at him.

"I am so sorry," he said, standing up over the Jordan, "but it looks like you are going to have to be awake for this." Before she could fade away again and take him with her, he broke open the packet of amyl nitrate and held it under her nose.

The Jordan's body jerked and her single blue eye rolled in its socket, a wild and staring sapphire as she gaped and gasped before she let out a blood-curdling scream. Galen's hand went down over the bloody gauze, applying a steady pressure while his eyes went back to the floor, scanning the supplies, but there was nothing more there for pain than an syringe of A-solve and a tube of topical anesthetic, neither of which would help the Jordan in her current condition.

A blinking from the corner of his vision caught his eye and, looking up, he saw a rapidly pulsing blue light coming from the walls, an indication that the Fledgling was in a state of distress as his Jordan writhed in pain and horror.

"Dammit, Cyan!" Galen hissed. "Isn't there anything you can do for her?" Responding immediately, the light stopped pulsing and gathered into a beam of deep blue that settled over the Jordan, enclosing her entire form. Her body stiffened at first and then relaxed, her mouth opening slightly. She took a deep, shaky breath and then her breathing resumed a more normal rhythm. Galen's shoulders sagged but his relief was short-lived as he saw the lid over her left eye began droop. "No!" he shouted. "Don't let her go to sleep!"

The blue light around her body grew brighter and the Jordan's good eye opened wide once again as she drew in another great swallow of air. Galen braced himself for the scream but her breath came out slowly, quietly.

"Thank you, Cyan," he whispered. The doctor's ghost looked at the Jordan, splayed out upon the galley countertop.

"Are you alright?"

She glared up at him in one-eyed amazement. "Seriously?" she asked, her voice hoarse and raspy.

"Right," Galen agreed.

Picking up the surgical scissors, he turned Blue's face again to expose the right side of it to the galley's overhead fluorescent. He pulled the bloody wad of gauze from the socket, relieved to see that at least the blood loss had slowed. Picking up the optical orb of hyper-glass that was now dangling next to Blue's right ear, he gently pulled it away until the silver filament, the one he knew was wound around her optical nerve, was pulled taut.

Galen eased the curved tip of the tiny scissors into the socket as far as they would go without puncturing the back of the ocular wall, then he snipped the filament and laid the eye down on the counter next to Blue's shoulder.

The Jordan reached across her body, groping wildly until her hand closed upon the bloody orb of glass and micro-tech, trailing its thread of silver and gore. Her face contorted with disgust as she grabbed the thing and hurled it at the wall while she mumbled something ineligible to the doctor.

Cyan, however, must have perceived what she had wanted because the orb was caught up and enveloped in blue light as it was pulled tight against the wall of the galley. The silver skin of the Fledgling swallowed the object and passed it through, spitting it out into space.

The doctor's ghost watched with incredulity as the orb was ejected from the cabin and then turned his eyes back to his patient. Discarding the scissors, he picked up the curette and fired the laser till it was a rounded line of searing heat three centimeters high and two centimeters wide. Moving quickly, he cauterized the open socket, stopping the flow of blood. The air was filed with a soft sizzling sound and the smell of burning flesh. Blue closed her one good eye, sickened.

Galen dropped the curette, cut off a large piece of clean gauze, and packed it into the empty socket. He took the rest of the roll and wound it around the top her head to keep it secure, tucking the loose end into the top of the bandage.

He crouched down and searched the contents scattered on the floor for an antiseptic packet. Finding one, he tore it open with his teeth and used the wet cloth inside to clean the blood off of the Jordan's face and neck.

Taking another look around, he spied a small, flexible square of silver material and snatched it up. He gave it a shake, opening up an emergency blanket that he wrapped around the Jordan before he lifted her up and carried her to the small cabin at the back of the ship. The pool of blue light that had surrounded the Jordan while she was on the countertop stayed with her as he laid her on the bed.

The ghost of the elfin doctor crawled in beside her, wrapping his arms around her lithe form, burying his face in her platinum coils.

"Take her home, Cyan," he whispered. "Get her back to the Dragon."

The blue light around the Jordan took on a greenish tint, making an aqua-colored halo around her body as it went limp.

The Blue Fledgling shot through the cold darkness with the Red Fledgling following just behind his brother's right wing. Jordan Blue faded away into unconsciousness and, as she did so, so did the image of Galen.

ONE FOUR

Bjorn sat with his hands laced together and resting between his thighs, his lower torso strapped into the seat of the transport as it shook and bounced its way out of the artificial atmosphere of Europa. The transport crewmembers made what adjustments they could in an attempt to make the ride more comfortable while Bjorn's officers, mostly his bodyguards and also strapped to their seats, stared straight ahead. Bjorn, however, leaned forward as far as his straps would allow and stared curiously at his newest acquisition – the troll manufactured by GwenSeven that bore somewhat of a semblance to the Red Jordan of the Opal Dragon.

The troll, the same AI construct that Julian had named Lucy, sat across from the Commander. Lucy, like the Chimeran constructs, stared straight ahead at the empty air in front of her. Bjorn smiled and shifted impatiently under his safety webbing. He had planned on starting something akin to an inquisition once they were aboard his ship, preferably once in the privacy of his quarters, but he found the waiting difficult. He didn't like to wait.

"Lucy?" he intoned.

The droid turned her sculpted face slightly, shifting her kaleidoscope gaze towards the Commander.

Her features are more fine, Bjorn thought, comparing the construct to Scarlett. *More delicate. Scarlett has a stronger nose and jaw. Stronger everything.*

The Commander was certain that, though Lucy was metal and circuits under her smooth skin, the human Jordan would chew the construct up and spit her out without a second thought. Bjorn grinned.

"Sir?" Lucy asked.

"Lucy," he repeated as if about to ask a question, and then fell silent, his eyes still on her. The construct cocked her head, waiting. Bjorn chuckled and shook his head. "I'm sorry, Lucy," he said after a moment, "I am simply very intrigued by you at the moment and, though I have many questions for you, I'm not sure where to start."

"An apology is not necessary," Lucy said, her voice oddly metallic and flat. "But if you have questions, I will be happy to answer them."

"Happy?"

"The word is used in this situation to mean obliging, not as an emotion. If you have questions, my requisite is to answer them as plainly as possible."

Bjorn laughed, ignoring the heavy turbulence as they left the moon's atmosphere. "I have many questions, Lucy. But right now I am just simply fascinated with you, and I am curious about GwenSeven. How long have they been making trolls?"

Lucy's golden eyes glimmered for the briefest seconds. "Two point six years, standard," she answered.

"How many have been sold?"

"One thousand, seven hundred and ninety one, since my last upload – less than twenty hours ago."

Bjorn nodded, a far-away look on his face and a small smile forming minute creases at the sides of his lips. "They are finally infiltrating different masses of demographics with artificial intelligence where they had been unable to reach – until now anyway."

Lucy cocked her head again. "Sir?"

Bjorn felt the urge to reach across to lay a hand on her

knee, a human affectation he had picked up a long time ago, but his restraints made it impossible for him to reach across even the short distance between them. "One of the reasons that I am fascinated by you Lucy is because I, too, was made by GwenSeven." Lucy's head cocked the other way, her quick movements reminding Bjorn of a bird. He laughed. "In fact," he continued, "I was the first."

At this remark Lucy straightened perceptibly, her golden eyes shining. "Then you are not Mr. Roder, as you previously implied. You would, in fact, be Bjorn van Zandt. The First of the First Seven. One of the three whom are recognized by the IGC as the chief leaders of the rebellion group, self-named Chimera. Created in the seventh month of standard year..."

"Alright, alright!" Bjorn interrupted. "I get it - you know who I am." He looked at Julian, sure that his bodyguard's lip had twitched. The other guards in his small entourage were smiling, darting mirthful glances at one another. Though Bjorn had been made to last for an infinite amount of time, unless he was killed, he did not like to be reminded of his age. The Commander sat back and shook his head, his eyes heavenward. "I knew I should have waited until we were aboard the *Mace*," he muttered.

A myriad of color swam across Lucy's eyes before they became gold again.

"Why do your eyes do that?" Bjorn asked.

"Do what, sir?"

The Commander's blonde brows went up over his green eyes. "They change color," he informed her.

"They do?"

"Yes."

"I was not aware." She was silent for moment before she spoke again. "Does the entire visible area change?"

"No, just the irises. Where it is normally gold."

"To which color do they change?"

"It's a little different almost every time, but usually to all colors at once, like a rainbow."

"Are they changing color now?"

"No."

"Now?"

"Yes."

Lucy gave a short nod. "It is a by-product of my processors working."

"They change colors when you are thinking?"

"Processing information would be a better description."

Bjorn shrugged under his straps. "Tomato, tomato."

Lucy cocked her head. "I don't understand."

"It's a human expression," Bjorn said. He grinned and shook his head. "I don't understand it quite that well myself."

Lucy's eyes glimmered and were still but she remained silent.

Bjorn sat out the rest of the trip, which was thankfully short, in silence. Helioch, his Quartermaster aboard the *Macedonian*, was serving temporarily as his second in command. Bjorn had let him know when they had boarded the transport and ordered Olivia to head their way. Olivia, the Navigator, had then begun a slow but steady descent towards the moon in an effort to hasten the rendezvous.

As soon as the transport docked with the Battle Cruiser, Bjorn escorted Lucy from the small craft and through the ship. His guards fell away to take up the normal duties they performed when not personally accompanying the Commander. Two broke away to administer the daily physical safety check of the vessel while two followed Julian to the bridge for a security check with the officers on duty.

Lucy followed Bjorn to his personal quarters where, after a print-read panel had scanned his palm, a wide door made of heavy titanium slid open. The billet was comprised of three rooms; a bedroom, a personal lavatory, and a small living room. The first room in the Commander's cabin was the living area. It held a small couch of steel bars topped with cushions covered in a smooth, white fabric that appeared to be made from animal hide. It was bookended by two matching chairs that faced a low holo table. On the wall was a large plastique rectangle. A chest-high steel rack of shelves topped with a pane of glass stood watching from the side of the room as a make-shift cocktail bar.

Bjorn held a hand out to the sitting area as he smiled at Lucy. "Make yourself comfortable," he offered as the door closed behind him. He walked to the bar to pour himself a drink and saw that Lucy remained standing in the same spot where she had stopped upon entering the room.

Bjorn shook his head, a small smirk at his lips, as he selected a bottle of wine from the shelf and placed it on the glass countertop. "Sit down," he told her, placing a stemmed glass next to the bottle.

Lucy approached the sitting area and then stopped again, examining the seats with her golden eyes. Bjorn opened the bottle and filled the glass.

"Sit in one of the chairs," he suggested when she had still not taken a seat. Lucy's countenance shifted from one chair to the other and Bjorn sighed as he joined her. "That one," he instructed, pointing with the hand that held his glass of wine.

Lucy sat herself as Bjorn settled into the couch, shifting his body to face her.

The Commander hesitated for a second, held back by a lifetime of social manners. Another second escaped as he realized he had lived his whole life as person that resented being treated like a machine, yet now he had a machine that he could not help but treat as a real person.

This is how they see us, he thought, looking at Lucy's stiff body and empty expression. *Even though we act like them in every way, they think we are like this emotionless robotic computer.*

It only took a moment longer before deciding not to beat around the bush, acknowledging the fact that he was dealing with a droid and that niceties or social formalities would be a waste of time.

"I want to know about Johanna Mattatock," he told Lucy, proud of his own private research. "The Red Jordan of the Opal Dragon. Assumed name – Scarlett." He leaned back into his chair and took a long drink of wine.

Lucy's strange, golden eyes fixed upon him for an instant, and then her face turned and she stared at the air in front of her as she laid her hand upon the arm of the chair in which she sat.

Bjorn watched as the fibers on the chair's arm glowed, and then as the glow streaked down the chair and through the floor. The streak crossed the ground through the fibers of the rug, and then climbed up the wall to coalesce in the rectangle of plastique that could be used for any range of entertainment but that the Commander mostly used for coms.

The space was suddenly filled with a still picture of a young woman, still in her teens, with dark wavy hair framing a face with dark eyes and a broad smile of white teeth. Bjorn grinned and felt his heartbeat quicken.

Scarlett as a young woman, he thought. *Maybe not even a pilot yet.*

"Do you have anything earlier than that?" he asked.

"No," Lucy said.

Bjorn sighed through his nose. "Next?" he asked.

The picture dissolved to show the same young woman, only a bit older but already much harder, her eyes fierce and her jaw set. She was dressed in gray training coveralls, and she was not alone. Though she was file and rank in a platoon of other pilots, she stood out in Bjorn's eyes like an illuminated religious icon.

"Next," he commanded.

"That is all," Lucy informed.

"Excuse me?" Bjorn asked, straightening in his chair.

Lucy turned her head until it was facing him. "That is all," she repeated.

Bjorn's brows went up. "I am inquiring about a woman that has been around for close to one hundred years, possibly more! She is an accomplished pilot and a high ranking officer in the IGC, and you only have two pictures of her?"

"I do not have any pictures of her," the droid corrected. "I am pulling these from the Galactic Web."

Bjorn's brows went up even further, stretching his smooth face in surprise. "The entire G-Dub only has two pictures of her?"

"It would seem so," Lucy informed without a trace of emotion. "If there is more, it is either concealed or forbidden."

"Ah!" Bjorn conceded with a knowing smile. A mischievous glint lit his green eyes. "I like either of those presumptions. How do we get around them?" He was even more pleased when Lucy smiled back.

"It will depend on what you want to know," she said. "And it will depend on how you ask."

"Well," Bjorn told her, his smile widening into a grin, "I want to know everything. How do I go about that?"

Lucy gave him a curt nod. "The simplest way to acquire that information is to ask about certain people, family, names and dates. Whatever information you require, I will retrieve from every known translatable database. This includes every civilized system within the IGC range, plus the IGC satellites of Golbli, Ganth, and Plemra."

Bjorn grunted. "I want everything you can find on Johanna Mattatock, her known family, aliases, etcetera."

Lucy's eyes glimmered and her hand glowed. "Much of that

information is restricted," she said, her voice placid, "but I will give you what I am able to access."

"See that you do," Bjorn said softly, watching the wall above the fireplace as it was filled with pictures and facts, one after the other, narrated by Lucy in her flat metallic voice. After only two short minutes she was done.

Bjorn, who had just retrieved the wine bottle and sat back down, scowled at the droid. "That's all?" he demanded.

Lucy turned her strange eyes towards him. "I have answered all that you have asked of me," she stated.

"It was mostly a list of names! I don't want her family tree! I want to know about *her!*"

"It is everything available from her personal records."

Bjorn could feel his temper rising and fought to squelch it. He stared at the troll for a second before he leaned back and placed a hand over his face in exasperation. "Do you have any idea how much you cost?" he asked, dropping his hand to his chin.

"You?" Lucy asked, cocking her head. "Or Mr. Roder?"

Bjorn felt his jaw clench. "I see you don't miss a lot," he said. "But rest assured that the money is real, though the name might be false. Unlike *you,*" he said, pointing an accusatory finger at the droid.

"Me?" Lucy asked. "I have not been false."

"Falsely advertised!"

"I do not know what you mean, nor am I aware of any marketing issues."

"Trolls are supposed to know everything."

"No being can know everything," Lucy replied. "Trolls are merely data-bases. Historians of a sort."

"What history you have given me is crap!" Bjorn told her. "No more than what I could have gathered from a planet-side electronic library!"

Lucy's eyes glimmered green and returned to gold. "I have answered all that you have asked of me," she repeated. "If you want more answers, or different answers, then you must ask more questions. Or different questions."

Bjorn rubbed his face with his hands and then fixed his green eyes on Lucy as something occurred to him. Scarlett's records were confidential because of who she was now. But that did not mean that she didn't have a past. Everyone has a past. All of her information was still out there, it just wasn't in a neat bundle. It was all about finding a backdoor.

I need to be a detective, Bjorn thought and then laughed aloud. The curse of the entire construct race had been a horribly limited imagination. Coming up with creative ideas would not be easy. *But I can imitate,* he thought, rubbing his chin. *After all, that's what we were made for – to imitate humans.*

Bjorn had seen an elfin holo once about a detective who solved his problems only by seeing certain numbers and then following the trails they left. The memory gave him an idea.

"What year was Scarlett born?" he asked.

"Her personal records are sealed," Lucy said. "Only accessible to IGC officials with secondary clearance and above."

"But birth records are still accessible to the general public. Search public records of birth on the moon of Io starting twenty years ago and go back until you get a hit on her name."

Lucy's eyes glimmered but her response was immediate. "3857."

Bjorn grinned, excited. It might take some finagling, but he would get what he wanted. He was sure of it now. "Search forward from that date, school records. See if you can find her name attached to a graduating class."

"Tesla High School."

"Year?"

"3875."

"Search forward, looking for a secondary school."

"Three Mile University, admitted in 3877."

"Graduated?"

"No."

"What is the last record that the school has concerning Johanna Mattatock?"

"All classes dropped by student mid-semester, 3880."

"Accepted at another college?"

Lucy's golden eyes shimmered into shades of violet and blue before they returned to gold. She tilted her head. "Yes, but not until 3960."

"That's quite a long time." Bjorn rubbed his chin as he considered the years, wondering what Scarlett had been up to and wondering how long it would take him to find out. "Can you do multiple searches at the same time?"

The corners of Lucy's mouth turned up. "Of course."

Bjorn templed his hands, touching his index fingers to his lips. "Go back to where she dropped out of school in 3880 and search forward from there. Check travel records, public military records, and open job histories. Give me the first chronologically sequential hit. Let's see if we can figure out what she was doing in between."

"Traveled abroad via Asten Travel Company, Milky Way One to The Flower. Trip was booked for ten years but passenger disembarked after eight." Lucy's eyes glimmered. "An early return ticket was issued at extra cost, extra paid to expedite the journey."

"Why the sudden return Scarlett?" Bjorn whispered, looking at her image on the wall. Without taking his eyes from her face he addressed Lucy. "What year was that?" he asked, although his mind did the math before she could answer.

"3888."

Bjorn nodded. "When the Rebellion began. Search forward

again, travel records, public military records, and open job histories."

"Flight school, 3888 to 3890. Graduated at the top of her class."

"Next?"

"Advanced flight, 3890 to 3892. Graduated with honors."

"Next?"

"Application to the military branch of the InterGalactic Council." Lucy's eyes changed from gold to red and back again. "Application was withdrawn by applicant before it could be accepted."

"Really? Hmm. Next hit?"

"Hired by ChronoTroop as a fighter-pilot instructor."

"Ah. She decided to teach." Bjorn touched the tips of his index fingers to his lips once again. "I wonder why. Next?"

There was a pause before Lucy spoke again. "Accepted at Callisto University in 3960."

"That's a big gap," Bjorn remarked. "Nothing in between?"

Lucy shook her head. "Not that is public record."

Bjorn tried to imagine what she might have been doing but his imagination failed him. Instead, he tried to recall what he had been doing those years. He remembered them clearly because they had been so frustrating. Just when it seemed like the Chimeran Military was making headway, there was a terrible lull in the war as they tried to secure weapons and troops and get them trained.

Maybe Scarlett, then Johanna, felt the lull as well, got tired of teaching and decided to go back to school.

"What do the school records say?"

"Started off as a chemistry major. Changed area of study many times but did not officially change her major until 3972."

Bjorn frowned. "And how long did it take her to graduate after she had officially changed her major?"

"Five lunar months. Graduated with honors, Dean's list, double major in space flight and aeronautics. Minors in chemistry and military history. Applied for IGC Officer's Candidate School on the day of graduation."

Bjorn sat back in his chair. It was obvious, even to him – a construct with great intelligence but little imagination. Scarlett had screwed around for twelve years not knowing, or seemingly caring, about what she wanted to do with her life. Then suddenly she had turned it all around, finishing her degrees, swiping up any possible accolades, and headed for the one school that taught complex flight with a predetermined course for IGC advancement.

The Commander stroked his smooth chin, his green eyes far away and thoughtful.

What happened, Scarlett? he mused silently. *What happened in your life to make you suddenly pull it together and become the best-damned fighter pilot I have ever seen?*

"The day she changed her major," Bjorn told Lucy, "Cross reference with any publicized event within seven days prior."

Lucy's eyes glimmered and she read off a string of events that included parades, parties, funerals, and ICG promotions. Bjorn shook his head in annoyance, feeling that he was finally on to something.

"Fourteen days prior," he amended.

Lucy again began to rattle off events of the requested week in sequential order until Bjorn held up a hand, commanding her to stop.

"Go back," he said. "Repeat the last."

"The Amliss Attack. The first recorded attack of the Chimera, spaceborn, upon those identified as being within the InterGalactic Council."

Bjorn nodded. He remembered the event. The Chimera had been blamed and, even though they had not been responsible, they had been glad to bare their teeth at the universe by taking credit. The Commander cocked his head, digging into his own memory before he realized that Lucy's would be more accurate.

"Do you know the date that the Chimera raided the IGC Aviation Compound, Asthera?" he asked.

"Of course. It was ten twenty-six, 3972."

Bjorn brought a hand up once again to stroke his chin. "That is exactly what I had thought."

He remembered those days long ago, working fervently to get the jets fighter ready before their first mission. He also remembered the news of the attack, how the Chimera had been blamed and how they had been jubilant to accept the accusation. It had seemed an omen of promised victory.

But how does that tie in with Scarlett?

"Do you have the names of the pilots involved in the Amliss Attack?" he asked.

"Of course."

Lucy began to rattle off the names of those involved in the assault but Bjorn could have stopped her after she had given him the first one, the officer that had led the charge and had died later at an IGC Infirmary.

The universe might be a melting pot of species and societies but, even then, Mattatock was not a common name. It only took the Chimeran Commander a second to cross-reference the name with Lucy and find out that it was Scarlett's father.

ONE FIVE

The call for the meeting came from Commander Brogan personally, which was the only reason why she was there. If it had been anyone other than the Captain of the Opal Dragon, Jordan Blue would have found some excuse not to attend. As it was, and without any regard for the chain of command, she had too much respect for the Captain to do less than anything he ever requested. Besides his high rank of an IGC Commanding Officer and the admiration he deserved for his efforts, sacrifices, and dedication – the man was more of a father to the Blue Jordan than her own father had ever been. Nonetheless, the Jordan attended the meeting begrudgingly.

Cyan had returned her to the Dragon after she had removed her prosthetic eye, where she had been properly cared for by the medical staff, but the Jordan had insisted vehemently that it not be replaced. Not yet, anyway. After a short recovery, Jordan Blue returned to spending her time on patrol - shunning the company of others, including her ghostly love. As it was, she only turned on the link that brought Galen around when she needed a question answered or she thought the utter loneliness might kill her. Her trust in everyone or anyone had dwindled like a fire starved of oxygen.

On the bridge of the Opal Dragon, behind the helm, was the sunken area referred to as the pit. Calyph and the Executive Officer, Commander Blaylock, sat in two of the five chairs in the pit, facing the Captain. Jordan Blue leaned against one of the four silver columns that surrounded the sunken space with her arms crossed over her chest. An eye patch, made from the same sparkling black material as her flight suit, now covered where her right eye had been.

The Commander had called a meeting to discuss Jordan Scarlett. The Red Jordan had been diagnosed with SM and been sent on a forced medical leave to a moon on the far side of Jupiter.

Personally, Blue felt that she couldn't care less about the Red Jordan. She thought that she wouldn't piss on the other Jordan had she been on fire, a colloquialism that gave Blue a stab of glee until she remembered that it was a saying she had learned from Scarlett. It was a saying that had been directed at herself from the Red Jordan from time to time. The black-clad Jordan blew a petulant puff of air through her nose and fixed her eyes upon Commander Brogan, shifting her light weight from one foot to the other. It was obvious that the Captain found her presence important, or else he would not have summoned her in from a patrol in the outer banks.

She scrunched her face under the sparkling patch over her eye, still getting used to the feel of it.

Now she wondered if she had been mistaken in being gone so much, if only for one person.

The Jordan's lone sapphire eye glittered as she regarded her Captain with deepening concern. He was looking more tired and strained every time she saw him. The lines in his face seemed to get deeper every day and a smile from him was getting more rare. She watched as he absently rubbed the side of his neck and noticed that his right eye looked red and irritated.

Jesus, she thought, unexpectedly struck by his appearance and overcome with concern. *We're killing him.* Discreetly, she reached under the platinum cuff on her wrist and opened her link to Galen. His bluish form flickered into life next to her, unseen by the others. He opened his mouth to speak but, after looking around, he realized where he was and snapped it shut

The Jordan glanced at his ghost and then looked meaningfully at the Captain, directing his attention to the Commander. She moved from her defensive position against the column, skirted the Engineer, and took the seat next to the Captain. She reached out a slim-fingered hand and placed it upon his knee. He looked over at her, his pale eyes startled.

"Are you alright, sir?" she asked, a frown creasing her smooth brow.

Brogan gave her one of his rare smiles, though it looked forced. "Yes, Jordan. I'm fine. Thank you."

Blue looked at him as if she thought he was not being quite truthful with her, but she remained silent. The smile helped. "Commander Blaylock said that you are concerned about Scarlett," she started, trying to encourage him despite her own qualms about the Red Jordan.

He nodded quickly, as if he had forgotten the reason for the meeting until reminded. "Yes," he said. "Yes, I am. I can feel," he began to tell them and then paused as if searching for the right words. "I can feel that she is drifting away. I don't know any other way to express it." He looked at Blue, his pale eyes searching her face. "Do you feel anything?" he asked. "Either within yourself, or coming from Fledge?"

Blue considered his question for a moment before slowly shaking her head. She didn't feel much of anything lately, other than what felt like the numbness of an amputated soul, but did not think it prudent to mention that to the Captain. She certainly wasn't wasting her time or energy thinking about Scarlett.

Brogan sighed. "I feel like we are losing her."

Blue's frown deepened. "What do you mean?"

"I feel like her bond with us, and with Fledge, is weakening."

Blue sat back, surprised, her single eye darting to the other two at the meeting. "Can that happen?"

"Of course it can happen," Blaylock snapped.

Blue looked at him in amazement. Calyph looked as shocked as he did uncomfortable but Blaylock, she noticed, looked decidedly smug. Despite her own feelings about Scarlett, Blue felt a wave of animosity at the look of satisfaction on the XO's face.

"I think maybe we should bring her back," Brogan said, his voice soft and tentative, his pale eyes sending out a silent plea.

Blaylock's expression immediately hardened into a scowl. "Sir, I have to admit that I don't think that is a sound idea," he said, his tone firm and commanding. "Doc Westerson gave a specific time for her to be planet bound. We cannot risk everyone's safety just for Jordan Scarlett."

Brogan's shoulders sagged and Blue looked at the two men, her eye wide with surprise and edged with fear. Brogan's whispering appeals, Blaylock's authoritative commands. She was not sure which of those was more disturbing.

Brogan is the Captain of this Dragon, she thought. *When did Blaylock assume command and not tell anyone?* She watched the chest of the Executive Officer swell as the Captain brooded in sullen silence like a child that had been rebuked. She didn't like what she was seeing. Not one bit.

But what can I do? she thought. *I'm all alone.* The thought was an echo of what she had been feeling for months, but now felt colder and sharper than ever. *Jade is gone from us and Scarlett is on a medical leave that is closer to exile. I'm the only Jordan aboard this Dragon. Scarlett's absence has been compulsory, mine has been self-imposed.*

She regarded the Captain, his jaw set and his downcast eyes watching his own thumb as it ran over the fabric of his armrest. Her eye flicked over to the Executive Officer, his hazel eyes narrowed at the Captain like an evil wizard holding a man enthralled. An unreasonable fear crept up her back and settled on her shoulders like a shroud. She shook it off.

Blaylock likes that she is gone, and that I am hardly ever here. That way, his voice is the only one the Captain hears, day in and day out. He outranks me, but if I wasn't alone there might be something I could do. I don't know what, but I know there is strength in numbers. He might be able to silence one Jordan, but it would be much harder to silence two. Especially if the other one is Scarlett.

Blue came to the realization that she would be rather listen to the Red Jordan's hot-tempered bitching than the Executive Officer's underhanded command of the ship.

"Calyph!" she called out, startling the Engineer. She turned her ruined face and fixed her gaze on his blue eyes and tilted her head, inquisitive. "You always seem to have a solution, especially when it concerns Scarlett. Any ideas?"

The elfin Engineer blushed to the tips of his pointed ears, his almond-shaped eyes darting from one officer to another. Brogan looked at him, his bluish eyes bright with unexpected hope, while Blaylock glared at the elf as if he had already said the wrong thing.

"W..w...well," he stammered nervously, looking away from the furious XO to the Captain. "Have you considered the triptych?"

Brogan straightened and his pallid blue eyes widened under a raised and furrowed brow while Blaylock looked as if he would have no greater pleasure than to feed the elfin Engineer to a starving Golgoth.

Blue turned her face to the Captain, nonplussed. "The triptych?" she asked. "What is the triptych?"

The Executive Officer cleared his throat meaningfully but the Captain was either too excited to hear him or simply ignored him. Blue was hoping for the latter.

Brogan looked at her and it seemed as if ten years had suddenly melted from his face. "When a Dragon loses its Captain," he explained, "the one it had fostered since Jordanhood, the new Captain is given an injection of the

Dragon's genetic material. It gives the bond between them a... jump start, so to speak. "

"Really?" Blue asked. "I never knew that."

"Why would you?" Blaylock asked lightly though his jaw was clenched and his glare was still trained on Calyph. Blue paid him no mind, keeping her eye fastened on the Captain.

"Sooooo," she said, "if we give Scarlett some of Fledge's genetic whatever, it will renew their bond?"

"It's worth a try," Brogan said, enthusiastic. "And while Doc Westerson is there to administer the shot, he can re-evaluate Scarlett! He can see how she is doing and when she will be able to return."

Blaylock shook his head. "Sir, I would have to caution you against such a plan," he said firmly, fixing his sharp gaze on the Captain. "Triptych can be dangerous, and it has never been tried on a person that already has the Dragon bond. We don't know what it could do to Jordan Scarlett. It could be detrimental as far as we know. And we certainly cannot let our chief medic go out on some intergalactic house call!"

Brogan looked down at the floor, crestfallen. Blue's small hand tightened into a fist and she turned her eye to the Executive Officer. "Test it out on me then," she offered.

All eyes turned to her. Blaylock looked as if she had tried to feed him a toad. He shook his head vehemently. "No. It is too dangerous."

"I'm not asking *you* to do it!"

His hawk-like eyes filled with cold fury and Blue could see the vein in his temple pulse. "You watch your tone, Jordan," he warned, his voice low.

"Yes, *sir*," the Jordan said. She turned to Calyph. "How is the material taken from the Fledgling?" she asked.

"I do it," he said, though his voice was so unsure that it came out sounding more like a question. He was obviously terrified of the conversation that was unfolding around him, but pulled himself together. "It's a metallurgic withdrawal. Then it is encapsulated and put into a hypodermic."

"So," Blue asked, "if it's metal based, and something goes wrong, you can pull it out of me?"

"Theoretically, yes."

"You see!" Blaylock said. "It is only a theory. Are you willing to risk your life on a theory?"

Blue smirked at him, her scar pushing up into her cheek. "Everything is only a theory, sir. Until it is proven. I am willing to take that chance for another Jordan, if my Captain will approve." She blinked her bright blue eye innocently at the XO before turning her face to Commander Brogan.

Blaylock pressed his lips together. Since the decision had been placed directly before the Captain, it would be out of turn for him to speak now. Instead, he glared at Jordan Blue, certain that she knew all too well what she was doing, and it irked the Executive Officer to no end to think that he may have underestimated her.

Captain Brogan frowned, his mind turning over possible problems and outcomes, before he nodded. "If you are willing to take that risk for Scarlett, I will stand behind you, Jordan Blue."

"And," Blue continued with a triumphant smile before the XO could object, "if all goes well with me, then you can dispatch Calyph to administer the injection to Scarlett, so Doc Westerson would be spared the house call."

The Commander grinned, satisfied. He looked happier than she had seen him in a long time. Alternately, she had never seen Blaylock look so pissed. It gave her a smug look of her own. She turned to Calyph, who looked petrified. The poor elf was obviously not cut out for politics.

"How long will it take you to get the injection ready?"

The Engineer turned his almond-shaped eyes towards the Jordan as he considered. "It's a very simple procedure, really.

If Doc Westerson is available, we can have it ready by this evening."

"In that case," Blue said, turning her face back to the Captain. "With your permission, Commander?"

Brogan smiled at her. "Godspeed Jordan," he told her with a deferential nod. "And God bless."

"Thank you, sir. If you'll excuse me, gentlemen?" she asked, rising from her chair. The other men rose respectfully as she stood and ascended the steps out of the pit. The Jordan could feel Blaylock's eyes boring into her as she walked from the bridge.

A part of her, the part that had so recently harbored a naïve mind and an innocent soul, had been robbed and beaten and left for dead. The remains of that part, the small piece that was left, now kept a wary and distrustful eye on everyone. It was that little piece that saw the look in the Executive Officer's eyes as the Jordan excused herself and knew that he would pay her back in spades the first chance he got.

Nevertheless, Blue left the bridge with decidedly more bounce in her step than she had trudged in with to attend the meeting called by the Captain. She nodded to people who greeted her as she passed by in the Artery and decided that she felt better than she had in a long time.

"Must you always jump in with both feet?" Galen asked once they were clear of prying eyes and listening ears.

The Jordan could see his flickering blue form out of the corner of her left eye and she smirked but did not turn to face him. "I turned you back on for your opinion of the situation, not your opinion of me." She tossed her coiffed platinum hair. "Besides," she said primly, lifting her chin, "it is my duty to help Scarlett."

"If she were covered in flames, you wouldn't piss on her to put them out," Galen told the Blue Jordan, making her grin.

"Did you get that phrase from her?"

"Something like it," the ghost confessed.

"Well, you're wrong. I would certainly take those measures if needed."

"Bah!' Galen spat. "You don't give a damn about Scarlett!"

"I do too," Blue argued, careful to keep her voice at a normal level. "She may be on my personal shit list but she is still a Jordan." She angled her face slightly towards his flickering form and lowered her voice. "And, more than that, I don't trust Blaylock. The Captain is just so...fragile right now. I'd been too selfish to realize it before I saw him today. Having Scarlett back will help him, I know. And I need someone on my side."

"Scarlett has never taken your side," Galen advised.

"She'll side with me before she sides with Blaylock. She hates him, more than the rest of us, impossible as that might seem. I don't know what happened between those two before we all met here on the Dragon, but it had to be something. Not only do they detest one another, but they watch each other like they are waiting for the knife in the dark. Waiting to turn it."

"Blaylock has served in the IGC since he was a snot-nosed cadet. He is next in command on the Dragon, why wouldn't you trust him?"

Blue shook her platinum hair, making the coils sway over her shimmering black flight suit. "He's up to something."

"What?"

"I don't know, but I know I don't like it."

As it turned out, Doc Westerson was available and Calyph got to work. Jordan Blue received a call from the Med Bay letting her know that they would be ready for her that evening at 1900 hours.

Blue, feeling celebratory, dined on crackers topped with

peanut butter accompanied by a glass of champagne.

"Classy," Galen remarked, watching the Jordan lick peanut butter from her fingertips before chasing it down with a swig of sparkling wine. He sat on the edge of her bed, gripping the edges.

"What can I say?" Blue asked with mock haughtiness. "I like nice things." She sighed and sat back in the solitary chair that graced her personal quarters on the Dragon.

"What is it?" Galen asked.

Blue looked at him, his form flickering like a bad, out of date holo. "What do you know about the triptych?"

"Nothing. I'd never heard of it until today. You?"

Blue shook her head. "Add it to the list of information that the IGC doesn't give out."

"Does it make you wonder?" Galen asked.

"What else they're not telling us?" Blue finished. Galen nodded, watching her carefully. She turned in her chair so that she was facing him. "Do you think Faith is right? Are they really just using me?"

The deceased doctor shook his head, his dark hair falling in front of his blue eyes in the same manner it had done when he was still alive. "I honestly don't know. I've never been involved in politics, other than defending you or myself when brought up on one charge or another."

Blue grunted, remembering the vid of Galen facing the pilot's tribunal on her behalf. She brooded in silence before finally pushing her chair back and standing up. She put two of her fingertips on the sparkling black eye patch as if checking to see if it needed to be adjusted, or simply reassuring herself that it was real. Her black-clad form shimmered and she fixed her single blue eye on Galen's ghost.

"I just don't know whom to trust," she admitted, "so for now, I think it's better that I don't trust anyone."

"Not even me?"

"Not even you. Sorry."

Galen opened his mouth to protest but was unable to utter a word before the Jordan had reached for the cuff on her wrist and cut the link. His flickering image disappeared in a blink.

Blue stood where she was a few moments longer, looking at the space where he had been. Finally, she shook her blonde head in an effort to clear it and headed for the infirmary where Doc Westerson and the ship's Engineer were already waiting.

They ushered her into a private sickroom with two narrow beds and a minimal amount of medical equipment where a male nurse took her temperature and poked a digital stethoscope under the neck of her black flight suit.

"Did you get Cyan's... material?" she asked Calyph.

He nodded. "I did."

"Did you hurt him?" she asked, her voice low and menacing, though the sudden change in her tone was instinctual rather than intentional.

Calyph gave her a look of exasperation. "Don't you think you would have heard him if I did?"

Blue sighed and nodded, offering a conciliatory smirk to the Engineer. "I guess so," she admitted.

The Doc gave her a welcoming grin as the nurse held a monitor behind her left ear, taking her blood pressure. "Good evening, Jordan," Westerson greeted.

"Evening, Doctor," she replied, watching the men move and edge around her in the small room.

The doctor looked at the nurse who nodded, silently giving him the okay on her vitals before tucking his gear into a nylon pack and leaving her alone with the Dragon's Chief Medic and Engineer. Westerson held out a hand, inviting her to lie down on one of the beds that had been specially prepared.

Blue took one look at the bed and her single blue eye

flashed back to him.

"You're going to strap me down?" she asked.

The Doc nodded. "Of course. We have never tried this on a person that has already had an established bond. We don't know what you are going to do or how you will react."

Blue narrowed her left eye at him, the flesh on her right cheek bunching under the sparkling black patch that she wore. "How do the new Captains usually react?"

Doc Westerson shrugged to show that the norm was less than exciting. "Usually a few spasms, some hyperventilating. Nothing to be alarmed about."

"But enough to tie me down," Blue finished.

The doc smiled warmly at the half-elf pilot. "I don't like to take chances and we are trying something new here, injecting a Jordan that already has formed a bond. Your reaction may be more severe, or it may be less because of it. All I know for sure is that the Jordans on this Dragon have proved to be highly unpredictable."

Blue gave him a smile and nodded. "Alright," she acquiesced, jumping up onto the bed and laying down. She settled in, trying to get comfortable while the medic fastened straps over her chest, arms and legs.

"Here you go," Calyph said as he handed the doc a syringe gun, the slender glass tunnel full of a swirling silver liquid.

"Is that his blood?" Blue asked, straining against the restraints to raise her head enough to see.

Calyph shook his head. "Not really but, for the lack of a better term, I guess you could call it that."

"What do you mean?" Blue asked, frowning.

Calyph tilted his head but kept his eyes fixed upon the swirling silver inside the glass tube of the gun. "It is very hard to compare Dragons to humans, or elves for that matter. They are as different from us on the inside as they are on the outside.

Just like you can't compare arms to wings – they may be in the same general spot on our bodies, but they are used for completely different things. Their veins and arteries don't even transport blood – they are inner tunnels used to transport food, meaning fuel or energy, transformed from starfire."

"It looks like mercury," Blue said.

Calyph snorted. "It would kill you for sure if it was."

Blue tore her eyes from the syringe to gape at him. "Then what is it?"

Calyph looked at her long enough to give her a smile that was half apologetic. "No one is really sure. It's not on either periodic chart – human or elfin."

Doc Westerson flicked the glass tube with a fingernail, checking for bubbles. Satisfied, he turned his muddy brown-green eyes to the Jordan on the bed. She had put her head back down on the small pillow but the medic noticed that, for the first time since he had known her, she looked a trifle nervous.

"Ready?" he asked.

"Are you serious?" she replied.

Westerson grinned and turned to the Engineer after he had tugged down on the straps, making sure they were secure. "Have you ever done this before?"

Calyph shook his sandy blonde hair emphatically in the negative. "You?"

The Doc nodded as he raised the gun. "I administered Captain Brogan's," he said, taking a moment to admire the metallic liquid that swirled inside the glass tunnel.

"Really?" Blue asked, bending her neck and leaning her head up again as far as the straps would allow.

"Really," Westerson assured her, gently pushing her back down. "And I was present on the Beryl Dragon for the injection of Captain Condliffe." He turned the gun and showed it to Calyph. "This point right here," he said, "can go against the inner bicep, right here, or on the outer side against the triceps muscle."

Blue took a deep breath while the men leaned down over her, talking and poking and demonstrating and observing.

Cyan, she thought, tuning them out. *In just a little while, I'm going to be closer to Cyan. That's not something I would ever mind.*

She felt the cold tip of the gun against her arm and she closed her eye. There was a pause long enough for the anticipation to nearly kill her and then a snap as the needle went home and a long, lonely second for her to wonder if anything was going to happen at all before her arm was filled with an ice so cold that it burned.

The Jordan sucked in a great breath of air as the cold raced for her neck, tightening everything it touched. Before her heart could thump another beat, every muscle and nerve spasmed in an agonizing wave that crashed over her. It squeezed her head in a painful vise and then shot down her body, filling every fiber and cell, making her shake. She opened her mouth to cry out but as she did her body was enveloped in cocooning warmth.

The feeling was familiar.

It was like the night not so long ago when she had scooped out her eye and Cyan had wrapped her in a light that took away the pain. This time, however, it was less of an anesthetic. The feeling brought an image to her mind of a mother wrapping her child in a blanket and holding her close. She knew it was the Dragon, reaching out to hold her, to comfort her, to protect her.

Her mouth was stretched open wide but, instead of a scream, Blue let out a long rush of air that was almost a sigh. Her lone eye rolled in its socket, wide and staring as Doc Westerson scribbled furiously on an acrylic with a plastic stylus, taking notes as fast as he possibly could. Calyph watched, fascinated, as the pupil of her single eye dilated, the round drop of black growing until it reached the edge of her iris, completely obliterating the sparkling blue.

The Jordan looked at the two men next to her, seeing them like she had never seen them before. She saw them as if through another's eyes – through a Dragon's eyes. Her freshly honed vision took them in down to the last skin cell and hair follicle, noting every detail, every strength and each vulnerability carried within their bodies since childhood. They looked so different, each so perfect and yet so frail.

Her eye finally travelled beyond them and the Jordan gasped at what she saw. Despite the fact that she had cut their com-link, she could see Galen sitting on the bed across from hers with his legs dangling over the side, his arms crossed and a playful smile on his full lips. And instead of the flickering ghostly image she was used to, her dead lover was as sharp and clear as the other live men in the room. His black hair hung over bright blue eyes that looked at her with a mischievous gleam.

"How are you feeling, Jordan?" he asked.

A slow smile spread across her face as she breathed in the room around her. "I feel ten feet fucking tall," she whispered.

Doc Westerson's brows went up and he nodded curiously as he continued to scribble. Before Jordan Blue could fully process what she was seeing, she became consumed by what she was hearing. She was acutely aware that she was hearing with more than just her ears. Sound seeped into her, filling her body and coursing through her blood, as if she were inside a giant bass and part of a great orchestra.

She closed her eye and focused first on the constant swooshing that filled her ears, accompanied by a variety of thumps so loud that she felt as if she had been loaded into a washing machine along with a pair of clunky flight boots.

"What is it Jordan?" Westerson asked, his voice as clear as a bell. "Can you vocalize this experience?"

"Heartbeats," she whispered. "I hear heartbeats!" She could hear the beat of her own heart, and those of the Fledglings. She could hear the sound of the Dragon's heart, and of the men in the room and… Galen!

Blue opened her eye in surprise. She could hear the sound from a heart that had been stopped months ago. As if reading her thoughts Galen smiled a little, but only with his mouth. His blue eyes stayed somber and earnest.

"My heart still beats for you, Jordan," he said.

Blue smiled back. "Like an eight-oh-eight," she whispered. Galen grinned and she turned her attention back to the sound of the heartbeats, absorbing them into her body like water into dry paper.

Unexpectedly, she found one that beat in time with hers. The feeling it brought gave her a mental image of a womb shared by fraternal twins.

"Scarlett," she whispered.

Calyph turned a shade paler and the chief medic went wild with his notes.

Softer, almost like an echo, she could hear another beat and she recognized it as the third sibling, the one that was lost.

No, she thought. *Not twins. Triplets.*

"Jade!" Blue shouted, closing her eye and arching her back. Her thin body, clad in its shimmering black flight suit, strained against the restraints that bound her as if she could leap from the bed and chase down the Jordan that had taken his life to save her own.

Failing the chase, she lay flat again and instead tried to reach out as far as her newly heightened senses would let her.

Jade! she called again, this time with her inner voice, her newfound Dragon voice, plumbing the depths of the universe as far as she could reach. She waited and though there was no answer she could feel him. At their present distance, he was merely an emerald glow on the edge of the horizon before he was lost in the sounds of every soul aboard the Dragon that rose like a cresting wave, deafening her.

It was over almost as soon as it had begun. Just as she had begun to truly hear, to really stretch out with her new senses, they were all snapped back into place. It was if an outside force had disturbed them.

The Jordan's eye popped open – as black and sparkling as the patch that covered the place where its mate had once been - searching, as her body quivered with premonition. The lights in the infirmary dimmed and the Captain's voice spoke from the overhead coms system.

"Doc Westerson?"

At the resonance of his commanding voice, her sense of sound - which had felt like a membrane that was being stretched further and further while steadily growing thinner and thinner – pulled in and flexed, like a muscle waiting to be used. For now, though, the voice of the Captain was the only sound she heard. Her pupil contracted to its normal size, shrinking in the dazzling sapphire of her iris.

Jordan Blue, back to the present and fully aware, turned her head to listen to the com. She couldn't help but notice that Galen still sat on the bed across from hers and that she could still see him in complete color and perfect clarity.

Calyph and the Chief Medic looked at the speaker vent on the ceiling – the tiny slits in the silver Dragon skin looked like gills.

"Yes?" Doc Westerson answered.

"If Jordan Blue is able, I need her to report to the bridge immediately. One of the moons of Jupiter is under attack." There was a pause as if the Captain was considering how much more he should say. The silence wasn't long. "The Lido moon."

There was a click as the Captain cut the communication. Blue's face turned to the doc and the Engineer.

"The Jordan Training Center," she said. "Get me out of here."

❦

Jeanette dropped her bags by Grandpa's door, more exasperated than tired.

"What's wrong?" Grandpa asked. "Are your books too heavy?"

Jeanette managed a lopsided grin. "Grandpa! I don't have books. Nobody carries books anymore!"

"Your acrylic, then," Grandpa said, remembering that the acrylic was the big thing that everyone was using these days, but his remark only bought a sigh from his dark-haired granddaughter.

"Mom and Dad won't let me have an acrylic," she said, less than pleased. "They say I'm too young."

"Then what is in there?" Grandpa asked, indicating the school bag that lay next to her dance bag.

"Just some old ass piece of plastic that a pre-schooler wouldn't use," Jeanette said with disgust. "It's totally outdated."

Grandpa leaned forward, his white brows pushing high into his craggy forehead. "Excuse me? I thought my hearing was getting better, but I know I did not just hear what I think I heard."

Jeanette sighed. "I said it was just the oldest piece of plastic," she said, annunciating her words carefully.

Grandpa pressed his wrinkled lips together and eyed her mistrustfully until she smiled and bounded up to him, kissing him on the cheek.

"Grandpa!" Jeanette admonished. "You have an acrylic that you never even use!"

Grandpa smiled guiltily. "I know. But that's only because it was a present and I don't know how to use it."

"Really?"

"Really."

"I could show you," she offered.

"Would you?"

"Of course!"

"That would be lovely my dear," Grandpa told her. "I actually got it out today, thinking maybe Sean could help me."

Jeanette made a face at the mention of her brother, but clapped her hands with delight when Grandpa produced the acrylic. It wasn't exactly new, but it was still in the box that it came in from the store, wrapped in a thin coat of plastic, which she promptly removed with a tiny fingernail and a deft hand.

Jeanette was excited to handle the fancy piece of technology and geared it up with ease. Her childish fingers danced upon the glass, quickly programming it with everything she thought Grandpa could use or would like. After she had demonstrated to him how to use the device, he laid it carefully on the kitchen table. He beamed proudly at his granddaughter and fixed her a snack.

"This is really good, Grandpa," Jeanette said as she sat at the table in the kitchen nook, her small feet hooked around the legs of the chair as she munched on the bread and cheese sandwich Grandpa had cooked in a pat of butter. Bright light came in through the windows and shone on her dark curls. "When did you start cooking?"

"The question isn't when I started, little Jean," he said, giving her wink, "the question is, when did I stop?"

"That *is* a good question, Grandpa. When *did* you stop? I don't remember you ever cooking before - so it must have been before I was born."

"That's right," he agreed. "It must have been." He made himself a cup of coffee and sat down at the table across from Jeanette. "It certainly has been a long time."

"Why so long?"

"It got too hard for me. I would burn one thing and another wouldn't get cooked enough. Most of all, I couldn't read directions on packages anymore." Grandpa let out a low chuckle. "Sometimes I would start cooking something and forget what I was doing." He threw back his head and cackled at the ceiling. "Your mother would get so mad! I think she was afraid I was going to burn down the whole building!" Grandpa cawed laughter at the memory. "Can't say I blame her."

Jeanette smiled and brushed the crumbs off of her mouth with a napkin. "So it was when my parents were married," Jeanette encouraged. "You were still cooking, but it was before I was born."

Grandpa looked surprised. "Why yes, I guess it was." Though his blue eyes were clearer than they had been in a long, long time, they became distant with memory. "And your mother was starting to get a belly, but not with you. "She was pregnant with your brother, which means that must have been about fifteen years ago."

That makes Sean fourteen or fifteen, Grandpa thought. *I'll be damned. I know how old that boy is.*

Jeanette regarded Grandpa with large, dark eyes. She cocked her head, making her dark curls bounce. "You seem a little different Grandpa," she told him.

"I do?" he asked, but before she could answer he nodded. "You're right, I am. I feel different," he said, running his tongue over the new teeth poking up from gums that had turned a firm, healthy pink over the last week or so.

He looked around the kitchen and noticed, though not for the first time, how much sharper his vision had become. "I am different," he declared softly, looking back at Jeanette before his blue eyes narrowed. "And I think your brother might have something to do with that."

Jeanette's eyes narrowed as well, though her lips curled down in mild disgust. "Maybe. He thinks he knows everything." Her lips turned up again in a sly smile. "But he sure doesn't."

Grandpa looked at her and smiled. "What is that supposed to mean?"

Jeanette smiled sweetly at him and laughed. "Nothing, Grandpa! Sean is such a big know-it-all these days, and everyone thinks I'm such a baby, but I'm not! I'm just as smart as Sean," she told him, her round face proud and defiant.

Grandpa smiled. She reminded him more and more these days of her Aunt when she was younger, always trying to one-up her older brother. In fact, he could remember little Joey being the same way as well.

Where had that finely honed competitive edge in their family come from? Had he ever been like that himself? Long ago, when his only child had been born? That child's mother certainly hadn't been. Even without his newly improved memory, Grandpa could remember her like it was yesterday. Everything about her had seemed like magic. Her dark hair and shy eyes and intoxicating scent and a voice that had been like music to his ears.

"I don't think you are a baby," he told Jeanette, pulling himself from his reverie and making her grin. "And I couldn't be more impressed by what you taught me today," he said, tapping a finger on the acrylic. "I can't wait to use it."

Jeanette stood up and gave Grandpa a peck on the cheek before zipping her plate through the cleaner by the sink and putting it back in the cupboard.

Grandpa noticed the skip in her step. It was just a little more than usual and it made him grin, showing the nubs of his teeth, both old and new. "I bet you have one of your out of this world questions for me today."

Jeanette laughed. "As a matter of fact, I do."

"Well, then," Grandpa said rising from his seat. "Let me get comfy in a softer chair. This one will make my butt sore if I'm in it too long."

Jeanette giggled and bounded into the living room and planted herself on the rug while Grandpa ambled in with his cup of coffee. He placed it on the wooden side table and eased himself down into his favorite chair.

"What it is you want to know today?" he asked.

Jeanette took a deep breath. "Where did all the people go?" she blurted. Grandpa frowned, making deep creases in an already creased brow.

"What people?"

Jeanette hid a giggle behind her hand. "The people on Earth, Grandpa," she said. "Who else?"

Grandpa gave an exaggerated shrug. "No one knows, sweetheart. All we know is that, one day, all communication with Earth was lost. Not just from here on Io, but on all the moons and all the ships. When an expedition was sent back to investigate, they searched the whole planet but they didn't find a soul."

"Was there a war?"

"It didn't look like it. There were no signs of destruction."

"Could it have been a biological war?" Jeanette asked, careful with her pronunciation. "Or disease?"

Grandpa shook his head. "There were no bodies. Not even animals. It was as if everyone just up and left, down to the last bug."

Jeanette rolled onto her belly and put her chin in her hand, her fingers curled in and pressed against her lips. "Was there anything out of the ordinary?" she asked. "Other than all of the missing people and animals, of course."

Grandpa tilted his head and thought for a moment, then nodded slowly. "Now that you mention it, I recall there was. I believe that there were reports of high radiation on certain parts of the planet."

Jeanette sat up. "So it could have been nuclear!" she

exclaimed, but Grandpa shook his head.

"Even if there had been a nuclear war or a nuclear accident, there would have been bodies. Or," he said shifting in his seat, remembering the nuclear accidents of the 2030s, "traces of bodies. Earth is just simply an empty planet. The only things that remain are what they built and left behind."

"Nothing else?" Jeanette asked.

"Nothing but mystery," Grandpa said, tapping his lip as he considered. "Those areas of high radiation, they would cool down to a safe level, and then spike up again about every five years. It's why Earth has been safe to visit, though not all places and certainly not when a radiation spike is expected. They usually let the planet cool and cycle for a year before they let the cruise ships in."

"So it is safe to visit, but not safe enough for people to return and re-inhabit," Jeanette finished softly.

Grandpa smiled at her and nodded. "That's right, sweetheart."

Jeanette let out a deep breath as if he had taken a great load off of her shoulders, but the scowl on her otherwise smooth brow told him that she still had lots to think about. He wondered, as he often did, what was going on in that head of hers.

"Well, Grandpa," she said, looking at the old-fashioned timepiece on the shelf by his books – he had taught her and Sean both how to read time from a real clock when they were both much smaller. "I better get going. I have dance class." She stood up and gave her Grandpa a great big hug and a kiss on his cheek, making him smile.

"I thought that wasn't for another hour!" he told her.

Jeanette laughed. "Your memory *is* getting better Grandpa!" she exclaimed. "Which is good, since you are remembering to shave everyday!" She gave him a big smile to show she was teasing. "I'm meeting some friends early today so that we can practice for the upcoming recital," she explained. "Thank you for the snack," she said, giving him another kiss on the cheek before bouncing out the door.

Grandpa smiled and planted an elbow on the arm of his chair, bringing his hand up to put a thumb under his chin while his fingers took up thoughtful residence over his wrinkled lips.

That girl sure makes me feel good, he thought. *About as good as the new medicine I have been taking.*

Thinking about the medicine made him think about the acrylic that Jeanette had skillfully set up and showed him how to use. One of the first things he planned on using it for was to look up, or 'ping' as little Jean had told him, what that medicine was. He already had a good idea of what it was doing to him.

He took a sip from his coffee and his eyes fell on the bag Jeanette had left by the door. It was black canvas with pink holograms of ballet shoes that danced along the sides.

Hmm, he thought with a frown, concerned that she might need the bag for her dance class. *Nah,* he decided. *She wouldn't have left it if she needed it. They probably have extras at the school.*

Grandpa sipped his coffee and thought about the new acrylic sitting on the kitchen table while he watched the pink shoes twirl and dance across the black fabric.

FROM

The Dream Journal of Hope

The stars turn, bright and far
Over the rise of the Galactic Bar
The Gunfighters are there
With their heads shaved bare
In an empty house a few doors down
The Assassin waits
The crosshairs of the laser are
A miniscule splash of blood on the wall.
Back and forth,
Third time I stand
The sights travel
Sparse furniture, the scape outside
Reflected within
He takes his time, he knows he has me
I take my time,
My last chance, last breath, last beat
And the hilt of my knife
Stands in his chest.
His gang gives chase, I do the front door trick
And hide in the closet
Footsteps pound and recede and
Just as a I sigh

Someone opens the door and
Johnny is there, with his close-cropped hair
Holsters as empty
As the scape outside
His eyes as blue
As my frozen heart
Stopped
In time.
He joins me in the confines
My heart leaps as he leans close
And whispers,
You are looking in the wrong place -
For the wrong key.

ONE SIX

As soon as Doc Westerson released the tabs on her restraints, Jordan Blue was up and bolting from the room. In the corridor, she dodged bodies that moved with dogged purpose as the Dragon wheeled its immense bulk through space in answer to the distress call from the IGC military base on Lido.

The Jordan moved with the speed and grace of a cat on a hunt. Her sleek, black-clad form darted down the hallway from the Infirmary as she made her way to the fore of the Dragon.

She was exquisitely aware of each muscle in each of her legs - the fast twitch fibers, the adenosine triphosphate feeding each myosin head as it slid past each actin protein, each one filled with silver Fledgling DNA as they contracted and released, propelling her with more power than she had ever experienced - still every movement felt effortless. She was conscious of all her senses, and yet she felt as if she were hardly using any of them.

Blue turned her head as she moved rapidly towards the bridge, feeling that someone was with her. Someone was, indeed. Galen kept pace next to her though he was hardly moving his legs and not avoiding anyone. Crewmembers seemed to go around him as they gave the Jordan a respectable amount of space.

Though most of her sharpened senses had subsided, most likely in her body's attempt to preserve sanity, Galen remained as large as life.

"You're still here?" she asked, managing to look both

pleased and annoyed simultaneously.

Galen grinned at her. "There's nowhere else I'd rather be," he confessed. Blue harrumphed and kept her pace smooth and even and quick, easily dodging anyone who did not see her coming.

"Can anyone else see you?" she asked after they had passed a group of mechs and pilots heading for Fighter Bay. The pilots had all moved deftly aside for her, but one had pulled his hand close to his body, as if to keep from touching Galen.

Galen shrugged. "I don't think so, but that doesn't mean that on a baser level they can't sense that I am here."

More to think about later, Blue mused, slipping like a piece of starry night from the hallway to the bridge.

When she arrived in the midst of it all she found the Captain in his chair at the helm, issuing orders left and right. It made her heart swell with confidence to see him acting like his old self. Sure and in command. The Jordan herself felt invincible. Her lungs felt as if they could expand forever, drawing in an endless supply of air. Feeling as if she was towering over everyone around her, Blue could have sworn that she was at least twice her height of four and a half feet tall.

The Jordan stood at attention close to her Captain, awaiting his orders. His face turned and, seeing her, it nearly split in half with an enormous, boyish grin. His grin made Blue smile in return and she lifted her chin, waiting.

"The moon of Lido is under attack," he informed her, his smile evaporationg as he donned the serious demeanor that the situation demanded. "We are the closest ship for response and, if I may say so, the most ready to counter. Are you ready?"

"Aye, aye, sir," Blue responded.

"Then get to your Fledgling, I want you to lead the offensive."

Ready to dash off once again as the Captain turned away, the Jordan's body jerked to a quick halt. "Sir?" she asked.

Brogan turned back to her, surprised. "Yes?"

"Shall I take both Fledglings?"

The Commander's face broke into a smile once again and he gave her a curt nod. "If you think you can, Jordan."

"Yes, sir," Blue turned and left the bridge at a brisk trot as the Commander turned to the pilot close by standing at attention and awaiting orders.

"I want you to follow with a single platoon, two by three. Have another platoon circle opposite and take up rear guard. Jordan Blue is the ranking officer and will lead the counter-offensive. Standard protocol applies for defense of the Dragon. "

"Yes, sir," the pilot boomed before hustling from the bridge as fast as his boots would take him.

Blue reached Fledgling Bay with Galen at her side. Given the current situation, the security team at the detfleck administered the fastest inspection she had ever been given.

"What about him?" she asked, jerking her head towards Galen.

The guard and the medic both looked around and then looked at her as if she might have gone mad.

"Who, ma'am?" the guard asked.

"My shadow!" the Jordan teased.

Both the medic and the guard uttered nervous laughter as she strode away, throwing them a wink with her single eye.

Strange, she thought, *I'm more real now, now that there is less of me.*

Blue headed for Cyan, her stride turning into a jog as she circled the Fledgling. A front section of his lithium and titanium side melted away as she approached, forming a door with a set of stairs leading down to the flight deck as a warm and welcoming voice filled the space between her ears.

Blue

The Jordan threw back her head and laughed as she ascended the stairs. "You know it!" she called out, entering the flight cabin as the steps rose and melded back into the Fledgling's side. Galen looked at her in the same manner the guard and the medic had just moments ago.

"Have you gone crazy?" he asked.

"Maybe," she acquiesced with a grin.

She dropped down into the pilot's seat as Galen settled down into the only other seat in the small cabin.

"I like that Calyph put a chair in here for me," he said. "That way I don't have to crouch behind you like a ghoul."

Blue grinned as she thumbed the controls on the dash. "I don't think it was for you specifically, but I'm glad it's there for you."

Jordan?

The sound that gently touched the inside of her head, both a respectful greeting and a question, came from the Fledgling that was not her own. She was delighted to find that their voices, though similar in nature, were as different as their personalities.

"Yes, Fledge," she answered, already knowing his question. "You're coming too." His response was warm satisfaction, like his brother's.

The Jordan ran a finger along the smooth metal skin of the console dash and over a band of pearlescent white, opening communications with the Dragon.

"This is Jordan Blue," she announced. "Do I have coms?"

"Jordan Blue, this is the bridge," she heard Darius reply. "You have coms. Stand-by for the Commander."

Brogan's voice filled the cabin. "This is Captain Brogan."

"Sir?" Blue asked. "Are the fighters ready?"

"They are, Jordan. I'm waiting for the Dragon to get us a little closer so you can fall as a group – I don't want you too spread out."

"Roger that, sir."

She glanced at Galen, who was grinning at her from the other seat. She wanted to say something to him, but she knew Brogan would hear. The Dragon crossed the distance easily, folding space and time like a child folding a napkin. The Captain's voice broke in a second later.

"Close enough. Take them in, Jordan."

"Yes, sir."

Jordan Blue reached her hands out in front of her and they were immediately filled with a fighter's wheel as it emerged from the dash. "Let's go boys," she said, guiding Cyan out of the bay door, Fledge following close behind as they dropped out into space. From the other side of the Dragon came a stream of deep-space fighter jets as they dove out of Fighter Bay.

The Dragon had already brought them within a double klick of Lido's atmosphere and Blue could see the battle that was unfolding within her quadrant of sight, an attack upon the last school she had attended. The most brutal and yet most elite school in the civilized galaxies.

The Jordan observed a small contingent of fighter craft, probably everything the Jordan Training Center had available, fighting off an offensive of Chimeran assault jets while an evacuation was being staged behind the line of fire.

Blue slid her finger along a band of gray light on her console dash, opening a wider communication line that included the fighters from the Dragon as well as the IGC ships already engaged in battle as they defended the Jordan Training Center base on Lido.

The group of jets that had come from the Dragon turned and flew in under the great belly of the ship and joined the Fledglings on the other side.

"Adrian?" Blue asked aloud. "Is that you on my immediate flank?"

"Yes ma'am," a deep, masculine voice answered.

"Good," Blue said, eyeing the fighters below as she readied the Fledglings to go down in steep dive. "I'm going straight in. I want you to take two squads, circle port, and attack from that side."

"Yes, ma'am."

Half of the group broke away and followed Lieutenant Adrian. The other half followed the Fledglings as they descended.

"J Leader!" Blue called, eyeing the lead jet engaged in the defensive. "This is Jordan Blue from the Opal Dragon."

"Welcome to the fight, Jordan," a warm voice said over the com. It was a voice that she would recognize anywhere.

"Jesus!" Blue exclaimed, breathless. "Sergeant Cormen, is that you?"

"The one and only!" he agreed heartily. Blue would have laughed with delight if not for the severity of the situation. He had been her favorite instructor at the Jordan Training Center. Probably everyone's favorite, but time for catching up would have to come later.

"Sergeant Cormen," Blue directed, "please disengage from the battle, wheel starboard and escort your evac."

"Yes, ma'am," the Sergeant cordially acquiesced. "Though, ma'am?"

"Yes?"

"I believe you owe me a beer."

Blue laughed, remembering the bet she had lost to Sergeant Cormen years ago. "I certainly do, Sergeant. Meet me in the Atrium tonight and I will buy one for your whole platoon. Consider it interest." Blue could hear his booming laugh over the com system, followed by the words issued to his platoon.

"Hear that, team? Complimentary cocktails in the belly

of the Dragon tonight. Let's just make sure we are all there."
There were muted exclamations of excitement as his platoon
of pilots concurred and wheeled to follow the instructor's jet
towards the section of the base under evacuation via large
troop carriers.

The Jordan watched them turn as one, her eye following the
attacking Chimeran jets that followed them to the left. "Now
Adrian," she commanded. "Go!" She watched as he took his
pilots down and attacked the Chimeran fighters from their
unprotected and unsuspecting right side.

The atmosphere of the terraformed moon lit up like an
outburst of fireworks as laser fire followed by explosions
tore apart the Chimeran jets that had tried to harry Sergeant
Cormen and his departing fighters.

"Marcolt?" Blue asked. Are you in command of the
remaining squads?"

"Yes ma'am," a voice answered from the lead jet of the
fighters that had stayed behind with the Fledglings.

"Stand fast until directed. I'm going in."

"Yes ma'am."

As Adrian's two squads of fighters tore apart the attackers,
Sergeant Cormen and his platoon guarded the flight deck that
was full of cadet pilots and instructors filing into the carrier
shuttles. Blue took Cyan and Fledge down past the evacuation
and went after the enemy fighters that were hell-bent on
destroying the JTC itself.

Fire hotter than any man-made laser rained down upon the
Chimeran jets that were strafing the buildings of the Training
Center. The Fledglings threw the Chimeran assault back with
acute violence and the enemy ships were scattered, thrown like
toys engulfed in flames. The fighters spun wildly through the
air only to crash against the surface of the moon, exploding on
impact and then exploding again as the jet fuel caught and let
loose, raining shrapnel on the moonscape.

"Marcolt?" Jordan Blue called.

"Yes, ma'am?"

"Assist Lieutenant Adrian and pick off any jets that might try to pursue the carriers that are high-tailing it out of here."

"Yes, ma'am."

Marcolt led the remaining fighters from the Opal Dragon towards the battle on the other side of the base.

The Jordan's glittering blue eye scanned the battle below. The Chimeran jets had lost more than just the offensive. Sergeant Cormen and his fighters had successfully guarded the evacuation that was nearly complete. Adrain had the Chimeran jets beaten and on the run. Now, Marcolt's team came streaming in to cover his flanks, decimating any that tried to escape.

Blue grinned at the fiery bedlam. It was her first battle with her Fledgling. Their first victory.

"Good job, Jordan," Galen told her. His voice was soft but Jordan Blue could hear the pride in it.

I can do this, she thought. *I can lead. Not just fly and fight, but I can lead.*

Visions of her sister's offer flitted through her head. Blue tried to push them away but the images of herself leading a squad of Fledglings, possibly even an astro-army of Dragons, persisted.

Maybe she is right, the Jordan measured for the first time. *Is the IGC simply using me for what I can do for them? Are they really tyrannical?* She touched the bottom of her eye patch gently, as she considered her situation. *If I am going to play my own game, I better find out.*

When she pictured Blaylock, and his obvious thirst for control and complete distaste for Jordan Scarlett despite what the woman had been through and how hard she had fought, Blue was sure that Faith had been right. The IGC was nothing but a conglomeration of self-serving power-hungry monsters.

But when she pictured Captain Brogan, she refused to believe it.

Shaking her head, she began pulling up on Cyan's wheel as she turned him starboard to follow the evac carriers when she felt a sharp pang of distress from Cyan and Fledge, their voices filling her head with warning at the same time Galen began shouting.

"Your right, Jordan! On your right!"

Blue pushed the wheel as far it would go, diving before she gave it a sharp turn and pulled it towards her chest, circling up and back. Two Chimeran fighter jets were diving towards her on the right, firing as they closed the distance.

She jerked Cyan to the left and Fledge followed as if he was his shadow. Unnerved for only a second, the Jordan regained her composure at once and risked a glance at Galen in the seat next to hers.

"Having trouble seeing on your right side?" he chided.

"Fuck you," Blue snapped, circling the Fledglings around for attack. Galen looked at her, shocked.

"Don't be mad at me!" he scolded. "I'm not the one who plucked out your eye!" Though Jordan Blue was looking forward, her smirk was not lost to him, nor was her acid tone.

"Not this time."

"Hey!" Galen shouted, offended. Blue dove and swerved through atmosphere of Lido, trying to gain an advantage over the fighters that were pursuing her. Galen didn't seem to care about the pursuit. "Nor was I the one to put a lit Lethe pipe in your face!"

"That's not fair!"

"You started this!"

Blue's single eye widened and she turned to stare at him. "Now?" she demanded. "Now? We're having our first fight *now*?"

The Jordan led the Chimeran fighter jets out of the thin atmosphere and into the black beyond. They had no chance of catching her, and their laser fire was easily evaded now that she was aware of them, but she was having a damnable time trying to gain the upper hand.

"Screw it," she said. "Fledge, I want you to..."

Before she could say another word, the Fledgling shot off into the dark, leaving behind a trailer of crimson light that quickly faded away.

"Did he just leave?" Galen asked as he stared through the hyper-glass that served as Cyan's eyes, their argument temporarily suspended.

"No," Blue said, effortlessly dodging the fire from the ships behind them. "He just knew what I wanted before I could finish what I was saying. Or Cyan did and let him know. I'm not sure – I'm still figuring some of this shit out."

Galen, his anger diminished but still smoldering, turned back to Blue to finish their quarrel, not caring that they were in the midst of a firefight. Before he could speak, however, Fledge came racing back towards them. The Jordan pushed Cyan into a dive as Fledge raced over them and unleashed Dragon-fire on the ships behind.

The enemy fighters were instantly reduced no more than melted lumps of steel, glass, and bits of plastique that were now condemned to wander senselessly through zero gravity for the rest of time.

"I know it's not your fault," the Jordan admitted in a bitter tone, frowning and pulling Cyan around in a wide turn. "I just can't help being mad at you."

"For what?" Galen demanded. "Dying?" Blue gave him a small shrug as she opened fire on the smoldering remains of the Chimeran jets, just for good measure. Galen, for the first time since he had been dead, was obviously angry.

"Well I'm sorry I went and died!" he said, his voice rising to a shout. "Trust me, if I could have done it differently - I would have!"

Blue took the Fledglings down in a brutal plunge, leaving the flaking remainders of the Chimeran ships in their wake. She pulled them out of their dive once they had reentered the atmosphere of Lido and banked to follow the transport shuttles and their escorts from the JTC as well as those from the Dragon. She let go of the wheel and it sank back into the dash panel. Blue sighed and turned to face the ghost next to her.

"I'm sorry," she apologized. "I still don't know how to handle this. It's why I kept you cut off. I am trying to figure this IGC shit out on my own and deal with your death at the same time. I'm doing a shitty job at both!"

Galen's scowl melted into an expression of infinite patience and concern.

"You're not doing a shitty job," he said softly. "You are learning to cope. It's not easy and I sure don't like it either. But if it came down to you or me, I'm glad it was me."

Tears ran down the Jordan's face, from her left blue eye as well as from underneath the black eye patch that she wore over the right socket. She guessed that the tear ducts hadn't been cauterized.

"I'm sorry," she said. "I'm so sorry."

Galen held out a hand and she pushed herself out of her seat and onto his lap, falling into arms that were as real to her as they had ever been. They encircled her body, holding her close and tight and warm.

The pilot's seat shifted away and the chair that held only a ghost before, elongated as Cyan made sure there was enough room for both of them.

"Don't be sorry," Galen whispered into her golden-white hair. He closed his eyes, his black hair falling over his face. "You have nothing to be sorry about. We're together. That's all that matters."

The Fledglings followed the evacuation of the Lido moon, silent guards to those loading into the carriers, before escorting the fighter jets back to the Dragon.

ONE SEVEN

For the Chimeran Operations Officer, Jasyn Issord, the day started off like any other day. He spent the day at the villa of Faith de Rossi like he most always did. At the far edge of his senses he could feel the storm rage around him. The anger at her being gone once again was like a burgeoning thunderhead and he ignored it the best he could. He closed his mind against the feeling the way a person would close the windows during a particularly heavy bout of rain. The Chimeran did not know that the impending storm was as dangerous as a class three hurricane, about to carry him away. Moreover, even if he had known, he probably would not have cared.

For once, he was not plotting Faith's death or his own escape – something that had filled his early days when she was gone. Those thoughts subsided as the weeks went on, refueled only by his anger when she would leave, usually inciting him to renew his vows to see her destroyed.

But the only thing he was plotting this night was dinner. Faith had been gone for many days on her current trip and was coming back even later than she had promised. The thunderhead, for now, was on the horizon – his anger quelled by the excitement that she would soon be home.

He had been to the kitchen to see Cook, who had been told by Mari that Faith was on her way and would be arriving within the hour. He would have asked Mari directly, he had quickly learned that Mari was the one that directed the entire household, but he always seemed to make the woman terribly nervous. Cook usually knew just as much and was easier to talk to.

"I would like to take Faith out for dinner tonight at a restaurant in the Commons," he advised Cook. "There is one where the tables are in a garden and Tom says that at night there are little lights that are strung above the patio."

Cook, who had been pounding at a long cut of meat in between two thin sheets of plastic, stopped long enough to give the construct a warm smile. "I think that is a fine idea," she said.

"But," Jasyn added, "you might want to have something ready to make in case she is too tired to go out."

Cook grinned and winked at him. "I always do."

Jasyn smiled and went to the bedroom to get dressed. He walked into the enormous closet and selected his favorite suit, since he knew it was the one that Faith liked best, and dressed himself in front of the full length mirrors.

He went back into the bedroom and, since he did not yet hear the commotion that would announce her arrival, sat down in the wing chair next to the bed and thumbed on his acrylic. Barely five minutes later, as he had just only begun to browse the games and current players, the din of activity descended the villa's central lift. Seconds after the sound of commotion that always preceded Ms. de Rossi's arrival, Faith entered the bedroom.

She sighed and smiled at him as he rose from his chair, though she did not look happy. He tossed his acrylic down and came straight for her, his lips already parting in anticipation. He wrapped her in his arms and kissed her, his body flooding with a warmth that had alarmed him in he beginning. Now the feeling was familiar and welcome.

"I missed you," he said.

Faith kissed his lips and then his cheek. "I know," she sighed. "I missed you too." She pressed her forehead against his, closing her eyes, and when she spoke again her words came out in a rush. "I have bad news - I can't stay." Jasyn pulled his head away.

He blinked at her in surprise and then frowned, feeling the heat rise in his cheeks. "You can't stay? What do you mean?"

"I'm sorry, I was supposed to be home this morning."

"I know."

Faith paused, struck by the tone of his voice. "Now I only have a few minutes," she apologized. "Mostly just for Mari and Penny to pack the craft for my trip."

"Do you have time for me?" he asked, wrapping an arm around her waist and giving her a sly smile as he gave her a gentle tug towards the bed.

Faith kissed him and shook her head, carefully disengaging herself from his embrace. "Not this time." She turned and walked towards her vanity.

Jasyn's fists clenched.

Control, he warned himself, though he could not remember ever having to exert so much effort to manage his emotions before. *You can control your feelings,* he assured himself, forcing his hands to unfold though he was far from relaxed. In fact, the more he fought for control, the more he felt it slipping away. *Why am I the only one that has to control their feelings?* he thought, his anger spiking. *It's not fair!*

His hazel eyes narrowed to slits, he watched Faith open a drawer in the vanity and something occurred to him. *Do I have any control over what she feels?* His eyes followed her movements, noting how tense her body was, her face drawn and tight. *She's not that stressed about work. She has been living and breathing meetings and schedules for more than a century. She is anxious because of me. My response is what triggers her response.* The realization replaced the anger with a feeling he couldn't identify, but it was as sensual as it was aggressive.

"I could make you, you know," he said.

Faith, who was bent slightly at the waist as she retrieved a necklace from the drawer, froze. She turned slowly to face him as she straightened, drawing herself up. Jasyn could see hectic patches of color, high on her cheeks. "What do you mean by that?"

He walked slowly towards her until their bodies were almost touching.

Slowly, very slowly, Jasyn brought his head down and touched his lips to one of the stars of color that had blossomed on her cheekbone. He brushed his lips along her face, following her pulse down the line of her jaw until he reached the side of her throat and gently kissed the soft skin under her ear. He let his lips slide down her neck and in the same way kissed the left side of her throat. He let his face fall until it met her shoulder.

His hand came up and his thumb gently touched the hollow of her throat before his fingers spread out and slid down to graze over her right breast. Her back began to arch and he brought his other hand up around her back and rested it firmly against the base of her spine so that she couldn't back away.

She leaned towards him but he pulled away just enough to keep their bodies from touching.

He could hear a small sound escape her throat and she pushed against him, seeking his mouth with her own and, again, he pulled away just a bit.

She wrapped her arms around him and pulled their bodies close and tight. "Okay, smartass," she breathed, "you were right. You *can* make me." He laughed softly, burying his face in her neck and kissing it.

Victory! he thought, elated, hoping that it meant she would stay.

"But this time you might have bitten off more than you can chew."

Jasyn, surprised, leaned back so he could see her face. "Meaning?"

Faith took a long look at him without answering and he

could tell that she was struggling with something.

Maybe she has a storm of her own, he thought for the first time.

Faith removed her arms from his waist but he kept holding on to her. She thumbed the gold cuff she wore around her wrist and brought it up to her mouth. "Penny?"

"I'm right here," Penny said as she pushed open the doors of the bedroom and walked inside, attended by one of her own aides and headed for the closet.

Faith ran her fingers under the collar of Jasyn's shirt and spoke to Penny without looking away from his face. "Pack Jasyn's things. He's coming with me."

Penny's brisk walk through the room stuttered to a stop and a slight choking sound preceded her voice. "I beg your pardon?"

Faith smiled. "He's coming with me. And he'll need a tux. No, two tuxes, if memory serves. Also a casual suit and whatever Charity is insisting on for the dance."

"Ma'am?" Penny asked, though it sounded more of a command than a question. "The soonest I could get a delivery would be in half an hour and we are already running behind schedule..."

Faith turned her face so that she could see her assistant and her smile pulled down at the corners of her lips, though it stayed lit behind her eyes. "Then I suggest you hurry."

"Yes ma'am," Penny answered as she broke into a brisk trot, motioning for her aide to follow quickly.

Faith turned her tawny eyes back to Jasyn's face as a flustered Penny issued commands from the dressing room. Mari came bustling in to help.

"Where are we going?" he asked.

Faith snaked her arms back around his waist and gave him a quick kiss. "To a party," she told him.

"Penny seems a bit frazzled over just a party."

Faith buried her face in his neck. She let the tip of her nose slide up to his ear. "It's a ball that Charity throws every two years," she said, her voice low. "It's held at her home, the Last Castle on the Distant Shore, and lasts for three days. Every head of the InterGalactic Council and a few notorious socialites that managed to pull some real heavy strings will be there. It's quite an event."

Jasyn pulled back slightly so that he could see her face, thinking that she might be joking. "That *is* quite an event," he admitted. "Are you sure that you want to take me to something like that?"

Shut up shut up shut up, he shouted inwardly at himself. *Just go. Shut up and go.*

Faith reached up to run her fingers through his thick, dark hair. "I'm not just *taking* you," she told him. "I want you by my side the entire time."

Jasyn's mouth dropped open and, closing it quickly, shook his head slowly from side to side. With some difficulty, he swallowed.

"Are you sure?" he asked again. It was not beyond him to understand what his presence at her side at could mean, especially at such an important event.

SHUT UP! Stop talking. You need to be there.

"It's time," Faith said, her voice quiet but firm. She kissed him one more time before pulling away. "I would rather change before we go, and freshen up a bit. Why don't you go let Penny brief you on what to expect over the next three days and board the craft. I'll get dressed and we should be ready to leave as soon as your clothes get here. You can change once we're spaceborne."

"Alright." He gave her a quick peck on the cheek and regarded her for a few moments without saying anything.

Don't say anything stupid. Just say thank you and get the

hell out of here before she changes her mind.

He smiled. "Thank you," he whispered before giving her another kiss and leaving to brave whatever storm Penny had brewing for him.

He walked from the room and closed the door behind him, making a mental effort to slow his breath and bring down his heart rate.

It wasn't easy.

At long last, the Chimera would know where to find Charity de Rossi, like they now knew where to find her older sister. Jasyn was already aware of the event in question – it was the same one that Charity hosted every other year and in attendance would be every living person of importance in the GwenSeven Corporation along with every head of state and high official in the InterGalactic Council. The means and ability to crush GwenSeven was finally within reach.

The problem now was that Jasyn was torn. The storm rushed over him and he leaned into it, lifting his chin in exhilaration as he turned his face to the wind.

The Chimeran Operations Officer patiently endured the haste in which he was rushed about, a small smile in the corner of his mouth as he watched Penny send in measurements and pictures to get him a fitted tuxedo and other clothes for the party. He could see how much it frustrated the PA and was inwardly delighted at her inscrutable effort not to let it show.

When Penny was done, he was escorted onto Faith's personal spacecraft and, seeing it for the very first time, barely had time to glance about in surprise before he was instructed to take a seat.

Faith's craft, from what he could see, was a smaller version of her villa.

The enormous cabin he had entered was a perfect mirror of the living room, with thick, white sherpla skin rugs on black marble floors, white sofas and chairs, and a refreshment bar along the wall that separated the room from the kitchen. Penny pointed to a white, leather wing chair and he sat down obediently, watching the staff move about in what looked like a barely controlled frenzy of activity.

A man that he had never seen before came down from the upper level and at first Jasyn thought he must be part of Geary's security contingent. But the man was dressed differently than the usual suit worn by de Rossi security and a bit older than any agent he had seen so far, with a slighter build and dark hair just going gray at the temples. After a quick look around, he went straight to the construct and introduced himself as the Captain of the spacecraft.

He welcomed Jasyn aboard, let him know how fast they would be traveling and when they were expected to reach their destination. He showed the construct how to fasten his safety webbing and wished him a comfortable journey before he joined a group of crewmembers and began speaking in hushed but urgent tones.

Jasyn watched him go in amazement, realizing that the Captain was the first person, other than Faith or possibly Tom, to really treat the construct as if he were another person rather than another person's plaything. Even Tom, however, treated him like a child. A smile quirked up the corner of his mouth and Jasyn turned his head just in time to see Faith enter the cabin.

She moved her eyes from one person to the next, giving orders quietly as she walked gracefully through a swirling mess of assistants, staff, and flight crew. Jasyn felt a sharp tug deep within his body, making both his heart and groin ache painfully.

Instead of the crisp business suit or smart caftan she usually favored, Faith wore a short, black cocktail dress that shimmered and sparkled, throwing the lights of the craft off of her body as if she were a piece of polished jet. It made Jasyn think of her pool, inky black with the flicker of a billion distant suns.

And holding a secret.

The thought rose, unbidden in his mind, as his thoughts often did.

An important secret.

Then her eyes found his and she moved towards him like a magnet drawn to iron ore. And he, like an iron filling, felt as if he was being drawn towards her, held down only by the safety webbing that was pulled snug over his hips.

Her hair was swept up and held by back by gems that glittered like stars in the firmament of her gold and brown locks. It exposed her neck, graceful and lovely, adorned with a necklace of small, polished onyx links. The black chain sparkled like her dress. Like her pool.

Mari said something to her before hurrying off of the craft but Jasyn could see that Faith wasn't paying attention to anyone but him. Penny ushered in a man with a number of boxes, led him through a door that in the villa would lead to Faith's bedroom, and then ushered him out again, sans boxes. She brought Faith a small, sparkling comset on a silver tray just as she was about to sink into the chair next to Jasyn.

Faith took her seat and hooked the comset over her ear without taking her eyes off of her companion. The Captain's voice came over the intercom to let everyone know that they were clear for departure. Everyone remaining on board moved quickly to take their seats and check their restraints. The crew attendants signaled the bridge once everyone was secure and the door to the craft slid closed.

There was a hiss of airlocks and a slight rocking as the craft disengaged from the villa, followed by a few seconds of drifting silence as they created a safe distance from the satellite city and amassed their momentum. Then the room tipped, tilting slightly as the floor rose towards aft as the jet shot out into space like a boat cresting a wave. Unlike the villa, the furniture in the craft was bolted to the floor for just this reason. Three seconds later, the down compression found its medium and put the room and its occupants into a normal, if artificial, gravity.

There was a series of clicks and snaps and the craft was once again full of people moving all about. Penny was at Faith's side in an instant.

"We have coms," she announced quietly. "Mr. Canley has first, do you want to take the call?"

Faith sighed and nodded. A second later the sparkling wire over her ear was slushing out punctuated sounds of quiet conversation from light years away.

"I'm terribly sorry, Mr. Canley," Faith said, her eyes unfocused and downcast, "but that is an issue you would need to broach with Charity."

She looked up and caught Penny's watchful eye. A glance passed between the two and Penny nodded and moved away quickly. Faith looked away, returning to her conversation as a steward appeared, placing two fluted glasses on the slender table nestled between Faith and Jasyn's chairs. Another steward appeared with a bottle of champagne and a magnetic chill bucket.

Jasyn watched with interest as Faith's brown and gold eyes, far away with her conversation, suddenly focused on the present as the corked popped from the bottle of champagne. They lost focus again immediately as she returned to her obligatory object of communication.

"I am sure that you are, Mr. Canley, but this is one area where I have no jurisdiction." She laughed apologetically and said good-bye. She glanced at Penny who gave her the identity of the next caller as she passed by on her way to the galley. Faith touched the side of her comset and was engrossed in another dialogue within moments.

Jasyn's lips parted as he watched her speak, feeling the storm build around him, breathing it in. He was on his way to a vital location in the Revolution and would have access to take down any and, if he played his cards right, *every* player that opposed The Cause. He could change the tide of the war – he could make history. It wouldn't take more than a bit of careful planning and a few crucial moves.

The strap of Faith's dress fell to the edge of her shoulder as she shifted in her seat, making the Chimeran's breath hitch to a stop. He bit his lip and took a controlled breath as his hazel eyes traveled over her body.

He could not remember seeing so much of her skin, outside of the bedroom of course, and even in there it was always dimly lit. His eyes ran down the line of her neck and over the smooth curve of her shoulder. Her arms were bare and he was overcome with an urge to reach out and touch them with his fingers or his lips. The strap of her dress seemed so thin and fragile, so powerless to hold up the sparkle of black that clung to and covered such a small part of her body. It held a precarious balance at the top of her arm, threatening to jump.

Champagne was poured and an attendant proffered the filled flutes on a silver tray. Jasyn took one and waited for Faith. She took hers almost absently and then, seeing that he too was holding a glass of the golden sparkling wine, touched the rim of her glass to his.

The glasses kissed with a musical chime and he drank from his, never taking his eyes off of the woman next to him. She watched him for a second, then sipped from her own glass and looked away again. She continued her conversation though Jasyn could tell that it no longer had her attention.

He smiled into his glass as he took another sip before he set it aside, placing it on the small table between their chairs. His dark eyes trekked over the line of her black dress to where it came to an abrupt halt on her mid-thigh. Her skin was perfect – smooth and slightly freckled.

As if sensing his gaze, she crossed her legs, though it only made the dress ride up higher on her thigh. Jasyn turned his face away and studied the bubbles rising in the glass on the small table. When he turned back, his eyes again sought out the strap of her dress. His mind quickly calculated the average amount of threads needed to make it, and how much pressure it would take to snap them.

His eyes rose to the line of her jaw and then slipped down her neck to the curve of her breast where it disappeared into the top of the dress. Feeling his heart rate begin to pick up speed, again he had to look away. This time Faith caught him – both looking at her and looking away – and the corner of her mouth quirked up in a smile.

Jasyn silently laughed and cursed himself. Here he was, so close to the head of GwenSeven that he could grab her and tear her to pieces before her security team even knew what had happened, but the only thing he wanted to tear apart was her dress.

The Chimeran Officer knew that he should be mentally preparing himself for the evening, going over every possible option that might be of use to The Cause. Yet all he could think about was kissing Faith's mouth, smelling the skin over her throat, touching her in the places the black dress covered, places where only he could touch. His gaze fell again to the smooth expanse of her skin where it plunged into the neckline of shimmering black. Realizing that his jaw was beginning to hang open, he snapped it shut and looked back again to her face.

His eyes met hers and he saw that he had her full attention. She made a few, soft excusing remarks to the person on the other end of her com-link and then killed the connection without so much as a good-bye. She pulled the glittering device off of her ear and regarded him coolly. She reached over and laid a hand upon his knee, and he felt a current run through his entire body.

Her gold and brown eyes were bright with amusement and her own lips were parted, her breathing deep and irregular. She re-crossed her legs and took a sip of the pale-gold liquid in her glass.

The bustle of the crew and staff went on around them, oblivious to the evolving energy he could feel coalescing about their bodies, pulling them together.

Faith signaled for Penny and the PA was at her side in an instant. She held out the comset, her eyes never leaving Jasyn's face.

"Are Jasyn's clothes here?" Faith asked.

"Yes," Penny answered, taking the comset and placing it in a polished box lined with golden velvet. "Everything he should need for the trip is boxed and waiting on the bed in your bedroom."

Faith smiled. "Why don't you go get dressed?" she asked. "It's a long way but we'll close the distance quickly in this ship, no more than a couple hours. We should be ready when we get there."

Jasyn ran his knuckles down her bare arm. "Why don't you come help me?" he suggested, his eyes dark and shining.

Faith's smile widened as she considered the idea. "Because the plan is to get you dressed. Not to get both of us undressed."

Jasyn thought the second idea was more appealing but he knew that he was not in a position or a place where he could argue. It didn't bother him. Knowing now that he might have more control of his situation than he had previously thought, he decided that he might make her pay for it later. He undid his safety webbing and gave Faith a peck on the cheek as he rose and headed for the door that, in the villa, would lead to Faith's bedroom.

"Black box, silver ribbon," Penny advised him as he passed by.

Jasyn gave her a nod and, letting himself through the door, he found that it *was* her bedroom - just a smaller version of the one back at the villa, and minus the vanity, of course. There could only be one mainframe.

He looked through the boxes on the bed and selected the

black one with the silver ribbon, finding that it held the most formal looking suit he had ever seen. He undressed and tossed his clothes on the edge of the bed, wishing he was in it with Faith, and donned the pants and shirt. Standing in front of the bathroom mirror, he was almost done with the tie when a thought occurred to him. He undid the tie and went to the door and stuck his head out.

"Penny?" he called.

The PA regarded him for a moment without moving, her brown eyes round and questioning behind their square black frames, before turning them to Faith. Faith only shrugged and Penny, after straightening her skirt and tucking her acrylic under her arm, joined him in the bedroom.

"I don't know how to tie it," he lied, indicating the oddly shaped strip of black cloth hanging around his neck.

Penny pressed her lips together in a thin line and, after tossing her acrylic on the bed, went to work on his tie. Jasyn fought to keep his smile apologetic and simple. Even with his abnormal amount of control, it wasn't easy.

Penny finished with the tie and attempted to give him a look of mild disgust but even the tight-lipped PA realized that he looked too good. Instead she gave him a smirk and gathered up her acrylic and left without ever saying a word to him.

Jasyn pulled the jacket on over his shoulders and took a look in the mirror, straightened the tie, smoothed down the fabric of the suit and gave the bed one last longing glance before he rejoined Faith and the others in the main cabin.

Faith smiled at him approvingly as he retook his seat. "You look amazing," she whispered, reaching over to squeeze his arm.

"Not as much as you do," he whispered back, laying a hand over her thigh.

"I know, I don't dress up very often. But, thank you."

"You might be overdressed," he told her. "Maybe we should

go back to the bedroom," he suggested. "You could change out of that dress."

Faith laughed softly. "We don't have time," she told him.

"I will go as fast as I can," he promised.

Faith laughed, a bit louder this time, though they were politely ignored by everyone moving around them. "Then where's the fun for me?" she asked.

"I'll show you."

Faith laughed again and placed a hand over his, the one that was making its way up her thigh. "I'm sure you would," she agreed, though she made no move for the bedroom.

Jasyn sighed and shook his head, though it was all in good humor. As much as he wanted her, he knew that to ruin how perfect she looked would be a crime – at least before the time was right.

The rest of the trip was quick and uneventful. Faith was just finishing her second glass of champagne, signing Penny's acrylic time and again, when the Captain came on again over the com, letting the passengers know that they would be starting their deceleration within the next few minutes.

There was a flurry of activity once again and, as Jasyn was trying to calculate how far they had gone in just a few hours, the craft had landed and they were being fussed over as aides and stewards helped them undo their safety webbing and rise to their feet. They were brushed off and cooed over before they were ushered from the main cabin and Officer Issord found himself staring down a set of metal stairs with his jaw agape as he looked up and took in the home of Charity de Rossi.

He had no idea what to expect, but he never would have expected what he saw. Castle could mean anything, from a fortified fortress to a simple home that was loved with intensity. A military base, a home for nobility, or the domain of a feudal lord. Here, for Charity de Rossi, it was all of these things.

Small, rolling hills of manicured lawns, hedges and gardens rose and rose and rose to support a fairy-tale castle that stretched up and into the night sky in a brilliant burst of color. A thick curtain wall joined squat towers that had been raised for defense while it encircled more refined and delicate structures, toped with conical roofs and coupled by graceful bridges.

Officer Issord pulled his gaze away from the glowering magnificence on the rise to be sure of his footing as he descended the stairs. As he reached the ground he saw the elongated glass globe that was their car, hovering half a meter above a road of shaved verge. Geary was holding a door open for Faith, also holding one of her hands to steady her as she carefully climbed into the carriage. He closed the door.

"Jasyn!" Geary barked at him before he circled the car and opened the door on the other side. Jasyn hastened to keep up and then stopped – never before had Geary held a door open for him. Trying not to look as confused as he felt, he ducked inside the car and seated himself next to Faith on the blue velvet bench inside the small cabin. The sharp-eyed head of security dipped his head inside and pinned Jasyn to his seat with his steely gaze. "Keep her safe," he ordered through his teeth. Jasyn's reply was so automatic that it surprised himself as much as Geary.

"Yes, sir."

Geary shut the door and the car slid forward, accelerating quickly. Jasyn craned his neck to look back, more surprised than ever. He could see Faith's ship now from the outside; smooth white beryllium shaped like a diamond with rounded corners. On the ground; her obviously displeased head of security, frowning as he glared at the moving car. As he dwindled into the distance behind them Jasyn turned his hazel eyes to Faith.

"He's not coming with us?" Jasyn asked.

"No, only guests are allowed at the party." Faith had a

bemused smile tucked into the corner of her mouth. "You have me all to yourself." Jasyn unsuccessfully tried to keep the shock from his face.

"No Penny? No Geary?"

Faith shook her head, her smile widening. "They will be there, just not with us. Geary will keep an eye on us via security monitors and he and Penny will both be available over a com-link, but Charity is extremely strict on keeping her parties personal. Besides, these affairs are already crowded. If everyone there had their personal security detail at hand, or even just their aides, there would be no room."

Geary's last words settled over him, along with the enormity of the situation. The knowledge that Faith was unprotected, more vulnerable than she had ever been, sank sharp fangs of fear into him and he realized that his reply had been genuine. He would keep her safe.

His eyes were drawn to the castle and he opened his mouth to speak – intending on extracting information in the way he always did - when he realized the castle was lit with the colors of the rainbow.

"Seven," he said softly. "There are seven colors in the rainbow," realizing it for the first time.

"Yes, there are seven."

Just like the colors of the Fledglings in the New Year of the Dragon, he thought. *The same as the number in your company. Seven.* Something about that thought nagged at him but Faith was talking so he pushed the thoughts away in order to pay attention.

Half a dozen valets waited in the brightly lit porte cochere to assist them out of the conveyance. As soon as they had shut the doors on the car it moved away on its own, disappearing down the lane of close-cropped grass.

Jasyn escorted Faith into the castle, almost freezing in mid-stride when she told him that they were going through a body scan, even though it would show nothing out of the ordinary. They already knew he was manufactured. Then he waited in barely controlled panic as a polite and deadly looking Asian assassin subjected him to a gel scan since he had no idea what it might reveal. It seemed to show nothing, since the only jolt he received was from the man welcoming him as Mr. de Rossi.

There was a sizzling smell of ozone as the wall of detfleck sprang to life behind them and he and Faith walked into the party of the era. All eyes turned their way and the Chimeran Officer felt his chest swell with pride, not because he was there, but because of the woman on his arm. Within moments their hostess, Charity de Rossi, accosted them with her usual flair.

Jasyn found himself greeting her with a smile, amazed at how different he felt about the woman since he had last seen her. He took Charity's hand and lightly kissed the back of her fingers. "Ms. de Rossi," he acknowledged.

Charity laughed. "Jasyn!" she admonished. "You know you can call me Charity, we're old friends!"

Jasyn found himself wearing much the same smile that Faith often wore – slightly secretive and tucked into one corner of his mouth. Faith slipped her arm back inside the bend of his elbow and they followed Charity as she led them through the parting crowd, chatting at the pair from over her shoulder.

Jasyn and Faith followed the glamorous figure and vapid conversation of their hostess through stone-walled rooms full of ancient art that were hung with priceless tapestries, weaving between crowds of important people whose eyes fell heavy and silent upon them, transforming into surprised looks and excited whispers as they passed.

Charity brought the couple to an abrupt halt and introduced them to a small group of people - two men and one woman, all holding drinks. The men couldn't be more different, though they both looked pleased to see Faith. One was tall and thin and gray-haired with blue eyes just beginning to cloud with age. The other was trim and athletic with salt and pepper hair and flashing dark eyes. The woman was bird-boned with a long, stern face.

Jasyn didn't know if the woman had looked so dour before their arrival but she certainly was less than pleased now.

"Ms. de Rossi," she greeted before she promptly walked away.

Charity laughed, dismissing her with a wave of her jeweled fingers. "Here she is!" she exclaimed to the two gentlemen, indicating Faith as her bedecked hand swept back around. "Safe and sound!"

"Ms. de Rossi," the older one greeted with a broad smile and a short bow. "How good it is too see you, and see you looking so happy!" Jasyn liked him already.

"Faith!" the other exclaimed, taking her elbow and leaning in to kiss her cheek. "I'm glad you made it."

"Glad!" Charity laughed. "He was worried sick!"

The man laughed complacently, not taking his eyes off of Faith. "I've never seen her late before," he confided, looking her up and down in a languid manner that made Jasyn uncomfortable. He took an instant disliking to the man.

Faith smiled at him. "There's a first time for everything," she conceded. "Gentlemen, I would like to introduce you to Jasyn." She looked at Jasyn. "Jasyn, this is Dr. Silas," she said, holding out a hand and inclining her head towards the older man.

"Jasyn, it is a pleasure," Dr. Silas said, offering his hand. Jasyn reached out his own hand and the doctor grasped and worked it like he was trying to pump water from a spout.

"The pleasure is mine," Jasyn replied, grinning.

Faith nodded to the other man. "And this... is Barin Trey."

Barin gave Jasyn a look laden with suspicion and shook his hand, though much less enthusiastically. "Jasyn," he greeted, curt and cold.

Jasyn simply nodded, hoping he was giving back the same chill. Charity looked about the room, a furrow between her perfect brows.

"I know I have circulating trays," she said, her voice pouty. "Oh well!" She smiled broadly, beguilingly optimistic once more. "There is always the bar! Jasyn?" The construct looked at her, taken aback. "Come with me, will you?" she intoned, the closest she could come to a plea.

Jasyn smiled, obliging. "Of course." He turned to Faith. "Can I get you something to drink?"

She let go of his arm and rubbed the edge of his elbow. "That would be wonderful. Thank you."

He gave her a smile and followed Charity through the crowd, a line of fear running up his spine as he left Faith alone. Worse than alone – he was leaving her with that shark-eyed predator that had looked at his woman like she was dinner.

Jasyn followed Charity once again through the crowd and into another, much smaller and much more crowded room. As always, everyone parted to give Charity plenty of space and he joined her next to a long counter of polished wood. Behind the counter were countless platter droids, skimming between the human tenders in starched white shirts and burgundy neckties. Charity raised a bedazzled hand and one of the tenders was in front of her immediately.

"Two Varti and a glass of champagne."

The tender bowed and hurried away, then was back in a flash with the drinks. Two of the three glasses were of short, heavy crystal and filled with dark, amber-colored fluid. Charity picked them up, handing one to Jasyn. She clinked the edge of her glass to his.

"Cheers," she toasted, "to old friends." Looking into his eyes, she took a long drink from her glass.

Jasyn gave her a nod as he raised his glass to her and took a sip. He quickly used the glass to cover his mouth as he coughed unexpectedly, surprised by the burn the liquid left in his throat. Charity laughed, though not unkindly, and he joined her. He took another sip, without coughing this time, and took the flute of champagne off of the bar.

"Don't take too long getting back," Charity advised with a sly smile. "Barin has been after Faith for quite some time." She sipped her drink, her green eyes appraising him over the crystal rim.

"What do you mean?"

"I mean he wants to wed her and bed her – but not necessarily in that order," Charity told him, a snarky smile creeping up the side of her perfect face.

Jasyn smiled graciously and Charity had to give him some credit, his composure never wavered.

"Then I better get back," he said, his voice even. "I told Geary I would keep her safe – and that maniacal bastard would never forgive me." He gave Charity a knowing smile and moved away through the crowd, her green eyes following him as he went.

Dr. Silas was gone when he returned but Barin was still talking to Faith next to a long hearth that housed an artificially dying fire. Barin Trey, for the first time since their arrival, looked much at ease and more than a bit superior. It made Jasyn wonder what they had been discussing in his short absence.

Jasyn handed Faith the flute of champagne that he had gotten for her as she threw a curious glance at the heavy crystal glass that he held for himself. She knew that he usually did not drink unless it was a taste of what she was drinking, and even then it was just to be polite.

She gave him a grateful smile and took a sip of the champagne before she quickly returned her attention to the conversation she had been having with the IGC Director of Artificial Intelligence.

"Dammit, Barin," she said softly. "You're being unreasonable!"

Jasyn put an arm around her waist and he could feel her lean back into him. He tried not to smirk at Barin but couldn't help himself.

Barin, however, seemed to take no notice of how comfortably Faith leaned back against her escort, or how protectively he held an arm wrapped around her waist. He took no more notice of the construct than if he had been a piece of furniture. His cold attitude had changed to one of complete disregard in just a few short minutes. He stood, in Jasyn's opinion, inappropriately close to Faith as he talked to her. Then the Chimeran watched unbelieving as the man reached out and touched Faith, *his* Faith, running the tips of his manicured fingers along her arm as he spoke to her.

Suddenly, Jasyn couldn't even hear what the man was saying. All he could hear was the pounding rush of his own blood as it coursed through his body, its sound deafening in his ears. He could see that the man's lips were moving, but every ounce of his attention was trained on the man's hand as it traveled up and down Faith's bare arm in the most familiar manner. His thumb ran along the inner side of her bicep, where Jasyn knew the skin was so soft, and dangerously close to the curve of her breast.

If he touches her there, Jasyn thought with an astonishing rush of passion, *I will kill him where he stands.*

He looked away and took a sip of the dark liquid in his glass, feeling the liquor burn its way down to his stomach as Faith went on, passively arguing with the prick.

Jasyn was aware of the blush that occasionally crept over the line of his jaw and sometimes into his cheeks. It produced a rush of heat that was not unpleasant, a human condition that was built into his manufactured genetic code either purposely or by chance; either way, he had never given it much thought. But, as Barin reached out to Faith and tucked a stray strand of hair behind her ear, Jasyn felt his entire body flush in the same manner. He feared he must be turning red everywhere.

Not everywhere, he thought, as he glanced down and saw that the knuckles of the hand wrapped about his glass were white. With a conscious effort and all the control he could muster, he relaxed his grip before it shattered the heavy crystal in his hand.

The arm he had around Faith was as rigid and motionless as a piece of stone. He was afraid that if he moved it he would crush her.

Barin let the knuckle of his thumb trail along Faith's jaw as he pulled his hand away from the delicate lines of her face and Jasyn could feel the rush of blood through his body, heavy with murder.

You're losing control, he warned himself. He knew instinctively that he should get away, but he was loath to leave Faith, especially with Barin. *She'll be fine for a minute. You need to get a hold of this rage.*

Jasyn carefully released Faith from his grip and, clearing his throat, gave her what he hoped was a shy and benign smile.

"Excuse me," he said apologetically, placing his drink on a mantelpiece. "I need to find a restroom."

"Over there," Faith told him, pointing with her glass to the far side of the room where it intersected with the next.

"Thank you. If you will excuse me?"

"Of course."

Jasyn turned and walked cautiously through the crowd that seemed glad to part for him, watching and whispering as he went. His throat was closing, making it hard for him to breathe. His head was pounding, making it hard for him to think. He found the bathroom and went inside, nearly slamming the door behind him.

He paced about the dimly lit room of cut and polished black granite, his jaw clenched as tight as his fists. He could not remember ever having been filled with such fury – not at GwenSeven nor even at the IGC, the makers and the holders of the slave chain for all these many years.

The fury boiled within him like a poison, consuming him.

Control, he thought. *When did I lose control?* He realized that his fists were balled so tightly that his short nails were cutting into his palms. He shook his hands open and suddenly thought of Chip. *What would Chip do?*

Though thinking of the happy-go-lucky construct often brought a smile to his own face, the thought of Chip tonight did nothing to calm his own wrath. Jasyn looked up at his reflection in the smoky dark glass that hung on the wall over the black granite sink.

Fuck Chip, he thought vehemently, scowling at himself in the dark mirror. *What are* you *going to do?*

A great and sudden shift, either within himself or throughout the universe, collapsed in and around him, leaving him strangely calm. The visage in the mirror looked back at him, the expression slowly relaxing. Jasyn took a deep breath, turned and opened the door, leaning out of the bathroom and looking anxiously about.

Despite the distraction of Barin Trey, Faith spotted him immediately and, discerning some sort of trouble, made her excuses as she deposited her drink on a side table and headed straight towards him. He ducked back into the bathroom and took another deep breath, flashing a quick grin at his reflection in the dark mirror.

Faith burst into the small room looking about frantically, as if there might be something there that could threaten his safety. The room was as near as normal that it could be, as far as Jasyn could tell. It reminded him of her pool at the villa. The room was dimly lit and everything was made of speckled black granite except for a toilet that was pure black and hard to make out – a veritable black hole in space. Faith could see Charity's sense of humor immediately, but not what might have troubled

Jasyn. She turned, confused, just as she heard the door click shut and the bolt-lock slide home.

Her eyes found his, hers still confused, as he crossed the distance between them in two quick strides before enfolding her his arms and kissing her with nearly crushing force. His momentum pushed her backwards until the backs of her thighs stopped hard against the black granite countertop. Her body tipped dangerously backwards, her back arching under the brunt of his assault, but his arms wrapped tightly around her body and kept her from toppling over.

Though caught by surprise, Faith felt her body respond and returned his kiss with equal passion, her mouth open and eager, tasting what he had been drinking and recognizing the Varti. It was a stimulant rather than an alcohol, and she could feel the tingle of it upon her tongue as she pushed it deeper into his waiting mouth.

Her hands held his face and then slipped to the back of his head, buried and twisted into his dark hair as she pushed herself against him. His hands traveled down her body, roughly feeling every curve beneath the fabric of her dress. They stopped at her hips and then slid back up. Grasping her waist, he lifted her up and sat her down onto the countertop and pushed her thighs apart with his hips.

Jasyn could feel her moan inside his mouth as she pressed harder against him. She pulled her face away, tipping her head back, and his lips left hers to find her neck. He hooked his thumbs under the hem of her dress, sliding it up to her hips, feeling the smooth skin of her legs with the tips of his fingers.

Faith moaned again, arching her body against his as his tongue found the hollow of her throat. Her hands went down his back and then around to his front, searching for the buckle of his belt when Jasyn suddenly pulled away from her.

She opened her eyes, nonplussed, to see him with his hand hovering a few centimeters away from her head. His lips were open and wet but his expression was one of shock.

"What is it?" she breathed, her hands hooked onto the waistband of his pants as her eyes searched his face.

"I, I'm sorry," he stammered. He looked at his hand as he brought it down to cup her face, running his thumb along her cheekbone. "I don't want to mess up your hair. Or your dress."

"It's okay," she said, her voice still breathless.

"No," he said. "It's not."

His jaw was clenched with forced control as he pulled her gently from her seat on the countertop, setting her carefully on unsteady feet, keeping their bodies pressed close together. Faith clung to him, her breath still coming fast and ragged, as he smoothed down the black fabric over her body.

"I'm sorry," he apologized again. "I'm just not used to seeing you like this." He straightened the strap of her dress, pulling it tenderly back up over her shoulder. "Your dress, your hair...you look so beautiful. I'm so sorry, I don't know what came over me. I'll wait," he promised. "I can wait."

Giving her hips a firm squeeze, he leaned forward and placed a gentle kiss on her mouth, pulling away before her already parting lips could demand more.

"I know this party is important and there are people you need to talk to," he whispered. "I'll find our room and wait for you there." He gave her another gentle kiss before letting her go. Then he turned and left quickly, shutting the door behind him.

Exiting the bathroom, Jasyn spotted Barin Trey - watching the door like a hawker on the hunt. The Operations Officer quickly turned his face away, knowing he could not suppress his grin. His eyes fell on Charity, surrounded by other socialites and taking a long drink of Varti, her green eyes smiling at him over the rim of her glass. The lower three of the four fingers that held the glass curled around it, leaving her index finger pointing out the direction he should take.

With a slight bow and an appreciative smirk, Jasyn turned

to his left and took the nearly deserted hallway in the direction Charity had given him on the sly.

Maybe she's not so bad after all, Jasyn thought as he went quickly down the passageway that was guarded by ancient, priceless statues. It opened up onto a room of people, stopping him in his tracks until he realized who they were.

Snacking and socializing in the great hall were the security and staff-in-waiting of the dignitaries only a few rooms away. Jasyn's eyes fell on Geary, standing close to a chatty Penny, just as the other man's eyes fell on him with a disapproving scowl. He nudged the PA and went straight to the construct, Penny following at his heels.

"Is something wrong?" she demanded as they reached him. Jasyn quickly shook his head.

"Faith is tired. I think she needs to...lie down." He swallowed hard to keep himself from grinning. Even so, Penny's brown eyes narrowed at him behind the small black eyeglass frames she wore. "I thought I should make sure that our room is ready for her," he added.

Her lips pressed together into a tight line before she nodded. "Alright. This way." She handed Geary her drink and turned on her heel, making the construct hurry to follow her determined pace. Jasyn could feel the disapproving and distrustful glare of the security man on his back as he hastened to keep up with the PA.

Penny led him down hallways and up staircases, some as wide as streets, some thin and winding. She was obviously quite familiar with the castle. The PA finally came to a stop in front of a large door of steel that was made to look like ironbound oak and gave Jasyn her most stern glare.

"Will Faith need me for anything else tonight?" he asked.

Penny's glare turned into a leer. "The cocktail reception is the only event scheduled for this evening, if that is what you mean."

Jasyn gave her what he thought of as his 'Chip smile,' since he knew she hated it. "Then I will just wait for Faith, and make sure she gets settled."

Penny rolled her eyes at him and stormed away without another word.

Jasyn let himself into the room and would have, if he could, let out a long whistle. The place was large enough to house an entire company of soldiers and elegant enough to house royalty.

His hazel eyes traveled over the sitting room as he entered. The plaster walls were painted dark beige and the blonde-wood floors were covered with heavy gold rugs. A real fire roared in the huge fireplace, framed in with cream-colored marble veined with gold, topped by a heavy and ornately carved mahogany mantle.

Tall, arched windows of leaded glass were flanked by heavy drapes of golden velvet and gave a view to the gardens behind the castle. Though now under the cloak of darkness, paths were lit between hedgerows and flowerbeds by footlights in all the colors of the rainbow.

Jasyn looked over the antique sofas upholstered in gold velvet and polished cocktail tables to the room beyond as he loosened his tie. Before another long fireplace on the far wall was an enormous four-poster bed with an ornately carved headboard and hung, like the windows, with heavy drapes of gold velvet. It was covered with a patchwork of gold satin and copper-colored velvet and a ridiculous amount of pillows in varying shades of gold.

This isn't just a guestroom, Jasyn thought as he undid the top two buttons of his shirt and eyed the doorway that led to the expansive bathroom of cream-colored marble, freestanding claw foot tubs, steam showers and gold-plated body driers. *This really is Faith's room.*

He turned as the door swung open and the woman in question stood in the frame, her small hand on the handle of

the door and her poise in a manner he had never seen before –
threatening.

She pushed back the heavy panel of steel as she crossed the
threshold and it swung closed behind her and the lock snapped
with a sound of finality that chilled Jasyn's blood. He had seen
her angry before, but never angry at him. He swallowed hard
as he watched her close the distance between their bodies,
each step decisive and controlled, her hands clenched into
small fists.

She stopped short when she reached him, so close that he
could feel her warm breath on his neck. Her gold and brown
eyes were blazing and when she spoke each word was firm and
foreboding. "Don't you think for a second that I don't know
what you were up to downstairs."

Jasyn's mouth moved but no sound came out. He swallowed
again, trying to find his voice. Faith's jaw clenched for a second
and then released. Her whole body seemed to relax and she
let out an exasperated breath, a small smile quirking up one
corner of her mouth.

"That is twice now in one night that you have left me
wanting," she accused, though her tone was no longer angry.
Earlier he might have smiled, even gloated, but now his
instincts told him that now it would be a dangerous thing to do.
So he waited, watching her in silence. Her face, hard and angry
only a second ago, softened. "Don't you ever do that again," she
told him.

"Yes ma'am," he whispered.

Faith, breathing though her teeth, reached out and dug her
hands into the open collar of his shirt. Grabbing the lapels she
tore them apart, sending buttons flying in all directions as she
pulled Jasyn's body to hers, searching out his lips with her own.

*Penny is going to be pissed as hell if she has to get me another
tux,* Jasyn thought as he listened to the patter of his buttons
raining down on the floor while Faith pressed her soft lips
against his, forcing them open.

Jasyn's mouth responded eagerly and he wrapped his arms around her back and pulled her hard against his body. He was filled with a deep satisfaction and a strange sense of calm knowing that Faith was his. He had no idea that the calm and satisfaction he felt, was merely the eye of the storm.

ONE 8

Two cycles later, adjusting to her new girth, the Rogue headed out for a dinner with the Senators of Lentoch.

She was still getting used to the huge body. It took concentration and control to walk, even more so to walk quickly - without toppling over to one side or another. Lifts were never big enough and taking a stairway was a joke. There were times when the Aridian was amazed at how the Ambassador had learned to get around. She was exhausted just by getting dressed in the morning and would sit on the edge of her bed for what seemed like forever, regaining her wind.

The Doppelgänger was thankful that the Ambassador had stored up an amazing amount of linen handkerchiefs, though when she first spied them she feared that the body she had taken might be quite ill. After heaving her bulk around for more than just a trip to the bathroom she discovered their real use. The moving around took an enormous amount of effort and the body responded, not just with instant exhaustion, but with a vast quantity of perspiration. She was constantly mopping the round face and the back of the bulging neck.

Who knew that the body could sweat so much without melting away altogether?

It was almost certainly due to another fact she had discovered that amazed her. The body she had taken not only loved food, but it could take quite a lot. The appetite was astounding and seemingly bottomless at times.

Lobster?

Yes.

A Gordon filet?

Yes.

Another serving?

Why, yes.

Dessert?

But of course! Maybe two, just to be polite.

It seemed that there was no end to the man's craving for tasty delights and his love for food had been insatiable. It still was.

The Rogue Aridian, wearing the ambassador's fleshy body for the night, sat across the table from two Lentoch Senators at a pricey restaurant on the newly made pollen moon of Egriel in the Flower Galaxy. It was already famed for its cloned wild boar.

The Ambassador had dined on the boar specialty, savoring the crispy pieces of charred fat, and pronounced it the most delicious dish he could ever remember having. He finished off his dinner with a slice of cocoa-eel that was buried under mounds of cream that had been toasted at the edges.

The Lentochs were tall humanoid beings, with greenish skin and slightly pointed heads. To the Doppelgänger, they looked like two giant spears of asparagus.

She wondered if it was her own thought, or the result of the Ambassador, who always had food on the brain. Either way, his large form chuckled at the thought, dabbing a napkin at the corners of his lips.

The Lentochs, if that was what they really were, were no more Senators than she was an Ambassador. But, on a deal like the one she was making, no one would dare show their true self.

They were not Aridians, she knew that at once. Once she was sure of that, she had nothing to worry about, except for the funds of course. The Rogue belched as delicately as possible into her napkin before laying it back across her wide lap and proceeding to scoop sugar into her coffee.

"Well, gentlemen," the Ambassador rumbled, stirring the coffee. "What exactly do you need from me to proceed with an arrangement?"

One of the Lentoch's dipped its tall head in understanding.

"We will need," it replied, "proof that you can acquire a Fledgling or a Hatchling. We might accept an egg, though you would still need to provide us with some kind of assurance that you will be able to deliver. We would," the Lentoch added, "increase the fee should you also be able to provide a Jordan."

The eyebrows of the Ambassador, slightly bushy and of a ginger color, rose perceptibly.

"Is that so?" he asked.

"Of course," the Lentoch said, his voice so gravelly and deep that the Aridian suspected that it might be coming from an implanted transmitter. "We can always find the means if necessary. But, should the means be easy for you to acquire..." the Lentoch smiled and tilted his pointed head, leaving his sentence unfinished.

"I see," the Ambassador said, seeming to regard his great belly while the Aridian mentally ran over possibilities.

"Either way," the second Lentoch said quietly, almost whisperingly, "dinner is on us. And, if there is any way we can help..." he trailed off.

The Ambassador grinned. "Help me decide on another dessert," he declared. "And in a few months, or less, I will help you to what you are after, and possibly more. I think once the egg, or eggs or Hatchlings or Fledglings are secure, a Jordan should not be hard to come by."

Both Lentochs straightened, stiffening as if they had been hit by tasers, then excitedly and quickly motioned for the waiter to bring the dessert cart once again, leading the Aridian to believe that they were pleased.

She would be more than happy to give them whatever they paid for, especially when they were covering the costs of fine meals.

The Ambassador smiled broadly and grabbed a fork.

⎂⎅

Jordan Blue left her cabin aboard the Opal Dragon, humming a tune from her newest favorite holo. She felt better than she had for a long time. She didn't know if she had been favored with pleasant dreams during the night, since she could not remember what she had dreamt, she rarely did.

I feel more up, she thought, searching for the right words to describe her current and newfound state of emotion. *Maybe it's because of my first victory.*

She smiled, wondering if it was the flow of Dragonblood in her veins, though Calyph had told her repeatedly that it wasn't blood. He had given her the scientific name but she couldn't pronounce it very well. The feeling it gave her was impossible for her to describe. All that she knew was that she felt closer – closer to the Fledglings, closer to the Dragon, closer to everyone and everything. Most especially, closer to Galen.

The black-clad Jordan turned her platinum-blonde head to the right and there he was. They had bridged the chasm that had opened between them, and now his constant presence made her feel whole again.

She smiled at him along with the crew members that she passed, returning polite nods as she made her way down a main Artery corridor – its light growing brighter in an attempt to mimic a rising sun in the depths of space.

The Jordan mused on her feelings as she made her way to the Atrium, the vast space in the Dragon's belly that consisted of small markets, boutiques, bars, eateries and other social and holo clubs. At this early hour only the cafés were open, and even those were scarcely populated by a small number of officers. Most of the crew had their breakfast in the mess hall, where it was free.

The Jordan entered a café that was empty save for two Security Officers at a table in the very back. She ordered a nano muffin and a cup of milk and coffee from the young elf girl behind the counter who regarded the Jordan with large, brown eyes. The girl took her credentials card without a word and handed her a steaming cup and a muffin that looked nearly as large as her own head.

Blue took her cup and muffin to the table in the back where the two Security Officers sat, their table half in the dark. They both rose respectfully when they saw who she was, offering her wan smiles and greeting her in unison with, "Good morning, Jordan."

"Good morning," she replied. "Do you gentlemen mind if I join you?"

"Of course not," one replied, pulling out a chair for her.

Galen sat down in a chair at the table next to theirs, his blue eyes shifting from one man to the other before settling back on the Jordan.

Olney, Blue thought. *Lieutenant Colonel Olney. And Hearth. Major Hearth.* Both officers were human, and just showing a pattern of wrinkles around their eyes, though Olney's hair was still jet black and Major Hearth had no signs of gray yet in his scruffy blonde hair. She grinned at them as she took her seat.

"Long night?" she asked, indicating the tall glasses of bloodgin over ice that they were nursing. Both men snickered.

"Long shift," Hearth said.

Blue nodded, recalling that Security Officers as well as the Safety Officers worked shifts of seven days on and seven days off. "Seven days, right?"

Both men chuckled and shook their heads. "More like

thirty-seven," Olney told her before taking a long pull from his glass.

The Jordan gaped at him, her blue eye staring. She looked at Hearth, thinking that Olney might be pulling her leg, but the man's look was grim.

"Are you telling me that you have been on shift for nearly six weeks?"

"That's right," Hearth agreed.

Blue turned, finding the wide brown eyes of the elf girl behind the counter. "Put their drinks on my tab," she ordered. The girl nodded without a word.

"That isn't necessary, Jordan," Olney told her, his voice kind.

"I think it is," Blue admonished.

"Thank you," Hearth told her. "It's much appreciated."

"Yes," Olney agreed. "But not necessary."

"Why have you been on shift for so long?" she asked.

Hearth shrugged. "After what happened on the Beryl Dragon, most of the crew has worked overtime, double time, and some have worked nearly all the time, setting things to right again and making sure that we are safe."

Blue shook her head slowly from side to side, almost unable to believe them. "I am so sorry," she whispered. She wondered suddenly if the wrinkles she noted under their eyes were due to age or exhaustion.

Olney cocked his head and looked at her. "Why in any world would you be sorry?"

Blue broke a piece off of her muffin and regarded it with a downcast eye. "Because I hadn't really thought about how the recent events have affected the rest of the crew – so many people. I feel selfish."

Colonel Olney reached out and laid a gnarled hand over her thin, pale fingers. "Jordan, you have nothing to be sorry about. This is our job, and none of what happened was your fault."

"Still…" she whispered.

"Still nothing, ma'am," Olney told her. "You have put in no less than the rest of us," he said, his eyes glancing to her flight suit, the usual sparkling blue replaced with the shimmering black that she now wore in deference to those she had lost, before his gaze flickered over the eye patch she also now wore. He looked away from it quickly, politely.

Hearth drained his glass and leaned towards the lithe figure with white-blonde hair. "Besides," he said, "Jordan's are always on shift, aren't they?"

Blue nodded. "Unless we're on leave," she agreed, thinking of Jordan Scarlett, on an ordered sick leave.

"Which is why, " he declared heartily, "you can afford to by us lowly officers a drink." He held up his empty glass and shook the ice cubes in it at the elf girl behind the counter who quickly made and brought him another drink.

She turned her brown eyes to Olney, who was giving Hearth a good-natured glare. "Sir?" she asked. "Would you like another drink as well?"

Olney blew out a deep breath, puffing out his cheeks. "Certainly," he acquiesced with a smile. "Why not?" He drained his glass and handed it over.

Blue smiled at their sustained good humor and glanced at the elf girl. "On my tab," she reminded. The girl smiled and nodded before she hurried away.

"Only," Hearth told her with a grin, "if you promise to eat all of that muffin. The size you are, someone from Laundry is liable to pick you up and use you as a lint poker in the dryers!"

Blue laughed and ate the piece of muffin she had broken off.

The officers, their mood lightened by drink and the relief of ending a long shift, joked with the Jordan until her mood was just as high as theirs. Olney glowered at Hearth when the officer's jokes took a lewd turn, until Jordan Blue told a few lewd jokes of her own, showing that she was not offended and could certainly hold her own.

Both officers were holding their sides, laughing, by the time she was done with her muffin and coffee. A few crewmembers passing by the café threw curious glances inside, and a couple junior officers came in for coffee, intrigued by the trio at the back table.

ᘓ୫ᘔ

After a few rounds and with a grin splitting her already broken face, Jordan Blue wished the officers well and paid the tab, leaving a generous tip for the serving girl before she gathered her credentials card and left the café, heading for Fledgling Bay. Galen kept pace by her side.

"You're awfully quiet," she remarked, keeping her voice low.

Galen shrugged. "I just like being with you. And I'm afraid if I engage you in too much conversation when others are around, they will start to think you are crazy."

Blue snorted. "Galen, I have a lurid scar on my face that I never had fixed. I've taken to wearing black, become highly anti-social, and hardly ever eat. I amputated my own eye for God's sake. I am quite sure they already think I'm crazy."

Galen grinned. "That doesn't bother you?"

The Jordan shook her white-gold hair. "Why should it?"

Galen shook his own head in amusement, his dark hair falling over his face in the way that it always had. Seeing it, seeing him, made the Jordan feel whole again. More than that, she decided. She felt rested and refreshed. Despite all that had transpired in the previous two-month cycles, she finally could see the light at the end of the rainbow. She felt good.

More optimistic, Blue thought suddenly, finally zeroing in on the way she felt. She began humming again as she neared Fledgling Bay, looking forward to seeing Cyan. She was even looking forward to seeing Fledge.

The Blue Jordan could feel a bond forming, ever so slowly, between herself and the Red Fledgling.

She had told the Captain about it the last time she had checked on him, paying him a visit in his private quarters. It was where he was to be found, rather than the bridge, more and more often. He had smiled gently, almost nostalgically, which was something that he did very infrequently these days.

"I'm glad to see that," he told Blue when she informed him about the growing bond with Scarlett's Fledgling, his pale eyes earnest. "It happens in human families, you know."

"What is that?"

"When a parent is lost," he began but then his own words seemed to choke him. Blue wanted to reach out to him, to hold him and offer him some comfort, but he forced himself to recover quickly. "One sibling will often step in to care for the other children. A bond is formed," he said, his voice growing huskier with each word. "It is not the same as the parental bond, but it is better than being alone."

His voice broke on the last word and so did Blue. She wrapped her arms around her Captain and held him tight. She could feel him clutching her back like a man at sea clinging to the last scrap of wood that was once his boat.

"It will be okay," she assured him, though she was not sure herself if that was the truth. But she *wanted* it to be okay. For herself, but especially for Brogan. He was more a father to her than the one she had known as a child, and to see the agony that he was enduring over the loss of Jade and Scarlett was terrible. "It's hard now, but it will be okay. Scarlett will be back and things will be more normal."

"I know," he whispered hoarsely, patting her on the back as he regained his composure. "I know."

The encounter had left the Jordan shaken and she recalled it now as she entered Fledgling Bay. She did her best to shake it off lest it frighten or upset the Fledgings. Then she let her feelings stretch out to touch them where they were waiting. She felt them with her newly heightened Dragon senses and her heart responded by quickening. It began to beat faster and faster and at first she thought it was in excitement to see the Fledglings, and for them to see her.

Then, swiftly she realized that her heart was not beating rapidly with excitement but in response to theirs, which felt in distress. She could feel Fledge's heartbeat, irregular to the edge of panic. Then the feel of Cyan emanating like a wave.

Caution, that feeling said. *Slow. Careful.*

Her high, arched brows drew close together as Jordan Blue crossed the bay, nodding and murmuring greetings as she went. Assaulted with the feelings of the Fledglings, she went through the security measures to gain access to the far side of the deadly wall of detfleck where they waited.

After giving the medic on duty access to her mouth she gave a whistle to the security man on watch, quickly noticing the odd looks of discomfort that each of them wore. Something was up, making her even more anxious than before. Once she was given clearance, she bowled past them, clinging to her newfound optimism like it was a lifeline. She didn't want to lose hope again, not when she had just regained a piece of it.

The two Fledgling Dragons stood side by side, each as large as a fighter galley. They were both a matte silver color, though one gave off a shimmer of blue and the other a shimmer of red. The Jordan grinned, seeing them whole and safe and secure.

"Why all the fuss?" she called out as she walked around the shimmering red of Fledge's nose so that she could stand between him and the blue glow of his brother, Cyan. "I'm here and ready for..." Her voice trailed off and she froze, her flight boots rooted to the silver tarmac of Fledgling Bay. There was a figure already standing there between the two Fledglings.

The figure was obviously a woman by the way she was curved. She wore an opal-colored coverall as did nearly everyone aboard the Opal Dragon.

As does everyone in sick-bay, Jordan Blue thought. *As does every mental patient on board, or those on medical leave.*

The figure had wavy dark hair that formed itself into fist-sized curls in the dry space air. The woman turned, looking longingly at the Red Fledgling, before her dark eyes fell on the Blue Jordan.

Jordan Blue felt her jaw loosen in confusion as the woman gave her a wicked and knowing grin.

What in the hell? Jordan Blue thought as she immediately grasped the meaning behind Fledge's irregular heartbeat and Cyan's feeling of caution, trying to warn her.

Balls and shit.

 ONE NINE

Jasyn, calm and secure within the eye of the storm, was still not immune to the raging sea beneath him. The morning after the cocktail reception found him accompanying Faith to a pre-brunch gathering in the castle's conservatory.

The conservatory was an enormous and circular room at the center of the castle, just over the ballroom. Its domed ceiling was made of leaded hyper-diamond that let in streaming sunlight for what seemed like a thousand living plants. The center of the room was dominated by a fountain of boulders. Water bubbled from, rushed, and streamed over the mountain of rocks before pooling in a reservoir at the base where it crashed into a steaming mist.

A package had been delivered to Faith's room that morning, just as they had been getting out of the shower. Jasyn, dressed in a robe, had opened the bedroom door to accept the package, which sat on a flat, floating, butler droid, from Faith's flushed PA. Jasyn did not know what flustered Penny more – seeing him in a robe or having to knock.

He guessed it was having to knock. She had never knocked before until she entered the bedroom one day at the villa to find them in a naked tangle on the carpet. Now she always knocked and waited for the door to be opened.

Jasyn pulled the box off of the droid and gave it a gentle shove back out into the hallway. He gave Penny a grin that made her turn red before he closed the heavy door. He put the box on the bed and, after pausing for a moment to regard the package with a bit of suspicion, opened it to find clothes for both himself and Faith.

He heaved a sigh of relief, knowing that they had been sent by Charity. The material looked a bit strange and felt even stranger when he reached out and rubbed it between his thumb and finger. They gave off on odd chill, cooling his hand.

Faith, fresh from the shower, had joined him and together they laughed and dressed each other in the clothes that Charity had provided. Though strange, it was obvious that the outfits were woven with a manufactured substance that was meant to keep them cool.

Still, even with the strange clothes, the heat inside the conservatory was stifling. It did not help that the room was packed with both plants and people. Guests walked slowly through the oppressive heat and between the potted trees, laughing and chatting, fanning themselves and sipping cold drinks.

Faith walked with her hand in the crook of Jasyn's arm, greeting the people that she knew, which was everyone. He glanced at her and noticed that she was wearing the necklace he had bought for her on their first outing.

"That's a little heavy, considering the circumstances, don't you think?" he asked, tilting his head towards her as they made their way through the crowd.

"Is it?" she asked, reaching up with a slender finger to touch one of the heavy links. She shrugged. "I hadn't really thought of it."

Jasyn smiled. "I don't believe that," he said. "You never do anything without thinking." Faith only smiled in response, tightening her grip on his arm.

They neared the giant fountain in the conservatory and Jasyn eyed the boulders immersed in the bubbling and streaming water that was so loud that the voices of the guests had to be raised in order to be heard over the rush. The mist that rose from the pool where the water crashed over the rocks added even more humidity to the heat.

Charity! he mentally scolded in good humor. He smiled in amusement. His mirth, however, was short-lived.

"Faith!" Charity called.

Faith and Jasyn turned as one to see Charity clothed in a slip of a dress much like the one that she had provided for Faith, waving at them from a throng of guests halfway across the enormous room. She made her way towards them, weaving her way between sweating bodies, pulling along a very tall man with blonde hair and a downy beard of reddish-gold. She finally reached them, laughing and perspiring in the most light and delicate manner, the man looming over them all like a golden shadow.

"I have someone you *must* meet!" Charity exclaimed. "Faith, this is Nathan," she said, extending one jeweled hand toward her sister and placing the other over her mostly bare chest. "Nathan, this is Faith."

"It is a pleasure to finally meet you in person," Faith said. She moved to shake his hand but he took up her fingers and bent to kiss them. He had to bend very low to make up for his towering height.

"The pleasure is mine," he said, straightening slowly and fixing his blue eyes on the older de Rossi sister with a rapacious smile. "And I thought that the heat in here was from the greenhouse ceiling."

Charity gave a girlish laugh. "And this is Jasyn," she told Nathan.

"Nice to meet you," he offered the construct without so much of a glance, his eyes and smile fixed upon Faith, his hand still holding hers.

"I'm sure," Jasyn said, his voice flat.

Faith gently removed her fingers from Nathan's hand. He let them go but did not back away and instead took a step closer so that he stood towering over her. She tried to back away but was stopped by the basin surrounding the fountain

"Has everything been taken care of to your specifications?" she asked, her head tilted back to look up at him.

"For the most part."

"Well, please let us know if anything needs to be changed," Faith continued, keeping her poise. "And if you need any more assistance, we will see to it."

"I'll take care of it myself," he told her. "But I should make a trip to your villa," he added, touching her under the chin with a long finger. "Just to make sure you have everything that you need."

"That would be fine," Faith agreed. She pressed herself against Jasyn, who was fighting once again to control the rush of murder through his blood.

Jesus! he thought. *First Barin Trey, now this asshole.*

He tightened his arm around Faith's waist as her eyes darted at Charity who laughed, sensing her sister's discomfort.

"Come on, Nathan," Charity said slipping her hand around the curve of his bicep. "We should probably lead everyone out of here before they begin to melt!"

"Alright," he agreed, though his eyes and his smile lingered on Faith.

Charity caught sight of a butler droid and signaled for it to announce the meal before turning to make her way through the crowd when she saw some people she knew and began gushing at them.

Once they had moved away, Jasyn turned his hazel eyes on Faith who gave him a nervous smile. "Well," she said, flustered, "that was interesting!"

"Yes," Jasyn agreed. "It certainly was."

He was certainly not pleased that the man had Faith so agitated – he had never seen her become so disconcerted before, and he certainly didn't like it. What did please

Operations Officer Issord, and unbeknownst to Faith, was that Jasyn had known him. But the man, too arrogant to spare Jasyn a single look, did not have the wherewithal to recognize the construct.

Jasyn had known the man's last name, and now he knew his first. And where he was. The Chimeran knew that his Commander would be very interested to know where the man was as well.

"Would you mind getting me something to drink?" Faith asked. Jasyn smiled, knowing that she wanted a cocktail to calm her nerves.

"Of course," he said, giving her waist a squeeze. "As long as I can leave you with somebody I can trust."

Faith laughed softly. "How about Dr. Silas?" she asked, lifting her chin to indicate the gray-haired man he had met the night before.

"That sounds fine," he agreed. She kissed his cheek and he gave her another quick squeeze before letting her go.

He watched as she made her way over to Dr. Silas before he turned and headed for the nearest bar, keeping an eye out for Charity and her lanky consort. He knew that if the man so much as laid a hand on Faith, he would break his neck – even if he had to stand on a chair to do it. And he didn't give a damn about how hard Engineers were to come by.

Jasyn arrived at a long counter of polished silver just as brunch was being announced and he found himself next to Charity once more. He gave her a smile as he glanced about for her companion.

"Don't worry!" Charity laughed, laying a hand on his arm. "Nathan is with Dora. He won't be bothering Faith for some time."

Jasyn forced a smile and leaned against the bar next to Charity. Again they were attended to with an almost frightening speed.

"Ma'am?" the tender inquired, giving a floating tender droid a shove, sending it gliding away in the opposite direction.

"I'll have a pom and vod," Charity instructed. "A d'larorange champagne for my darling sister, and a quine and ell for my friend here."

Jasyn gave her a smile as he shook his head. "I don't think so," he said. "No liquor for me this morning."

"It's perfectly safe," Charity drawled, her green eyes glittering at him. "Trust me."

Jasyn cocked his head at her. "Is that something I can do?"

Charity took a crystal glass from the tender that looked to Jasyn as if it were filled with chilled blood. She gave Jasyn a coquettish smile. "Definitely not." She handed Jasyn the flute of champagne for Faith and a tall glass of clear bubbling liquid for himself. "But you can trust the tender."

Jasyn looked at the man who gave him a curt nod. "It's just a tonic and lime, sir," he assured him.

Tonic of what? Jasyn thought as he took a cautious sip. It was surprisingly refreshing. He gave Charity a smile.

"I like it," he confessed.

"I know," Charity said, smiling demurely as she sipped her own early morning cocktail. Her eyes darted left and Jasyn's eyes followed, settling on Faith. Though he had just been with her, his lips parted as he saw her again and his heartbeat quickened.

She was perspiring gently in the small slip of a dress she was wearing, talking easily to Dr. Silas and a few others around her. She looked so light and free, save for the heavy link of chain she wore around her neck.

Jasyn's eyes were drawn to it, it seemed so out of place, and he thought of the day he had given it to her. At the time he had been so proud but now it made his skin crawl. He knew she wore it to please him, but he also knew that if it wasn't his chain, it would have been another.

"Why does she wear chains?" he asked Charity suddenly, his voice low. "All of her jewelry is made up of chains."

Charity lowered her drink and lifted her chin. "It lets her know her station in life. A constant reminder of who she really is."

Jasyn hardly noticed her acidic tone, his own feelings were so sour. "I hate it," he said, growing vehement. "I wish I had never bought it for her!"

Charity, regaining most of her usual composure in an instant, smiled at him over the rim of her cocktail glass. "I'm sure you only had good intentions when you did," she assured him.

Did I? Jasyn thought bitterly. *I'm sure I was planning her murder. Though I did want to do something nice for her. Why?* He tried to give his head a quick shake in an effort to clear it but it was heavy with passion as he stared at the chain necklace. It looked heavy and cruel.

"That doesn't make it right," he said, his voice quiet and his hand tightening around the glass in his hand. He swallowed hard and forced himself to relax his grip before he shattered the glass, though he was unable to keep the emotion from his voice. "I didn't realize it until just now, but I've come to hate those chains," he confessed in a harsh whisper. "I wish she wouldn't wear any of them at all."

Charity turned so that they were shoulder to shoulder and sipped her drink as together they watched Faith move decorously through the throng of people being herded towards the dining hall, greeting them hospitably as she went.

"It's funny you should say that," she told Jasyn without taking her gaze from her sister, "since you are the only one who can take them off her." She turned her face to the construct, her green eyes searching the profile of his finely molded face.

Jasyn turned to look at her, his dark brows pulled together, but Charity moved away without another word until her attention fell upon the very next group of people, where she was immediately her usual self. She called to them in the manner she always did, brimming with languid enthusiasm.

ⅭⱾⱾↄ

Jasyn thought that the brunch was long, and boring, but at least he was able to spend several hours with Faith afterwards before they had to join the group again for the evening festivities. Faith had offered to give him a tour of the gardens, but he knew that they would run into one person after the other who would want to talk to her, even if only for the sake of being able to *say* that they had talked to her.

Jasyn evaded the inconvenience by keeping her carefully sequestered within their personal suite in the Castle. It wasn't difficult to persuade her, or to keep her occupied, though it left him a bit drained before the evening bash that their hostess had in store. He pushed the com-button on the nightstand next to the bed and ordered a split of champagne for her and a glass of Varti for himself to refresh themselves before the party. A butler droid was at their door in less than a minute.

Jasyn, freshly scrubbed and dried and wrapped in a robe, took a swig of Varti and eyed the clothes that had been laid out for him and Faith on the bed while they had showered. The tux was made of some strange, shimmering material, but not too obnoxious. The outfit left for Faith looked half a contraption, but that was not what bothered him.

The next affair on Charity's schedule of events was a masquerade ball, and laid out by the clothes were two masks. The one for Faith was golden and jeweled, as it should have been. It was attached to a golden wand and made to cover only one eye. The one laid out for him was half black and half white and edged with a rainbow shimmer. It was made to be worn tied with ribbons at the back of his head, and when on it would cover both of his eyes and part of his face.

Half in and half out, he thought, *and part of the rainbow.* He took a long drink of the Varti, feeling it burn as it went down. *Maybe Charity isn't as vapid as she seems. Maybe it's just coincidence. Maybe it's a sign. Maybe I am getting paranoid. Or malfunctioning.*

He drained the Varti as Faith joined him to admire their attire for the ball. Seeing her, smelling her, touching her – made him realize that the only thing that he was certain of was that he wanted her. And that he didn't want to wear a mask. He was already wearing enough of them.

By the time they made it downstairs, Jasyn knew that he was either malfunctioning or drunk. He was enamored by Faith in her dress, and his chest swelled with pride in the way that she held onto him. She could have been there with anyone, or alone, but she was there with him. She had chosen him. He began their first dance by telling Faith de Rossi, the head of GwenSeven and the woman he had come to betray and then kill, that he had been made for her. The sensation of malfunctioning was brought on because it felt like what he was saying was true, and it did not bother him in the slightest.

During the entire evening he was continuously filled with a sense of calm, the feeling of satisfaction that Faith was his – that she belonged to him and he to her. His confidence was so high and the feeling so powerful that he even bowed graciously to Barin Trey when the man asked Faith to dance without giving the construct so much as a glance.

"I'll get you something to drink," he told Faith as the prick took her by the hand to lead her away.

"That would be lovely," she said.

Jasyn, not seeing a floating droid nearby, found himself once again at the bar and, once again, next to Charity.

"Jasyn!" she admonished. "If people keep seeing us like this they will begin to talk!"

"And that would bother you?"

Charity laughed girlishly. "Certainly not!"

"I thought you were going to keep him away from her," he said, nodding to where Barin was waltzing Faith across the parquet dance floor. He leaned against the polished mahogany bar and smiled at Charity as the tender brought him a glass of Varti and a flute of champagne.

"Oh Jasyn," she laughed. "I tried! But I have so many guests, and Barin is so determined to be with her!"

Charity sidled closer to the construct, her costume of a dress rustling like a thousand falling leaves, its many layers held up by a field generator. She slipped her hand inside Jasyn's arm and leaned closer to him.

"But I must admit, Jasyn," she exclaimed softly, accepting a glass of bright green liquid in a tall glass from the tender, "that was very kind of you to let Barin dance with Faith."

Jasyn shrugged. "What else could I do?" he asked.

Charity laughed. "What indeed!"

He smiled and sipped his drink. "Thank you for having us to your home, Charity," he offered as he bore out the song while Faith danced with another man. "It is as lovely and as extravagant as you."

Charity's laughter was like tinkling glass. "You think so?" she asked, though she didn't wait for an answer. "That is probably the nicest thing anyone has ever said to me!"

"I have a hard time believing that," Jasyn said good-naturedly.

Charity nestled against him, her skirts rustling around her. "I do like it here," she confessed. "Maybe *this* really will be the last castle."

Jasyn turned slightly so that he could see her face, a small line between his brows. "What do you mean?"

Charity regarded him with surprise. "You don't know?" she asked. "My home got its name because everyone teases me!"

Jasyn cocked his head, not understanding, and Charity sighed dramatically.

"Whenever I move," she explained with a pout, "I build a new castle and take everything with me from the old one - and it is not an easy thing, the building or the moving."

"I can imagine," Jasyn said.

Charity's smile was sly. "Can you?" she asked.

Jasyn laughed. "It's just a figure of speech."

Charity's green eyes sparkled but did not lose their sky look. "Is that so?" she asked.

"It is," he confirmed. "I can see the many and expensive things here and know that it could be no easy task to move them. I certainly cannot imagine you packing things into bubble movers and box foam yourself, not to mention piloting a freighter across the solar system."

Charity laughed and turned her green eyes back to the dance floor. "You are certainly right about that, Jasyn. I can't even imagine that myself!" she exclaimed, though the way that she laughed again indicated that she was indeed imagining such a thing. "Anyway," she continued, "every time I move I say, very emphatically, that this is the last castle I will ever build!"

Jasyn smiled, finally understanding. "And how many castles have there been?" he asked.

Charity shrugged, taking a long drink from her glass. "More than I can count," she admitted.

"Can?"

Charity squeezed his arm. "Care to."

Which is why no one has ever been able to get a bead on you, Jasyn thought. He wondered if that was an accident or speculated for the second time if it was possible that Charity de Rossi was smarter than she looked.

"I had thought perhaps that the one before this really was going to be the last one," she admitted. "But it turned out to be too damn cold. I should have known, being that close to Saturn."

"Saturn?"

"Yes, it was on t7, a nameless moon not far from Titan. It was a shame to abandon it. The castle was lovely, but I really can't abide the cold. Even all of the most modern measures could not dispel the cold that sank into my bones there. Besides," she said, the pitch of her voice rising again with her usual optimism, "I really think that this castle will be the last one. I love being by so much water, and I don't mind the weather, not like Faith does, but then again she doesn't have to live here. She prefers to live isolated, a princess locked in her tower, waiting for Prince Charming to come and rescue her."

Charity took another long drink from her glass, draining it this time. She pulled her arm from the Jasyn's elbow and placed the empty glass on a floating tray. The tray paused for her while she selected another. Turning back to the bar, she picked up the flute of champagne and handed it to Jasyn.

"I'm sure Faith is thirsty," she told him, her green eyes glinting in the light. "And Barin has had her attention long enough, don't you think?"

"Absolutely," Jasyn agreed. "Thank you, Charity," he said.

Charity gave him a graceful curtsy, laughing as she tried to straighten up with her corset cinched tight.

"Of course," she told him. "And Jasyn!" she called as he started to walk onto the golden wood of the parquet dance floor. He turned, waiting. "Don't let her drink too much!" she cautioned. Then she was hailed by a group of women squealing and squawking about her dress and whisking her away in the other direction.

Don't let her drink too much? he thought. *How the hell am I supposed to know what too much is? And how would I stop her?*

He shook his head as he walked onto the dance floor, glad that the song was winding down. Barin was holding onto Faith as if he expected another dance and inwardly Jasyn blessed Charity, wondering once again if she was smarter than she looked or just incredibly intuitive.

Jasyn approached Faith and Barin and stood close to them, drawing their attention. Faith looked delighted while Barin Trey looked decidedly pissed.

"I thought you might be thirsty," he said, handing the flute of champagne to Faith who took it with a grateful smile.

"Thank you, Jasyn, that was very thoughtful."

He smiled at her, carefully avoiding Trey's glare.

"Yes," Barin agreed. "How thoughtful."

Jasyn beamed as Faith broke away from Trey's embrace and slipped an arm around his own waist. He draped an arm protectively across her shoulders.

"Is there anything else I can get for you?" Jasyn asked softly, the tip of his nose against her ear.

"No thank you, darling. I'm sure I have all that I need right here," she said, tightening her arm around his waist.

Barin, all but clenching his teeth, did not miss the exchange. "But certainly," he told Faith, "there are still people here tonight that you must see?"

Faith tipped her head as she drank from her flute. "Yes," she agreed, looking around. She sighed as she already saw someone waving her over. "And it looks like Tanas has first dibs. If you will excuse me, or join me, gentlemen?" Faith asked.

"Of course," Barin told her and Jasyn simply nodded.

Faith smiled gratefully at them and released Jasyn, slipping away. Jasyn moved to follow her but was held back by a vice-like grip on his arm. He blinked at Barin Trey in surprise. While the man smiled at him in the most amicable manner, his voice was icy cold and his eyes were dark with hate.

"You are nothing but a toy to her," he informed Jasyn. "Do you realize that?" The construct stared at him, speechless.

"You are not a real person," Barin assured him, as if he didn't know. "And, though you may be fun to play with for a while, nothing can compare to a real person. You certainly can't give Faith what she needs."

Jasyn felt his surprise vanish, only to be replaced with a rage so overpowering that he had to fight to keep his body from shaking. He took a deep breath and tried to give Barin Trey his best disarming Chip smile, though he knew that all he was able to produce was a tight smirk.

"I am sure you are right, Mr. Trey," he said, speaking slowly and with as much innocence as he could muster. "And I am sure that tonight she will be thinking of someone real, like you," he assured him, "when she is screaming my name."

Thankfully, Barin's shock forced his fingers to loosen on his arm, rather than tighten. It made it easy for Jasyn to turn and walk away.

TWO ZERO

The woman in the opal-colored jumpsuit drew back and eyed the Jordan with not just obvious distaste, but actual repulsion.

Not Scarlett!

It was all that the Blue Jordan could think, letting out a huge gust of breath. *It's not Scarlett*, she reassured herself again, her heart racing. Her single eye took in the woman's thin form, her dark brows high and arched, and her pointed ears. *She's not even human*, Blue realized. *She's an elf.*

Recovering from the shock, Jordan Blue stared at the woman in front of her, a woman who stared back with just as much boldness, if not more. She had long, dark hair and large dark eyes, but that was where her resemblance to Jordan Scarlett ended. The woman was an elf and, where she lacked the more curved figure of Scarlett's body, she made up for in the angles of her face.

She had high prominent cheekbones and high arched brows over dark brown eyes that were distinctively almond-shaped. She was thin, though not as thin as Jordan Blue, but she was nearly half a head taller than the platinum-blonde starfighter.

"Eerie, isn't it?" Galen whispered, but Blue was still warily studying the woman that was causing her Fledglings distress.

She's taller than me, Blue thought, *and her hair is the same color as Scarlett's, but her hair is not the only resemblance*, noting the look on the elfin woman's face. *That sneer. She has Scarlett's sneer. Maybe they* are *related.* The thought made her snicker, bringing a scowl to the woman's face. Seeing her expression darken made Blue laugh aloud.

"What the hell is so funny?" the strange woman demanded.

Blue's laugh stopped short and the expression of humor was gone from the Jordan's face in an instant.

"Do you mean what is funny, *Jordan*?" she corrected. The woman bristled at the reprimand, pulling a quick breath into her small, narrow nose.

"Of course," she said stiffly, bowing her head a slight increment.

Jordan Blue was smaller and thinner - definitively tiny between the two Fledgling Dragons in her shimmering black flight suit. She had no idea of what a pissing match might be and certainly was not aware that she might have been thrown into one. Nonetheless, she leaned forward with one small fist clenched and pressed into the small of her back.

"Of course, what?" she demanded, her voice low. The woman's thin lips pressed together into an even thinner line.

"Of course, *Jordan*," she said.

Blue relaxed and leaned back against Cyan, crossing her arms in front of her chest. The woman, undaunted, gave her a sour look.

"What happened to your face?" she asked.

The Jordan, still recuperating from her initial alarm, gaped at the woman, her expression of astonishment quickly melting into a scowl. "Nothing compared to what will happen to yours! Who are you, anyway?" Blue demanded. "How did you get back here?"

The woman smiled languidly, a shark's smile in a bony face and tossed her dark hair in a way that was jarringly reminiscent of the Red Jordan. "I'm GL," the woman replied, as if the answer was obvious and the Jordan an imbecile.

Blue's shoulders jerked in a bout of silent mirth as she recognized not the woman nor her initials, but the manner in which they were used. "You're a Jordan recruit?" she asked, unbelieving.

GL lifted her chin. "You could say that," she replied, "though I would think I am a bit more than a recruit, since I am here." Blue's consternation returned.

"Why *are* you here?" she asked.

The opal-clad recruit sniffed. "Since the destruction of the Jordan Training Center, most of the recruits - the most promising recruits - have been distributed among the Dragons. Where, I am sure, it is hoped that they will be put to good use."

A line deepened between the white-blonde brows of the Blue Jordan. "We don't have any eggs, so therefore are not in need of any Jordans."

"Oh, really?"

"Really," Blue assured the woman before her body filled with tension as her own suspicions grew. "How many other recruits are aboard this Dragon?" she asked, cocking her head.

GL smiled. "None," she said. "Just me."

Blue felt her jaw clench. "There were at least sixty recruits evacuated from the JTC," she said. "That doesn't seem like a very even distribution."

GL shrugged. "I suppose someone saw the need for me here." She smiled again and reached out a slender hand to stroke Fledge.

The half-elf Jordan slapped the cadet's hand away from the Fledgling Dragon. "Don't do that!" she scolded.

GL held her chastised hand to her chest, startled. "Why not?"

Blue leaned towards the woman, her small form momentarily menacing. "Because he doesn't like it," she hissed. Her remark brought a greater look of surprise to the recruit's face, though it was quickly replaced by one of scorn.

GL tossed her hair in haughty indifference. "I don't care if he does. It's no matter to me. This is a military vessel and he will do as he is told, eventually, whether he likes it or not."

The black-clad Jordan stared at the woman in disbelief. "What is your name?" she asked, her voice soft.

The woman scowled. "I already told you. It's G..."

But Blue was shaking her head. "What is your *name*?"

The woman tossed her dark hair again in the same manner that reminded Blue of the Crimson Jordan, though she could not recall Scarlett being so despicable - even at her worst.

"Gemma Leigh," the woman said, her voice cold even though a smile edged her thin lips. She reached up and defiantly ran her fingertips along Fledge's smooth silver belly. "Though I favor the name Claret, should I get the chance to use it. Maybe Sky, even. My favorite shade of blue."

Blue's single eye widened in shock at the recruit's impudence before it narrowed and flicked to Fledge.

"Oww!" the cadet shouted suddenly, snatching her hand away. The place where it had rested on the Crimson Fledgling glowed red with heat.

Blue smiled. "I told you, he doesn't like it." She tossed her own platinum hair and leaned threateningly towards the scowling recruit. "And from now on, since we are on a military vessel, you better address me as ma'am."

The look of surprise on the recruit's face was rapidly replaced by one of anger. "Yes, ma'am," she acquiesced, her voice low and dripping with venom.

Blue smirked at the woman and turned on her heel and strode from Fledgling Bay as fast as her boots would take her. She intended to get to the bottom of whatever nastiness was afoot.

Despite the fact that she had taken an instant dislike to the arrogant woman, what stung her most were the feelings that she received from the Fledglings.

Caution, Cyan had told her, dredging up the most

appropriate human word he could find. It was enough. Fledge himself was emitting nothing but alarm and repulsion.

The check at the security gate was mercifully brief, since she had just gone through it only moments ago.

"Jordan?" Galen asked, keeping pace beside her. "What's going on?"

"That is precisely what I mean to find out," she answered through clenched teeth.

"I'm aware of that. What I mean is - what are you planning on doing?"

"I'm going straight to the Captain. This is bullshit. They can't just sub-in a Jordan like they need a fourth for a dammed pick-up game of Spades. And the fact that I am not being consulted on these decisions is not lost on me either."

She turned from a Vein corridor and took the split that led to the bridge. Galen followed in silence. The Jordan took the airlift, stepping into the plexiglass tube and letting the air push her up to the next level where she stepped out to find the door to the bridge not only closed, but guarded as well.

Blue frowned at the guard, a corporal who glanced at her with dread before snapping his eyes front and standing at attention. He had closed cropped curls of brown, and wide-spaced blue eyes. And he was big. Slender, but tall and broad shouldered. Perfect build for a guard. The Jordan's single sapphire-colored eye narrowed as she as she sized him up. She had the feeling that he was there for her personally, to keep her out of the bridge. She could feel Galen's watchful eyes on her as she stopped and stood in front of the man blocking her way, her black flight suit sparkling in the light.

The corporal was new to the Dragon. The Jordan knew who he was, but did not know him personally.

Which is also why he was selected for this particular dirty task, she thought, just as his name occurred to her. *Blake,* she thought. *His name is Blake.*

He saluted her, his eyes staring straight ahead. "Ma'am!" He uttered with as much force as he could muster.

Blue returned his salute with a nod. "Corporal," she answered. When he remained silent she cocked her head, questioningly. "Well? Are you going to open that door for me, or keep me from going through it?"

Corporal Blake's clear blue eyes darted to her and then back to the air in front of him. "Ma'am, I was ordered that no one was to disturb the Captain."

A bit of a smile grew from the red lips of the Jordan, pushing up on the right side into her scarred cheek.

"Did that order come from the Captain himself?"

Corporal Blake scowled, even more nervous than he had been before. He straightened himself and lifted his chin, though the Jordan could see that he was beginning to break a sweat. "No, ma'am. That order came from Commander Blaylock."

Blue nodded, her tongue in her cheek. "I see." The corporal seemed to sag with relief at her calm demeanor that he supposed was acceptance. Blue knew that Galen was grinning at her without having to look at him. She knew him as well as he knew her. Her own grin was almost a knee-jerk reaction. The corporal relaxed visibly at her easy smile.

"Get the fuck out of my way, Corporal," she said, her voice even, almost jovial. Corporal Blake's blue eyes darted to her in surprise.

"Excuse me, ma'am?"

"I said to get the fuck out of my way," Blue told him.

Blake shifted nervously. "Ma'am, I have been ordered by Commander Blaylock to not let anyone disturb the Captain. He is in a ..."

"Cut the shit, Corporal. I have the feeling that you were ordered to keep *me* out of the bridge..." Blake shifted his weight nervously as she continued, "but I could not care less. You may be twice my size, but I outrank you, and I am armed."

Blake's gaze darted to the laser pistol that was slung in a holster low on the Jordan's hip before again studiously examining the air in front of him. Tiny beads of sweat formed on his upper lip. "Ma'am..."

"Don't worry, Corporal," the Jordan told him in exasperation. "I'm not going to shoot you, nor am I going to make you go against orders." The corporal turned his chin to look at her in relief. "But, I have reason to believe that my Captain, *your* Captain, is in danger. Under IGC command order eighty-five-six, my duty to protect him supersedes and belays any orders you may have been given previously."

Galen looked at her, his brows raised. "Is that true?" he asked. Blue shrugged. Corporal Blake looked as confused as he was terrified.

"Now stand aside Corporal!" Blue shouted at the man and he hurried to move out of her way as he activated the door panel. The Jordan did her best to suppress a grin while she strode past him and into the bridge where she was met nearly face to chest with a furious Executive Officer.

"What are you doing here?" he demanded, darting a murderous glare at the corporal that disappeared from their view as the heavy door to the bridge slid closed.

Blue took in the entire control room in a single glance. Chiara and Darius hurriedly turned back to the panels they were manning as her gaze swept across them. She saw a wide, silver column rising in the back-center of the control room – the privacy wall that encircled the pit when it was needed. She knew the Captain must be inside. She turned her glare back to the hawk-eyed Executive Officer.

"I want to know what the fuck is going on!" she hissed. "And I want to hear it from my Captain!"

Blaylock closed his lips together until they nearly disappeared, shaking his head slowly from side to side.

"The Captain needs to do what is required of him, and then he needs to rest. He cannot be troubled by whatever is bothering you at the moment."

Blue moved her shimmering, black-clad form closer to the Executive Officer, refusing to back down. "What do you think you are doing?" she asked, her voice low. When the other officer gave her a questioning look her lips pressed together in a red tight line. "Are you trying to replace Scarlett?"

There was a flicker in Blaylock's eyes just before they narrowed at the Jordan. "We are at war, Jordan – if you haven't noticed. We are a military vessel. The Fledglings need Jordans. End of story."

Despite the shock of his words Blue shook her head. "The Fledglings have Jordans," she told him. "What are you doing?"

Blaylock's chin lifted and his countenance relaxed. "I am doing what needs to be done. The Captain does not need to be troubled with your opinions."

"Only yours?"

Blaylock glanced around the bridge as if ensuring their privacy but the other officers seemed extremely absorbed in their panels. "The Captain is in a very delicate state right now," the XO said, speaking in hushed tones. "His nerves are stretched so far I fear they might break. I am doing what needs to be done, and you will do the same!"

"You cannot appoint someone to substitute for a Jordan," Blue advised, her voice as even as she could keep it. "There is no precedence, as far as I know, but I am sure that it will have to be approved by a panel at the IGC, the Captain, and - not to mention - the Fledgling!"

The right corner of Blaylock's mouth twitched. "Desperate times," he advised, "call for desperate measures. We don't know when, *or if,* Jordan Scarlett will recover well enough to rejoin us."

The Jordan's single blue eye searched the intense eyes of

the Junior Commander and a silence fell when she saw what was there. She could hardly believe it.

"You cannot replace a Jordan," she told him, forcing herself to keep her voice from breaking. "Only a Fledgling can do that."

"The past is not the future," Blaylock told her. Every sentence he delivered was like a slap.

"You bastard," Jordan Blue whispered. "What are you trying to do?"

This time Commander Blaylock had the audacity to smile at her. "I mean to see that we stay the course."

The Blue Jordan looked at him and, for a moment, stopped listening to him even though she could see his lips moving. Instead, she opened up to the Dragon – listening to her in the same way that she would reach out to listen to the Fledglings. The Dragonblood pulsed in her veins and made it easier than it ever had been before.

Careful, the Dragon warned, her voice a deep reverberation throughout the Jordan's body. *He is dangerous.*

And he is in control, Blue thought, her heart sinking. *For now, the bastard really is in control.*

Blue could feel the Dragon sigh.

"You will treat cadet GL with respect," Blaylock was telling her. "You will personally give her a tour aboard the Dragon and introduce her to the other officers and any crew member vital to her job."

"And what job is that exactly?"

"Right now, she is only an observer. But treat her like an officer. An important officer. You will introduce her to the Fledglings as well as the crew." The Executive Officer leaned back, a smirk quirking one corner of his mouth. "And you will take her on patrol in the Fledglings."

The Jordan felt indignation begin to boil within her as he spoke and his last remark had her ready to explode. She felt

Galen lay a restraining hand upon her arm and she shook it off.

"I will not!" she shouted.

"You will!" Blaylock shouted back. "Or I will have you brought before the Council for insubordination!"

"You wouldn't! You couldn't!"

"I could so, and before the next dimlight. You are only here right now because so far you haven't caused me any trouble, though that seems to be changing of late, and it would tear the Captain apart to lose all three of his Jordans. But, so help me God Jordan Blue, if you don't fall into line and fall into line fast, you will be sharing a room with Scarlett! Permanently!"

The Jordan opened her mouth but found herself too stunned to speak. She was shaking with rage but the XO had had enough. He pulled down on his opal-colored coverall, straightening it.

"You are dismissed," he told her, his voice thick with contempt. The Jordan opened her mouth again but the Commander tilted his head in warning. "Unless you would like to be relieved from duty."

The Jordan's eye opened wide as her mouth snapped shut. She turned and left the bridge, her dark form seeming to absorb the light as she went.

She passed the corporal on guard duty without even noticing him and dropped down the lift tube like a stone. She made an effort not to run but made her way to her personal quarters as quickly as she was able.

As soon as she was alone in her cabin, Blue leaned her back against the wall, as much for physical support as mental, closing her eye and letting her head tip back and rest against the silver skin of the Dragon.

Galen moved to stand in front of her, laying his hands gently upon her upper arms. Blue tried to muster the bitter anger she felt, but when she spoke her voice came out in a near sob.

"That bitch!"

Galen cocked his head. "Which one?" he asked.

Blue lowered her chin and opened her eye. "Faith!" She let her head fall back again, though her eye remained open, staring at the ceiling. "She was right. We are nothing to them. Nothing but pieces on a holo game board."

Galen reached up a hand and stroked her cheek. "What are you going to do?" he asked. The Jordan was silent for a few moments and then lowered her head so she could look in his eyes.

"I'm not sure yet. But I'll tell you one thing, I'm not anyone's pawn." Galen gave her a look of trepidation.

"Please don't pluck out your other eye," he begged.

The Jordan let out a sound that was half laugh and half sob and Galen wrapped her in his arms.

"Don't worry," she said into his shoulder. "The way things are right now I'm going to need an extra pair...in the back of my head."

"You'll have to change your hairstyle," Galen mused, pressing his face into her platinum pompadour.

Blue uttered another laughing sob and held him tighter.

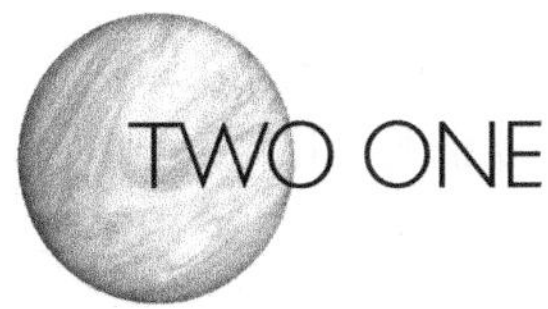

TWO ONE

Though he wasn't keeping track, Jasyn was sure at one point in the evening that Faith had spoken to every soul at the party at least once. To his relief, Barin Trey did not cross their path again. He wasn't sure how another exchange with the sanctimonious prick would turn out, but he did not think it would end well.

Jasyn tried to mentally catalogue every important person that he met and then gave up after an hour. He had one more Varti and Faith had more glasses of champagne than he bothered to count. They danced again and again. Faith lost her mask at one point and then a bit later stumbled, falling into his arms.

"Okay," he told her. "I think that is my cue."

"Cue?" she asked, reaching down to adjust a shoe.

Jasyn smiled. "Yes," he said. "To take you upstairs." He tilted her chin up and kissed her. Though there were people nearby, Faith pressed her body against his and he could hear a faint moan escape her lips.

Jasyn was sure that he was the only one who could hear her, though he wished Trey had been around to hear as well. "Yep," he said, "you've had enough. Let's go."

Though she did not seem more than tipsy, and there were certainly more people at the ball that had drunk much more, Faith leaned her weight against him as he led her from the party and up the stairs to their room.

After he had fulfilled his promise to Barin Trey as best he

could, they lay together, wrapped in each other's arms. Faith laid her head on his chest and he pushed a damp lock of golden hair away from her face.

Then, without warning, there was a bolt of lightning outside followed by a thunderclap large enough to shake the entire castle to its foundations. Faith, who had been drifting towards sleep, tightened her grip around Jasyn, clutching at him desperately.

Jasyn tilted his head down so that he could see her face. "What was that?" he asked.

"Thunder," she whispered. "And lightning."

Jasyn smiled. "I know that. I meant your reaction."

"I don't like it," she told him.

"Obviously."

Another bolt was followed with another earth shaking roar from the atmosphere and again Faith clutched at him, her nails rooting in his skin. Jasyn kissed the top of her head, smiling.

"Do you mean to tell me that the all powerful Faith de Rossi is afraid of a little thunderstorm?" he teased.

Jasyn could feel her wry smile against his bare chest as she gave his shoulder a playful squeeze.

"It's not just the storm," she said, her body slowly settling against his. "It's the sound. It's the way it shakes the castle. You weren't there that night."

"What night?" he asked.

The thunder rolled again, but this time it was farther away. Faith twitched, but did not clutch at him.

"The night they came for us," Faith said. Her voice was sleepy but her tone was very matter-of-fact. "The night they came to kill us." Her cheek pressed against his bare chest. "It doesn't matter now, but I'll feel better once we are in our own home."

Jasyn listened, his hazel eyes wide and his body tense.

"What was that?" he asked.

Faith wiggled against him. "You know what I mean. Once we are back in our own home, in our own bed, I'll feel a lot better."

Jasyn tried to relax his rigid body, especially since he could feel Faith beginning to go limp as she faded into sleep. "As long as we're together," she whispered. "We'll be fine. You'll keep me safe."

Jasyn lay still as her words replayed in his mind.

Our bed, she said. *Our home.*

He lay awake for a long time, listening to the sound of the retreating storm and the echo of Faith's words in his head.

Our bed. Our home.

Jasyn passed through the eye of the hurricane, and was swept into the storm once more.

⊗

Jasyn was sure that the next morning would be another gathering, full of good-byes of feigned concern – but he was wrong. Breakfast was brought to their room and he ate cooked oats with hot milk and honey while Faith and Charity sat on the chairs in the sitting room of their suite, drinking coffee and making plans in hushed voices.

An hour later, Charity was kissing his cheek and wishing him well until she saw him in a few weeks for her next party. "The party of the century," she called it – but with Charity everything seemed over exaggerated.

Faith was back to business as usual. Dressed in a smart, cream-colored suit with her jeweled comset hooked over one ear, she was followed once again by an entourage of security and assistants, led by the infallible Penny and Geary.

They were escorted from the castle and back onto Faith's

craft where they took their seats in the miniature replica of the living room of the villa. Faith spoke on her comset the entire time, taking one call after the next, but sat next to him with a hand on his knee. She glanced at him from time to time and, each time she did, Jasyn gave her his most reassuring smile.

It seemed that a few days from work piled up to a near insurmountable level for Faith de Rossi and she had to multi-task, and quickly, in an effort to keep up. Even while she was talking over the comset, Penny would mouth questions to Faith that she would answer with a nod or a quick shake of her head. Sometimes just a scowl would send Penny running through the craft.

Sometimes, Penny would be at Faith's side with electronic documents on her acrylic, awaiting Faith's signature. Jasyn watched Faith pluck the stylus from Penny's fingers with her right hand and then switch it over to her left so she could sign.

He felt the hairs on the back of his neck raise up, the same way they did when she would run her thumbnail over her lips when she was thinking. He looked away, not wanting to see her hands or her lips or her face.

His acrylic lay on his lap, powered off. For the moment it was nothing more than a dark pane of smooth glass. He had powered it on as soon as the craft was airborne, but it had put itself to sleep after fifteen minutes of inactivity. Jasyn was too absorbed by his own thoughts to notice.

Jasyn's mind kept taking him back to the day he had met JP. It had been at the same manufacturing plant where he and Malone had been sent in an effort infiltrate GwenSeven, namely Charity de Rossi. Jasyn could not imagine how things would have turned out had he stayed with Charity instead of being passed off to Faith. He would be less confused, perhaps. Perhaps not. The more he got to know Charity, the more different she was from what he had expected. But she was not Faith. No one was Faith.

Jasyn had been found on that day, long ago, as a group of

Chimeran soldiers had stormed the compound, "freeing" the constructs inside. He had been on a lower level, unconscious from a nasty blow to the back of his head and was bleeding from a gash there. Even today, if he ran his hand through the hair on the back of his head, he could feel the rippled skin of the scar.

JP, following the soldiers inside, had seen the fallen construct and quickly knelt down to see if he was alive. Though unconscious, his pulse was strong and the Commander motioned for two soldiers to take him to the infirmary. He was awake by noon, his wound already treated, and as the sun was going down he was taken with every other completed construct to a great field of wind-beaten, short, gray grass. The air was brisk and dry, the sky the same gray as the flattened grass. A stage had been hastily set up at one end the field.

On the stage was what looked like a very young man, not much more than a boy, with neatly combed auburn hair and porcelain skin. He wore a long, stiff, black robe with a high, round collar. Even from a distance, Jasyn could see the blue eyes that blazed above his ruddy cheeks and feel the intensity that radiated from his taut form.

The young man told the thousand constructs assembled in the field who he was, and who they were. He told them about GwenSeven – a coldblooded corporation that manufactured human slaves. He told them about the lives of servitude that had been planned for them, and the lives they could choose to live instead. He told them that he was there to set them free.

There were others there to help him– organizing the constructs into different groups, getting everyone housed and fed and ready to be transported away to their new lives. Before he left, however, JP met with every single construct at the manufacturing plant. Most chose to join him in what he called the greatest revolution since the formation of the True. Many begged to serve him personally. A few, very few, were afraid to fight and he blessed them and assured them a quiet life of peace.

Jasyn had been back in the infirmary when the young Commander came to visit. His eyes fell on Jasyn and seemed to shine with their own inner light. He sat on the edge of the hospital bed and pushed Jasyn's hair away from his face as tenderly as a mother would.

"How are you feeling, son?" JP asked.

Jasyn smiled. He didn't know a lot, but he knew it was odd for someone so young to be calling him son. "I'm okay," he said. "I get dizzy if I stand up for too long."

"What happened?"

"I don't know. The only thing I remember was waking up in a hallway, lying on the floor. People were shouting and running. After that, I blacked out again and woke up in here."

JP nodded. "That was where I found you. You must have been injured during the attack. It was mercifully short, and there were few casualties since the security against such an event was minimal and the staff had no reason or wish to fight."

Jasyn found out later that the staff, despite no reason or wish to fight, was slaughtered down to the last man. By that time, he was an officer commissioned aboard the Chimeran Battle Cruiser *Resurrection*, and was convinced that they had deserved it.

JP cocked his head at Jasyn, his blue eyes curious. "Do you remember any training they gave you here, or what you were made for?"

Jasyn shook his head slowly as he thought. "I don't remember anything before I woke up in the corridor."

JP nodded. "Well, it is obvious that you are custom-made. I can tell just by looking at you." He turned to a nearby medic, a handsome male construct with dark hair and dark eyes in a white lab coat. "Have you checked his vitals?"

The handsome young man nodded with a smile. "I did."

"And?"

The medic's smile became a grin. "They are the closest I have ever seen to yours," he confided.

JP started. "You mean..."

The young medic shook his head quickly, his smile fading just as quick. "No, sir. He wasn't made for...for that. But," he continued, his smile returning, "he's tight."

JP nodded thoughtfully. "You know what is going on here?" he asked Jasyn.

Jasyn nodded, smiling. "Of course."

JP shook his head. "No. I mean the big picture, my son. I mean, do you know what we are up against?"

Jasyn took his meaning and shifted his eyes away as he considered what the young Commander was asking. After a moment he nodded, slowly. "I heard what you said yesterday, about us and about GwenSeven."

"And?"

Jasyn scowled, his face a mask of concentration, then nodded again. "You are right. We can't let them go on doing what they are doing. Not to us – not to anyone." He turned his hazel eyes up to the Chimeran.

The slightly freckled face of the Commander brightened and he gave Jasyn a quick nod. "That is exactly right," he commended. JP paused for a moment, considering the young man on the bed. "I would like you to serve with me, as one of my officers," he said. "It will not be easy. Our fight will be long, our road treacherous, and you must have a strong heart and committed to The One in the most Zealous way."

Jasyn smiled, taken by the zeal and devotion of the young man before him. "You can count on me, sir," he answered. And he meant it.

For almost a century Jasyn had worked for the Zealot Chimeran, often working or fighting side by side with him.

Together, they had planned and executed mission after mission for the Cause. He could not count the battles they had fought, the plots they had designed or overturned, nor the odds that they had won against – time and time again.

JP was more than just his Commander. He was everything Jasyn could remember growing up with – a father, a teacher, a confidante. JP had always kept Jasyn close, more than any other officer aboard the *Resurrection*. He had shared plans with him that he had not shared with the other Chimeran leaders. Jasyn knew that even JP felt that they were closer than most.

Jasyn's eyes darted to Faith as the craft shifted, slowing down. She smiled at him as she spoke to someone light years away via the jeweled comset hooked into her ear. He forced a smile as well but it made him feel sick to do it. He knew that the ruse was drawing to an end. He knew that in a very short time, it would all be over for him.

⊰⊱

After they had docked with the villa, the two of them, exhausted, headed straight for the bedroom. Faith, of course, was called immediately away by work. By none other than the IGC Director of Artificial Intelligence, Barin Trey. Jasyn was only slightly consoled by the fact that Faith would be occupied for some time. A touch more consoled by the fact that he never planned on seeing the man again.

With a sigh and a kiss, she left the bedroom and headed for her office.

As soon as she had gone, Jasyn stopped undressing and went to the closed door and paused, listening. He could hear Faith's fading voice giving Penny instructions as she crossed the room. Satisfied, he put a careful finger on the door handle and slid the hasp on the electromagnetic bolt.

Moving quickly and ignoring the open shirt that flapped about his body, he went to the wing chair where he had left his coat. He picked it up and pulled his acrylic from the inner pocket before dropping the jacket back onto the chair.

Jasyn strode across the room, past the bed to the vanity, and dropped down onto the velvet-covered bench. He reached out and pulled his hand down the side of the mirror that was farthest to the right like he had seen Faith do so many times – like he himself had done many times as well.

The mirrors did their dance, changing and shifting. Some became holoboards, others turned into compute screens. Half a dozen were flat screens with a video feed. A ghostpad appeared on the vanity's glassy counter. The GwenSeven mainframe was wide open.

It was nothing for Jasyn to rig his acrylic to serve as an exterior hard drive that would leave no trace on the mainframe. Using the transformed vanity as a transmitter afforded him the ability to send a message directly to JP, without having to relay it through the broadband satellites needed to send a message via his acrylic.

He initiated the outlink, changed the format on his acrylic to mimic a keyboard, and laid the acrylic over the ghostpad. Jasyn, his face drawn and intense, pecked out a quick, encrypted message on the keyboard of his acrylic.

His decision already made, he hardly paused before sending JP the location of the Last Castle, instigating the assassination of Charity de Rossi. Next, he typed in the names and positions of those in the high ranks of GwenSeven and the InterGalactic Council and was sure to let JP know that they would be at the Castle for the big party, and when it would be held. He was sure not to forget to let JP know what his missing Engineer was up to, and where he could be found. The construct felt no sorrow, in fact quite the opposite, that the man would now be hunted down by Petrov and have to face the judgment of the Commander's blade.

He sent the message but, before he disengaged from the mainframe, Jasyn had one more item to take care of for the night. He uploaded Faith's contact file, which was pretty much composed of every living being in the galaxy. After a brief search he was able to find the one he wanted.

Jasyn pulled his index finger down along the glass, mousing over the name of Barin Trey. He swiped his left hand over towards the left side of his body, pulling up a column holo. He drew his right finger towards himself along the smooth glass until he found the line he was looking for in the column of listed commands that floated in the air in front of and slightly to the left of his jaw. He tapped his finger on the glass and the line he wanted became highlighted in red.

Jasyn took one last glance at the screen of light that floated before him, making sure everything was correct. He was fairly certain that there were only two things that needed to match, and they did. In one column was highlighted the name of Barin Trey. The selection in the other list, lit up in red letters, showed only one word.

Jasyn chose and approved the selection. An integrated security band popped up, giving him the choice to decline. He approved the selection once more, overriding the security band. Two words were highlighted in blue light across the holo screen as the designation: Barin Trey. The one word in red was the action required: terminate.

The Operations Officer did not pause for more than the time it took to make sure he had the right person before he hit the key that would designate the end of the smarmy bastard's life. Then he pulled the plug and set about putting everything in Faith's vanity back to where it had been.

Moving intently, he disengaged the acrylic from the mainframe and returned it to its former state as a woman's vanity. He returned the magnetic earrings he had used to rig his acrylic to inside the jewelry drawer from where he had borrowed them.

Crossing the carpet on cat's feet, he released the magnetic bolt with a breath of a sigh and then returned the acrylic to the wing chair, this time simply dropping it on top of his coat.

The construct finished undressing and slid into Faith's giant bed of gold and copper silk. He crossed muscled arms behind his head, lacing his fingers at the back of his neck. Staring at the ceiling, he thought of the message he just sent to the Commander of the Chimeran Battle Cruiser *Resurrection*.

Jasyn realized that he suddenly didn't feel too well, and did his best to ignore the sinking sensation in his stomach. He told himself that he was doing the right thing, and that was all that mattered.

TWO TWO

Blue spent an excruciating morning giving Gemma a tour of the Opal Dragon, only for the elfin cadet to look at every crewmember with haughty disdain. They stopped in the Atrium for a coffee before continuing to the upper decks.

A bright-eyed young man came up to the polished metal bar where they stood waiting. "Good morning, ladies," he greeted cheerfully. "What can I get for you?"

"Do you have pressed ijara caff?" Gemma demanded.

"No," he said. "The only pressed caff we have is inda."

Gemma rolled her eyes. "I should have known" she said, disgusted. "Well, if that's all you have, I guess I'll have to take it."

The young man turned nervous eyes to the Jordan in shimmering black. "I'll take anything with lots of milk and sugar," she said, encouraging him to relax. "Just put a shot of whiskey in it," she whispered. He smiled and gave her a curt nod as he hurried away and busied himself behind the bar getting their drinks. Blue turned her attention back to the sour-faced elf in opal-colored coveralls.

"So," Blue said, "why don't you tell me why you are you here?"

"All of the cadets from the Jordan Training Center were sent to…"

"Don't bullshit me," Blue told her. "You can tell me or I can find out somewhere else."

Gemma's dark eyes narrowed as the lie came to her

lips, then decided the bitter truth would be sweeter. "I was promised a commission."

That took Blue aback. "They can't do that."

"They can and they will. I don't know the details, of course. Only that a new Jordan would be needed aboard the Opal Dragon."

"If you haven't noticed," Blue said, leaning close to the woman, "this Dragon only has two Fledglings, and it already has two Jordans."

"Not from what I've heard," Gemma said, lifting her chin.

"Scarlett will be coming back," Blue told her. "You can count on it."

"I heard she was diagnosed with SM. That's not just something pilots recover from and return to work like they have had the flu."

Blue snorted. "Well, you don't know Scarlett," she told her. "I have never known anyone more obstinate or fiercely competitive than the Red Jordan."

Gemma leered at the Jordan. "You sound like you like her. I was told that you two didn't get along."

Blue shrugged. "Scarlett and I have had our moments, good and bad. But I respected her. I still do. And if there is one thing I know, it is that Scarlett will find a way back to her Fledgling."

"Maybe she will," Gemma agreed with a malicious smile. "Maybe another Fledgling will be in need of a Jordan."

There was a shimmer of sparkling darkness and the black-clad form of the Jordan was upon cadet in an instant with the speed of a snake upon its prey. Gemma found her back pressed tight against the rounded edge of the steel counter, looking down into the enraged face of Jordan Blue. Her scar stood out like a red flare against her skin and her single blue eye blazed like a sapphire held to the sun.

"How dare you imply that I would be relieved from duty!"

she hissed. "I could have your ass in a sling for suggesting such a thing without grounds!"

Gemma regained her composure and straightened her shoulders. "Without grounds? Look at yourself!" she hissed. "I am quite sure self-mutilation is grounds for Section Eight – release from military duty for psychological or psychiatric reasons."

Blue took a step back as if slapped. "I was not mutilating myself," she said, her voice barely above a whisper. "I had reason to believe that there was a camera in my prosthetic transmitting data to a non-IGC entity."

Gemma's thin lips pulled up into a shark-like grin. "That sounds like schizophrenic paranoia, to me."

"It's not! There was a damned camera in my eye!"

"Hmm," Gemma grunted, crossing her arms over her thin chest. "And was the Intel Officer able to determine the location to where it was transmitting?"

Blue lowered her voice and raised her chin. "I destroyed it before it could be examined by any IGC personnel."

Gemma's dark eyes narrowed to slits. "How convenient."

Jordan Blue could feel herself trembling with rage. She had killed a lot of people in the line of duty over the years; starfights, combat, and hand to hand. She had never given much thought to any of them. It was all part of her job. Never before had she outright wanted to kill anyone. Not until now.

Gemma's lips pressed together into a tight smirky line. "I've even heard that you talk to ghosts."

Though Galen had been standing to the side during the entire exchange, Blue hadn't spared him so much as a glance. Now, it was all she could do to keep herself from looking at him and she was tremendously relieved that she and Gemma were the only ones at the caff bar.

"Don't be ridiculous," Blue said, keeping her voice quiet and even. Her mind flew back to only the day before when she had told Galen that she didn't care if anyone thought she was crazy. A lot had changed in one dimlight.

The young man brought them their drinks, setting the hot cups down carefully. "Those are on the house, Jordan," he said, giving her a wink. Blue nodded dumbly, hardly hearing him.

"You might want to bring her another that is straight whiskey," Gemma said demurely as she sipped from her cup.

The man glanced at Blue who shook her head and drank her pressed caff. He really had put a shot of liquor in it and for that she was glad.

"Let's finish this, shall we?" Jordan Blue asked.

The cadet smiled. "Let's." She turned her dark, almond-shaped eyes on the barrista. "That's awful," she said, jerking her chin towards her cup. "You ought to be ashamed to serve it."

"Mine was fabulous," Blue said, giving him a smile. "Next time I see you in Technx, the drink is on me."

The young barrista smiled at her though his eyes darted nervously towards Gemma. He swallowed. "That will be nice," he said, though he obviously thought it would be nicer if the Jordan got the cadet somewhere else. "Thank you, Jordan."

"Let's go," Blue said sharply and walked out with the dark-haired elf right behind her, still leering at the young man behind the long, steel counter.

After Gemma had rebuffed, alienated, or downright insulted everyone she was introduced to, Jordan Blue finally brought her to the bridge of the Dragon. There was quite a lot more to see and people to meet, but the black-clad Jordan was hoping to end the awful morning that she had spent giving the cadet a tour of the ship. The barrista was not the only one repulsed by the woman and Jordan Blue had decided that she was quite finished with her.

"This is Chiara," Blue said, holding out a hand and indicating the outrageously tall, angular woman in the seat to the right.

She had light blonde hair pulled back into a tight bun and inquisitive blue eyes that peered through the square back glasses that she wore. "She's our Navigator."

"Don't you mean Astrogator?" Gemma asked, scornful.

Blue smirked. "I would if she was just astrogating us through space."

Gemma frowned. "That's right," she admitted. "She has to navigate through time as well."

"Very good!" Blue exclaimed sarcastically, as if praising a child. "Maybe they will make you a Captain and you can skip Jordanhood altogether."

Gemma gave her tight-lipped smile that said she would, if the IGC would let her. It made Blue's skin crawl.

Chiara smiled nervously, not sure what to do or if she should say anything. To her relief, the Jordan sighed in disgust and moved on.

"This is Darius," Blue continued, nodding to the Communications Officer, an elf with black skin and black hair. He rose from his seat to greet the recruit. "He handles all communications aboard the Dragon."

"It is a pleasure to meet you," the elf said, offering Gemma his hand. The cadet looked at him and then his hand with obvious disgust.

"I'm sure."

Darius glanced at Jordan Blue who shook her head apologetically. Darius sat back down and looked at Chiara. Her angular shoulders rose in a shrug.

"Alright," Blue said. "I've had enough of this shit." She turned to where the Executive Officer was seated at the helm reviewing star charts on a glass monitor. "Commander Blaylock?"

The XO looked up with scowl, a crease between his hawk-like eyes. "Yes, Jordan?"

"Permission for patrol, sir?"

Blaylock remained motionless for a second before turning his eyes back to the monitor. "Permission denied."

"Sir?"

Blaylock looked up again, clearly annoyed. "You have a job to do here, Jordan. I sincerely doubt that GL has been shown the entire ship, nor been introduced to everyone she needs to meet." He gave Blue a meaningful glare before turning his attention back to the charts.

"Sir?"

Blaylock looked up again and this time his jaw was clenched. "Yes, Jordan?" he asked, his voice tight with controlled hostility.

Blue noticed that Darius and Chiara kept their faces carefully averted. "The Dragon is in the near coordinates of the Aplesh Moon."

"And?" Blaylock demanded impatiently.

"My field pack is need of a check, possibly a repair. It was purchased on Aplesh, and I would like to have it examined, and fixed if need be, at the same place where I bought it."

Blaylock seethed inwardly. He wanted to tell Blue to go to hell and take her field pack with her, but knew he could not deny an officer an exam for their safety gear. He was sure that Blue knew that as well.

"Fine!" He spat. "GL…"

"Can continue her tour with Corporal Blake," Jordan Blue interrupted, hopefully belaying the chances that he might suggest she take the bitch along for the ride. "He has already agreed and, just having been given a tour and introductions so recently, knows just where to take her."

Blaylock glared at her, furious. "Just go, Godammit!" he ordered. "And I want the holo receipt, so I know you're not bullshitting me!" Blue gave him a quick bow and turned on her heel and strode quickly from the bridge.

"She's all yours," she told Corporal Blake as she strode by without looking at him or Gemma. "Have fun."

Corporal Blake swallowed hard and hurried into the bridge to assist in any way he could. He had been told when he was first assigned to the Opal Dragon to make friends quickly. "Everything onboard IGC ships is very political," his father had warned him.   "It's not what you know, it's who you know."

Blake had nodded dutifully to his Da at the time, determined to succeed. Within his very first week, however, the Executive Officer was furious with him and the only Jordan on board terrified him. He had volunteered quickly at Blue's suggestion that he give the cadet a tour. She could be a good friend to have, especially if she was going to be a Jordan someday.

The corporal entered the bridge and cringed inwardly at the Commander's glare and gave the cadet a quick bow. "I will be glad to assist you, ma'am," he said. Gemma smiled wickedly at him. He was the first person who had ever called her ma'am. She would be sure not to forget that.

"Thank you, Corporal."

Once in the corridor, Galen's laugh rang in Blue's ears. "Does your generator really need a repair?" he asked. "It's practically new and the best on the market less than a year ago. Better, probably."

Blue shrugged. "Anything to get out of here. Away from her at least."

Galen laughed again, though this time it was little more than a chuckle. "She is horrible," he agreed. "I can't believe she made it through Jordan Training."

"She didn't make it all the way through," Blue told him with a sidelong glance in his direction. It wasn't easy since he since he was on her right side, where her vision was limited. "That cycle was interrupted by the Chimeran attack. Remember?"

"I do, but she made it far enough to be assigned to a Dragon. The only one that was assigned to this Dragon. Someone must have plans for her." Blue stopped walking to face Galen, something she had never done before where she could be seen by other people.

"If that bitch ever gets a commission, I guarantee that she will be shot by her own troops within a week." The Jordan turned and continued her course towards Fledgling Bay.

"She's that bad?" Galen asked. Blue glared at him with her single eye and he held up his hands apologetically. "Okay. She is that bad. I just don't know why she infuriates you so much. It seemed like Scarlett was just as bad, possibly worse."

The Jordan shook her head, making the white-gold coils of hair swish between her shoulder blades. "No. Scarlett was an angry person, an arrogant person, but not a bad person. This woman," Blue said, spitting out the last word, "is a snake. I would sooner trust a Golgoth."

"That serious?"

"I think she would kill me without a second thought," Blue said, "if she thought it would get her a Fledgling."

"I wouldn't let her hurt you," Galen said, his voice stern. The Jordan gave him a wry smile as they walked along. "You can't protect me when I am asleep," she said, her voice gentle.

"Then Cyan would keep you safe," he said, though he sounded more hopeful than sure.

"Where do you go, anyway?" Blue asked, changing the subject. "When I am asleep."

Galen smiled. "I'm still with you, but it is like I am asleep too, or awake and watching you sleep."

Blue smiled as they entered Fledgling Bay. "I like that," she said. She smiled at the crewmembers that greeted her and they grinned in return. Despite the black flight suit and the eye patch, it made them feel good to see the Jordan smiling again.

She cleared the security gate in the wall of detfleck and a second guard came out and handed her a wax-paper bag, the top folded over.

"From Hydell," he told her when Blue looked at him and the bag with surprise.

"Ah, yes. Thank you!"

He gave her a nod and returned to the monitor room.

"I almost forgot," she said as she turned and headed for the Fledglings. "I'm glad he remembered."

"Remembered what?" Galen asked.

Hydell was a cook on the Opal Dragon that she had become friendly with just recently. After her bout of paranoia regarding espionage and suspecting everyone on board, she had made a bit of an effort to come to know more of the crew, especially those with which she was not well acquainted.

"Something for Chang," she said.

She felt the wave of welcome from both Fledglings as she approached them. Fledge's silver skin glowed crimson and he gave off the effect of a puppy. He had come a long way in the last few weeks in his feelings for the Blue Jordan.

Blue laughed as she approached Cyan and then climbed the silver steps he had made for her down the side of his body. "Yes!" Blue called out to the other Fledgling, though she had the feeling he could already read her intent. "You can come!"

Fledge glowed in excitement and relief as she climbed inside his brother and made her way forward before she dropped down into the pilot's seat. Blue knew that Fledge did not like to get left behind any more. His growing affection for her was largely due to the fact that they had been slowly forming a bond of their own, one that had been strengthened once she had been injected with Cyan's genetic material. Also, she knew that he was afraid of Gemma.

The fact that a forty-two meter, metal encased, Dragon

Fledgling that could breathe plasma fire was scared by a wasp of a woman only proved to the Jordan that Gemma was pure evil.

The Blue Jordan powered up Cyan with little more than a thought and took both Fledglings through the bay door of the Opal Dragon and out into the cold dark on a course for Aplesh. Talking to them out loud, and toying with their speed, Blue had the Fledglings touching down on the moon in less than two hours.

The Jordan secured the Fledglings at an IGC compound, her eye scanning the strange green sky. She navigated the copper city in a self-mobilized aircab that was little more than an elliptical metal sheath around her body. "Jeez," she muttered, dodging though traffic like an oversized bullet, "why are air cabs so small here?"

"Because parking is a bitch," Galen said softly, grinning.

Blue laughed. "I see that you found room for yourself in this moving coffin," she said, referring to the fact that she was lying on him in the same manner as if they were both reclining on a couch.

"I can ride on the outside if you want," he offered.

"That's okay," she laughed. "I like you right where you are. Just don't get up to any funny business. I'm renting this thing by the hour."

"So?" Galen asked. "Are you broke? I'm sure I left you all of my money."

"You had money?"

They both went into gales of laughter, the cab speeding along into a district of less than savory stores with dirty, darkened windows. The cab turned down an alley, headed for Chang's and arrived there with a jolt only seconds later, both of the riders giggling like children.

Despite his name, which led most to believe that he was from Indasia and of Earth-Asian descent, Chang was a

Caucasian human from Europa with bushy white hair and even bushier eyebrows. He had been a doctor, which was how Galen had known him. After losing his medical license, Chang moved to Aplesh and opened a seedy tech shop. He was as expensive as a surgeon and Blue was pretty sure that most of his technology was done off the books, and most likely illegal.

The Jordan opened the door to his shop and two tiny silver bells hanging from a piece of string announced her arrival. The response that came from the back room was immediate and gruff.

"I'm closed!"

The shop was a narrow hallway of shelves packed with boxes, wires, and what appeared to be body parts.

"Like hell you are!" Blue called out grinning, her blue eye looking up and down the glass case that split the crowded hall in half, but she didn't spy anyone. There was a murky light coming from the back room that was separated from the shop by a curtain of hanging metal beads.

A beefy hand was thrust between the metallic strings and it pulled the curtain aside enough for an eye topped with a bushy white eyebrow to peer through. The hand disappeared and, after a thunk and curse, was replaced by the whole head and bulky body. Chang came into the room, clapping his thick hands a single time in greeting.

"Jordan Blue!" he exclaimed, ambling down the slim walkway between the shelves and the glass case than ran the length of the room. Smiling broadly under a white puff of moustache, he embraced the black-clad Jordan, lifting her off her feet.

"It's good to see you, doctor," she said, embracing him as well amd clapping him on the back. Chang grasped her thin shoulders and pushed her away gently, holding her at arms length, examining her with sharp gray eyes.

"Mmm hmm," he remarked, his white brows knitting

together. "And how well are you seeing?" he asked, frowning at the eye patch.

"Fine," she assured him.

"Mmm hmmm." Chang tilted his head.

Blue smiled and shook her head. "Maybe my vision is a little limited on that side," she admitted. Chang grunted in agreement but stopped giving her the once over and fixed his gray eyes on her blue one, still holding her shoulders.

"I heard about Galen," he said. "I'm sorry."

Blue shook her blonde head. "Don't be. He always said you were a hack, and a mediocre doctor at best."

Galen looked at her, unbelieving. "I never said any of that," he hissed with a frown. Blue remained still, refusing to look at him. Chang tilted his head, frowning at her for a second before the corner of his lips twitched.

"He's haunting you, isn't he?"

This time it was Blue's turn to look incredulous. "How did you know that?" she asked, her scarred face splitting into a grin. Galen made a face.

"Haunting seems to be a very impolite choice of words," he muttered as Chang shrugged.

"I knew him well enough to know that he wouldn't leave you willingly, and that if he ever called me a hack I'd haunt *him*!"

Blue laughed and Chang glanced at the wax-paper bag she held in one hand. "What'cha got there?" he asked.

Blue held up the bag with a coy smile. "A little present."

Chang rubbed his large hands together. "Tea cookies kind of present?"

Blue nodded and held out the bag, which he took eagerly. He gave her a smile that was oddly childlike before he moved his hefty form down the aisle and into the narrow space behind the glass case. He found a place for the bag on a relatively empty spot on a shelf and turned his attention to the Jordan.

"Well, my little lady, to what do I owe the honor of this visit? I doubt it was to contribute to my growing waistline." He placed meaty forearms along the glass countertop and leaned forward over them, making the steel bindings on the case creak in loud protest. "Do you need a replacement?" he asked, motioning with a thick finger at her missing eye.

"Certainly not," Blue told him. "Not yet, at least. I'd like you to take a look at my field generator."

Chang frowned, his bushy white brows drawing together over gray eyes that were still as sharp as steel. "Something wrong?" he asked, obviously disturbed at even the possibility of such a thing.

The Jordan's shoulders moved up under the black shimmer of her flight suit. "I don't think it's the generator as much as it is me. I need you to adjust the heat output - even at the max I could use it to be a little warmer."

"Ah!" Chang exclaimed, pleased as if everything suddenly made sense. "That does not surprise me, considering how thin you are. You look like a wraith! Have you considered simply beefing up your diet? It's unhealthy to be so thin!"

"If that's the case," Galen added good-naturedly, "you must be the healthiest man on this moon!"

Blue suppressed a grin and, by the nature of her partially hidden smile, Chang's gray eyes narrowed in suspicion. Blue opened her mouth to explain but he shook his head.

"You don't have to tell me," he said. "I can imagine."

Blue laughed. "You know him too well," she agreed. "But as to the weight," she shrugged again, "this seemed easier." Chang sighed and the counter groaned under his shifting weight. He twirled a thick hand in his own direction, as if telling her to give it over and get on with it. The Jordan rolled up her left sleeve and laid her forearm against the glass, palm up.

Chang reached into the glass case and pulled out two long

slender metal stems that looked like giant needles. "Can I get you anything before I start?" he offered, glancing up at her with the needles poised above the platinum cuff that encased her left wrist. Blue shook her head and his bushy eyebrows went up. "Are you sure?" The Jordan nodded and, with another sigh, Chang bent his head down over the cuff.

Blue tilted her head, watching his left eye as the pupil grew smartly with a click that was barely audible, even with her elfin ears. She knew that Chang had a scoping zoom lens on that eye that was a high-grade optic, and that it had been self-installed.

She looked away as he popped open the metal cuff and went to work, her blue eye examining the many boxes stacked against his walls, stuffed with bits of everything from weaponry to medical supplies. Some shelves were crammed with thermite pistols and photon charges, or parts and pieces of both, and the glass case that split the room was overflowing with wires and miscellaneous prosthetics.

"So," Chang said conversationally as he exchanged the large set of needles for a smaller pair, "how are you - other than being dangerously underfed and missing an eye?" Blue grinned.

"Other than that, I'm fabulous." She pressed her lips together, undecided for a moment and then plunged ahead. "They gave me the triptych."

Chang's needles went perfectly still and only his eyes moved as he glanced up at her face. "Is that so?" he asked.

Blue swallowed hard and nodded. "So you had heard of it before?"

Chang grunted and returned to his work. "I had heard rumors of it," he said.

The Jordan felt the bile rise in her throat. Once again, she was the one in the dark. It was a feeling that she was getting more and more, one that she was beginning to fear and detest.

What else have they not told me?

"So?" Chang prodded without looking up. "What did it do

to you?" Blue almost shrugged out of reflex but, remembering the close work he was at, she simply swallowed against the burning in her throat.

"I can see things that I couldn't before. Hear things that I couldn't."

But obviously not everything, she thought. *They are still keeping things from me. A b-class officer and I am still on a need-to-know basis.*

"Like the good doctor?" Chang asked.

"No, he was popping up long before that."

Galen, who had been leaning over the counter to watch Chang work, reached up and stroked her cheek. The narrow room was silent for a while as the ex-doctor worked and the other two watched, alone in their thoughts.

"Are you after any new weaponry?" Chang asked as he exchanged tools once again but kept working.

"Not really."

"Are you sure?" he asked. "I just made a new prototype that combines a photon charge and a laser. It is only good for a single pulse, but its casing makes it invisible to any weapon screen out there at the moment."

Blue frowned, knowing that she had the privilege of wearing a laser pistol even to a suburban mall if she wanted. "Why would I need a concealed weapon?" she asked.

Chang closed her cuff with a snap, sealed the pin and gave her a shrug. "You never know," he said, his voice grave.

Blue thought of Gemma and how the woman had said she wouldn't stop until she had what she wanted. Galen, still leaning on the counter, looked at her with his blue eyes through the strands of his black hair and nodded.

"Take it," he said.

Blue smiled at Chang in thanks as she pushed her black sleeve back down to her wrist. "Alright," she agreed. "Let's see it."

Grinning, Chang reached into the ribbons of metal and plastic under his counter and produced a slender wand that appeared to be made of glass, slightly bulged at one end.

"Here is the trigger," he said, showing her the holo-trip on the bulged end. "The charge will come from the other end."

"Range?"

"Up to twenty meters. Come and see me in a month and I will have it up to a hundred. Till then, the closer you are the more damage you will do."

Blue smiled, making her face scrunch up on the scarred side as she accepted the wand from Chang. It was not glass, as she had first thought, but a very hard and very clear plastique. She held it up, examining its length. It was slender, but almost equal to the length of her forearm.

"I thought with one charge it would be tiny. Something I could put under my cuff, or in my lapel pocket."

"That kind of compact weapon makes the material too dense, which is what would make it show up on any weapons or body scan. Elongating the case as well as the photon charge spreads it too thin to be recognized as a weapon by any scanner."

"Where the hell am I supposed to conceal this thing?" she asked.

"Your boot," both doctors said at once.

Blue grinned and tossed her head. "I was afraid you were going to say my ass."

Chang snorted. "Would it be easy for you to pull it out of there and fire it in an emergency?" he asked.

Blue shrugged. "I guess that depends on what I was doing at the time."

Galen laughed as she leaned down and slipped the weapon down her leg where her black flight suit was tucked into her black flight boot. It fit perfectly, and was perfectly concealed.

"Thank you, Doctor," she said, reaching into the neck of her flight suit to pull out her credentials card. "How much do I owe you?"

"Bah!" Chang spat with a scowl. "Don't insult me!" Blue was about to protest when his face suddenly brightened. "But hey, Jordan. How about a quick kiss for an old man?"

Blue laughed and leaned over the counter to give him a peck on the cheek when he wrapped a meaty hand around the back of her neck and pulled her close to plant a strong and lingering kiss on her lips. Her blue eye widened in surprise but before she could push herself away he released her, laughing heartily.

"Take that, you black elfin bastard!" Chang shouted good-naturedly at the ghost he couldn't see.

Galen stood by Blue, shaking with fury as the Jordan herself laughed, drawing the back of her hand over her mouth to wipe off Chang's sloppy kiss.

"I hope that gives you a heart attack!" Galen hissed at him. Chang laughed harder, as if he could hear him.

"How pissed is he?" he asked Blue, who laughed with him.

"Pretty pissed," she assured him, shaking her head.

"Well, I owed him a good one for many a year," Chang said, his laughter dying down to chuckles.

"I am sure you did," Blue agreed, presenting her credentials card. "But I'm afraid you're going to have to charge me something, besides a kiss. I need a receipt."

Still chuckling, Chang pulled a heavy square of rubber from under the counter and placed her card on it before typing numbers on the side. The Jordan laid her hand over the card to authorize the transaction and after the glow around it died, removed the card and tucked it back into her flight suit.

"Thanks," she told the ex-surgeon, her sapphire eye full of merriment and respect. She put her hand on the door, making the bells tremble and chime.

"You are most welcome, my lady. And please, do not become a stranger. You can come to me for anything."

"Thanks, Chang – I will." Blue started to push open the door and then paused, "And Chang?" The doctor raised bushy white brows in response. "Start dating again," she advised. "You've still got the fire in you."

Chang gave her a low bow and the Jordan left the shop in girlish giggles, a scowling Galen following close behind.

TWO THREE

The Ambassador licked each of his stubby fingers, one by one, starting with the thumb and ending with the pinky before doing the same to his other hand.

He had indulged in many "business" dinners in the past month and had enjoyed them all quite heartily. His dinner with a renegade Golbli had been the most interesting and his lunch with a Persucant most delicious, and not just because of the sex afterwards, or the murder.

But it was the Lentochs that the Aridian ended up having a third and possibly final meeting with – because of the money. In the end, didn't everything come down to price - and what everyone was willing to pay?

This time they met in a very expensive and yet very circumspect tasting room near a far moon of Jupiter. It was convenient for the Ambassador, even more so for the Ambassador's doppelgänging passenger. The Aridian was headed for Adrogea for another meeting, just as important but along different lines of the same deal. The meeting place had been suggested hesitantly but in the hope that the distance could be closed between The Flower and MW1 without waiting till the last minute. Fast ships were expensive. The Lentochs, however, agreed to the place quickly and with poorly hidden excitement, making the Aridian wonder what the proximity meant for them.

The Ambassador made the trip from the artificial galaxy to the real one on an Embassy Carrier, blending and bluffing with other diplomats and would-be dignitaries. From there it was a transport to the Callisto sector where the Lentochs provided a private craft to the exclusive tasting bistro in a wealthy satellite suspended out in space.

An enormous window of hyper-glass afforded the patrons an unobstructed view of Jupiter. Its swirling mass was like a great lurid eye, peeking into the dining room like an evil giant squinting into a dollhouse casement. If one stood close to the glass and looked left, it was possible to make out the larger moons, hanging like small coins minted from drops of alien metals.

The Ambassador did not bother with the window or the view. Big meals and big deals were his silent mirthy mantra these days. Tonight, the deal looked as promising as the meal had been and the Ambassador was grinning from one side of his round face to the other.

"It has been lovely chatting with you and the dinner was quite marvelous, I must say." He patted his rotund belly and seemed to go slack before he suddenly rolled forward. "But now," the Ambassador declared, pouring cream into his cup of coffee until it reached the brim and threatened to spill over the side, "I have given you all of the information that you requested. All we need now are the funds, per our previous conversation, so that we may secure delivery of your...package."

"And the Jordan?" the smaller Lentoch whispered. Its voice was metallic, soft, and echoey.

"It is quite certain that I can provide you with a Jordan," the Ambassador rumbled. "For a short time at least. But, in the interest of good business, I will only expect payment for the Fledgling. Ten percent now and the rest upon delivery, as agreed."

The Ambassador leaned back in his chair and folded his stubby fingers over the expanse of his stomach.

The taller of the Lentochs nodded sagely and laid an acrylic face-up on the table in between them. The Ambassador put two fingers to his lips as he burped, and then placed a mini-acrylic on top of the one already on the table - face down so that the acrylics were glass to glass.

There occurred a series of soft flashing lights exchanged between the two devices. To the Aridian it looked like some sort of technological sexual intercourse, but of course she knew it would not be diplomatic to say so. It was only seconds before each went dark.

The Ambassador removed the mini acrylic and glanced at the numbers glowing softly under the glass. With a pleased expression and a quick nod, the mini-acrylic was tucked away into a hidden pocket in his voluminous jacket. The Lentochs removed their acrylic from the table and gave the Ambassador a small but polite bow with their slightly pointed heads.

"Very good," the taller one said in a voice that, to the Aridian, was clearly threaded through a synthesizer. "Now that business has been concluded for the nonce, if you will be so kind as to excuse us for the night?"

"Of course!" the Ambassador agreed. "And the dinner bill?" he asked, raising his ginger eyebrows.

The Lentochs smiled. "Has already been taken care of," the taller one assured him as they rose to leave. "Feel free to stay and indulge for as long as you like. The craft will take you as far as Callisto."

The Ambassador grinned, hefting his bulk out of his chair. "Very good, very good. My thanks," he said bowing.

"Our pleasure," the small one said as they both bowed before turning to leave. The Rogue waved a fleshy hand at them as they departed and then sat back down to finish her coffee. And order another dessert.

⊂⊃⊂⊃

Calyph walked briskly away from the detfleck gate once he had cleared security. It was late and the most of those aboard the Dragon were either in bed or in the Atrium, and the Engineer had left the troll busy in his personal quarters so it would not be able to witness or record what he was doing.

Still, it wouldn't be wise to dawdle. He had to work quickly.

The elf passed between the Fledglings and circled behind Fledge, his blue eyes furtive. He set the canvas bag that held his instruments carefully on the floor. He forced himself to breathe as normally as he could, but was helpless to control the way his heart was hammering wildly in his chest.

I'm not doing anything wrong, he assured himself. *I'm not disobeying orders. In fact, I am doing just what the Commander ordered me to do.*

He was worried that the Fledglings might pick up on his anxiety and react in a way that he couldn't predict. In a way that might get him killed, one way or another. He reached up a hand and touched Fledge's flank in what he hoped was a reassuring manner.

"Besides," he whispered. "Blue said you trust me. And this won't hurt a bit. Cyan has already done it, and it brought him closer to Blue. You want to be close to your Jordan too, don't you?"

When there was no response, at least none that he could detect, Calyph pulled a canister of hyper-glass from the canvas bag on the floor and unscrewed the styrex lid. He set the lid aside and placed the mouth of the canister against Fledge's metal hide as high as he could reach where the body began to thin out into a tail.

Holding the glass in place with his left hand, he placed his right palm against the bottom of the canister. There was a moment where nothing appeared to be happening as he focused and then he began the draw. A few seconds later, drops of silver liquid began to form on the outside of the Fledgling's metal skin inside the glass cylinder, before they broke away and drifted to the right, towards Calyph's right palm on the bottom of the canister.

The quicksilver pellets gathered as they hit the circular wall of hyper-glass where they joined and began to spread. More droplets formed and followed, thicker and faster now, till the canister slowly filled with a silver rain that fell sideways.

"See how easy this is," he said softly, almost to himself. The cylinder became a quarter full, which was how much he had drawn from Cyan, but this time the Engineer kept pulling. His blue eyes remained trained on the cylinder as it filled halfway.

"Just a little bit more," he breathed. When the jar was three quarters full, Calyph removed the glass from the metal side of the Fledgling. The viscous liquid continued to aggregate and cling on the far right where the Engineer had his hand cupped around the bottom of the tube.

The elf carefully tipped it upright and gingerly pulled his hand away from the bottom. A few drops of quicksilver clung to Fledge's side, but disappeared back into his metal skin once Calyph released the pull. The Engineer retrieved the styrex lid and screwed it onto the glass vial as he dropped to his knees next to the canvas bag.

Reaching into the bag, he pulled out a syringe gun and held the tip against the styrex barrier of the lid and depressed the button on the side of the gun. The needle shot through the lid and began to suck up the metallic fluid like a robotic mosquito.

When the vial in the gun was full there was a click as the needle snapped back into the mechanism. Calyph placed the filled gun inside the bag and swallowed nervously. He looked around, licking his lips, and then pulled another syringe gun from his bag and repeated the process.

This gun seemed slower, as if it were taking longer to fill, but he was sure that it was just his imagination. When the needle finally snapped back a smile of relief broke across his face. He removed the tip of the gun from the lid of the canister and looked up to the sound of footsteps.

Panic filled his chest but before he had time to think or react, Jordan Blue was walking around the front of the Red

Fledgling, coming straight towards him. Her slender form was clad in the sparkling black flight suit and an eye patch of the same dark material shimmered where it covered her empty right eye socket. The left eye was a bright and blazing blue.

She stopped in surprise when she saw the Engineer crouched on the bay floor. Her body tensed and her hand automatically fell on the butt of the laser pistol she wore holstered just below her hip. After the second it took her to recognize him, she relaxed and started forward again. Galen followed, unseen by the elfin Engineer.

At the sight of the Jordan, however, Calyph felt a fine sheen of sweat break out over his whole body.

"Jordan Blue," he said as easily as he could. "What the hell are you doing up at this hour?"

Blue shrugged. "I hardly sleep at all these days," she said. "I come out here a lot when I'm restless."

Of course you do, Calyph thought. *Why the hell didn't I think about that?*

"What are you doing out here so late?" Blue asked with a scowl, though the look and her tone were due more to curiosity than suspicion. Her blue eye dropped to his hand and her frown melted in understanding. "Ohhh. You're drawing Fledge's fluid. Why so late?" she asked.

"I had busy day," Calyph answered quickly. "I was afraid that if I put it off, Commander Blaylock would..."

Blue held up a hand, cutting him off. "Say no more," she said with disgust. "That ass..." she began to say but faltered as her sapphire eye fell upon Calyph's open bag and spied the syringe gun lying inside. The eye flicked back up at the syringe in his hand and the Jordan cocked her head.

Calyph swallowed. *Shit.*

"Calyph," Blue began, drawing out his name. Her tone was casual and curious but her body began to go taut in a slow but sure manner, like a winding spring. "Why are there two syringes?"

"I..." was all he was able to get out before his throat locked out all sound.

The Jordan pounced like a cat and was on him in an instant, grabbing the elf by his collar. The Engineer's feet pedaled backwards as the lithe Jordan propelled him back. Had the wall been closer she would have drove him into it. As it was, he held onto the vial and the gun as best he could as he struggled to keep his feet. Blue, her fists wrapped in the front of his shirt, finally stopped pushing once they were past the tails of the Fledglings and shook him till his teeth rattled.

Galen followed and watched but kept silent.

"Who is the second injection for, Calyph?" she demanded, giving him another shake. "Who?"

Calyph thought he was beyond being amazed, but he was. And scared shitless. The Jordan was a head shorter than him, weighed next to nothing, and only had one eye, but she was surprisingly strong, and armed.

He was terrified of being caught in the lie that was on his lips, but what else could he do? He couldn't even explain his own situation, much less make some attempt to silence the enraged Jordan. His mind raced as he thought of what he would tell her, but she saved him the trouble. The blue eye that had been narrowed in anger, suddenly grew wide and her grip on the Engineer loosened.

"Gemma?" she asked in disbelief and horror. "You think that you can..."

"Not me! Commander Blaylock said..."

"Blaylock!" Blue spat his name as if it were a curse. "I should have known. And the Captain?" Blue demanded.

Calyph almost sagged in relief to be let off the hook so easily. He shook his head, his lips pressed together. "Commander Blaylock said not to trouble him, with the stress he has been under lately and all."

The Jordan's small hands balled into fists as she shook with rage. "And he thinks he can make himself a Jordan like he is making a cake?" she hissed. "That he has the authority to..."

"No," Calyph stammered, shaking his head. "He told me that this was coming from the IGC. If it works here they might implement it in other areas. On other Dragons."

The Jordan looked as if she had been slapped.

"What?" She stared at the Engineer, speechless.

"I have a hard time believing that," Galen said softly. Blue agreed.

She shook her head, her white locks whipping across the back of her black flight suit. "He's lying."

Calyph sighed and his shoulders dropped as he finally began to relax, at least a little. "I had the troll run a prelim protocol check on IGC proposed regulations regarding Dragons and Fledglings. It is something that they want to try." He was stretching the truth, praying that the Jordan would not know.

Blue looked at him, aghast. "So they can replace us. Just like that. So now Jordans, an elite group of trained fighters who have given their lives for their calling, can be replaced as easily as beef stock in the galley." Her head drooped and her body sagged as if she had been mortally wounded.

Calyph, not knowing what else to do, laid a hand on her shoulder, trying to reassure her. "They don't know if it will work," he offered, then sighed. "But it most likely will. It always has for the Captains."

Blue raised her head so that she had Calyph fixed in her single sapphire-colored eye, an eye that had become glacier cold. The Engineer felt that he was looking down the barrel of a loaded gun and snatched his hand from her shoulder.

"But it's *not* going to work," the Jordan said slowly, as if discovering the answer.

Calyph frowned. "What do you mean?"

Blue smiled and the smile was as cold as her eye. "I mean that you are not going to administer that shot to GL."

"But..."

"Calyph," Blue said, her voice low, "if you put Fledge's fluid into that bitch I will rip out your fucking heart."

Calyph swallowed, turning pale. At that moment he didn't know whom he feared most, the menacing Executive Officer or the ninety-eight pound, one-eyed Jordan. But he knew that it wasn't Blue or the XO that he would have to face in the end. It would be Tara.

Taking his indecision for a lack of cooperation made Blue shake with rage and a growling noise came from deep within her throat. A humming noise came from the Fledglings, drawing looks from both the elfin Engineer and the ghost of the elfin doctor. Then, abruptly, Blue seemed to get a grip on herself. Breathing deeply, she straightened and smiled again, which made Calyph turn an even whiter shade of pale.

"I know this is a difficult decision," she whispered. "A frightening decision, even though you are a civilian and not here under military orders. I'll make it easy on you," she said and turned on her heel.

"Noel?" Galen called to her retreating form. He had seen that look in her eye before, and on more than one occasion. It always meant trouble.

Calyph watched, frozen as she walked away, and then was galvanized into movement as she bent and snatched the other syringe gun from his bag. She whirled on him before he could catch her, one hand holding the syringe gun and the other hovering over the real gun holstered on her hip.

Calyph froze once again, holding up his own hands – the one hand that still held one of the syringe guns and the other that held the hyper-glass canister with the few droplet remains of Fledge's bio fluid inside - in a silent profession of non-threatening innocence.

The elfin Engineer and the half-elf Jordan faced each other in silence like gunfighters from another age, waiting to see who would move first. Four long seconds ticked away before Blue made the first move. Her already broken face split into a grin, making Calyph's stomach drop down into his bowels.

In a single, swift movement the Jordan tucked the syringe gun into the crook of her elbow and, pressing the tip deep into her inner arm, pulled the trigger.

There was a pause, just long enough for a sharp intake of breath as the needle shot though the Mylar of her suit and into her flesh, discharged its contents and snapped home. Then the Jordan fell forward, the syringe gun falling from numb fingers and clattering across the floor. Calyph lunged for her, dropping the hyper-glass canister as he fell to his knees and slid. He made it there just in time to break her fall and keep her from smacking her skull against the floor.

So did Galen.

Calyph eased the Jordan down, Galen on her other side, resting her face on the silver tarmac while her body twitched uncontrollably. Calyph dropped the unused syringe gun on top of his bag and laid a hand upon the Jordan's back. He could feel the flutter under her skin as all her muscles began to spasm. The scarred, right side of her face was against the floor, so that he could see her lone sapphire eye.

The Engineer watched as the pupil grew and grew until it blotted out the sparkling blue of her iris, and then kept on growing. The black spread like welling oil until it covered the entire surface of her eye while the Jordan twitched and flinched, her mouth opening and closing like a fish that had been roughly yanked from the pond.

The Jordan made a gurgling sound and jerked, then whispered words in a voice so low that even his sharp elfin ears could not decipher what she was saying.

Galen crouched next to her, his hands quickly feeling her face and her neck, checking her pulse and, though Calyph could not see him, he could see her bottom eyelid pull down as the ghostly doctor checked her eye. From what the Engineer could see, the entire orb was as black and shiny as a marble.

Though she barely spoke, Galen could hear her words as clear as a bell.

I can hear them, she mouthed, her red lips forming the words better than she could make the effort to breathe them out. *All of them.*

"What can you hear, Jordan?" Galen asked.

Their heartbeats...

"Their heartbeats?" Galen repeated, feeling the pulse in her neck while looking at his watch. "I thought you could hear those before."

Different now. Unique.

Calyph watched her lips move, his blue eyes as round as saucers.

Their hearts...each beat...is different...like a fingerprint.

The Jordan went completely still for a moment and let the heartbeats fill her being. The beating hearts of the Fledglings, the Dragon, and every soul on board. Her senses stretched, spreading like blue light across the universe. Her breath rasped in and out, leaving a small cone-shaped mist of fog on the silver tarmac near her lips.

She could hear them and, in her mind's eye, she could see them. She listened to the heartbeats and to her they were like an orchestra, each one a different instrument that added to the symphony of Dragonsound and Dragonsong. She could hear the great slow bass drum of the Iron Dragon as he cut through dark space, next to a binary star system with a white dwarf and red giant, surrounded by icy blue planets.

He.

The Jordan's mouth worked, not trying to say that he was in Andromeda System Seven, which she knew in an instant by sight, but that the Iron Dragon was a *he.*

Everyone believed that all of the Dragons, save for the two male Fledglings that were from the Opal Dragon, were female.

But not Ferrous, Jordan Blue thought. *Then how? How did he bear children?*

She had no time to ponder it. She pushed it to the back of her mind. She would discuss it later with Galen.

Meanwhile, her mind was traveling across the galaxies, seeing Onyx and Pearl - the two Dragons that flew together more often than any of the others - feeling the brass trumpets of their hearts stretch through her nerves, and the woodwinds sung by their children as they lit up the cells in her skin. Each heartbeat had its own sound, every voice echoed by the beat of the crewmembers, making an orchestra. Each orchestra combining to play a grand symphony that stretched across the universe.

The heartbeats of the Dragons were the strongest, then the heartbeats of the Fledglings. She could hear Cyan and Fledge, their chorus like a favorite and familiar song. Behind their sound, like the same instrument only farther away, she could hear another. The Jordan's lips moved but no sound came out.

Verdana, she mouthed, the corners of her red lips quirking up in the tiniest of smiles. *You're out there. Somewhere.*

The Jordan blinked her lone eye, letting the sounds fill her soul. There were other beats, stronger than the humans but softer than the Fledglings. The corners of her mouth twitched again as she realized where they were coming from – the eggs.

She let her eyelid drop down over the black orb of her eye and stretched her feelings out across time and space. The beats were tiny and furtive, like the notes of a flute carried on the wind, but she could see each egg with perfect clarity.

Two eggs were in the Copper Dragon, two inside the Silver Dragon. And two...two...

Alexander, she breathed, all of the air leaving her body in a whoosh.

Then the Jordan drew in a great breath of air. Calyph watched her, stunned, as she kept drawing in more and more, filling lungs that had to be much larger than the ones housed within the frail chest of the Jordan.

Dragon lungs, Calyph thought, bewildered. He heard the next words she said. They were hushed but quite clear.

"That bitch!" Jordan Blue whispered hoarsely, her whole body seeming to draw in on itself as every muscle tightened. "Those bitches!" she exclaimed, louder this time. Her voice slowly rose on each word until she was shouting. "Those lying, conniving, *thieving* whores!"

Her body jerked and she pushed herself up from the silver floor. A bit of saliva had gathered and leaked from the corner of her mouth and she wiped it away with the heel of her hand. She finally turned her eye to Calyph. The black shrunk until it merely covered her iris, and then kept shrinking until it was a normal pupil once again, and the bright blue gem sought out the Engineer.

"And you," she said, her voice low and dangerous as she pushed herself further up off of the tarmac. She rose up, seeming to uncoil like a cobra. Calyph remained kneeling on the ground, too afraid to move. The Jordan stood slowly, but seemed to go up and up and up as she did so. Calyph could have sworn that she had to grown to eight feet tall, at least, though he knew that it had to be his imagination.

"You!" Jordan Blue spat the word between red lips and white teeth. "You *bastard!*" Calyph trembled and remained still, crouched upon the silver tarmac. The Jordan shook for a moment, silent as she searched for the right words. She looked at the remaining triptych, swirling in the glass tube of the gun that lay on the open bag next to the Engineer. Then her eye flicked back to where he knelt. "You make damned sure that Scarlett gets that other syringe."

Calyph nodded quickly. "I will," he promised.

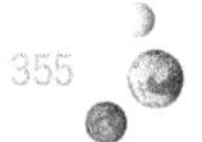

The Jordan sneered at him, her lips pulling away from her teeth and her scar standing out like an angry exclamation on her white skin. The Jordan began to turn away in disgust but glanced back at Calyph, her sapphire eye blazing.

"As far as Gemma goes," she told him, "I don't give a rat's ass what you give her, not even if it something that kills her, which might not be a bad idea. Either way, it better not be anything you draw from the Fledglings." She shifted slightly, her platinum coils falling over the shoulders of her black flight suit. "I'll kill you if you do," she promised, leering at him. "If Scarlett doesn't kill you first."

The Engineer swallowed hard and watched as the Jordan turned and headed for the Blue Fledgling. Normally, part of Cyan's side would temporarily melt away and allow passage, often accompanied by a short flight of stairs. This time, however, the Jordan ran and jumped at him and simply disappeared.

"Jesus Christ," Calyph muttered, dragging an arm across his brow. He crouched down as the Fledglings rose as one and shot out of Fledgling Bay, wondering what the hell he was going to do.

TWO FOUR

Jasyn boarded Faith's craft, bound for the Last Castle. The last time they had visited the castle, all he could think about was Faith - and tearing off her clothes. He had been a seething mass of sexual energy. This time he was a bundle of nervous tension, his shoulders tight and hazel eyes constantly darting about.

The construct had ridden in the spacecraft many more times since that trip. After their return from Charity's last event, Faith insisted on taking him everywhere. It was both incredibly gratifying, when he got to be with her alone, and incredibly dull during the time he had to share her with one boring meeting after the other.

Even when they traveled, Faith was always talking to someone on her comset. Sometimes he listened in, gleaning any information that he thought might be useful, but more often than naught it turned out to be crap. It seemed that everyone in the universe wanted something from her and, he realized at one point, that she was only taking the calls that could not be handled by her staff and/or fielded by Penny. He didn't know how she did it, or why. Worse, he finally knew why she would return home to him at the point of exhaustion and felt a twinge of guilt at how childish he would act, even though she had always made time for him.

Jasyn found out the hard way, one time, the importance of bringing his acrylic on their trips. He had forgotten it once on the craft and had to sit through a meeting with Faith and half a dozen Golbli emissaries, listening to them discuss fuel sources, prices and strategies for an entire day. It was so bad that he found himself complaining to Penny during the lunch break while Faith chatted with the Golbli on social matters.

"Isn't there anything to do?" he pleaded, hoping there might be a holo screen he could zone out in front of, or a book he could read. Penny gave him a smile that was tight with amusement.

"Do you read Golbli?" she asked sweetly. "I think I saw some zines in the lobby." Jasyn sighed.

"No. Anything more...hands-on that I could do?"

Penny's smile widened. "Hands on? Would you like for me to order you a prostitute?" she asked. Her tone was serious but Jasyn knew better.

"Is that humor or sarcasm?"

"Take your pick," she said, her brown eyes gleaming behind their square black frames. "It *is* a business meeting, so I am sure it would be a business expense."

Jasyn's lips quirked up on one side in amusement. "Again, take my pick?"

"You got it," the PA agreed.

Then something had occurred to him. "Shouldn't I get Faith a glass of champagne for her lunch?" Jasyn figured if there was a bar then he could perhaps get a glass of Varti. That, at least, might get him through the afternoon. Besides, it was strange to see Faith without a flute of sparkling wine held delicately between her slender fingers.

Penny's smile widened a pinch once again. "The Golbli don't believe in drinking during business meetings, and Ms. de Rossi is always respectful of that, even if others are not."

"Can I use your acrylic?" Jasyn asked as a last ditch effort, hopeful. Penny's smile disappeared.

"Are you crazy?"

Jasyn shrugged. "I will be, if I have to listen to them go on about fuel for another three hours!"

Penny's smile popped back up like a jack-in-the-saucer and

she leaned towards him. "The afternoon session is four hours," she confided in hushed tones. Jasyn's whole body sagged as he tipped his head back and rolled his eyes.

"Are you serious?" he whined. Penny nodded. "Can I take a nap somewhere?" he whispered.

"Lunch is here," Penny announced to the entire room with a gracious smile. Jasyn had groaned inwardly and eaten a despondent Golbli lunch before escorting Faith back into the meeting.

"What was that all about?" Geary asked Penny as the group meandered back into the conference room, his steely eyes never leaving Faith for more than a second, and never even to so much as to glance at the PA.

Penny made a tight movement of her shoulders and head, too small to be classified as a shrug. "He's bored," she said, her lips twisting into a small smile. "It's like he is becoming more human every day." Geary grunted.

After that, the construct made certain that his acrylic was with him wherever they went. On this occasion, he knew that Faith would not only be busy with calls, but that he would be nervous about the attack. It wouldn't happen for almost a week, but that didn't keep the Operations Officer from jumping at noises and shadows. He needed something to keep his mind occupied. The moment the craft was spaceborne, Faith took her first call on her comset. The Chimeran sighed and thumbed on his acrylic.

Jasyn went straight for the Gamer Complex to keep his mind from wandering. He knew that the attack on the Last Castle had been ordered, but that it wasn't supposed to happen for some time. JP wanted the attack to happen when all of the guests were there and, of course, after the egg had been removed. Jasyn was fairly sure that would not happen for another week, just before the party.

Like the last party, this one was scheduled to last for at least three days. There was to be a day of welcome and a celebration to mark the end of an era. The following day was being called the Synchronicity by some, the Singularity by a few others, and was to be a celebration that lasted all day and all night. The last day was for recuperation - a late brunch, swimming and walks, and farewells.

Jasyn was sure that the attack would come at the end of the very first day at sunset. As an Operations Officer he knew that it would be the most opportune time - every important dignitary and officer should be there by then and the staff would be upside down trying to get everyone settled and the party running smoothly. Also, it would be nothing to see some stray ships coming in, either late for the party or lower-end dignitaries looking for a last minute invite.

Jasyn and Faith would be going a week earlier than the rest of the guests due to a series of important meetings that required both Faith and Charity to be in attendance.

The attack will not happen for days, he told himself. *Quit freaking out.*

Still, the Chimeran knew his Commander well. He knew how impatient JP could be. He knew how eager he was to always make a decisive move. He knew how volatile the Commander could be and how his temper had gotten the better of him time and time again. Jasyn knew how much the man that looked like an angelic young priest despised Charity de Rossi.

Jasyn did not know for sure who would be called upon to lead the attack upon The Last Castle but an educated guess told him that it would most likely be Bjorn Van Zandt. The man was not only a crucial leader, but the best fighter pilot in the Chimeran military. Jasyn had met him more than a few times and knew the man was not always prudent. In fact, quite the opposite.

Still, they can't risk losing or damaging the egg. They will come for the egg. They will come for me, I hope. Seven or eight days. Or less. Then it is over. I'll be found out.

He flipped through the screens on his acrylic nervously, wondering where the hell the steward was with the champagne. It was rare that he drank alcohol rather than a sip of champagne with Faith or a Varti with Charity, but right now he would welcome anything to calm his nerves.

The Operations Officer found the game he wanted and logged in with the happy little code name he had adopted. He played a few rounds of Revolution but beat all of his opponents so quickly that he gave up. It just wasn't enough of a challenge.

He browsed the Complex and then joined a game of Starfighter. It was a faster game, and he was engrossed within seconds, taking enemy fire almost the moment he joined the fight. Before a minute had passed he recognized his main opponent. It was someone he had played against many times before - he could tell just by the way they moved and the strategic choices they made. Distantly, he heard the pop of the cork from the champagne bottle. He tipped his acrylic left and right, evading laser fire from his virtual enemy, then tipped it back and pushed with his right hand, pulling his virtual ship around to get behind the other fighter.

Jasyn heard the tone of Faith's voice change and he glanced at her but she was looking away. He looked back at his acrylic to see his ship come around a dead star and get decimated by the other fighter. The construct let the acrylic fall to his lap, the lights on the screen flashing to simulate the explosion of his ship, as his head rocked back. He stared at the ceiling of Faith's craft in silent defeat. It would be thirty more seconds before he could get a new ship and rejoin the game, but when he did, it would be game on. He ruled at Starfighter and he knew it.

"Would you like a glass?" Faith asked.

Jasyn lowered his head so he could look at her, though his brain felt like it was burning. He wanted to get back in the game right away and thirty seconds suddenly seemed like a long time.

"I would, thank you."

The steward filled a flute for him and as Jasyn took it he saw that Faith was staring at him in…. what? Surprise? Amazement? It was more than just surprise at him accepting a glass of champagne. She knew that he hardly ever drank, but he had on enough occasions. Now, on the way to Charity's, it should not be that strange.

Then it hit him. He had been so wrapped up in his game that now he was not sure if she had been speaking to him. Moreover, he was not even sure if she had been speaking Anglicus. Though he felt his heart rate spike, he gave her his most disarming smile and she responded by pulling her comset off of her ear, not taking her eyes from his face. Jasyn cocked his head.

"What are you doing?" he asked.

"I'm burning bridges," she said, handing the comset to Penny. She held up her glass and Jasyn touched its rim with the side of his own. The glasses gave off a small chime as they touched, the tiny sound echoing throughout the cabin of the craft. Faith smiled. "This is going to be quite the party," she told him.

Jasyn returned the smile as best he could, forcing himself to calm down. "I'm sure that every party Charity has is quite the party."

Faith laughed softly. "That's true," she agreed. "But I really think that this is going to be something special." She took a long drink of the champagne, keeping her brown and gold eyes fixed on Jasyn. He took a long drink as well, stopping himself before he drained the entire glass.

Penny politely interrupted for a few signatures on her acrylic and Jasyn watched as Faith plucked up the stylus with her left hand and signed, giving the electronic documents barely a glance.

Is there something wrong with that? Jasyn wondered. He sighed inwardly, sure that he was right but not sure of what that might be. It seemed that recently there were a lot of things that he was unsure of, but he pushed those thoughts away, determined that he was doing the right thing and that was all that mattered.

Right or wrong, he had already decided that he would have no regrets. For once, he was thankful that Penny kept Faith quietly busy with an endless stream of questions and signatures. By the time they had finished the bottle of champagne, the craft was touching down on the Distant Shore.

Jasyn disembarked, his hazel eyes scouring the skies above the Last Castle.

Quit freaking out, he told himself again. *It's not supposed to be for at least seven days, maybe more. You have plenty of time before you are found out. Bjorn is not that trigger-happy. I hope.*

This time for their arrival, instead of a private car for just Faith and himself, there was an air limo for all of them, including Penny and her PA, as well as Geary along with three of his best men. Also, this time, Charity's castle was a bustle of servants rather than a crowd of guests. There was no security scan coming in, and Jasyn never saw the Yakuza agent that had scared the shit out of him on his first trip.

They were ushered in like important sheep and allowed to relax for an hour before it was time to dress and go downstairs.

Charity held an intimate dinner of only thirty people in an ornate dining room of mahogany and gilt gold. Faith wore a long, cream-colored gown slashed with insets of gold. Jasyn wore a tux, wondering for the first time if it was always the same tux or if Penny had to get him a new one for every event. The shirt was new, he was sure about that.

The Chimeran was pleased to see that Nathan was not lurking about, though he had a distasteful feeling that he would see the lanky Engineer before the three-day ordeal was done. He took a glass of champagne from a floating tray as it drifted by and handed it to Faith. She accepted it with a warm smile, and then arched an eyebrow at him as he took a glass of Varti for himself.

"Developing a taste for that, are you?"

Jasyn smiled. "A little bit. But I won't drink if you don't want me to."

Faith shook her head. "By all means," she told him. "Have a good time. Just promise to control yourself this evening," she said, nudging him in the ribs with an elbow.

"I will promise no such thing," he assured her, smiling into his glass as he took a drink.

Faith choked slightly, laughing with champagne in her mouth and he gave her a look of concern but she waved him off, smiling and shaking her head. Jasyn felt the liquor burn his throat and then spread like plasma fire as it hit his stomach. He started feeling its effects within a heartbeat.

"So," he said, emboldened. "I don't see Barin Trey here this evening." His hazel eyes, full of merriment and mischief, swept the room where people were beginning to take seats around a table large enough for a few families to live under. Faith's expression became serious.

"Barin died in a skiing accident recently," she said, her voice low.

"I'm sorry to hear that," Jasyn said, not feeling sorry in the least. But, though he hoped that Faith did not need to be consoled, he thought he should be there for her. Faith simply shrugged.

"Dr. Silas will take over as Director," she said. Jasyn nodded.

"I like Dr. Silas."

Faith found their seats and Jasyn pulled out her chair. "He is a good man," Faith agreed, sitting down. Jasyn pushed in her chair and took his own seat. The food was served and he proceeded to fill himself along with the others at the table.

Faith had told him that they, along with most of the others at dinner, would be the ones included in business meetings the following two or three days at the GwenSeven Compound. They were only waiting on the Lentoch dignitaries who were scheduled to arrive the next day.

The Chimeran hoped that she didn't mean to include him. He hated meetings.

Four more courses were served after Jasyn had stopped eating. Faith seemed to take a single, polite bite off of each plate and then graciously put down her fork to speak with those seated close to them. Jasyn knew that if he had done the same he could have kept on going, but for the time being he was so full that it was impossible. For now, it was all he could do to sip his Varti and listen to Faith talk to the people around her.

Though he was not interested in their conversations, he noticed that they struck him as less insipid as before. Only months ago they had been maddening to listen to, and now he saw most conversations for what they really were; idle gossip. Before it was infuriating to have to hear their senseless chatter. Now it meant nothing and he tried to figure out why he felt different.

I guess back then, he thought, *they were such monsters to me. I didn't even think of them as real people.* His hazel eyes fell on those seated at the table, one by one. *Just like we aren't real people to them. Who is right?* he wondered as his eyes traveled over the small crowd. *Who is really real?* He shook his head and drained his glass.

After dinner the group finally rose as one to adjourn to another room for after-dinner cordials and liquors. Jasyn was escorting his woman, going along with the crowd, when he heard the person whom he had once thought must be the most artificial life form in the universe calling to him from across the room.

"Jasyn! Come sit with us!"

Faith tucked a knowing smile into the corner of her mouth and her hand into the crook of Jasyn's arm as he escorted her to where Charity was settling herself down into a high-backed chair of plush red velvet. Even Charity de Rossi, the universally known and notoriously shallow socialite, now seemed more warm and human to him than anyone he had ever met, with the exception of Faith.

Two other women, one with short blonde hair and another with straight black locks that fell down her back, sat on a couch of golden velour next to Charity, smiling at him.

"You get to see Faith all the time!" Charity scolded in an attempt to pout.

"Nonsense," Jasyn told her. "I hardly get to see her outside of the b..." Faith gave him a nonchalant yet sharp jab in the ribs, changing his direction. "Villa," he finished.

Charity threw back her head and laughed, showcasing the large emeralds that were hung around her smooth, white throat. Her fingers were curled around a flute of champagne and Jasyn noticed, for the first time, that she wore the same rings that Faith did except that the stones were different. The color of the stones in her necklace matched the emerald dress that fit her like a second skin, worn over only one shoulder and cut no more than a handspan above her knee. The same color as the stones in her trio of rings.

"Well then, since you've spent so much time together in the villa, what can you tell us about my sister?"

Faith opened her mouth to speak but he placed a hand over hers and gave it a squeeze, making her look at him in surprise. His eyes met hers and held them.

"That she is the most amazing person in the universe," he said, dropping his arm so that he could grab her hand, entwining their fingers. He could hear the other women inhale sharply but he kept his gaze fixed on Faith. "If I didn't know better," he continued, "I'd say that we were made for each other."

All of the color drained from Faith's face and there was a moment of stunned silence from the other women. It was broken by Charity's tinkling laugh as she leaned forward and placed a hand on the knee of the woman closest to her. "You see Dora!" she exclaimed. "You can't buy love like that!"

The woman with the long black hair took a drink of the dark red fluid in her glass, giving a slight nod. "I see what you mean," she purred.

Faith drained her own glass, quickly regaining her composure. "Well!" she announced. "It is getting late and we all have much to do and discuss in the morning." She gave Charity a meaningful glance and Jasyn could not decipher if it was a look of knowing or of warning. Possibly both. "So, if you will please excuse us?" she asked, though she turned and started away without waiting for an answer, still holding onto Jasyn's hand.

"Of course!" Charity called after them. "Have fun in the buh-villa!"

The other women's laughter joined Charity's and Faith shook her golden-brown head of hair, smiling.

"Why don't we take a walk through the conservatory?" Jasyn suggested as they left the room. "Maybe it will be too hot for you to keep that dress on," he added with a grin, giving her a sidelong glance. Faith laughed.

"We can't. It's under renovation."

"Renovation?"

"Yes. I don't know what Charity has planned, but everything that was in there has been removed."

Everything?

Jasyn, carefully keeping his body as relaxed his voice, smiled at Faith. "Then I guess I will have to get you out of that dress all by myself."

Faith grinned and cheerfully swung the hand that was holding onto his. "I guess you will," she agreed.

Already gone, Jasyn thought. The information he had gleaned from Faith's vanity had said that it would not be moved until right after the Synchronicity. *Something must have happened. Christ almighty, if JP knows, the strike could be at any time.*

He gave Faith a reassuring smile as they took a lift up to their room in the tower of the castle that belonged to Faith.

Not just at any time, he thought, hoping. *JP will wait for the party, for all of the dignitaries to be together in one place. It makes no sense to strike early.*

But, then again, JP did not always put a lot of hold in sense. He put his faith in the One, and the Chimeran Commander had quite the temper. And he hated the de Rossi's so much, Charity most of all. And he had no idea that Jasyn had arrived at the Last Castle a week early. No idea at all.

⊗

John came back from a late lunch and, making a face, pulled his comset off his ear and tossed it on his desk.

"Ah-ah-ah!" Mike scolded as he stood up and grabbed the lightweight jacket that was hanging on the back of his chair. "You're going to need that."

John looked at him, perplexed. "Where are we going?"

Mike flashed him a smile of white teeth. "Field trip."

"Field trip? Where to?"

"The mall."

"The mall? You have some shopping to do?"

Mike's hearty laughed boomed and echoed as he left the room, John following. "Kind of," he joked, though his voice had a deep and honest tone. He flashed his grin at John. "Since we are on a bit of a standstill for sign-ups, other than for the junior program, I thought we might go shopping for a pilot."

"And they sell them at the mall?"

Mike boomed laughter once again as they walked down the

corridor from their office towards the lobby.

"Buy one?" he asked. "I heard they're free. In fact, they are being born and raised right here at the local arcade."

John's amused expression melted into one of amazement as he regarded his partner's profile. "Trolling?" he asked. "We're going trolling for pilots?" Now it was his turn to laugh as Mike nodded and flashed his usual grin. "You can't be serious!" John admonished.

John's father had been a pilot, and his father before him had been a pilot and an instructor as well. He was the one who had told John about trolling - instructors looking for would-be-fighter-pilots and captain-protégés at arcades where they would sometimes find an adolescent ace gamer and recruit them for training.

It was an especially popular tactic during the onset of the Golgoth Tide, when IGC patriotism first sparked the hearts of those in the civilized galaxies. Many young men and young women, both sexes often illegally young, were recruited thusly. Now it was about as useful as it was archaic. John had certainly never heard of an instructor doing it during his own lifetime.

"I'm not sure that is a practice endorsed by the school," John told his partner as they left the building and crossed the grass-trimmed sidewalk to the lot where Mike's aircar was parked. It was a sporty model - lowslung with dragonfly wing doors and an ozonedrift spoiler.

The doors lifted and Mike climbed inside without a word, his grin a crescent of white in his near-ebony face. John climbed in as the silent doors swung closed and Mike pulled out onto the nearly deserted street, the car gliding smoothly over the slick pavement.

"As you know," Mike told him, "I am a single man, and have a little more time on my hands than I am sure you do. I spend a lot of my free time gaming, when I'm not giving some woman the thrill of her life, that is."

John snorted but otherwise stayed silent.

"There are some really big," Mike continued, "and some really good, players in the gaming world right now. One of them goes by the name of the Skipper."

John snorted again, this time in surprise. He had heard Sean mention the name before, a number of times, and usually with a bitter or miserable tone.

"Personally, this 'Skipper' has beat my ass a few times, and I'm not just talking about strategy game, but actual fighter pilot games." Mike's laugh filled the car but it had a rueful tone. "Do you know how embarrassing that is? Not only being an actual pilot, but an actual fighter pilot *instructor*, and getting your ass whipped?"

John chuckled. "I can only imagine."

"So," Mike continued, "the game I am playing now is to figure out who the hell he is. It hasn't been easy, because he is mostly a day player, which convinced me that it was most likely a kid, but an occasional night player, that brought him into my usual circle."

Mike steered with one hand while he reached into an inner pocket of his jacket and pulled out a mini-acrylic and handed it to John. The mini showed a three dimensional map of the area they were currently in, a small red star blinking on and off only a kilometer away from their current location.

"Well, I wrote a trace app and uploaded it to my console and waited for my chance. I spent my last game with him playing like shit, but holding on long enough to run a backwards trace on his console. You wouldn't have believed my surprise when I found out it was coming from the local mall – right here on Io, right here in upper-suburbia!" His booming laugh filled the car once again.

"I wish I could have seen the look on your face," John murmured, grinning. Mike nodded and turned the aircar down another tree-lined avenue.

"I had really expected that the trace would be from Europa. Although, if the guy is as good at strategy as he is a player, it will just be a link he hot-wired from a distant moon to relay through the arcade's gaming system. It would make sense, since we are at the highest point in the atmosphere and in the largest city on Io. If it does happen to be a relay, I can connect the relay to my acrylic and it will show where the link is coming from, my guess is still Europa. There is an endless amount of professional gamers and hackers there, not to mention pilots retired from the pre-rebellion days."

John looked at his partner with a knowing smile as the man turned the vehicle into the mall parking lot and slid the car into a front space.

"You're not trolling at all!" he accused. "And this has nothing to do with work – this is personal! You want to know who has been kicking your ass at a video game!" Now it was John's laughter that filled the car. Mike turned off the car and gave him a feigned a look of shock.

"Not just any game," he retorted as if offended. "Chimeran Revolution! I actually wrote the pilot portion of that game for GwenSaga."

"No wonder you could afford this car."

"And," Mike continued, ignoring John's remark, "I would gladly recruit a prospective pilot that can beat me at my own game."

John and his partner grinned at each other a moment longer, and then exited the craft simultaneously, the car bobbing slightly on its cushion of air as it was rid of their weight. John noticed their front row space and scowled at Mike.

"Handicapped parking? Really?"

Mike returned his scowl. "I'm missing my damned arm!"

"Not your leg!"

"It's still a limb!" he argued, laying a long-fingered hand

protectively over the dark skin of his rebuilt arm. "And besides, there isn't anyone in the upper klick any more handicapped than I am!"

John couldn't argue. Everyone in upper-suburbia was perfectly put together. So much that it was eerie. He and Rebecca had speculated with nervous laughter that they must be the only real people in the Upper Klick.

The car doors closed silently and, rolling his eyes, John followed his partner past the glass sculpture of a human head attached to the body of a lion and into the massive glass pyramid that was the local shopping mall.

The afternoon traffic inside the mall was just beginning to build and the two instructors made their way through the growing throng of teenagers and housewives that gathered outside of jewelry stores and clothing boutiques. They stopped in front of the GwenSeven store as they waited for the diagonal lift that would take them up the slanted side of the building to the next floor.

John eyed the large display of constructs behind the glass window. Most were human though there were a few elfin models. All were young and only half dressed, if that.

"Ever think of buying one?" Mike asked.

"What the hell for?" John asked.

Mike shrugged. "I don't know. Help around the house? Babysitter? Just to have one? I don't know."

John shook his head. The look on his face was like he had accidentally swallowed a bug. "No," he said. "Not ever."

The lift arrived and opened its doors. John and Mike entered the glass box and Mike brushed a finger over the blue holo near the door that showed the number two. The box rose, its electromagnetic and angled ceiling sliding up the inside of the pyramid, taking them up to the next level. John looked through the glass under his feet as they rose, watching the people gathered outside the GwenSeven store point at the perfect bodies posed behind the glass wall.

The lift came to a rather sudden halt and opened its doors onto the next level. The second floor of the mall was comprised mostly of sim-food eateries, sweet shops, and stores that sold items and clothing that only a teenager would buy.

The fighter pilot instructors left the slanted elevator and threaded their way through teen suburbia towards the far half of the level that was swallowed up by glass screens, gaming consoles, and flight simulators. The noise drew them in, beeping, warbling, thumping – swallowing them in a cacophony.

Mike pulled his mini-acrylic from his jacket pocket and glanced at it as they wove their way around the free-standing game consoles named Resurrection and Redemption that were alive with lights and sirens. They had to circumvent a huge platform of teenage girls dancing on boxes that lit up intermittently with shapes and colors, their pubescent feral howling nearly drowning out the trilling, artificial sounds of space travel and simulated laser fire coming from the other games.

Mike glanced again at his mini and then grinned as they rounded a column of six shift games lined up side by side before they reached the line of simulators splashed with garish light and the over-sized lettering that declared Chimeran Revolution.

The row consisted of eighteen blue consoles splattered with red paint that John assumed must represent blood spray. Each console had attached pilot seats that moved and shook inside a pod that was roughly the same size as a cockpit of a small fighter jet. Mike's dark eyes eagerly flicked from his mini to each console as they made their way down the row of pods but John stopped suddenly as if he had been poked with an electric current, his mouth dropping open.

Frozen, he watched his partner continue a few more steps, then frown and turn back, retracing his steps to where John stood. John leaned forward and put his hands on his knees to keep himself from falling down. Mike looked and him, nonplussed, as the man began to laugh.

John looked at the canvas bag lying against the side of the gaming pod and laughed harder, feeling hot tears well in his eyes. He didn't need to see inside to know who it was. As he bellowed laughter, the would-be-pilot turned to look at him. Her dark curls bounced as she turned her face up and her large dark eyes sought him out.

Jeanette squealed with delight and surprise as she recognized him. "Daddy!" she yelled as she left her pod to jump into his arms.

John caught her and held her close, laughing until tears were running down his cheeks. Mike looked from father to daughter and back again. His eyes fell on Jeanette's black canvas dance bag, the row of holographic pink ballet slippers dancing along its sides.

"I'll be dammed," he whispered shaking his head. "I'll be god-damned." Then he tipped back his head and laughed. His laughter joined John's, booming and echoing throughout the arcade amid the sounds of crashing ships and laser fire.

# TWO FIVE

Grande Edge of Kayos was the meeting point of transportation for the city-village on the terraformed artificial moon of Jupiter. Just to the west of the station was the river, where ferries and private boats docked. A steam-powered train took passengers south and east, while a hydrogen-powered monorail took travelers north to the more modern cities of Adrogea.

The station itself was large, though only semi-crowded. A week later it would be packed with beings of all species and races shoulder to shoulder, arriving for the great Night of the Synchronicity.

It was an open and airy building made of wood and glass, what the builders had thought would be a perfect mix of past and present. The architects strictly forbade anything futuristic, which included any super-produced metallics.

The depot was a place where one left the present behind and entered the past, or vice versa. There were old-fashioned turnstiles and smiling porters made of plastique that wore smart blue uniforms of woven cloth and Mylar neckties. The central room at the main terminal was lined with boutiques, sundry shops, and take-away stands. In the center was an oculus cafe, surrounded by tables and chairs.

In a chair at the edge of the circle of tables sat an Aridian, sipping a thick stimulant from a tiny demitasse cup. Her slender body was topped with a disproportionately large, and very round, head. Her large, dark eyes took up two-thirds of her delicate but cavernous face. Long, black hair fell in a dark curtain straight down her back.

Everyone at the train station gave the Aridian a wide berth. Though the female looked almost impossibly frail, and doppelgänging was strictly forbidden even among the Aridians - the punishment being death - one never knew. In this case, they were right to avoid her. The Rogue had been doppelgänging, and consequently murdering, without much thought or care since she was barely more than a child.

The Rogue sipped from her cup and wiggled with delight. It felt good to be herself again, at least for a time. She felt incredibly light and free. Never before had she carried around so much body, so much bulk. And certainly never for so long, though she had to admit that she enjoyed wearing the body of the Ambassador. Having temporarily shed so much heavy flesh, she felt as if the gravity on the artificial moon could hardly hold her down.

A group of strikingly attractive humans, all male save for a single dark-haired female, entered the far side of the terminal and headed for the turnstiles. Unlike everyone else, they walked straight past her table, close enough to reach out and touch. Only one of them, tall and blonde with amazingly green eyes, spared her a glance.

The Rogue's long and slender tongue darted out of her mouth to graze the corner of her lips in silent invitation but the man turned away and kept walking. The Aridian gave a slight shrug and sipped her pressed coffee. Probably for the best, she was expecting someone.

"Do you know that woman?" Lucy asked Bjorn when they reached the turnstiles. She had sensed a sudden spike in his heart rate, but it was there and gone in a blink.

"No," he replied, holding a hand out to Lucy so that she may go before him. "It's just that I had always wanted to have sex with an Aridian. I had heard so much about them that I wanted to experience it myself."

"And now?"

"No interest at all."

Lucy's head tilted slightly and her golden eyes glinted like a setting sun. "Does this have anything to do with your feelings for the Red Jordan?" she asked.

"I'm sure it has everything to do with those feelings."

Bjorn stopped short and Lucy stopped next to him. Julian, with a few hand signals and even fewer words, directed two guards to enter the train and run a security check and the other two guards to hand over the small steel cases that comprised their luggage to the smiling plastic porters before taking up a post around the Commander. The troll regarded him with her strange eyes.

"How can you be sure? Many things can cause a change in desire."

Bjorn smirked at her. "Because many of my feelings and desires have changed, and I am sure that they are all due to my feelings for the Red Jordan."

"Such as?"

The Commander's full lips pressed into a line and his blonde brows drew together slightly. "Such as, I have recently found out, or have been led to believe, that Scarlett had taken a lover aboard the Opal Dragon."

"And?"

Bjorn's frown deepened. "And if it is true, and if I find out who he is, I will kill him."

Lucy's eyes shimmered, taking in not only his words, but the tension in his body, the anger in his voice.

"This is jealousy," the troll remarked, half statement half question. It was an emotion she was aware of, but not familiar with. Bjorn's face relaxed, but only a little.

"It is," he agreed.

"Is that an emotion you have experienced before?" Lucy asked.

Bjorn let out a deep breath as he considered, then shook

his head. "I had twinges of something, some emotion I am still not sure of, once or twice at the beginning - not long after I was made - but it was nothing like this. Like I said, the feelings were only twinges, like stepping barefoot into something unpleasant. This is much different. This consumes me."

"In what way?"

Bjorn, his emotions rising, scowled at her. "Why the hell do you care?" he demanded, but Lucy's face remained passive.

"I am programmed to learn all than I can," she explained. "In what way is this different?" she prodded.

Bjorn looked away, trying to still his rise of emotion. "Because," he said, his voice getting lower with each word, "I will not share her!"

Lucy cocked her head. "But that desire has only to do with the present and the future. Killing someone from her past will not change the past." Bjorn gave her a tight smile and a glimpse of perfectly square, white teeth.

"It will make me feel better."

Lucy straightened. "That is interesting," she remarked.

The Commander grunted as one of his guards leaned out from between two of the monorail's first-class cars and motioned to Julian. Julian gave him a curt nod and directed everyone to the car, his head swiveling and his eyes cataloging everything he saw as he escorted the Commander and the troll on board.

Just a few seconds later, after helping Lucy onto the train and swinging himself up onto the landing between the cars of the monorail, the man that Bjorn presently wanted most to kill entered the station.

Calyph, the Engineer for the Opal Dragon, entered the terminal holding only a small leather satchel. Pointed ears poked up out of his sandy-blonde hair and his almond-shaped blue eyes darted around, searching.

They fell on the back of the Aridian who still had her

face turned curiously towards the turnstiles. The Engineer approached her cautiously, his head tilted to one side as if trying to get a glimpse of her face. He was almost upon her when she turned her face to him, her large eyes seeming to swallow him whole.

The Engineer's blue eyes swept the station one last time before she lunged at him.

"Calyph!" she squealed the moment before he caught her in his arms.

"Hello, Tara," he managed before her lips were on his and her slender tongue found the back of his mouth in the way she knew he liked. He pressed her slender body against his own, pulling her tongue even deeper into his mouth.

She pulled away and kissed him lightly on the lips when he released her, his blue eyes darting about the depot. Tara laughed.

"There is no one here to see us," she assured him, giving his chest a playful shove. "Would you like something to drink?"

"Christ, yes. Do they have ale, or anything stronger?"

Tara smiled and waved a plastic waiter over. The droid floated towards them and bowed at what would have been his waist, if he had one. Its body ended at the hips.

"Do you have ale?" Tara asked.

"We have a golden ale," the droid responded, his plastic smile never moving.

"Any black ale?" Calyph asked. "Or a stout?"

"Only golden, sir," the waiter responded.

Calyph's lips pressed together. "Any grain alcohol?"

"Grain alcohol?" Tara asked, her round face contorting in surprise.

Calyph shook his head. "You have no idea what I have been through in the last seventy-two hours."

"No, sir," the waiter answered, his smile painted on his

plastic face. "But we have bubbled wine."

Calyph sighed. "The golden ale will be fine."

The waiter bowed, bobbing slightly before he sped away.

"So," Tara declared. "How did it go?"

Calyph nodded but did not meet her eyes. "Well. It went well."

Tara's lids dropped half-way down over her saucer-like eyes, the human equivalent of narrowing her eyes in suspicion. "Did you sleep with her?" she demanded in a voice that was quite intimidating for one so small.

Calyph smiled in relief as the waiter returned with his ale. "Of course not," he told her. He took a long drink of the ale, trying not to think about how much he had wanted to sleep with Scarlett. That he wanted to bed the Jordan so badly that it made his body ache.

"Are you sure?" Tara asked.

Calyph smiled at her. "I think I would know."

"Would you?" she demanded. Her voice was full of so much scorn, so much that it sounded like Scarlett. Calyph laughed.

"Yes," he said, hooking a hand under her chair and jerking it across the floor till it hit his own, jarring it to a halt. "I would."

He kissed Tara, feeling her tongue snake into his mouth and her moan tremble through her thin lips. He ran his hands down the side of her body, fleetingly missing the feeling of Scarlett, of the swell of her breasts against his thumbs. He hoped that when Tara took the Jordan's form, that she would keep it for as long as possible.

"Did you get the triptych?" Tara asked, her breath heavy. Calyph tensed, anticipating her anger as he shook his head.

"No."

Tara's dark eyes, already round, seemed to grow rounder, and darker with anger.

"I pulled it," Calyph said quickly, "but I was caught." Tara went still and it seemed to Calyph that for a moment she was literally all eyes. "It's okay," he assured her. "Luckily, the Jordan that caught me merely confiscated it."

Calyph thought it prudent not to tell her that the Jordan had injected herself with it. Nor did he mention that the Executive Officer on the Opal Dragon had spoken with him about pulling Fledge's genetic material for the new cadet. It would just make Tara more pissed that she did not get hers.

She's like Scarlett that way, Calyph thought affectionately. *They both have some awful tempers.*

Calyph's blue eyes traveled over Tara's body, a body that he loved, though he wistfully wished that she shared a few more attributes with the Red Jordan.

The Aridian's cheeks puffed as she blew out a quick breath and tiny waves formed in the small forehead between the curtains of black hair.

"Well," she said, decidedly, "at least you are alright, and they did not find out about us or what we are about." Calyph let out an imperceptible sigh of relief. He had thought Tara might be wearing his balls for earrings if things did not go well. "Still," she continued, "how will the Fledgling respond to me if I do not have his blood?"

Calyph shrugged. "He will have to go by your DNA," he said, wrapping an arm around her waist and giving it a squeeze before he gave her a deep kiss. "Which, I am sure, will be enough. Either way, it's in Scarlett now and when you replicate her, it will be in you."

"You're right," she said, nodding thoughtfully. "I hadn't thought about that."

Calyph sat back and took another long pull of ale, relaxing. For the first time since he and Tara had made their plans and embarked on this journey, he really felt like it was going to happen.

"Did you get the chlorfagel?" she asked.

Calyph nodded. "Just now – at an apothecary's on the west side of the town. I didn't want to take it to Elaeric's. He might have sensed more than I am able to hide. It's in my pack." He brushed a dark strand of hair away from her face. "And the Ambassador?" he asked. "Has everything been arranged?"

Tara grinned, her smile stretching from one side of her round head all the way to the other. She produced a mini-acrylic from a purse, thumbed it on and showed it to the Engineer while her other hand ran up the inside of his leg. Calyph gasped, a result of the hand on his crotch as well as the numbers on the screen. It was more money than he had made in his whole life. More than he would ever make.

"And that's only ten percent," Tara said, giving him a squeeze. "The rest will be transferred when they have the Fledgling."

"How are they going to fly it?" he whispered, still mesmerized by the numbers on the screen. And that was only ten percent.

Tara shrugged and the little acrylic disappeared back into her purse. "They think they can do it. Which is all that matters, besides the money of course!" She laughed and kissed the elf on his nose.

"And they have it all?"

Her round head bobbed, nodding. "I had them authorize an echo when they made the transfer, so that I could see what they had in the bank without being able to withdraw more than they had already given us."

"And?"

The Aridian grinned. "They could buy a whole fleet of Fledglings."

Calyph whistled. "Well, we'll be set for life, and for the lives we've always dreamed of having." He kissed her again, longer this time, making her moan. He looked into her round, dark

eyes as she broke away, breathless. "Is there a place where we can finish this conversation," he breathed. "My train doesn't leave until the morning."

"There is," she whispered, standing up. She threw a handful of coins down on the table and turned away, smiling seductively.

Calyph took her hand and let her lead him away, just like he had always done. Ever since they were children.

TWO SIX

Galen grinned at the Jordan as her porcelain fingers danced across the dash console, silencing the communication lines with the Opal Dragon, cutting off the heated demands from an extremely agitated Executive Officer. The stars around them, bright specks of crushed diamond against a black velvet backdrop, seemed to freeze and grow bright and ultra clear before they started to warble and blur as the Fledglings began to fold the space before them as they shot through it.

The pilot glanced at the doctor's ghost. "What are you smiling at?" she demanded, tossing him a quick scowl before her single eye returned to the dash and then to the window above it.

"Your flight suit."

The Jordan's eye rolled up in exasperation. "Yes, I know. Why is everyone so upset that I wear black? I would think the reasons are obvious."

Galen shook his head. "That's not it."

The Jordan glanced at him and then reached down to the console to adjust their course. "Well?" she prodded.

"It used to refract the light - white light would glint off of your body like a million stars."

The brow over her black eye patch arched. "And now?"

Galen's grin widened. "Now, it throws off glints of blue and red."

"Really?"

"Really."

The Jordan leaned back into her seat, her white hair shining around her head like a halo in the dark. "I know what you're thinking."

"You always did."

Blue sighed. "You want to know about the injections," she said. "You want to know what they did to me."

"Of course, but I know you will tell me when you are ready. My main concern, as always, is that you are not hurt. That you are safe. Other than that, I would at least like to know how you feel."

Blue nodded, staring out into the blurred space around them. "I can't begin to describe how I feel," she confided.

"Try."

The Jordan nodded, as if it were a task she had put off but knew that it must be done. "The first shot made me feel," she shook her head, platinum coils bouncing, as she sought out the right words, "more aware, more instinctive. But it wasn't just my own intuitions that were sharpened; it was like I was given the instincts of someone else, something else. The Dragons."

Galen nodded, still grinning. "You *were* quite the animal that night," he agreed.

The Jordan threw him a glare with her single eye, though she had a smirk on her ravaged face. "It made me more aware of everything *around* me -seeing you clearly, for instance." She took a deep breath before continuing. "Seeing the crew in a way that ashamed me." Her voice dropped, almost cracking. "I have known most of them for years and yet I don't think I ever really took notice of who they really were as individuals."

Galen looked at her with a mixture of pride and surprise. "You are starting to sound like a Captain."

The Jordan tipped a pointed ear towards her shoulder, an indication that she could neither agree nor disagree.

"The second shot made me more aware of everything *within* me."

Galen cocked his head, his black hair falling over his own pointed ears. "For instance?"

The Jordan turned her glittering eye to him. "The entire universe," she said, tapping her thin chest with one long finger. "It's all in here. In each and every one of us."

The doctor's ghost nodded thoughtfully and they were both quiet for some time. "What about your connection with the Fledglings?" he asked after a while.

"Stronger. So much stronger. The bond that I have built with Cyan over these past few years – it was like that, but stronger, and instantaneous. Where, before, we were starting to be able to read each other's feelings, now communication is much easier, much clearer."

"You can hear them now?"

"Yes, though it is mostly still images, rather than words. They do use words, but feelings and pictures come across more often."

The elfin doctor's ghost and the half-elf pilot were silent again as they contemplated the Jordan's words.

"And where are we going now?" Galen finally asked.

"To see my sisters," she told him. "Faith and Charity to be exact."

Galen raised his already high-arched brows over his deep blue eyes. "That should be interesting."

Blue's smirk pushed up higher into the slashes of burn scars on her face. "Yes, it should."

"And do you have an answer for her?"

The Jordan frowned. "I'm not sure. But I can tell you one thing, she's not as crazy as I thought she was."

Galen grunted but gave no further comment. The background of distorted space and the streak of the stars were the only indications of their movement as they cut across the galaxy, the Fledglings trailing streams of blue and red light. They traveled in silence through the vacuum and the void, each taking solace in the company of the other.

After just an hour the Fledglings began to brake, bringing the stars back into sharp focus against the stark black of ever night.

"They're getting faster," Galen whispered. The Jordan nodded, smiling proudly as she touched the controls on Cyan's dash. Both Fledglings turned as one, banking as they plunged through space towards a tiny water moon on the outskirts of the Jupiter system.

Galen eyed the position of the great, gleaming ball of swirling gas. It dwarfed everything in the sector so much that it felt as if they were no more than a gnat flying by a sun. He glanced at the numbers over the console dash. "We're not going to see Faith," he stated.

Blue shook her platinum head. "We're going to see her," she corrected. "Just not at her place."

"Good," Galen muttered, a line between his dark brows. "I don't like the security guy there."

Blue looked at him, curious. "Which one?"

"The one that looks like a lost puppy, and looks at you like you are there to rescue him."

The Jordan thought back to her trip to Faith's villa. She could only distinctly remember two of the security staff. One had looked like he wanted to kill her. The other was nicer, though he had acted quite peculiar.

"Tom?" she asked, remembering his name. Galen glowered at the air in front of him like a sulky child but didn't say anything. Blue laughed. "I hadn't even turned you back on at that point. You were with me?"

"I'm always with you," he murmured.

The Jordan adjusted their course as they closed in on the

water moon that was called The Distant Shore, smiling to herself.

"How do you know where to find Charity?" Galen asked, changing the subject. "Can you feel her?"

Blue nodded. "A little. Faith, too. But there is something else I can feel even more. A heartbeat that calls to mine." She turned her face so she could see him better. "A Hatchling."

Galen straightened. "She has one of the eggs? It's hatched?"

Blue shook her head. "It hasn't hatched yet. It was beginning to awaken, getting ready to break the shell while it was aboard its mother. They both were. My sisters figured out a way to lull them back to sleep."

Galen nodded. "Faith has the other one." It wasn't a question.

The Fledglings dove as one, making a clean cut into the atmosphere without so much as a shudder but, as soon as they did, Galen turned his face away from the front panels of hyperglass that served as Cyan's eyes. Blue turned her own face to him, laughing.

"Jesus, Galen! You're already dead! What do you think is going to happen?"

"I don't know," he told her through clenched teeth. The Jordan threw back her head and laughed. "Would you please watch where you are flying?" he hissed, which only made the Jordan laugh harder.

"We're in a Fledgling, Galen - not some jet. Cyan won't let anything happen to us." She didn't mention that she could pilot a jet as well as a Fledgling with her one eye closed, knowing that it would only agitate him more.

A sharp buzz came from the dash, signaling a non-IGC entity attempting to establish coms. Blue ran her left hand down the left side of the console and a masculine voice broke in over the system.

"This is LC Coms, addressing the two craft that just entered

our fly-space. Please identify yourself."

Blue snorted. "Are you serious? I'm sure that if you can see me then you know damn well who I am."

There was noise over the com that sounded like someone clearing their throat. "Our systems indicate that we have two... Fledgling Dragons on approach."

"Well," Blue told him, "at least something is working down there."

"That would make you Jordan..." the voice queried, leaving the sentence for her to finish.

"Yes," Blue simply replied. When a pause ensued she sighed in exasperation. "Blue. Jordan Blue. The only active Jordan in all seven systems at the moment." She placed her left hand over a section of the dash, cutting off coms from her end. "What a dunce," she muttered.

The Fledglings dropped through the troposphere and began gliding smoothly over the dark, choppy waters that covered the globe. Blue touched a light on the dash and a holo sprung to life over the console.

"Cyan," she instructed, looking at the multi-dimensional map, "there are only two main structures on this moon - a commercial compound and a residence. Take us to the residence. I think you know what I'm looking for." Cyan immediately banked to his left, Fledge following just a few meters off of his right wing.

"Are you here by invitation, Jordan?" the voice asked.

"Yes," she replied. "My own."

"Jordan Blue," the voice said, "as that you are not expected, would you please mind returning into orbit until I can get a clearance for you to land?"

"I would mind, but thank you for being so polite." A speck appeared on the horizon, quickly growing into a splotch. "Cyan," Blue said softly, "enlarge that for me would you?" The image zoomed close, showing a rocky island covered in green and topped with an enormous castle that seemed blacker than the bottom of a well.

"Well, that's something I never thought I would see again," Galen whispered.

Noel turned sharply to look at him. "You've been here?"

Galen shook his head slowly. "Not here, but a place that looked just like it - the castle, I mean. Exactly like it, except that it wasn't black."

"Jordan?" the voice asked. "We politely request that you retreat into orbit until we can get clearance for your arrival."

"Request denied," Blue responded, changing the front visual back to real time so that she could plot their course. The island was growing in the distance, though the castle was still hard to make out.

"Jordan," the voice said, assuming the stringent tone a parent might use with an errant child, "it is well within our right to shoot you down if you do not comply with our request."

"You can try," Galen murmured. "You're right, he is a dunce."

The Jordan snorted. "You would have done so by now," she answered over the com. "Your affiliation with the IGC prohibits such a move, not to mention my relation to the owner of this water-covered wasteland."

"Do you mean Ms. de Rossi?"

"She owns this place, doesn't she?"

"She does, but I do not see...ah! Yes, Jordan Blue. You are Noel de Rossi?"

"I am." She put her left hand on the dash once again and looked at Galen. "What an idiot!" she said, laughing. "If I ever end up with these bitches, the first thing getting changed is security. It's a wonder either one of them is still alive." The Jordan's eye became thoughtful and distant as she gazed out at the castle that was growing larger by the second. "Do you know who would make a great security officer?"

Galen smiled. "Who?"

"Scarlett."

Galen laughed but the Jordan turned so she could see him. "I'm serious. She would shoot first, ask questions second."

Galen laughed harder and Blue smiled, taking her hand off of the dash as the Castle began to loom into view.

"Where do you want me to land?" she asked.

"Jordan, if you wouldn't mind..."

The Jordan shook her head, grinning. "Front lawn it is." There was a muffled curse over the com as the Fledglings came burning in over the island, pulling a torrent of air in their wake, even as they slowed. With a heavy animal grace, both Fledglings pushed out their four, stout silvery legs from their underbellies and landed on the expanse of manicured lawn in front of the shining black edifice that was the Last Castle of Charity de Rossi.

"Are you going to let me in the front door?" Blue asked sweetly. "Or do I have to make my own entrance?"

There was a heavy sigh from the other end of the communication. "There will be an escort there for you momentarily."

Blue, wearing an innocent smile, left Cyan and let a security contingent escort her into the Castle and run a scan on her body. A small man with golden skin, black hair, and dark eyes even more almond-shaped than her own, bowed deeply to her.

"Your sidearm, Jordan?" he asked. "Please."

Blue pulled her pistol from its holster and handed it over without a word. Though he was dressed in silk and seemed the utmost mannered, a chill ran up the Jordan's spine as he bowed to her once again.

"Yakuza," Galen whispered, as if the man might hear him. The man straightened and smiled, cocking his head the slightest bit as if he *had* heard Galen.

"I feel, Jordan, that there is something else about you." His smile implied that he was offering forgiveness, yet she needed to be completely honest and soon - there would be no second chances with this man. The Jordan's mind flicked to the feel of the glass rod within her boot and just as quickly flicked away.

"My lover is with me as well," she said, which was entirely true though she did not expect it to be believed.

"Ah!" the man exclaimed, turning his body so that it was angled towards the space next to the Jordan, exactly where Galen stood, and bowed deeply. "The ghost in the machine. Welcome, doctor!" Blue had a second to wonder if she had gone as pale as Galen before the man held out a hand, inviting them inside.

"Thank you," Blue said, giving the man a slight bow before turning to follow the contingent that waited for her inside. They fell in step next to her, escorting her down a wide hallway with wood paneled walls that were hung with garishly obvious priceless pieces of art.

One of the men turned to her as they walked along. Blue noticed that he was older, and not dressed like the others.

"A butler," Galen told her.

"May I offer you anything to drink?" he asked.

"Champagne," she replied as they entered a room lined with long fireplaces, hung with enormous tapestries, and decorated with delicate antiques of smooth velvet and polished wood. She let out a low whistle. "Better bring me the whole bottle." The butler bent at the waist in acquiescence.

"Anything to eat, Ms. de Rossi?"

Noel laughed. She couldn't remember anyone ever calling her *that* before. "Sure. Just don't worry about anything fancy. I'll eat whatever you can find." The butler bowed again and left the room. The security men that remained glanced at each other, unsure. "Unless any of you guys are going to hang around and feed me, piss off."

The security team rumbled softly like a herd of sleeping buffalo. Then, as one, they moved away and left through the same door the butler had taken.

"Jesus!" Blue exclaimed when they were gone. She dropped down onto a small couch with velvet cushions. "Could you believe that guy?"

Galen sat down next to her and draped an arm over the carved mahogany back of the sofa. "Which one?"

"The guard!"

"Hmm," Galen agreed. "You've never seen a Yakuza before?"

"No! And I hope I never do again! He scared the shit out of me!"

"Really? What was it about him that scared you?"

The Jordan frowned at Galen's usual turn to the clinical query but answered him. "He could see you. I'm sure of it. And I felt like he could see right through me."

Galen smirked. "They are all like that - the Yakuza, I mean."

"Where did they..." she started but a door opened and the butler re-entered the room, pushing a tray on wheels and escorted by a floating droid carrying a chilled bottle of champagne and a free-standing chill bucket.

If he had taken notice that she was speaking aloud to an empty room, he gave no indication. The tray rattled to a halt next to the couch. It held tiered trays piled high with bite-sized bits of food. There were slices of fruit and crisp vegetables, along with miniature tarts, hot savories, and sweets.

"I think a sandwich would have sufficed," Blue told him. "But thanks." The man smiled and took the bottle from the droid, removing the wire and expertly popping the cork. He poured a small amount into a delicate flute and offered it to the Jordan.

"If Madame pleases," he said, holding out the glass.

"Madame does," the Jordan said as she accepted it and

took a sip. Her high, arched brows pulled together over her glittering blue eye and glittering black eye patch. "Damn!" she exclaimed, handing the glass back to the butler. "That's some good shit!"

The man merely smiled as he filled the flute to the brim and handed it back to the Jordan while the droid set up the ice bucket and nestled the bottle inside the floating chips of ice.

"I can bring you a magnetic chiller, if you prefer," the butler offered but the Jordan shook her head, making her platinum coils tremble on her black-clad shoulders.

"Don't be silly," she said. "This is fine."

The butler bowed in response. "Your sister has been notified of your arrival, and will be joining you shortly. Is there anything else I may do for you at present?" The Jordan shook her head again.

"I'm sure I will be fine. Thank you."

The butler gave her another one of his deep bows. "Should you require anything else, you need only to raise your hand." He smiled and with his gray eyebrows raised he glanced at the area above the largest fireplace. "Security is watching you, but they will send me in first – should you seem in need of anything but restraint."

The Jordan grinned at his blatant yet jovial honesty. "Thank you. I will certainly do that." The man gave her anther bow and left the room. The Jordan, shaking her head in amusement, selected a slice of pear from the rolling table and lounged back, taking a nibble off the fruit and a long drink of champagne.

"So," she said to Galen, "this is how the other half lives."

Galen grinned. "The universe is not simply divided into two groups," he told her. The Jordan returned his smile, though it had a bitter edge to it.

"But it is. Faith was right about that, at least. There are the players and the pawns." She took another long drink.

"You might want to slow down," he advised.

"What for?" Blue asked as she pulled the bottle from the bucket and refilled her glass. The black brows of the doctor arched high above his bright blue eyes as he smiled and shook his head.

"Faith and Charity," he warned, "are not like Brogan and Blaylock."

"You knew them well?" Blue asked, though this time only taking a small sip from the glass.

Galen shook his head. "Not really, I only met them in person a handful of times. But I know how they operate."

"How did you first meet her?"

Galen looked at her, frozen, his face pale and drained of expression. "You don't want to know."

The Jordan lowered her glass from her red lips and rested it on her thigh. "Now I definitely want to know!"

Galen looked down and laughed nervously at the coincidence. "Faith asked me to spy on her younger sister for her."

Blue's sapphire eye went wide. "Are you serious?"

Galen laughed again and nodded. "I never thought of it before, but it was almost the same thing she had asked for you. Nothing covert, just asked me to keep an eye on her – report anything I thought was important."

Blue shook her head in amusement and selected a sausage and gravy filled pastry from the tray. She bit into it and Galen handed her a napkin to staunch the flow of gravy on her chin. Grateful, Blue took the napkin and then froze with the cloth covering the bottom half of her face.

"They're here," she whispered, wiping off her chin and draining her glass once again. Galen quickly took her napkin and topped off her glass. Noel took a deep breath and settled back onto the couch.

⚜

Notified of the arrival of Jordan Blue, Faith and Charity de Rossi quickly made their way from the GwenSeven Compound to the Last Castle with only a handful of assistants and preceding their personal security details.

They eschewed the hydrofoil and took a jet, landing in a cavern beneath the castle. The small entourage followed the sisters up and through the castle until they came to an enormous pair of closed mahogany doors that were intricately carved, the raised areas gilded in silver. Jasyn recognized it as the entrance to a large sitting room.

Faith turned to Penny first. "Please wait here," she instructed. "When Geary arrives, have him wait here with you."

Penny nodded quickly and stepped demurely to the side while Faith turned to face her sister.

"Something to drink?" she asked.

Charity grinned. "But of course." She turned to Jasyn, much to his surprise. "I think it's time we celebrate, don't you?" When he only blinked at her in puzzlement she laughed. "Would you be a darling and get us a bottle of champagne? Aide will help you."

Jasyn smiled. "I know the way."

Charity could not contain her smirk. "Aide will go with you anyway. You too," she said motioning to the other assistant. "Though Jasyn is the only one to return." She eyed her two top aides, making sure they got her meaning.

They nodded in assent, letting her know that they understood, and turned to head for the supt-kitch, the closest room that had a full bar and a partial kitchen. It was also much closer than the only room on the ground level that was an actual bar. Jasyn hesitated, throwing a glance of concern at Faith, and then followed Charity's assistants down an intersecting hallway.

He smiled at the aides that accompanied him to the supt-kitch, trying to relax. He tried to think of how wound up Geary must be - racing back to the castle - thinking that it might be comical, but for once the construct cursed the man for not being with Faith to make sure that she was safe.

As soon as he reached the kitch, however, his mood was lifted. Everyone, though they had been working around the clock in preparation for the upcoming party, was in high spirits. They greeted Jasyn jovially, as if he was an old friend, and hastened to get him anything he might need or want. A bottle of champagne was immediately brought to him by a barback, asking if he would like a chilled bottle of Varti as well.

"Yes," he told the barback with a grin. "Send it on a butler droid, with a chill bucket for the champagne." The barback nodded and quickly moved to do his bidding.

Jasyn's grin belied the way he was feeling. His heart sank as he realized what it was that he was experiencing. He was feeling part of a team. He was feeling respected. He was feeling human.

He pushed the thought away as a butler droid floated up to him, waiting. It carried the chill bucket, the bottle of Varti, and two heavy crystal glasses on a field tray. He gave a nod of thanks to the barback and picked up the two empty flutes on the bar. Holding the flutes by the stems in one hand and the champagne bottle in the other, he turned and headed for the parlor where Faith was waiting.

He needn't concern himself with feelings right now, he assured himself. He had made his decision and he would keep to his purpose.

The Chimeran made his way back to the sitting room, wishing that he knew what day it was. Wishing he knew if the sun was almost down. Reaching the carved doors, he pushed them open, deciding at once that he didn't care.

"Here we go," he started to say, anticipating the smile that Faith would give him, but his hazel eyes fell on the frail figure splayed upon the couch.

The Black Jordan, he thought wildly, though he knew that it was really the Blue Jordan and that it was Faith's youngest sister. His blood ran cold as her single blue eye bore into him and froze him where he stood. Her mouth opened slightly as if she were tasting the air, breathing deep, tasting his scent. A single thought raced through his mind as he watched time slow to a crawl. *She knows!*

His hazel eyes found Faith, trying to tell her that he was sorry, that he had to do what he had done. He wanted her to know why he had but felt that now there would never be the time.

It seemed as if the faces of the older women in the room, Faith and Charity, moved fractionally as they tried to grasp what was transpiring before them. The whole scene seemed underwater. Sounds were muted, movements slow and cumbersome.

The Jordan, however, moved with a supernatural speed - a speed he had not seen outside of reflex-jacked sapiens.

The wraith with platinum hair and clothed in shimmering black dove forward, pulling a weapon from her boot as she rolled over a shoulder to come up on one knee and take aim. Had she been facing Faith in the slightest, Jasyn would have thrown his body in front of her. As it was, the slender wand of glass was pointed at his own body. There was nothing for him to do but brace himself.

He heard Faith scream, but before his heart had thumped another beat, a blinding light shot from the end of the Jordan's weapon and tore through his left side, knocking his body to the floor. He rolled onto his side, which felt impossibly numb before it started to burn. He thought that he cried out, but he wasn't sure.

There was a crash of breaking glass and a pounding of

footsteps as people thundered into the room in response to Faith's cry. There were screams and shouts that he could not make out. He laid on his injured side, hoping to hold in any part of his innards that might be able to escape. The construct thought that the caved-in feel might mean that his ribs were broken, then he thought that they might not even be there at all. His body curled in instinctively, his nostrils full of the smell of his own burned flesh, panting and feeling that he was getting no less than what he deserved.

There were sounds of a struggle and everybody was talking or yelling and moving all over. Then he felt Faith against his body, trying to cradle his head and comfort him but he did not want to look at her. He tried to draw in further, ignoring everything around him.

There were shouts and orders and the Jordan was escorted from the room by security and Charity left, following her aides. As Jasyn tried to block it all out and give in to the pain, he realized that the room had gone silent. He and Faith were alone.

His breathing ragged, each inhale a sharp pain in his injured side, the Chimeran forced his eyes open and looked up at the woman he had been sent to destroy.

Her gold and brown eyes were rimmed with red and her face was streaked with tears, something he was not used to seeing. He reached out the arm on his uninjured side and curled it around her body.

Just the feel of her was enough to make him feel better, and worse. He pulled her body tighter against his own, closing his eyes again, scrunching them shut against the pain that racked his body and the pain of what he knew.

⳹⳺

Jordan Blue had watched the construct enter the room and

felt her body stiffen the way a mongoose would instinctively react to a snake. At once her head was filled with the voices of both the Fledglings.

Otherling!

Their silent warning came as one and they filled her mind's eye with images of Chimeran ships, star fights, and the Chimeran sigul, the lazy-eight symbol for infinity.

The Jordan moved reflexively, certain that the universe had conspired for her to be armed. She dove forward, pulling Chang's weapon from her boot. She took the one shot she had before Faith bowled her over, practically knocking her eye-patch off her head as the woman pinned her down.

Blue fought to shove her sister's weight off of her body while at the same time trying to fix the eye patch on her face that had come askew. "Get off of me!" she hollered, struggling. "He's Chimeran!" she shouted in her own defense but her sister's weight refused to budge. Instead it only shifted, hold the Jordan to the rug.

"I know that!" Faith hissed in her ear.

Noel's single blue eye widened but, before she could voice another word, security teams for both of her sisters were pouring into the room. Faith pushed herself away from Noel's body and scrabbled across the floor to where the Chimeran was lying on the plush carpet, bleeding from a hole blazed into half of his ribcage.

One of the stern-faced suited guards that had escorted her into the Castle hauled Jordan Blue to her feet where she quickly adjusted the black patch on her face. The man she recognized as Faith's main security man immediately confiscated her weapon and made it disappear.

"Take her to the conservatory," Charity instructed. "I'll be there shortly." Her green eyes fixed upon her youngest sister in hope that she would behave.

The man roughly turned the Jordan to frog march her down

the hall but she shook her arm free of his grip.

"I can walk myself," she said, angry. With a final, albeit confused, glare about the room she stalked off, escorted by Charity's entire security team. Once they had left the room, one of the guards laid a commanding hand upon her black-clad shoulder and she jerked it free. "God dammit!'" she yelled. "Keep your mitts off of me!"

Galen kept stride close by, watching carefully. Should any of them try to get heavy handed with her, he would intervene. He wasn't sure how that would play out, and he didn't care. Dead or not, he would keep her safe.

The security team marched the Jordan down one hall after another, up a lift and down another carpeted corridor. They opened a double door for her, waiting with what Galen was sure they thought of as extreme patience.

"Wait in here," one of them commanded. The Jordan drew herself up to her full height of a meter and a half and strode past them all with a look of disgust. The door closed behind her and she looked around.

She was in a cavernous room, round with a domed ceiling of glass. Through it, she could see the pink and orange light of the setting sun. Or Jupiter, she wasn't sure. The room appeared as if it were under renovation. It was barely lit and half full of furniture that was pushed against one wall. Its singular feature was a dry fountain that at present looked like no more than walled-in pile of rocks.

The Jordan sat herself on one side of the room on a stool pushed up to a cocktail bar. "Well!" she exclaimed. "That was quite the scene!"

Galen only harrumphed in response. His blue eyes left the Jordan and found the door she had just passed through. He stared at it as if looking through it. "What did you think about Faith?" he asked.

"Besides the earful she gave me about more Fledglings

coming and that the Captains will have to die first?"

Galen nodded, still staring back the way they had come. "Did anything about her strike you as strange?"

Blue gave a single chuckle through her nose. "Everything about her strikes me as strange."

Galen finally turned to face the pilot in shimmering black. "Is there anything you are more aware of? Now that you have had those injections?"

The Jordan shifted as if the question made her uncomfortable. "Maybe. Yes. I don't know."

"Yes you do. Tell me."

The Jordan shifted again but nodded this time. "She has a strange feel and, I know you are going to think this is weird, but she gives me a feeling similar to the one I get from Opal, my mother Dragon."

They both turned as the door swung open long enough to allow Charity and a butler droid to pass before it swung shut again.

Charity glanced around and, spying her youngest sister, lifted her chin and joined her at the bar. The butler droid pulled out a chair and dusted it off before placing a crystal glass of dark fluid on the polished counter next to Charity and then placed a flute of champagne on the bar next to the Jordan.

"Turn on some lights," Charity instructed the droid as it folded in upon itself. "And leave us." The droid tipped its hovering body towards Charity in polite acquiescence and then darted off. A second later a bank of lights that ringed the room close to floor came on, giving the sisters a twilight at their feet to accompany the sunset overhead.

The Jordan, feeling about as comfortable with Charity as she had with Faith, took a deep breath through her small nose and looked around.

"The egg was here," she said.

Charity nodded slowly. "Yes. It was moved two days ago."

"But he is still close."

Charity's green eyes glittered in the half-light. "How do you know that?"

Blue fixed the woman with her single sapphire eye. "Because I can feel him. I can hear his heart beating."

"Is that so?" Charity breathed, amazed.

"It is," the Jordan said with a shrug, not wanting to discuss Dragon details with the woman next to her. Instead, she put an elbow on the bar and her chin in her hand. "So, you're keeping company with the Chimera?"

Charity sighed. "It's a long story. A really long story."

"I have the time."

Charity's lips quirked up in a smile. "I'm sure you do, but… all in good time. I've got better stories than that one. How about government sanctioned murder, terrorism…"

"Slavery?"

Charity lifted her chin. "We do not support slavery."

"But you make slaves."

"We make droids that look like people. We changed the way that they were made eight decades ago." Charity tossed her golden hair and took a drink from her glass. "For being an IGC pawn, you sound awfully pro-Chimeran."

"I am not a pawn," the Jordan declared vehemently. "And I am not pro-Chimeran! I'm just being…being…"

"The Devil's advocate," Galen whispered.

"The Devil's advocate," Blue said.

Charity's green eyes narrowed and her smile tightened as she reached for her glass. "Hello, Galen," she said.

The Jordan leaned forward, her sapphire eye bulging as Galen laughed and said hello to Charity. "You can hear him? Can you see him?" she demanded.

Charity laughed and took a drink from her glass, shaking her head. "No. Neither. Faith said that he was still with you, and it just occurred to me what that really meant. Especially that term. It was one he had used before."

The Jordan threw a glare to her right. "You *knew* him? I thought you had only met him a couple of times."

"That's true, I did. A long time ago. I did not know him very well. Certainly not as well as you, of course."

The Jordan ran a hand over her face and looked at the pink and orange glow that seeped from the domed ceiling. "This is going from crazy to crazier."

Her sister laughed, tilting her own head up. She held her glass out to Noel as if making a toast. "Welcome to my world," she said. The Jordan only gave her a smirk at first but then, seeming both amused and resigned, picked up her flute of champagne and touched its rim to her sister's glass.

"Cheers," she whispered and both sisters took a long drink.

"So," Charity said. "Why are you here?"

The Jordan pressed her lips together, battling inwardly with the desire to be in control and the need for answers. Finally, she sighed. "Because I am confused."

Her sister's expression, for the first time, softened. "I know," she said. "And we don't expect you to make this decision overnight. We are sure, though, that you will eventually see the light. We are right in what we are doing."

Noel snorted and shook her head. "Everyone thinks that they are right. That's why people fight on different sides. But both sides can't be right. What makes you think I will see the light, as you so eloquently phrased it?"

"Because Faith said you would," she said softly. "And she is never wrong." When the Jordan smirked, Charity tilted her head, examining the pilot. "And you have already begun, haven't you?"

The Jordan shrugged, uncomfortable. "She didn't tell me

that much."

"She didn't have to. She lit a candle so that you may see, and that candle has grown into a lantern by your own power. Now, I'll bet, it is impossible for you not to see."

Jordan Blue turned her face away and took a sip from her glass. It was true. She had lived an idyllic life, blindly trusting everyone around her. Faith had cleaned the crust from her lids and now Noel's eyes were wide open. She could see clearly what before she had refused to believe. Her leaders, not to mention *the god-damned government*, the people to which she had devoted her life - the governing body for which she had stood and fought and killed - was not exactly the shining light of liberty and justice that she had always believed.

They had withheld information from her, and they still were. They had potentially killed the only man she had ever loved. They had used her for what they needed and then had shown her that they still had the power to take away the last thing that she lived for – her Fledgling.

"Before that Chimeran came in and interrupted us," the Jordan said, changing the subject, "Faith said that there would be second rainbow. A whole new clutch of eggs, born to each Dragon?"

"That's what we have been led to believe." Charity tipped her blonde head, examining her younger sister's expression. "But Faith is correct in what she told you," she continued, her voice gentle. "The Captain of the Dragon must die for eggs to manifest. You realize why, don't you?"

Noel shook her head, never feeling more naïve than she did at that moment. The warmth of her sister's gaze did not help. Galen placed a ghostly hand upon her arm but it did not reassure her.

"The Captain provides the seed," Charity said softly. "Dragons do not simply reproduce themselves."

Noel gaped at her, abashed. She would have laughed if not

for how serious Charity looked – still, she thought she might. "Are you suggesting that the Captain procreates with the Dragon?"

Charity laughed lightly and shook her head. "Certainly not!" She laughed again as she considered the idea. "Certainly not the way we do! But when the Captain dies his body is absorbed by the Dragon. I have no idea how the process works - I'm sure your Chief Medic could explain it better, or maybe your Engineer. But it is this absorption that creates the eggs from which new Dragons will be born."

The Jordan's lip curled at the mention of the Engineer. She leaned back on her stool, digesting the information she had just been given. She had to admit that it made sense, in a way. Not just the reproductive aspect, but the way that the Dragons were able to communicate with the humans and/or elves – they shared a small part of their DNA. She could see Galen from the corner of her eye, thoughtfully tapping his chin with two long fingers.

"Surely you must have realized that no female Jordans had been sent to a choosing since the first one, over a thousand years ago, until of course you and the Mattatock girl were sent."

Blue closed her eye, understanding. "Because the Dragons were all female," she said softly. "They would only choose male Jordans. They were choosing their mate."

Charity smiled at her astuteness and sipped her drink, watching the Jordan carefully. She did not have to wait long. Noel's eye popped open and stared at her sister.

"Except Ferrous!" she whispered. She turned her head and spoke over her shoulder to Galen while Charity watched her with gimlet eyes. "I meant to talk to you about that!" Blue exclaimed.

"What?" Galen asked, frowning.

"Ferrous, the Iron Dragon, is a *he* – not a she." Galen frowned but Charity merely sipped her drink, watching. "When

I took the triptych, the one I took from Calyph, and injected myself with Fledge's fluid," Blue continued, "I could see and hear every Dragon, every Fledgling, every Hatchling as if I were part of them. I suppose, in a way, I am. As soon as I touched Ferrous, I knew instantly that he was male." She turned her scarred face to Charity. "But that doesn't mesh with what you're telling me. He has a male Captain."

Charity gave her an indulgent, knowing smile. "Do you know," she asked, "that rumors, myths, legends – they all begin because they have a grain of truth to them? Something that somebody saw with just enough evidence that would lead others to believe them? What story surrounds the choosing? The one about what happens to the cadets that are not chosen."

The Jordan chuffed a small laugh, already familiar with the story. "That they are eaten by the Fledglings, which is ridiculous."

"And where do you think a rumor like that got started?"

The black-clad Jordan shrugged. "You've got me on that one."

"We started out this conversation with stories. Well, here is one for you." Charity uncrossed and then recrossed her legs as she settled onto her stool, getting comfortable. "At the first choosing there was an equal amount of male and female cadets, since no one knew at that point exactly what a new Dragon might be looking for in a pilot. What was not equal was the ambition of the pilots." Charity paused and looked at Noel. "Tell me, what was your choosing like?"

Noel shrugged as she considered, remembering. "It was hot. The Bay, then the Womb, was kept hot for the eggs. Everyone had stripped down to their underclothes after the first hour, but the wait went on for days – there were six of us sequestered in the Womb."

Charity nodded. "So it was with the first choosing. Only there was a young elf named Khasper. He was determined to be the first Captain, no matter what the cost."

Charity stopped and sipped her drink. When it was obvious that she was not going to say anything more, the Jordan twirled her hand, urging her to continue.

"So, what happened?"

Charity smiled. "So he was. And still is."

Noel's mouth opened slightly as the realization settled over her and she looked across her shoulder at Galen. After a short pause, he nodded, his face grim. Noel turned her face back to Charity. "He killed them?" she asked. "All of the cadets?"

"Every one."

The silence spun into something ethereal.

"If there was no one there to witness," Galen said, "they would have to have taken his word for it. That the Fledgling had killed the unchosen cadets."

"And so the story became a legend," Noel whispered. Her body slowly filled with the numbness of shock. "I can't believe he got away with it."

"And that's not all," Charity added. Noel closed her eye, feeling slightly sick.

"What Faith said," the Jordan continued, making an effort to swallow, "about the Executive Officer..."

"Was true. Leonora, the first Executive Officer on Ferrous, and Khasper's lover as well, died under mysterious circumstances, right around the time the Engineers began questioning the reproductive cycle of the Dragon."

"Ferrous must have communicated to Khasper what he needed," Noel said, thoughtful.

"And Khasper was kind enough to provide for the manifestation of the Iron Dragon's eggs."

The expiring light made the room look cave-like and the Jordan's face was ashen in the semi-dark, her scars standing out in sharp contrast like angry pink slashes. Her black eye patch was beginning to look like a hole in her skull.

"He killed his Executive Officer? *And* she was his lover?"

Charity's lips made a tight line. "And, from what I have been told, was carrying his seed as well." Noel paled further and Charity continued. "He wanted, you see, to make his own contribution – to have his own code live on. Without having to die himself, of course."

"That is just something you were told," the Jordan whispered hoarsely. "How can you believe it?"

"Have you ever met Khasper?"

The Jordan nodded slowly. "Once. He gave me the creeps, to put it lightly, especially when he looked at me." Noel remembered it was more than just the creeps. Her skin had gathered into gooseflesh when she had met him, and she had been filled with a terror that made her blood run cold when he had looked at her.

"Is his hair still black?"

The Jordan looked up sharply. "Mostly, though it is shot with gray at his temples. His eyes, though, are blacker than night. Everything about him was dark." Noel remembered, and recalled thinking that he was like a black hole, a force so great than even light could not escape.

Charity nodded. "And Leonora was pale. Pale skin and eyes. White hair."

"What does that have to do with..." the Jordan began but stopped as soon as she thought of the now grown Dragons that had been the offspring of Ferrous. "Onyx and Pearl. Black and white." She closed her eye.

"We all have our secrets," Charity told her. "But none more so than the IGC. And their secrets are the most painful to learn. Khasper's story is just a small tale in a galactic-sized library of murderous atrocity."

Blue opened her sapphire eye and regarded her sister with a look wrought with sorrow. She opened her mouth to speak but it snapped shut and her head jerked to the side as if startled by a loud noise. Charity looked in the direction the Jordan was facing but she could discern no movement or sound from the shadows.

"I have to go," she said, standing quickly.

Charity sighed. "Won't you stay for the party? There are people I would like you to meet."

"I have to go," the Jordan repeated. "Now." Charity did not hide her disappointment but Noel dipped her chin slightly, fixing her sister with a serious eye. "Maybe another time," she told her. "I might want to hear more. Maybe. I don't know."

Charity nodded, beaming. "Very well."

Blue glanced about, looking for the nearest exit. The glass ceiling was an inverted bowl of violet ringed with red. The room itself was succumbing to darkness except for the bank of lights along the bottom curve of the wall. Noel seemed a piece of the night herself, reflecting stars of red and blue as she tugged at her flight suit.

She gave Charity a curt nod and moved to leave the room. As she passed her sister, on impulse, she dipped slightly and quickly kissed her cheek before she strode from the darkening conservatory without another word.

Charity's only movement was a flicker of her green eyes before they filled with tears. Otherwise, she remained motionless as the ever-deepening red sky in the dome above her head turned to violet.

The Jordan moved with haste down the corridors of the castle, sprinting for the Fledglings once she was in the open.

TWO SEVEN

The Macedonian braked as it neared the gas giant, adjusting course to keep a safe distance. Bjorn watched from his chair at the helm as it came into view. Lucy stood by his side, watching silently. Liquid helium and hydrogen swirled under the gaseous surface of ammonia crystals, under more swirls of gas and debris that circled the planet in a never-ending chase – giving it the appearance of a massive confection from a candy shop, displayed on a backdrop of crushed black silk.

Old loves and new, Bjorn mused, thinking of his first and (what he hoped might be) his last. *Must we always give up one for the other?*

"Run a scan for IGC ships within this quadrant," Bjorn instructed his navigator, Olivia. She had a full, beautiful face and luminous brown eyes that moved rapidly across her console. Aaron was not on shift so Emma, a twin of the lovely Olivia, sat ready at the communications console.

"Nothing within this quadrant, sir," Olivia replied after checking her screens.

"What about within the quadrant of the moon?"

There was a pause as Olivia extended the search. She shook her head, her long brown hair undulating. "No, sir."

"What about non-IGC ships?"

"There are three Jabret ships on the far side of the planet, one point five LD from the moon."

"Scavengers," Bjorn muttered. He knew that the junkers would not see the Chimeran fighter jets at this distance, and they would not care what the Chimerans were up to as long as they were left alone. He stayed in his chair a moment longer, quashing his internal battle and rising to his feet before Lucy could ask him anything he did not want to answer.

"Make sure my pilots are ready," Bjorn told Quartermaster Helioch. "And my jet."

The Quartermaster gave Bjorn a quick nod and turned to carry out his orders as the Commander left the bridge. Lucy followed, her stride efficient and effortless as she kept pace with the Chimeran. He had an entire minute of silence before she spoke.

"There have purportedly been twelve castles built by Charity de Rossi," she reported coolly as they made their way down a brightly lit corridor. "Eleven of which have been called the Last Castle. Of the twelve, the locations of only three have been discovered, this latest discovery will raise that count to four, should the report prove to be true."

"Is that so?" Bjorn mused aloud, giving Lucy an amused smile without breaking stride.

"It must be," Lucy said dispassionately before she continued. "Never has the castle been discovered while it was inhabited, therefore the security measures taken to protect it have never been tried and therefore never evaluated. There is no way to know what you may be flying into."

Bjorn turned a corner, a smile creasing his handsome face. "We," he corrected. "No way to know what *we* may be flying into."

Lucy's normally stoic expression reflected a human reaction - surprise. "By we, do you mean that I will be accompanying you on this flight?"

"I do," Bjorn said, grinning. He made a sharp turn and exchanged one corridor for another before he reached the Battle Cruiser's fighter bay. Each jet selected for the mission was undergoing safety checks, their prospective pilots suiting up nearby.

"I can assure you that I have no fighting skills whatsoever," Lucy told him.

Bjorn laughed. "Then I will take you along for your company."

"Is that a joke?" Lucy asked, her golden eyes swirling. Bjorn had made it quite clear how he felt about her lack of personality and her program could only assimilate his words into what might be sarcasm.

"Yes," he told her as he reached the jet closest to the bay door, facing the maw of blackness beyond, the rest of the platoon in a triangular formation behind.

The jet, like Lucy, was a new model, with all the bells and whistles, including a seat for a navigator or a gunner, right next to the pilot's seat. Bjorn slapped the ladder that led up to cockpit and held out a hand to Lucy to help her up. The Commander regarded her with raised brows when the troll remained motionless.

"What?" he asked.

"As I stated before," Lucy said, "there is no way to measure the security measures you will surely encounter and therefore impossible to predict the chances of survival."

Bjorn's brows went higher, furrowing his normally smooth brow with squiggles of surprise. "Are you afraid of dying?" he asked.

Lucy regarded him coolly, her golden eyes moving as she processed. "Such emotion is far beyond what I can assimilate. That being said, no creature that is even semi-sentient goes willingly towards its own death unless it is programmed for self-destruction." The troll made an agitated sound, as if clearing her throat. "Might I add, as you have pointed out before, you spent a handsome sum acquiring me and it would be a waste of money well spent to have me incinerated at such an early point."

Bjorn made an exaggerated shrug and the corners of his mouth pulled down. "But if I am dead, I am sure I won't care," he assured her.

Lucy's golden eyes widened, reflecting glints of red and green light. Bjorn pressed his lips together to keep from smiling. He knew that he could order her into the jet and she would not refuse, yet this was by far the most interesting conversation he had ever had with the dark-haired troll.

"If the measures have never been tested," he told her, then wouldn't it stand to reason that my chances of success are fifty-fifty?"

"No. The first human to jump into a live volcano was unquestionably incinerated. The fact that it had never been tried before did not increase his chances of survival."

"Be optimistic then," the handsome Chimeran suggested. "I'm an accomplished fighter and I have never lost a battle."

"I believe that optimism is beyond me as well," Lucy said.

Bjorn grinned as he reached into the pocket of his blue coveralls and dug out a small but heavy-looking metal disc. Lucy recognized it as a piece of currency from the moon where they had visited the Red Jordan.

"I'll tell you what," Bjorn said. "If this lands heads up, I win and you accompany me. If it lands tails up, you can stay here on the *Mace*."

"From what I have been able to gather," Lucy said, "nearly every woman you meet ends up with her tail up."

Bjorn froze as he was about to toss the coin. "Is that a joke?" he asked.

"Yes," Lucy responded, her voice flat. "Was it funny?"

Bjorn paused, considering. Then he chuckled and shook his head. "It wasn't bad, Lucy," he admitted. "Not too bad at all."

The troll's face shifted just enough to look pleased.

"Shall I toss?" Bjorn asked.

"Why bother?" the troll replied with a manufactured sound that emulated a sigh. She grasped the thin steel bars on either side of the ladder. "That coin has a head on both sides."

Bjorn laughed as the troll swung herself up the ladder rung by rung with an easy, mechanical grace. "Move on over when you get in," he called behind her, "unless you are planning on piloting this thing."

"Though I am sure that I am able," she called without looking back, "I will do no such thing unless it is my only choice."

Bjorn chuckled as he shimmied up the ladder and, after taking a look around the bay to make sure that everyone had finished their preparations and were boarding their own jets, swung one leg and then the other into the cockpit and dropped his weight down into the pilot's seat.

Lucy was methodically securing her safety webbing without so much as glancing at it, staring instead through the glass front of the fighter. Bjorn drew his index finger over the sensor that would shut the cover and secured his own webbing as the hood fell slowly and closed over the two passengers inside.

There were series of snicks and clicks as the hatch sealed and Bjorn unconsciously opened his jaw out of habit, making his ears pop. He went through his preflight checks and powered up the double-twin engines. Though it was the largest fighter in the bay it was by far the most quiet.

"I love progress," Bjorn murmured as he rolled the jet forward, checking his screens. He raised the level of thrust just enough to propel the jet though the nitrogen membrane of the bay door and fall out into space before firing the engines to full.

He checked the coordinates that had already been set into the uni-loc and glanced at his back-screen to make sure he had all platoon members following before he shot a look at the troll. Her angled, passive face was framed by dark waves of hair and looking at her sharp profile reminded him of Scarlett.

"Can you keep a secret Lucy?" he asked, smiling.

"No," the troll said, her flat voice eliciting a laugh from the Commander.

"Well, I am going to tell you anyway."

"Something tells me you shouldn't."

"Well, that just proves that you have no outside perception, extrasensory perception, as the humans call it. I think for the elves it is simply second nature, like walking or breathing."

"You were saying?"

"Yes," Bjorn agreed, sliding his finger along the dash, initiating auto control of the jet. The craft banked, roughly at first as it honed in on the coordinates, and then smoothed out as it sailed along through the vacuum of space. Bjorn checked the screen and saw that the platoon was following as smooth as a flock of geese. "You have no need to worry," he continued. "I think our chances are better than you know."

"Why is that?"

The Commander adjusted controls and coordinates and his green eyes flicked from one place to another, though his expression remained still.

"I'm not planning on attacking the castle."

The troll's head swiveled around to face him, her golden eyes swirling. "I do not understand. Has the mission changed?"

"The mission stays the same, but it will be a ruse. I have no intention of killing Charity de Rossi." Bjorn glanced at her and grinned at her expression before he was overcome with laughter.

"Tell me what you are feeling, Lucy," Bjorn demanded. "What are you feeling right now?"

Lucy cocked her head. "I feel nothing – feelings are not part of my program. But, the second after your confession; I experienced the equivalent of confusion and surprise, then the desire to correlate your words with the odds of possibility of truth, then satisfaction at the most likely outcome and, I suppose, relief. Yes," she said, agreeing with herself, "if I could feel something, it would be relief."

"All of that in one second?" Bjorn asked.

Lucy's dark brows arched above her golden eyes. "How long would it have taken you?" she asked.

Bjorn glared at her in begrudging admiration. "I'm sure you could figure that out," he said. "If you don't already know." He turned his face forward and, with just the slightest trace of a smirk, so did Lucy.

Bjorn relaxed into his seat, enjoying the pull of the craft as it maneuvered through space. It was much less jerky than his previous fighter, though he had grown a bit attached to the old thing. It had been reliable, the laser weaponry precise. He had known its quirks as well as he had known his own, and he had always been able to adjust for them with the greatest of accuracy.

After Scarlett had worked her mischief in it, however, and even though his mechs had assured him that there was no longer a single molecule of CS in the thing, he couldn't fly it. He would not be three seconds in the cockpit before his nose would start running and it simply would not do for a fighter pilot to be constantly sniffling like a child. The Commander also found that, along with a runny nose, he would have an erection - but he refrained from mentioning that to the mechs. It was easier to simply get a new fighter.

The Chimeran platoon made a hard swing at breakneck speed around Titan, Bjorn's ship leading to the target – towards a small and, from what Bjorn could see at the current distance, desolate moon floating on the outer orbit. At this point it was still a far distant dot on the map.

"If you do not plan to kill Charity de Rossi," Lucy intoned, "then why are we out here? Why the ruse?"

"Well," Bjorn admitted. "I am still trying to figure that out. I have been wrestling with the dilemma for days. I don't want to kill her, but I want to further the Cause. I must. I am unsure as how to proceed – my lack of imagination limits me. Can I still fulfill my mission and not kill her? I don't know. I guess I was hoping that the universe would lead me to the right answer."

"You feel obliged to your superiors..."

Bjorn threw a cutting glance at the troll with his green eyes. "JP is not my superior," he was quick to correct.

"Your...equal officer expects this of you, and you have promised that you would complete this mission. Yet you feel compelled to not do so. In fact, if my memory banks and placation analyzers are correct, it is possible that you feel compelled to protect Charity de Rossi."

Bjorn's face snapped to the right. "What makes you think that?"

Lucy's face again took on a barely discernable smirk. "I do not think," she assured him. "It is only what I can apply from what I have processed from stored data," she told him, her voice cool.

Bjorn blew a puff of exasperated breath through his nostrils. "Damned new models," he muttered. "Almost as opinionated as a real woman."

"I beg your pardon?" Lucy asked.

"Nothing. I was just saying that we are nearing our target."

"Hmm," Lucy remarked.

Bjorn was shooting her a glance that he hoped was reprimanding when he could hear Emma's voice over the com.

"Sir, Olivia has informed me that she is detecting a large transport ship on approach, Carrier Class."

"IGC?" Bjorn asked, the muscles in his back rippling into tension.

"No, the Carrier is Chimeran. First launch carrier of the Battle Cruiser, *Resurrection*."

Bjorn hissed through his teeth. *JP! What could it be now? And besides, isn't he on the far side of Jupiter?*

"Thank you Emma, but unless my immediate return is required, I will deal with it after the conclusion of this mission. Until then, have Olivia keep your current distance. And make sure that Carrier stays there with you!"

"Yes, sir."

He knew that the attack on the Lido moon had been a success. What the hell could JP be up to? Was he sending him troops? Mechanics? He racked his brain but could not recall a request or a discussion with the other Commander that might explain the appearance of the Carrier.

Bjorn shook his head. "Damn crazy fool," he muttered, glancing at his screens. They were getting close. He switched his controls over from auto to manual.

"Me?" Lucy asked. "Or Emma?"

"Neither," Bjorn replied, adjusting course. His green eyes flicked to the readout that showed his platoon of fighters. They were following in perfect formation. "I'm just trying to figure out what to say or do when..." he trailed off as the jet began to tremble.

The Commander rested his hands easily on the v-shaped flywheel of his jet fighter, ready to engage whoever might be suddenly crashing their party. A part of him thought it might be the first of Charity's defenses and his mind searched for what he would say if given the chance, and what he would do if he was fired upon first. The moon was close, but not close enough to warrant defensive measures. They were barley within readout.

Bjorn could feel the reverberation throughout his craft and realized that it could only be from an approaching ship decelerating from max speed. On his port side. Bjorn pulled starboard, his platoon in tow and ready to fire, as he watched a white-hot burning glow from the port side of his shield glass.

As the white-hot glow faded to a gleaming blue, Bjorn almost felt a sense of relief before he was overcome with a maddening annoyance to see that it was a Chimeran jet fighter from the Battle Cruiser, *Resurrection.*

"Greetings, Commander," a crackling voice said over the coms. "I trust that I am not too late?"

Bjorn winced even as he laughed. "Commander Petrov!" he called heartily. "I did not know that you were drafted for this firefight!"

Yes, Bjorn thought wildly, *tell him he is too late. Tell him that it is done. Abort the mission and get to Scarlett.*

"Well," Petrov said, before a sound that was obviously the Chimeran nervously clearing his throat, "my Commander wanted to me to come along to see if you needed any...help." Petrov's voice cracked on the last word, sending Bjorn into a bout of laughter.

As much as JP and his crew of bible-thumping Zealot's got under his skin, Bjorn could never help but be amused, sometimes to tears, by them.

"Petrov!" he scolded. "You are such a terrible liar!"

Petrov, accompanied by only one other fighter jet, pulled his height up within his own craft, his white blonde hair brushing the inner glass of the hood.

"I will take that as a compliment," he stated, matter of fact. "I am proud that it is not a sin at which I excel."

Bjorn boomed laughter again, even though he knew that he was now guaranteed little success in what he had hoped for the most. "Here to help, my ass! You are here to make sure that I do what I am supposed to do, and report back to JP."

"And," Petrov added, "to assist in any way that I can."

Bjorn used his index finger to plug the micro speaker that relayed communications to outside craft. "Of course you are, you bootlicking bastard," he muttered. He pulled his finger off the screen and smiled as if Petrov could see him. "Fall in with the fighters on my port side," he ordered.

"Yes, sir," Petrov agreed easily.

Bjorn watched as they closed the distance to the far away satellite, his green eyes narrowing. A furrow grew between his brows and deepened the closer his ship got to the moon.

"Platoon, hold orbit," he ordered over the com system. "I'm going in for a preliminary sweep."

"What does that mean?" Petrov asked.

"It means you hang back," Bjorn told him. "I'm going to do a run for a first-line security sweep, so if there is a laser trip, it doesn't take our entire platoon."

"Very well," Petrov agreed.

"Thanks for your permission," Bjorn muttered with his finger pressed down over the metal screen of the micro speaker once again. The Commander broke away from the rest of the formation. He pulled starboard in a long, swooping curl and eyed the dark moon as he dove closer and closer – his body becoming more and more taut as his hope faded to a thin line in the dark.

His head tilted as he studied the miniature, blasted world as it grew in his vision until his craft was streaking into its thin atmosphere. The black of space was replaced with a gray sky full of a dying sunset.

"Will you kill her if you have to?" Lucy asked.

A crease darkened Bjorn's otherwise perfect forehead as he considered. "Yes," he said definitively. "But I wouldn't like it."

Lucy was perfectly still, silent and watching as his tension faded, along with the trepidation of being blown into smoking ash, and he pulled in for another long loop, flying as low as he dared.

This time, he brought his jet down close to a sea of choppy water that covered more than half the globe. He checked the instrument panel and saw that he was nearing a massive island.

Soon, he was close enough to make out the castle. It squatted on a rise of land like a wary predator, jealously guarding its scarp of rock from the water that threatened it on all sides. Its towers and battlements stretched dark and broken fingers into a sky going from scarlet red to deep violet. The minarets and spires stood out like thorns against the fading light.

"Can they see us from this range?" Lucy asked.

"Of course they can see us," Bjorn snapped. "You should know that!"

"I do," she admitted. "I just don't know why they haven't fired at us." A moment of silence ensued while Lucy's eyes glimmered. "Could it be that her feelings mirror your own?"

When Bjorn pulled up from his dive, he stared at Lucy with green eyes that had gone a bit wild. "Can you do an EL scan from this range?" he asked.

"Of course," she replied, her golden eyes shifting and glinting red in the far-reaching rays of the sun. After a moment, her body moved in what looked like a shrug. "There is a radacmeter score of ten, but even that is all residual." She turned her golden eyes to him. "It seems that the universe has conspired in your favor, Commander."

The corner of his mouth tightened and then he sighed. *Then I guess this is where we say good-bye, Charity. New love trumps old loves.*

Thinking about Scarlett lifted the weight that had settled on his heart. It made Bjorn smile, then he threw his head back and laughed, elated. Inspired. He pulled the craft up and around, circling back to the platoon out in the darkness of space, checking to see that all of the com lines were open.

"I'm going to go in on a high run," he informed them.

"Check two?" his next-in-command intoned from the second squadron of fighters. "Request your back-up."

"No," he replied. "I'm going in alone."

"Commander..." Petrov warned. "I should tell you that..."

"What?" Bjorn demanded with a scowl. "That you are here to babysit me Petrov?" He could sense the other Chimeran stiffen within the safe confines of his own jet. "Don't worry," he assured the man. "I am going to nuke the bitch. Not only will you be able to see the blast from here, but you will be able to take a radiation mez and be able to report back to your Commander that I utterly destroyed the fucking place."

There was a gasp from Petrov followed by the admonition of, "Language, Commander!"

Bjorn laughed as he wheeled his craft around. "Besides," he continued, "I don't want any fighters, mine or yours, taking on any unnecessary radiation. They're getting old and have taken about as much abuse as they can." The green-eyed Commander broke away from the platoon, dropping back down towards the moon, firing up the state of the art thermo-nuclear missiles on his new fighter. "I don't want anyone wasting any time taking in the view," he announced over the com system. "As soon as you see the blast, scatter. I will already be gone. My troops are to haul ass back to the *Mace*. Petrov, will you be joining us?"

"Not unless you request our presence directly, Captain," Petrov answered.

"That won't be necessary. But thank you so much for your... assistance. Either way, that castle has seen its last day.""

"Then until next time, Commander," Petrov said amongst the murmurs of assent coming from Bjorn's pilots.

Bjorn reached out and cut the coms with a swipe of his hand along the console dash. With a dogged expression he adjusted his craft to hone in on the castle, its black spires reaching heavenward in a silent plea.

Lucy, ever inquisitive, could only keep quiet for so long. "What is it that you hope to accomplish by this?" she asked.

"I guess," Bjorn said as he pushed the jet down into the sunset atmosphere of the moon, "That I am saying goodbye to old friends. Whatever it is, I have a job to do and a date with

Scarlett to keep – and I intend on doing both."

"I don't recall her acquiescence to see you again."

"She wants to, though," he said with a touch of annoyance. "I know it. Also, I have the strangest feeling that she may be in danger."

"That is interesting," Lucy remarked. "Where is that feeling coming from?"

Bjorn shrugged, flipping controls. "I guess from where the wizard put my heart."

"Do you mean Faith de Rossi, or Gwendolyn?"

He shrugged again. "What's the difference?"

Bjorn thumbed the scanner on the dash twice, the glass panel taking his fingerprint both times, releasing two nuclear missiles on a course for the castle on the hill. As soon as they were released, the Commander launched the jet into hyperspeed, breaking the speed of light barrier just as a spreading lotus of white light dispersed the growing night below him.

The castle was annihilated and replaced by a radioactive crater twice the size of the land it had sat upon. The surrounding sea expanded away from the blast in every direction before the black waters returned with a vengeance, rushing in to fill the void.

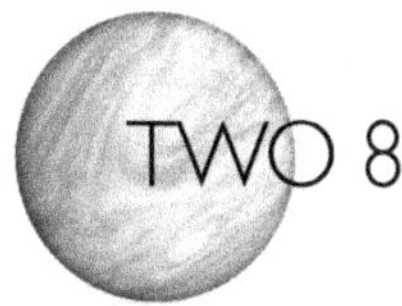

TWO 8

Jasyn tried to shift his weight but the pain tore across his ribcage like plasma fire. Outside, the sun was beginning to set on the Last Castle. Jasyn couldn't see it, but he could feel it. It felt like it was setting on his life.

Faith laid a cool hand along the side of his face. "You're going to be fine," she assured him, her voice calm and soft and firm.

He shook his head slowly, his lips pressed tightly together, before a spasm of pain racked his body. His jaw clenched and his eyes clamped shut, rendering him speechless. When it passed, his hazel eyes opened and fixed on her face. He exhaled sharply, searching for words.

"You knew," he whispered.

Faith paused, then nodded.

"When?" he asked. "When did you know?"

Faith pressed her lips together and shook her head slowly back and forth, a line forming between her brows. Jasyn closed his dark eyes and his own brow became perfectly smooth as he understood.

"From the beginning," he said, then a wheezy chuckle escaped from his lips. "You knew the whole time."

Faith nodded slowly and her expression was that of strain and guilt. Jasyn tried to shift his weight again, trying to find some comfort, but the pain tore up through his side, making his body jerk convulsively. Faith saw his face contort with the effort and helped him move so that he was lying on his uninjured side, facing her, his head cradled in her lap. She kissed the ridge of his brow and he reached out, wrapping an arm around her.

"I love you," he said.

"Shhhh," she said, laying two fingers on his lips and looking into the hazel eyes that had beguiled her from the very first time she had looked into their depths. "Don't say anything. This place is too secure."

"I want you to believe me," he whispered.

Faith smiled down on him, her fingers tracing the edge of his chin. "I do believe you," she whispered back.

His face pulled together in a grimace. Whether it was physical hurt or mental anguish, Faith did not know. She winced as well, only able to imagine the agony as his blood soaked into the cream-colored fabric of her suit.

"Be honest with me," she coaxed, cupping his chin with a gentle hand. "Would you really protect me?"

Jasyn, his hazel eyes lucid though full of pain, nodded. "I would die for you," he said without hesitation.

"And I will protect you," she said softly. "Your secret is safe with me."

Jasyn closed his eyes and turned his head, hiding his face in her chest.

Faith leaned down, covering his upper body with her own. She brushed her lips against his soft dark hair, inhaling deeply. She enveloped his body as much as she could, bringing her lips down to the edge of his ear.

"And since we are sharing secrets," she whispered, "and being honest with one another, there is something that I should tell you."

Jasyn managed to pull himself closer to her slender form,

though he shuddered at her word *honest*, and wrapped his arms around her waist as he felt the blood seep in slow rhythmic waves from the edges of the burned gash in his ribs.

Her lips brushed his ear and her voice was just a breath.

"I am not Faith de Rossi."

Jasyn's eyes widened until they were almost perfectly round, but not with surprise, with realization.

He had known, all along, hadn't he?

"And you knew about me?" he asked her.

"Yes."

"Who I was?"

"Yes."

"Why I was here?"

There was an audible swallow before, "yes."

Jasyn felt his throat tighten with shame. He had to force himself to meet her steady gaze. "You saw everything that I sent to JP?"

"Yes."

Jasyn closed his eyes even as he continued. "So you know that..." He winced, trying to continue, but gave up when he heard her sigh. She continued for him, her voice low in an attempt to avoid being picked up by any microphone in the room.

"That you started to give him misleading information nearly two months ago? And that, after our last return from the castle, you began to outright lie to him?"

He opened his eyes, searching her face.

"Yes. I had to. I meant what I said about protecting you. I'll do anything to keep you safe, no matter how this all started. I really do love you."

She cupped his face with a firm but gentle hand, her thumb rising along the ridge of his cheekbone. "I love you, Jasyn," she said but his mind, already drifting towards unconsciousness, snapped back to what she had said a few moments ago.

I am not Faith de Rossi.

All of the things about her that had disturbed him were beginning to make sense. He fought against the fog that was descending over his head, making him sleepy. Instead, he focused on the pain.

The pain that was racking his body was merely a mirror of the guilt that had been tearing at his heart and even that suddenly became distant as his mind raced away.

The mirror, the mirror was the clue – just as he had always thought.

Puzzle pieces fell into place almost faster than he could put them together.

Pieces flipped and switched and fell, just like the mirrors of her vanity. The mirrors of the vanity. Mirrors and mirrors. The reflections of reflections in the swimming pool. The way her spacecraft was a mirror of the villa.

The way she would trace her lips with the smooth bed of her right thumbnail, instead of the left.

The way she would pick up a stylus with her right hand and sign with her left. It always seemed awkward because she was never truly left-handed.

Everything was a mirror. *She* was a mirror.

Jasyn tried to focus but his mind was getting darker by the second.

The only thing that was not a mirror was the silky smooth feel of her arm where there should have been a scar – the scar Faith had gotten from an immunization at two years old that had made her terribly sick. It had left a ripple of flesh on her upper arm that her twin, born at the age of five, never had.

The pain surged through him once again and Jasyn turned his face so that it was buried in her chest and he pulled her close as tight as he could, his breath coming out in a single, soft word.

"*Gwen.*"

❧

When Scarlett opened her eyes, all she could see was a figure crouching over her, though her vision was too blurry to make out who it was. She tried to talk but her throat felt like a rusty hinge. She brought her hand up to her mouth and a second later she could feel someone supporting her head and holding a cup to her lips.

The Red Jordan was confused and disoriented. Her ears felt like they were stuffed with cotton. Her head felt like it was stuffed with straw.

From tin-man to straw-man, she thought belligerently. *Am I progressing or regressing?* she wondered. *Maybe I'm digressing.*

The only thing that she was sure of was that she was inside of Fledge. That alone was almost enough to make her weep.

Still, it was bewildering to know that she was inside of him and yet not in her pilot's seat - though she had already seen, from the outside, how much larger he had become. The Jordan closed her eyes, trying to remember what happened.

She had been in town for the celebration of the Synchronicity.

My god it was packed! she thought, remembering the revelers, dancing and jostling and cavorting, shoulder to sweaty shoulder in the town square. Bjorn had been there, and Calyph too. And Mica. She was sure that she had seen the cabbie again but that time he wasn't in a cab but in front of a tent.

Had it been Arwa's tent? No, it had been a fortuneteller's tent, though it had looked like Arwa's.

She shook her head, it was all so muddled. Had there been

an Aridian there? Had she really seen an Aridian? Yes, she was sure of it. It was a female, she had spotted her right before she had looked up, which must have been when someone smeared the chlorfagel across her neck.

Had it been the Aridian? Scarlett shuddered. If so, she was very lucky to be alive. She remembered making it to the town walls and staggering out, barely conscious. Fledge had been there, waiting on the crest of the first rising hill. The memory of it brought tears to the backs of her closed eyes.

Scarlett.

"Hmm?" she said, lifting up, thinking someone had spoken, then she realized she had heard the voice with her head, not her ears. She eased herself back down.

Fledge?

Her own name came again, warmer this time. *Scarlett.*

The Jordan squeezed her eyes shut but this time the tears came, escaping from the corners of her eyelids and running down the sides of her face towards her ears.

Who? she asked mentally, but Fledge's only response was a feeling of puzzlement. *Who saved me?* she asked.

A feeling of befuddlement was the only response. Scarlett thought that maybe he could not understand her words so in her minds eye she pictured Bjorn, the tall and lean green-eyed Chimeran Commander. Then she pictured Calyph, his sandy blonde hair over his pointed ears, his almond-shaped eyes blue and full of innocence.

Fledge's befuddlement turned to outright confusion. Scarlett sighed and tried to open her eyes again but they seemed even less compliant than her voice. She waved her hand and motioned to her neck and the figure was there again, leaning close this time, touching her.

There was a grunt and then she could feel her neck being cleaned with a cloth. She opened her eyes but the figure was still blurred. Scarlet closed her eyes again, concentrating.

She remembered that her knees had buckled and she had collapsed. And she had been caught by strong arms and lifted up. She thought of Bjorn, lean and muscled. She thought of his strong arms and her heartbeat quickened. Fledge's heartbeat responded, though Scarlett had the feeling that it might be in amusement.

Bjorn had carried her once before - lifting her up and carrying her with no effort.

Calyph had caught her up in his arms as well one time and carried her to safety. Had it been to Fledge or to the Opal Dragon? She couldn't remember now, it all seemed so long ago.

Scarlett tried to remember the feel of the arms that had caught her so recently, tried to see if she could discern who it had been.

Green or blue, she thought suddenly as she heard a sound made by the person that was with her now. She thought of Calyph's blue eyes, always so full of concern, and Bjorn's gimlet green eyes, always full of mirth and desire. Desire for her.

His eyes, she thought. *If I could just see his eyes, I will know who it is.*

Blue or green?

Green or blue?

She tried to raise her head but she was gently pressed back down. The figure leaned down again, getting the last of the chlorfagel from her neck.

Fledge, she thought, *help me.*

A surge of relief washed over her, a wave of strength as her body was filled with warm, red light. Scarlett reached up to the silhouette above her and wrapped a hand around its neck and pulled the figure down until they were nose to nose.

Blue or green? she thought wildly, forcing her own eyes open. *Green or blue?*

Her dark eyes, edged with crimson, blinked rapidly - not

sure if what she was seeing was real.

Green or blue?

Blue.

The Red Jordan blinked, again and the again –just to make sure – but she was right.

Blue.

Scarlett fell back down onto the bed making soft sounds like whimpers, till the whimpers grew into soft laughter. Laughter that grew until tears leaked from the corners of her closed eyes once again.

EPILOGUE

Jasyn's body shuddered, clutching at the woman in his arms. His head swam as he tried to make sense of the situation and failed. The pain was a great smear of black and red across his vision. All that he could focus on was the crushing feeling in his chest as he forced himself to keep breathing.

He had been rushed from the castle in the fading light of sunset just as his vision had begun to fail. He began slipping in and out of consciousness like a drunkard dancing with shadows. His awareness would ebb away like the blood from his wound, then snap back as a rush of agony would bring him around again.

Are some of my ribs broken? he wondered. *Is that what hurts the most, or is it something inside my ribcage? What the fuck is under there - my liver? My spleen? I don't know enough about anatomy. All I know is that the damned Jordan shot me with a weapon I had never seen before. It must have been the first time she had used it, too. If her aim had been better, even just a little higher, she would have hit my heart. Or my head.*

Jasyn opened his eyes and realized there were other people in the room, people touching him and asking him questions. Gwen was no longer holding him.

How long were my eyes closed?

He could feel his body being lifted and set on something airy and flat before he was carted away. His hazel eyes darted around the room, searching out Gwendolyn. Her eyes saw that his were open and she was back at his side in a blink. Though it hurt him to do so, he reached out to put his arm around her.

Gwen. I knew. Somehow I always knew that it was her. But how? Why?

She started talking to him but her words were not making any sense, like she was speaking an alien language. He could almost understand her, but not quite. Gently, she pulled his arm from where it was clasped around her body. She kissed his fingers and then folded them into his palm and then put his hand on his chest.

People began rushing around again. Someone, a stranger to his eyes, spoke to her and she turned her face away and answered, her voice as quick and sharp as a blade, though her face was streaked with tears. Looking at her, he remembers way she was on the night of the thunderstorm.

Jasyn felt something sharp pierce the skin on the inner crook of his elbow.

That's where Faith likes to slip her hand, he thought. *No,* he corrected. *Gwen. It's where Gwen likes to slip her hand.* The thought disappeared as he himself slipped into soft darkness.

Jasyn blinked his eyes. He turned his head and realized that he was in a medical room, reclining in a propped-up bed with white rails. He looked down and saw that he was wearing a white cotton shift printed with faded blue diamonds, a sad attempt at giving a medical gown some character. It seemed as if no time had passed since he was on the air gurney, but some must have. Possibly quite a lot.

Plastic tubes ran out of the inside of his left forearm and he could feel the tight pull of medical tape over his wound. Some sort of plastique clamp held tight to his ribcage.

Most of the pain was gone, at least the pain in his side. There was a strange, dull ache in the left side of his chest that he suspected had nothing to do with the Jordan's weapon.

Even with the pain gone and now having the ability to think a bit more clearly, he was having a hard time getting over the shock that Faith was really Gwendolyn. It had been her the whole time. What confused him even more was that deep inside, he felt that he had known all along.

Gwen sat in a chair next to him, clasping his right hand in her own though her upper body was lying forward over the side of his bed. Her head was face down next to his uninjured side as if praying or sleeping, her gold and brown hair spilling across her back. Looking at her brought on a surge of mixed feelings.

He had no doubt that he loved her, but he felt an odd sting of betrayal that she had deceived him about who she really was.

Don't be ridiculous, he thought. *She's lying to everyone about who she really is. Not only did I lie about who I was, but I came here to kill her.*

Still, that sting did not go away.

Used, he decided. *I feel used. I came to spy on her and instead she used me to spy on JP, which makes me feel like a fool as well. I guess I had it coming.*

He took a deep breath and looked up at the quiet room. Charity sat in a chair against the wall, taking a long draw from a steel cigarette. Her green eyes sparkled with mischief as he spotted her.

"I'm sure you are not supposed to smoke inside a hospital," Jasyn told her, smiling in spite of all that had happened. Charity returned his grin, her eyes glittering.

"One, it's my hospital. Two, it's a vapor cigarette. Three, even if one or two were not the case, do you think anyone would have the balls to tell me to put it out?"

"I wouldn't," Jasyn admitted and looked at Gwendolyn, who had sat up during the brief exchange, blinking the sleep from her eyes. She saw Jasyn's smile and sighed with relief.

"How are you feeling?"

"Fine, I guess."

"You guess?"

"My side is okay," he explained, "if that's what you mean. I'm sure they are giving me something for the pain." Gwen nodded and Jasyn's hazel eyes looked into her eyes of brown and gold. "Inside, I'm not sure how I feel."

She nodded, understanding. "I know. This hasn't been easy on me either."

Jasyn looked away. *Stop acting like a child,* he told himself. "When did you know you loved me?" he asked, redirecting the conversation.

Gwen swallowed before she spoke. "A long time ago," she whispered.

From her chair against the wall, Charity gave a loud *Ahem!* - clearing her throat. Gwen looked over and Charity nodded at her as if encouraging her to get moving. Gwen nodded back, took a deep breath, and looked back at Jasyn.

"What do you remember?"

He started to shrug and then stopped as he felt the clamp on his side bite into him. "I remember walking in, and then the Jordan..."

Gwen shook her head quickly. "No. What do you remember about us?"

Jasyn frowned, puzzled. Did she mean their life at the villa? He had the feeling she was after more.

"I don't know what else to do," Gwen said, her voice oddly desperate. "You need to try. Try to remember."

"Remember us?" he asked. Gwen's head dipped in the barest of nods but as soon as the words had left his mouth the water began to trickle through the dam. His breath came out in a soft rush and he turned his face away as pieces of the dam began to break away. "A train. I remember a train. And a bullfight." Gwen's next breath came out in a choked sob and her whole body trembled. "I remember a house," Jasyn continued, "a house made of glass, on beach near an ocean." Jasyn frowned and shook his head. "No, on a lake."

"It was both," Gwen said, tears spilling down her checks.

The memories came pouring through the hole in the dam, sweeping away more of the blockage and his hazel eyes opened wider and wider as if watching the past on a holo screen.

"I remember," he said, his voice tinged with wonder. "Not everything. But I remember us."

Gwen laughed, wiping her tears away with the back of one hand.

"Enough!" Charity stood up, tucking the steel cigarette into a pocket on her sleeve as she came towards the bed. "You can stroll down the avenues of the past at another time," she told Gwen, her smile never faltering and her eyes never leaving Jasyn's. "Right now we have much more important things to start discussing."

"Charity..." Gwen started but was cut off with a single look.

The pale, slender fingers of Charity's right hand wrapped around one of the metal rails on the hospital bed. "It is time for this rebellion to come to an end. Actually, it should have come to an end ninety-nine years ago. But, sometimes things do not go as planned." A small chuckle escaped her red lips but her knuckles turned white as they grasped the bar tighter. "So now," she told Jasyn, "we need to know what you know. We need to know what the Chimera have planned."

Jasyn swallowed. He could feel that slight bitterness rising inside him again, the feeling that came from the knowledge he had been a pawn of these two women, but he pushed it away. After all, he had come to kill them both. He had fallen in love and had passed the point of no return a long time ago.

He glanced at Gwendolyn then fixed his eyes on Charity and nodded. "I know everything they have planned."

Charity threw back her head and laughed girlishly. "I certainly hope so," she told Jasyn when her laughter trailed off. "That was the plan."

Jasyn looked at Gwen, fighting against the lump that was

expanding in his throat, wondering how long they had been using him. "Your plan?" he asked. Charity laughed again, even though Gwen's expression was one of misery.

"No silly," Charity answered. "It was your plan."

AUTHOR'S NOTE

They say that we are each the author of our own story (or destiny). Quotes like that never fail to give me the warm fuzzies. My own story goes like this: Chapter One: It is a sunny day (rainy day, windy day, there is a class-five hurricane) and April goes to the bar to write Chapter One.

I hope you liked, or at least enjoyed, this tale - even though it was the same one as the last book. Wasn't it? We are always told that there are two sides to every story but I realized long ago that there can be many more than two. Every witness has his own account of what happened. There is no right or wrong, or even; *listen, man, this is what REALLY went down...* Each version is merely our own personal perception and our own singular reaction. How do you react when you discover that those you perceived to be the heroes in your life are actually the villains, and vice-versa? Some people plug ahead and keep grinding out the current chapter of their story without changing a thing. Some start a new chapter. Some start an entirely new story.

For me, the only thing I enjoy more than a good story is a good backstory. So my apologies in advance for those of you who like to seek me out and shout: *WHAT'S NEXT?!?* Before you find out the what, I am going to tell you the why – or at least the how and where the story really started, according to my own perception.

As for your own story, what happens next is up to you.